490

W9-BDG-081

THE
BLACK SWAN

THE
BLACK SWAN

Mercedes Lackey

DAW BOOKS, INC.
DONALD A. WOLLHEIM, FOUNDER
375 Hudson Street, New York, NY 10014

ELIZABETH R. WOLLHEIM
SHEILA E. GILBERT
PUBLISHERS

For color prints of Jody Lee's paintings, please contact:
The Cerridwen Enterprise
P.O. Box 10161
Kansas City, MO 64111
1-800-825-1281

Frontispiece by Larry Dixon

DAW Book Collectors No. 1120

DAW Books are distributed by Penguin Putnam Inc.
Book designed by Stanley S. Drate/Folio Graphics Co. Inc.

First Printing, May 2000

1 2 3 4 5 6 7 8 9

Dedicated to all those
who have ever dreamed
of becoming a swan

CHAPTER ONE

THE newest girl had finally cried herself into exhaustion at last and slept, her tear-streaked face half hidden in her disordered hair, head cradled in the silken folds of Jeanette's midnight-colored skirt. Moonlight flattered her; if it had been the pitiless light of the sun that bathed her features, they would have been blotched red and altogether unattractive with three nights of hysterical weeping. The silvery light of the moon was more forgiving; it hid the red in her swollen eyes and cheeks, and turned the tears lingering on her lashes into drops of crystal. She looked pitiable, with a tragic, frail beauty that would have softened the heart of anyone but her captor, von Rothbart. His will was proof against any mere woman.

It had certainly taken this wench long enough to reconcile herself to her situation. Odile would have liked to sigh with vexed impatience, but her father's training held firm, and she schooled her features into marble impassivity, keeping her gaze fixed at a vague point somewhere out on the moonlit lake. A cool zephyr touched the water, dissolving the reflected moon into dancing ripples.

From the water's verge, a close-clipped lawn rose in a gentle incline toward her, punctuated with mathematically designed flower beds, perfectly shaped trees, and topiary bushes. Despite the beauty and tranquillity of the manicured park land surrounding von Rothbart's dwelling, Odile would rather have been inside the manor, but her father's orders kept her here, watching carefully over the new one, to make certain she did herself no harm. One never knew; suicide was a mortal sin, but the fear of sin might not stop her.

Three nights of steady weeping, three days of disconsolate drooping in the shadows of the great willow, ignoring food, company, comfort—I can't ever recall anyone but Odette taking that long to resign herself to her situation. After all, her position is hardly a tragedy—and she has only herself to blame for her captivity.

The soft twitter of very young voices reminded her that some of the maids probably *preferred* their new life to their old. Odile couldn't see the youngest members of her father's flock, but she knew where they were; off in the shelter of the rose arbor to her left, weaving moonflowers into crowns or making dolls out of blossoms. Elke, Ilse, Lisbet, and Sofie were very happy as they were, and why shouldn't they be? They'd been grubby little peasant girls before they'd come into von Rothbart's flock. *Here*, instead of coarse shifts of linen and rough-woven skirts of wool, they had soft silk gowns that never grew shabby or dirty. Instead of toiling from dawn to dark in the hard labor of a peasant hut, mucking about in pigsties and cow byres, they were waited upon by Eric von Rothbart's invisible servants, their own duties only to wait in their turn upon Odette and Odile. Such service was a light burden; Odette required little of her handmaidens but company, and as often as not, she didn't even require that. As for Odile, she much preferred to do without their service and company altogether; their company was deathly boring, and the invisibles were far more satisfactory servants.

Tonight, for instance, distressed by the new one's ceaseless caterwauling, Odette had retreated to the island in the middle of the lake before the change came upon them all. There she was, still as a white marble statue, as still as Odile herself, seated with folded hands in the shelter of the tiny "temple" in Greek mode that von Rothbart's fancy had placed there. The pitched white roof and white columns glimmered in the moonlight; in her misty gown of pale silk, Odette could easily have been a statue or a spirit perched there, mourning the past glory of lost kingdoms, and not a living woman, mourning her own sins and losses.

Her handmaidens, separated from her by the waters of the lake, conducted themselves much as they would have had she been among them. Some drifted through von Rothbart's gardens, some trailed bare feet in the cool water, some spoke in slow, sad voices, relating the same tales of their past they'd told twenty times before. A dozen, including Jeanette, hovered over the new one, inarticulately trying to comfort her, or at least bring her quiet resignation to her fate. In the soft, diffused moonlight, they all looked alike, all clothed in maidenly white, all differences of hair color and complexion silvered over into the same tones of ethereal white-blue, all movements in the same slow, graceful gestures, as if they all dwelt underwater. Like Odette, they could have been spirits—well, all but nine of them. Nine, including Jeanette and Odile, wore black instead of maidenly white. Eight of the nine wore their sober gowns in ceaseless mourning for what they had lost, in a vain attempt to wrest forgiveness from an unforgiving and inplacable master. Odile wore black, because her father wished her to, to signify symbolically that she was no creature of Odette's retinue.

Von Rothbart placed a great deal of importance in symbols; as a sorcerer, he knew the power they contained. As his daughter and only student, Odile had instinctively felt that same power before she had the words to articulate it.

As his daughter, she would much rather have been inside the manor, watching him work or studying on her own. How could these women bear to spend so much time doing *nothing*?

If I were to be charitable, I could assume that Father's enchantments fog their minds, or despair makes them too lethargic to care, she thought, scornfully, mimicking her father's attitude. *But I think it likelier that they are unaccustomed to using their minds very much at all.*

A burst of muffled giggling came from the rose arbor, and the four little ones emerged to dance a solemn pavane on the grassy lawn as sourceless music wafted through the garden, matching their steps to the soft notes. A few of the others joined them after a time, but Jeanette made no move to do the same, and Odette in her aloof isolation did not even change her position, though she certainly heard the music.

Odile determined that the new acquisition was so exhausted by grief that she would likely sleep until dawn, and slipped away from the garden full of girls. With nothing to keep her among the idle maidens, she wanted only to get back to her studies, which at least had the value of novelty. The Great Hall drew her as a lodestone drew a needle, and she glided silently up the sharply carved stone steps, past the granite guardian owls perched on plinths to either side of the door, and eased the heavy oaken door open so that it did not creak and disturb her father at his own work.

Within, the vast and echoing central hall lay deserted and practically unlit except for two torches in sconces on either side of the entrance. The faded, smoke-stained banners of conquered enemies long past and liegemen long gone hung limply from the blackened beams above; if she had not known the subjects of the tapestries of dragons, wyverns, manticores, and other beasts that covered the walls, she would not have been able to make out the dim forms imperfectly picked out in tarnished gold thread and clouded gems. There was no fire, not even ashes in the cold hearth, and the great wooden chairs arrayed along the walls held nothing but dust. Von Rothbart's magical servitors were singularly blind to the accumulation of mere dust unless she reminded them of their duty in that direction. She crossed the flagstone of the hall and passed into the next chamber, a narrow guardroom, which was just as empty. Ahead of her, lights sprang into existence, as the invisible servants anticipated her direction. The library was next—also empty—then the stairs to her father's tower where he worked his magics and devised new ones. The tower door was locked, but no light shone from the crack beneath it; von Rothbart was not there. Nor was he in the cellar where some of his supplies were stored, or the dank and depressing dungeons, and when she checked other storerooms and even the stillroom, it was clear that she need not have gone to the trouble of trying to be as quiet as the servants. Von Rothbart was not in his residence.

Odile considered the empty manor with some astonishment; there was only one likely reason for her father's absence, and he had never before gone a-hunting a new bird when the latest prize was not yet settled. This was new behavior, and she dared to wonder for a moment what was going on, poised on the threshold of the library as her mind spun a web of speculation.

Then, with a frown, she shattered the web and whirled about, winding her way back through the tangle of empty, ill-lit rooms to her own little workplace. *Curiosity annoys Father*, she reminded herself, with a touch of apprehension. *Questions annoy him even more.* She had not been von Rothbart's daughter for this long without learning to keep curiosity within bounds and questions to a bare minimum.

Curiosity was best confined within her magical studies, and when she reached her workroom, she lit all the lanterns in it with an impatient gesture, bringing a flood of light to the space.

Her workshop was a smaller, simpler version of her father's, less cluttered because she did not keep failed experiments littering the benches, nor did she start half a dozen projects at once. She spared a glance and a brief flush of pride for her last successful task, the scrying mirror beneath an insulating black silk shroud.

But she had a more ambitious task ahead of her, and one that her father did not know she was attempting. She didn't want to face his ridicule for her audacity, or his amusement at her failures, for she'd had several already.

But tonight, knowing that she was alone in the manor, without any interfering energies from her father's more powerful magics about, she felt more confident of her success than she had since she'd begun this task.

She rang a tiny silver bell, and immediately felt the whisper of air that meant one of the servants was at her elbow.

"Bring me a live mouse, then watch to see if the new one is about to awaken, and summon me if she is," she ordered, tossing a tiny silver cage over her shoulder without looking. It vanished in midair, and she gave no more thought to it as she busied herself with the rest of her preparations.

The cage with its quivering, frightened occupant was on the workbench precisely when she needed it, and she picked it up in her left hand. She closed her eyes, whispered the guttural syllables of her memorized incantation, calling up a stream of power motes with the circling fingers of her right; living bits of light that danced and sparkled with colors far brighter than those of the true gems of the tapestries in the Great Hall.

The mouse shivered, its whiskers quivering with terror, as she directed the motes to swirl around it in an ever-decreasing spiral. The brilliant colors reflected in its terror-widened black eyes as the motes entered the cage and paused for a moment, surrounding it with a ring of enchantment.

Then, like a swarm of bees attacking an enemy, they swiftly engulfed the tiny creature, covering it from nose to tail. Every hair shone with light, delineated for a brief moment in a glowing opalescent shimmer. It gave a single squeak of pure panic, then stiffened and dropped to the bottom of the cage as if dead.

Hovering over the cage like an anxious parent, Odile waited and watched, to see if this trial would bring success.

She knew the precise moment von Rothbart entered the manor, for the hovering crowd of invisible servants that had collected about her, creating whispers of moving air no stronger than the breath of a moth, suddenly vanished, deserting her at the summons of their master. The attraction of her minor magic was nothing to the magnetic pull of the master of the manse. A thrill of anticipation shivered the back of her neck, and her heart beat a trifle faster—but of all her feelings, hope was the strongest at this moment of success. *This time—maybe I can impress him this time—he'll smile, he'll tell me I'm a worthy pupil, wor-*

thy of the name von Rothbart and the mantle of a sorceress.

The soft footfall in the door behind her warned of her father's presence—the invisibles would have told their master where she was as a matter of course. They wouldn't converse with her or any of the flock, but they told her father everything that passed in his absence. He would want to know why she was here instead of watching the new one, and if she had obeyed his instructions not to leave her unwatched while she was awake and in her proper form.

She whirled gracefully—von Rothbart insisted on grace; clumsiness was an offense to his senses—but did not even raise her eyes before sinking into a deep curtsy, her black silken skirts pooling beautifully around her. His boots, of the finest, softest sable leather, were all she saw of him for the moment.

"You may rise," the deep voice said from a point above her head, speaking without inflection of any kind. He did not yet know whether she deserved punishment for leaving her duty; he reserved judgment in the absence of information. Above all things, von Rothbart was suspicious, he had seen so much betrayal. But he was also just, and would not condemn without cause.

She moved out of her curtsy as gracefully as she had fallen into it, only raising her eyes to her father's red-bearded face when she was once again fully upright. She studied his expression carefully, but as usual, there was nothing to read there. The faint smile could just as well have been painted on. It was a carefully cultivated mask of pleasantness, and meant nothing.

Von Rothbart was a powerful man, descendant of warriors, and the warrior blood that flowed in his veins showed in the rippling muscles of shoulder and arm, leg and chest. Many sorcerers, he has told her, let their bodies become weak as they concentrated on magic to the exclusion of all else—and subsequently, when confronted with a warrior protected against their magic, were easy to slay.

"You, of course, will have other weapons than strength to bring to bear against such a lusty young man, and will have no need of force," he had said, his mouth twisting in a cynical smile. "You will only need to lure him into complacency, and you can remove him with a cup or a hidden dagger. You are female; such actions are second nature to your kind."

She had hidden her hurt, as she always did when he said such things. He had taught her to conceal her emotions at all times, for emotions were weapons, and it was not good to put a weapon in the hands of anyone else, even one's father. And even though the words hurt, she knew he was right. In such a situation, she *would* take the easier route to disarming an open enemy. But why must he always drive home his contention that women came to treachery as easily as breathing? Could he not at least see that even if *most* women were treacherous by nature, she was the exception to that rule? After all, she was his daughter, body, mind and soul; he had the training and raising of her, in the image he wished. His thoughts were hers; why could he never acknowledge that?

She brought her thoughts to heel with a wrench, and pummeled her rebellious emotions as a housewife would pummel unruly dough. She could not read his mental state from his face, nor from his clothing; it was the same black-and-brown doublet, shirt, and hose he had worn earlier this evening. He *did* wear his owl-feather cape now, though, which meant he had been flying, and that was another clue to where he had been, for he seldom flew unless he was hunting another traitor to bring to just punishment. But why was he hunting again, so soon? How could he be bored with a new captive when as yet he'd paid scarcely any attention to her?

She gave voice to none of her questions; women should remain silent until spoken to, even the daughter of a sorcerer who was a magician in her own right. She was as impeccably trained in proper manners as in all else.

"You have been practicing." It was a statement, not a question. His eyes narrowed, although there was not as yet any accusation in his tone. "And what of the new one?"

Not quite a rebuke, but a reminder that one waited in the wings, if she had neglected her duty out of boredom. "She sleeps, sir," she reported confidently. "And I gave the Silent Ones orders to warn me if she showed any signs of waking. Had they done so, I would have abandoned whatever I was doing to follow your orders that she not be left alone while awake."

"Good." No more than that, but the threat of rebuke passed, and she felt it. "Her progress?"

"She has accepted her fate, if not her fault," Odile told him. "She shows resignation, but no sign of repentance. I believe that she will join the flock in the morning, and acknowledge the fact that there will be no rescue from the punishment her own folly has brought to her."

"As I would expect from a woman." The scorn in his voice was as habitual as the pleasant expression of his face. "And what is your progress, since I find you at your proper studies?"

Rather than answering him directly, she turned, and carefully lifted the little silver cage from her workbench, handing it to him. He held it up, peering at its occupant from beneath a pair of heavy, fox-colored eyebrows.

"A sparrow?" he said, for the moment looking puzzled, since he had no idea what she had been attempting to master. "I see nothing remarkable about it."

"Hold it in that beam of moonlight coming through the window behind you, Father," she urged, her excitement building despite her effort to control it. She knew what the result would be, having made the trial herself already. When he saw for himself what she had mastered, surely a word of praise would come from his lips, surely for once his eyes would warm with approval!

He held the ring at the top of the cage between his thumb and forefinger, and moved the cage until it was squarely in the path of the moonbeam. The tiny bird inside fluttered its wings in helpless alarm, but the moonlight fell squarely on it, and it could not evade what was coming.

The moment the light touched it, the bird froze in place. It shivered violently, then the shivering increased, until for a moment it was a vibrating blur in the thin, blue light. It uttered a terrified chirp, and dropped to the floor of the cage, still vibrating in every feather.

Then it wasn't a bird at all, but the mouse that the Silent One had brought her earlier that evening, a mouse that picked itself up from the bottom of the cage and squeaked with profound unhappiness.

Odile looked up at her father, glowing with pride and expectation. She had mastered the transformation spell that enabled her father to control his captives, keeping them in the form of swans by day, and maidens only as long as the moon was in the sky. Granted, it was only a mouse—but it was a small step to go from mouse to maid, smaller by far than to master it in the first place.

So she waited, holding her breath, hoping for a word, a sign, the least hint of praise.

But von Rothbart stared woodenly at the tiny

mouse, saying nothing at all—then turned his hard gaze back to his daughter. "Can you remove the magic?" he asked, as she had known he would.

"Yes, Father," she affirmed, but her heart was beginning to sink although she gave no sign of her disappointment. *He isn't impressed. I had been so certain he would be—I was wrong. I thought I had accomplished something important, but it must be that I have only done what I should have.* The approval she craved more than food or drink would clearly not be forthcoming. Once again, she had failed to exceed her father's expectations—and he had made it abundantly clear that merely fulfilling them was not worthy of praise.

"See that you are certain in the spell and its removal," he said gruffly, an odd glint in his eyes for a moment, a glint she did not understand, and was not entirely certain she really saw. "Magic is useless if it cannot be reversed or removed."

With that, he put down the cage and waited. Stifling a gulp of disappointment, blinking eyes that stung for just a moment, she removed the magic, taking the sparkling motes of power back into herself as they drained from the mouse, until it was no more than an ordinary, if severely confused, house pest.

Von Rothbart turned, his feather cape rustling softly, and left the room without another word.

Odile watched her father's back, swallowing involuntary bitter tears of disappointment and rejection, feeling her head droop a little as her heart sank with dejection.

Still, her fingers were steady as she reached for the cage to release the captive. She unlocked the catch, pulled on the door—and frowned. The door was stuck—but it had moved freely enough before.

She moved the cage into the light, and examined it carefully; to her astonishment, the cage was now mildly deformed, making the door stick rather than moving freely on its hinges. There was only one way, one time, that could have happened—when her father had picked up the cage to examine its contents and then held it as the sparrow became the mouse. His powerful hands had, for some reason, contracted around the top and base of the cage, subtly deforming it.

The sky lightened from black to gray as dawn neared. All over the gardens, birds shook themselves awake, and a few tentative songs replaced the chorus of frogs and crickets. Von Rothbart was in his suite with the great door shut; if he was not already asleep, he soon would be.

Odile, however, had one more duty to perform before she retired to her bed, and it was one she did not begrudge spending the time on.

This morning the moon would set and the sun rise at nearly the same moment, and the setting of the moon marked the moment when the maidens would undergo their own transformation. As Odile paced down the steps of the manor, the maids cast wary glances at her, then abandoned their tasks, taking her appearance to mean that their evening was at an end. They rose from their seats, dropped the flowers they had been gathering, deserted their dances in mid-step, and drifted to the water's edge, gathering there on the soft grass in a rough group. Jeanette awakened the new one and, rising, took her by the hand to draw her to her feet and lead her to join the rest. Even Odette left her seat in the shadows of the marble pavilion and came to the water's edge on the island. Odile followed, but did not actually join the group, keeping a delicately calculated distance between herself and her father's captives.

They all waited, in silence, as the moon touched the horizon, then descended.

When the last sliver of pale disk slipped below the horizon, the maidens stiffened, then dropped to the ground in awkward curtsies, as if faint, their silken gowns puddling around them.

A peculiar, opalescent mist rose about them, a mist that separated into pockets surrounding each girl, then closed in on them. Odile watched closely, eyes narrowed and forehead furrowed, drinking in each subtle nuance of her father's magic, searching for the refinements she had clearly not mastered.

The mist shivered, the girls trembled, then the mist settled over them, obscuring their forms completely in shimmering whiteness for just a moment.

Then the first rays of the sun touched and banished the pockets of mist—and the graceful heads of von Rothbart's flock of enchanted swans rose from their recumbent, feathered forms, dark eyes shining softly in the rosy dawn light.

By ones and twos, they stretched out their necks, ruffled their feathers, and stepped into the water of the lake. Eight black swans swam amidst the white ones, dipping their heads in willing obeisance to the most beautiful and graceful of all as she glided toward the gathered flock from the shore of the island refuge, a swan wearing a tiny golden crown on a necklet resting on her snowy breast.

Odette was as flawless and lovely as a swan as she was as a maiden, and Odile experienced a twinge of jealousy, and tried to banish it.

If she had been as beautiful of heart as she is of face and figure, she would not be paddling in Father's pond wearing nothing but feathers. She allowed her control of her expression to slip just a little as she met the mournful gaze of the queen of the swans. Her lips twisted in a sardonic smile. *You brought your fate upon yourself, no matter how much you would like to deny it, Odette. If you had paid half as much attention to the state of your soul as you did to your mirror, you would still sit at your father's side.*

But the swan turned her eyes away, and led her flock across the lake, taking them into the shelter of the reeds where they could not be seen. Odile wasn't worried; they couldn't escape, and in the form of swans, they couldn't work any harm on themselves. Her father's spells prevented them from flying off unless he led the flock, just as they prevented the maidens from leaving the grounds and gardens.

But she paused at the edge of the water as the last of the swans vanished into the reeds. The surface of the lake, unruffled by bird or breeze, mirrored the pink-streaked clouds overhead. There were no mirrors in the manor; von Rothbart forbade them. She knelt on the bank and leaned over to look at her reflection, automatically putting her hand to her hair to smooth it from her brow.

Her reflection looked back at her, solemn blue eyes above sharply defined cheekbones, skin pale as porcelain, hair of spun silver. She studied herself, critically. *Not unattractive, but too thin and too odd for beauty. My hair is the wrong color, my eyes are too pale. No, I am no competition for any of the swans, and certainly not as beautiful as Odette.* Surrounded by beauties as she was—even the four little swans were lovely, and getting more beautiful as time went on—she could not help contrasting her appearance with theirs.

Even her father had made comments. *"Take more care with your looks,"* he would say in irritation. *"Peasants look more pleasing than my own daughter. My captives look like queens, and my daughter a drudge."* And yet, she was not supposed to take overmuch care of her looks, either—for he would chide her for vanity if he thought she spent too long in the hands of the Silent Ones. It was hard not to feel jealous of the so-perfect Odette, supernaturally lovely without effort.

In a burst of impatience, she flicked her fingers in the water, destroying her reflection, and rose to her feet. Her duty was at an end for the night, and she could seek her own bed until the sun dropped below the horizon tonight. While she slept, the Silent Ones would see to it that the swans were fed, with bread and grain, with crisp greens and savory herbs.

Odile walked slowly toward the steps as the early sun gilded the granite and gave it a spurious warmth. Birds caroled joyfully all around, the same birds that shivered in silence and fear when von Rothbart donned his feather cape and took to the sky as a great owl. Now the garden that had been a study in soft black and silver-blue last night showed the true colors of its palette—yellow lilies and white, pink, and red roses, the blue of cornflowers, the purple of violet and pansy, the gold of calendula and chamomile. Fragrances spicy and sweet filled the air as flowers opened their petals to the sun. Phlox and meadowsweet nodded as she passed, gentian and lupine lifted heads as proud as Odette's to greet her. In many ways, she hated to sleep the day away, and sometimes would scant herself on sleep in order to drink in the sun and morning air.

Not this morning, though. She was in no mood to enjoy the birdsong or the riot of flowers, and besides, the spell she had worked so hard to master had worn her out. She stifled a yawn with one hand as she slowly mounted the stairs, and the thought of her soft bed in her darkened room had more appeal than the azure sky and emerald lawn.

Magical work never seems to tire Father, she thought resentfully. *Why does it always exhaust me?*

The door opened as she approached. Von Rothbart was certainly asleep at this point, for if he had not been, there would not have been a single one of the invisible servants free to open the door for her.

She passed through the portal, and it closed behind her. The two torches in the Great Hall had already been extinguished, and the golden morning light poured through the clerestory windows high in the walls, shining on the strange creatures frozen in the weave of the tapestries, glinting from dim jewels, as dust motes danced in the slanting beams. In the shadows below, Odile made her way to her bedroom, where thinner beams of light played and flirted through cracks in her shutters, and a gentle breeze sighed through the same cracks and brought a hint of the garden into her chamber.

Invisible hands helped her shed the gossamer folds of her midnight-silk gown; more helpers brought her a wispy sleeping shift the color and texture of dawn clouds. It slipped over her head, and she tugged it into place, while the servants tidied everything up. The bed covers turned back beneath the ministering of another of the Silent Ones, and Odile needed no further invitation than that. She climbed into bed, and the bed curtains slid shut around her, cutting off the playful sunbeams and leaving her in lavender-scented darkness as profound as the night.

Now, at last, she could lose herself in sleep, and perhaps in her dreams her father would be pleased with her.

CHAPTER TWO

WITHIN the cedar-paneled robing room, a handful of women hovered over their ruler, speaking
in carefully modulated voices. The queen hated what
she called "cackle and gab," and this soothing murmur
was more like the hum of contented bees. Seated at
her dressing table, cosmetics spread before her in a
palette of open jars, Queen Clothilde frowned at her
mirror: The traitorous object revealed far too many
wrinkles around her eyes, and too many silver hairs
among the blonde. *I must try the saffron rinse after
all, I suppose, ruinously expensive as it is—or bring
back the fashion for henins and wimples to hide hair
altogether.*

"The gold-spangled headdress and the red-gold coronet," she ordered, in a voice scarcely louder than
that of her women, and the ladies hurried to fetch the
precious objects from the wardrobe. With the spangles
to distract the eye, and the reflections from the ruddy
gold adding bold color, her silvering hair would be
less obvious. There was nothing to be done about the
wrinkles, except to paint her face carefully with egg
white and alum to tighten her skin and try not to smile
or frown once it dried.

She attended to her face herself, and did not allow
her ladies-in-waiting back inside her chamber to dress

her hair until after she had done all that art and arti-
fice could contrive to erase what time had done to
her. *Alum and egg white at the eyes and mouth to
shrink the skin tight, powder to cover the shine.* . . .
She dipped tiny brushes in the pots on her table; rose
quartz held the carmine for the lips and cheek to
counterfeit the blush of youth, malachite the kohl and
mica to add depth and sparkle for the eyes, all im-
ported at unthinkable expense from the Holy Land.
Charcoal powder in sweet oil, made into a paste, darkened her lashes and brows, and a touch of belladonna
in the eyes themselves gave her a wide and doelike
innocence. Alabaster held the alum, and she mixed
the egg-white concoction fresh each morning on a
matching alabaster palette. Talc ground to powder she
dusted over her face with a hare's foot, softening the
effect of cosmetics so that only the most experienced
eye could tell that she used them at all. When she
was satisfied with the effect, she beckoned to the door
without turning her head, and an augmented group
crowded into the room.

While her ladies combed and arranged her hair,
then put on her jewels, headdress, and coronet, her
ministers stood at a respectful distance, presenting her
with some of the less-urgent questions of the kingdom.
Items of a truly pressing nature and great importance
were saved for the Council Chamber, but there was
no point in taking up the time of the Council with the
trivialities of household matters.

In fact, these matters were so very trivial, that had
she not insisted on having final approval of *everything,*
she need not have troubled herself with more than
half of them. More often than not she didn't pay a
great deal of attention to the droning of her ministers
in the morning, once she had the gist of what they
were droning about.

This morning, however, was different. "Repeat

that," she ordered sharply, losing her usually tranquil tone as something she thought she'd heard actually struck her with palpable shock. Her Minister of the Household started with surprise at the snap in her voice.

He recovered his aplomb immediately. "I said, Madame, that as Prince Siegfried's eighteenth birthday is but six months away and fast approaching, Your Highness should take thought to an appropriate celebration. He will, of course, be assuming the crown once his majority is achieved, and the subject of his coronation will be handled by the full Council rather than your Privy Council, but the celebration is a Household concern. It would be advisable, for instance, to invite eligible young women to present themselves with a view to a swift engagement, and a marriage following the coronation. The young women of your court are amiable enough but—" he hesitated, "—hardly suitable in rank, much less in dower."

Clothilde stopped herself from clenching her jaw out of habit, and from frowning only by reminding herself of the recent application of egg white. "I will take thought for all of these things, Heinrich," she said smoothly, schooling her voice to dulcet sweetness. "You may trust me to arrange everything for the celebration; I would hardly care to put such important arrangements for my beloved son in the hands of anyone but myself. Is there anything else?"

"Only your signature here, Madame," said the Minister of Supply, presenting his list of household expenses to her. She freed a hand long enough to inscribe her name and press her signet ring into the hot wax of the seal, and the men retreated, leaving her alone with her women.

She allowed them to fuss over her a little longer, then dismissed them with a wave of her hand. They gathered up their combs and brushes and bowed themselves out, leaving her alone with her thoughts. After a moment, she rose from her dressing table and retreated to her private sitting room, taking a seat on the thronelike chair nearest the window and picking up her embroidery. But she set no stitches, for it was her thoughts that held her full attention.

They were not pleasant thoughts, for although she had taken pains not to show it, the Household Minister's words had come as a violent shock to her system.

Can it really have been eighteen years already? Her throat tightened with dismay. *How could the time have passed so quickly?*

For eighteen years she had held supreme power in this kingdom, answerable only to the Emperor himself—and the Emperor rarely bestirred himself to take interest in anything outside of his own court. For eighteen years, since the death of Siegfried's unlamented father, hers had been the strong hand on the reins. King Ulrich had been a foolish man, a poor ruler, and no one had been particularly dismayed by his death shortly before the birth of his son—least of all his widow Clothilde.

Though the ministers were quite taken aback when they attempted to rule me as they had ruled him. She permitted herself as much of a smile as would leave the egg white undisturbed. She had foreseen that something might happen to make her a widow, for Ulrich was a heedless sportsman, reckless in the hunt and the joust, throwing himself into all manner of hazards and trusting to his luck to save him. Sooner or later, she had expected that luck to run out, and eventually it had. By that time, with charm, tact, and her considerable beauty, she had already taken pains to win the loyalty of Ulrich's knights; when the ministers and nobles attempted to put her in her place, there had been a brief scuffle and an execution or two, but on the whole, she had assumed the throne without a great deal of difficulty as Siegfried's regent.

But the throne was mine only as Queen Regent, in trust for my son. . . . She repressed another frown.

That was the rub; she had always known, somewhere deep inside, that she would not be the reigning monarch forever, unless a similar accident occurred to her son. She had been *very* careful of his health in the earliest years, for she knew that several of the defeated nobles were watching her sharply at that point, but once he was of an age to be turned over to tutors, she had encouraged the same reckless behavior in him as his father had shown. Sadly, he had never been quite reckless enough; meanwhile his eighteenth birthday had seemed unthinkably far in the future, and there had always been plenty of time to consider what to do when the time to turn over the throne neared. Now it was here, and somehow she had been caught unawares; no accidents had occurred, and he was healthy and fit.

Nevertheless, she *had* laid enough carefully prepared groundwork to have a number of options. A contrived accident, however, she dismissed out of hand. This close to the fatal day, it would be very suspicious. *Siegfried is not as foolish as his father, but at least I have seen to it that he is ill-prepared to rule.*

It had been simple enough to beguile the intelligent child with scholarly tutors, to distract him with books and learning, to immerse him in Greek and Latin to the exclusion of those skills a ruler required. Romances and minstrelsy proved another distraction; he was an indifferent poet, but she had encouraged that pursuit to the exclusion of more practical matters. In fact, she had so petted and praised his scholastic efforts that he was inclined to trot them out like prize horses whenever the occasion warranted, and often when it didn't. That offended the sensibilities of her plain and illiterate nobles, who considered learning to be a foolish waste of time at best, and effete at worst.

When his physical energy demanded an outlet, hoping for heedless risks to life and limb, she encouraged him in the same pursuits that had put his father's life at hazard, then heaped fond praise on him to inflate his pride. Horse, hawk, and hound were his passions, shared with his best friends; he played at jousting and bested even hardened warriors. His love of lore might be considered effete, but no one could accuse his mother of coddling him and shielding him from manly pursuits. And none of this was of the least practical use.

He was an outstanding horseman, a fearless rider willing to take any jump and ride any beast—but he knew nothing of strategy or war tactics beyond the little he had learned from his books. He was a masterly scholar, and had managed to annoy every unschooled noble in his service at one point or another by trotting out his superior intellect and knowledge on every possible occasion. An outstanding jouster, he offended seasoned warriors by considering their experience to be the self-aggrandizing bluster of men whose time had come and gone. He could defeat almost anyone in single combat, but if he ever had to fight in a real pitched battle, he would probably be pulled from his horse and killed by a swarm of peasants with pikes before he knew what had happened—and he was so utterly self-confident that he dismissed any advice as the pessimism of old men. He knew how to command, but not how to rule; how to flatter a woman, but not his knights and ministers; how to bend a horse to his will, but not a man. The maidens of the court adored him, as did the heedless young men, but the older men, the ones who held the power, were not so blinded by his personality and overall good nature. Only tradition would make them insist on crowning

Prince Siegfried as their king—but they held so stubbornly to tradition that it would be easier to persuade the trees of the forest to walk than it would be to persuade them to pass him over in favor of his mother.

Why must men be such utter idiots?

She had hoped, after all these years of successful rule, they *might* have been willing to retain the status quo—but Heinrich's words today had made it clear that the old men *would* follow tradition over common sense. Women could and would only be regents, keeping thrones faithfully in trust for their sons, and handing them over without a murmur the moment the little fools reached the magic age of eighteen.

Indeed.

Well, if they would insist on tradition over good sense, she would have to take another path—and something the minister had said suggested the tactics she might take.

Siegfried was romantic, susceptible to women, and had no sense at all where a lovely face was concerned. His tutor had encouraged him in his fantasies, filling him with tales of knights and their chaste ladies, of love from afar, of endless quests undertaken for the sake of a pair of enchanting eyes. He was a ripe fruit ready to fall into the white hands of the first maiden who was clever enough to appeal to his notions of romance and chivalry.

Or into the hands of the first maiden who is coached to appeal to those notions. Yes! Yes, this is what I have been searching for! She nodded, lowering her lids over her eyes in satisfaction. *That* was the way of handling this situation; she needed to find an empty-headed beauty of sufficient rank to qualify as his bride, one she could manipulate into keeping him busy and distracted as he tried to live up to the image of all those ballads—

One who can persuade him into some impossible

quest, perhaps, to prove his love for her? One who will encourage him to enter every tournament possible to honor her?

A possible goal, but not one she could count on. No, better to simply provide him with a foolish little toy to occupy his attention, while his mother took the burdens and difficulties of rule into her own conscientious hands. Even the old traditionalists would be content with the situation, so long as they had a king in name again.

I can call myself the First Minister, or some such thing. And whenever he shows any interest in ruling, I shall present him with all the tedious mundane matters—then coach his wife into some crisis or other to distract him. Her right hand closed unconsciously over her left, covering the signet ring as if to keep it from being wrested from her. *Or—if she is delicate, her first pregnancy may well kill her, and he will be plunged into inconsolable mourning for as long as I need to keep him there.* There were many possibilities branching from this path—enough to satisfy even her ambition.

Her success would depend on finding the right girl, though. Her plans would fall apart if Siegfried's bride could not be properly manipulated. She could not go hunting such girls herself; for this, she needed help. Fortunately, that help was close at hand.

She summoned one of her ladies from the outer room where they sat over their embroidery and sewing. "Bring me Uwe, the minstrel," she ordered. "I have a headache."

The lady bowed and silently left the room. In a reasonable time, Uwe appeared, bearing his lute, with an expression as calculatedly bland as Clothilde's own.

Uwe owed everything to Clothilde: prosperity, fame, and above all, security in his position. That, for a minstrel, was above price, for he knew that even if he became ill or old and useless, he would retain all he had now. He was, gratifyingly enough, one of those who knew how to gracefully acknowledge his debts without being disgustingly servile. In public, he showed the same face as every other minstrel—a sort of poetic arrogance, a barely veiled scorn for all those who could be made or broken by a carefully worded song. In private, he was wholly and completely Clothilde's creature.

He sat down on a stool conveniently near Clothilde's chair and began to play, but not to sing. That was for the benefit of her ladies in the outer chamber, for the sound of his playing would cover their quiet conversation.

"I have a task for you, one that will entail some traveling," she said softly, leaning back in her chair and closing her eyes, in order to better feign the head-ache she had claimed.

"That presents no problem," he replied, just as softly. "Command me."

She saw no reason to hedge her words. "Siegfried should be wed as soon as possible. I need you to find suitable candidates—of proper rank, with beauty enough to dazzle him, fragile and charming, utterly brainless, and possessing wills of butter. But above all, they must be maidens who will be more than happy to be advised and counseled—ruled, in fact—on all things by their so-considerate mother-in-law."

He chuckled, a sound that he covered with a partic-ularly intricate fingering passage. "To be presented at the prince's coming-of-age celebration? An excellent and most thoughtful plan; surely he will fall helplessly in romantic love with at least one. Siegfried should be proud to have a mother so considerate of his welfare. How many?"

"Four, I think. I will provide you with invitations to present to the parents, once you make your selection." She curved her lips into a faint smile; it was so gratifying to have *one* person clever enough to understand what she required without having to be given every little detail. "I leave the rest in your hands."

"I live to do your will," he responded, as she had known he would. "Is your headache better?"

"Entirely cured." She extended her hand to him. He kissed it, then rose and took his leave.

She watched him go with detached admiration. In her younger days, when he had first appeared at her court and caught her attention, she had enjoyed a brief affair with him. She had done so in order to have yet another hold over him, but had found it remarkably pleasurable on many levels. Pillow talk with Uwe had been instructive, and had contributed to her early success in winning over her nobles.

She had been quick to notice when he tired of her, as she had known he would—and perhaps it had cemented his loyalty when she had let him go, indeed, had directed his attention to one of her ladies, and arranged for that lady's husband to be elsewhere at opportune times for Uwe. That had been only the first of many such arrangements on her part, showing him that although she was a woman, she was not prey to the weaknesses of women; she had even presented him with an attractive and obedient servant—female, of course—so that he was relieved of the need to charm before he satisfied himself. From time to time after their initial affair had concluded, she had welcomed him again into her bed, secretly of course, and he had been as satisfactory there as elsewhere.

She roused herself from her reverie; there were things to be done. With great care for the drape of her gown, she rose from her chair and entered the outer chamber. With a gesture, she summoned her ladies from their own handiwork, gathered them around her and left her chambers, descending from

the Royal Tower by the worn stone staircase to the
Great Hall.

As she entered, the assembled courtiers bowed and
curtsied, and she paused on the threshold, hand
cupped once again over her ring.

The Great Hall's lofty ceiling, lost in the shadows,
boasted no captured battle banners hanging from the
crossbeams. That was an innovation on Clothilde's
part; displayed bravely above the heads of her courtiers were banners portraying the arms of everyone of
any note in the Court. The most important hung closest to the throne, of course, but *everyone* who boasted
a title and arms, even if it was no higher than esquire,
could look up and see his arms on display there.

It flattered everyone without obviously *being* flattery, and everyone who looked up remembered that
it was Clothilde who had put their arms in the Great
Hall, replacing the trophies of past kings.

The battle flags now decked the formerly bare walls
of the garrison hall. This also flattered Clothilde's soldiers, because she had told them that the battle flags
should be in the custody of those who were truly responsible for capturing them in the first place.

Whitewashed plaster coated the stone walls of the
Great Hall, keeping out drafts and insulating the
room from the damp that came with walls of stone.
False columns painted on the plaster, with false
walls and statuary painted between, made the room
look larger than it was, and a gallery painted above
the columns held the likenesses of the knights and
ladies of Arthur's fabled Round Table looking down
on the courtiers of Clothilde's court. In her husband's
time, there had been no gallery above the painted
columns, and the columns themselves barely stood out
against the cracked plaster, stained with decades of
smoke and soot.

Like the Great Hall, Clothilde's male courtiers had

changed since her husband's time; no longer did they appear in garments worn, shabby, or stained. Even the oldest and most recalcitrant had been coerced into well-made, clean court-garb by wives, sisters, and mothers.

Perhaps they did not care before because the Hall was too dark for anyone to see what disgraceful state their men appeared in. A good proportion of men, as she well knew, did not care what they wore, nor how stained and disreputable it was, so long as they did not freeze or bake.

She paced gravely up the middle of the Great Hall, as her courtiers moved respectfully aside for her. Reaching the dais, she took the three steps in the same grave manner, then turned, bowed her head in acknowledgment, and took her seat on the throne.

Her herald stepped up to the front of the dais, knocked his staff three times on the floor to signify that court was in session, and the first of the day's audience seekers presented himself as his name was called.

Clothilde clasped her hands together in her lap and sat with the perfect stillness of one of the painted figures above, listening with an expression containing equal parts of gravity, attention, and concern.

Siegfried was nowhere to be seen, of course. Court bored him, for Clothilde had seen to it that he only knew the most tedious aspects.

As she sent one petitioner away satisfied, and prepared to welcome a wealthy trader, she considered her court, *her* court, the court that she had made out of the dribs and drabs her husband had ruled. Her resolve hardened.

She would never tamely hand what was hers by right over to her fool of a son. Never.

Her hand covered that emblem of her power, her signet ring, and it warmed until it felt alive. Siegfried would not have that power; she vowed it more fervently and with more feeling than she had made her wedding pledge.

And if all her plans failed, if there was no other way to keep the power of the throne in her hands—it was still possible for deliverance to come in the form of a so-tragic accident.

"Hah, Dorian, you'll never disarm me *that* way!" Siegfried taunted his opponent as he countered a clumsy attempt to knock his sword from his hand. Sweat poured down his back and neck, and he had a bit of a headache from squinting through the slit in his helm, but he wasn't even breathing hard. This little exercise was just enough to get him warmed up, and he was enjoying himself to the hilt. He replied to the move Dorian had attempted with an expert version of the same blow. As his sword hit solidly, the vibration of the strike ran up his arm until he felt it in his shoulder, calling up a momentary ache—but at that point, it was no matter. Dorian's blade went flying, and the young man swore, shaking numb fingers as he backed out of the way of Siegried's blade.

"Dammit, Siegfried, can't you disarm a fellow without taking the use of his hand?" Dorian shoved up the visor of his helm with his uninjured left, and glared at the victor. Siegfried laughed and doffed his helm altogether, casting it carelessly into the hands of his squire who caught it expertly and set it aside for cleaning.

"I warned you that you were no match for me," Siegfried responded, still laughing, as he handed his sword to his second squire. He walked toward Dorian, pulling off his gauntlets as he did. "I warned you, but you insisted on trying my paces. Just because you've gone off to the Emperor's court and learned a trick or two doesn't mean you can come back and give me a drubbing."

"Yes, well, now I am well and truly defeated, and won't be able to close my fingers for the next hour, and I hope you're satisfied," Dorian said sourly, a scowl turning his handsome, fair face into a mask of irritation. His own squire hurried to his side and pulled off the gauntlet on the injured hand.

"Don't sulk, Dorian, you look like a thundercloud," admonished Siegfried's best friend Benno, slapping the defeated knight on the back as the maidens who'd gathered to watch the contest giggled behind their hands. "Here we've got the prettiest ladies of the court come to welcome you back and cheer you on, and you're going to frighten them away with your black looks!"

Dorian cast an involuntary glance at the colorful little knot of girls in their delicate linen gowns and embroidered surcoats, braided hair coiled neatly under light veils, and managed to smooth his expression into something more acceptable. "All the same, Siegfried, it's damned hard, coming back after all this time to have you trounce me first thing without even having to catch your breath!" the knight complained, with less heat. "Don't you think you could at least have let me win just this once, as a courtesy to somebody you hadn't seen in three years?"

"Siegfried doesn't hold back for anyone, not even me," Benno broke in playfully, before Siegfried could say the same thing. Siegfried raised an eyebrow at him, but added nothing to that; after all, it *was* true. "Once his blood gets stirred up, he just forgets everything but fighting. If you ask me, there's a bit of the berserker in our Prince."

"Er, well, you're probably right," Dorian grumbled,

but he seemed mollified. Siegfried snorted, but kept his thoughts to himself. *He hasn't changed, not in three years. Still can't admit it when he's beaten, and expects a man to hold back for him. Holding back doesn't serve any purpose even in practice, and doing less than your best isn't honorable.* Just because Dorian had some high-placed relative in the Emperor's Court he seemed to think he had the right to special privileges here. *Hah! If that relative is all that close and highly placed, what's he doing back here, then? He's nothing more than another hanger-on, that's clear, or Dorian would be in the Emperor's personal train of knights by now.*

Siegfried did feel a twinge of envy, though; Dorian had all the luck! Three years at the greatest court in Europe, and the mere thought of all the opportunities for adventure that must have been given him made Siegfried want to gnash his teeth. *If I'd been allowed to go—I surely wouldn't have come back here! By now I'd have won a hundred tournaments, and I'd have all that ransom and armor to prove it. I'd be the Emperor's Champion, or else I'd have gone on a quest to rescue a kidnapped lady, or maybe I'd have killed a dragon.* The fact that Dorian had accomplished nothing of the sort only made Siegfried more certain that *he* would have covered himself in glory.

There was no reason to tell Dorian that, however; he must feel badly enough, going home without anything more than his knighthood to his name, not even a single tournament laurel to decorate the crest of his helm.

"Why don't you come on the hunt this afternoon with Benno and me?" Siegfried asked instead, as the squires unlaced his mail shirt. Dorian shook his head.

"My father ordered my presence; heaven only knows what for," Dorian grumbled. "I'll tell you what I'm afraid of—I think he's been bride hunting for me, and I'm about to be chained down to a homely sack of turnips with a face like a sow whose only virtue is a father with equally fat lands."

"Oh, well—but if her dowry is rich enough, all you have to do is get her with child and then take your pleasure elsewhere," Benno replied cheerfully, his bright blue eyes sparkling. "Plenty of girls about—fat lands means pretty serf girls, for one thing, and there's not a few lonely ladies need a generous fellow's company. As for the bride herself, put out the candle, have her women douse her with scent, and it won't matter what she looks like. Get her with child once a year, and she won't have anything to complain of."

Siegfried frowned; that was no way to talk about a highborn maiden, even if she did have a face like a sow. He hoped the maids watching them hadn't overheard, and changed the subject back to the hunt. "We're looking for a new hunting ground; we've hunted so much around the palace that we need to let the game come back. Are you sure you can't get away to come with us?"

"Absolutely certain; Father was—insistent." Dorian had lost his anger with Siegfried in his annoyance with his father. "But there will be tomorrow, I hope?"

"And the next day and the next, until we find someplace with decent game." It was Siegfried's turn to slap Dorian companionably on the back; Dorian stood firm against a friendly blow that would have flattened a lesser man, and his stock rose a bit in Siegfried's estimation.

Dorian went off to disarm. Siegfried stripped his own armor off and left it to his squires to gather up. The maidens drifted off to the gardens when it became plain that the prince had no intention of seeking out their companionship or providing further amusement with another bout. Siegfried signaled to a servant in royal livery waiting against the wall for his orders.

"Fetch us some bread and cheese and a couple of wine flasks from the kitchen and bring them to the stable," he told the man, and turned to his friend. Benno was a little shorter than Siegfried, darker, and considerably lighter; what cemented their friendship was a common interest in learning, not fighting. With Siegfried's tutor, they often discussed Greek philosophy or Latin literature far into the night. "I'm not of a mind to get pulled into my mother's toils this afternoon. What say you to going straight to the stable and riding off before anyone knows what we're about?"

"I'd say that's a good plan," Benno agreed readily, as he would agree with almost anything Siegfried suggested by way of amusement. "Will you ride your black today or the bay?"

"The bay, I think; he's the better jumper." Siegfried was looking forward to a good, challenging ride over rough ground; for some reason, he'd been suffering from a growing discontent since late spring, and he couldn't seem to shake the feeling except when he was doing something active. Music made him melancholy, he was dissatisfied with his own attempts at poetry, and the books he used to love left him feeling stale and flat. He wanted something, but he didn't know what it was.

A good war, maybe, is what I need; a fight worthy of a man. Not that I'm likely to get one. No evil sorcerers about, and no one threatening to lay siege to us. Much as he loved his mother, there was no denying the fact that her court was that of a woman—slow, sleepy, and dull. Peace was all very well for old men and females, but a young man needed something to get his blood stirred up.

He and Benno strolled across the yard to the stable, leaving his squires still picking up his arms and armor for cleaning. His shirt stuck to his back, and he couldn't wait to be mounted and out of the still air within the castle grounds. There was no breeze to cool him here in the courtyard, and he ran his hand through his sweat-matted hair to get it out of his face as he entered the shadows of the stable. A groom hurried to meet them, but Siegfried passed him by, too eager to wait for his beast to be brought to him.

Benno ordered his dun hunter saddled; Siegfried himself saw to the harnessing of his bay, throwing blanket and saddle over the strong back, then tightening the girth as a stable boy got the bridle onto the beast's head and the bit into his teeth. Siegfried took over fastening the throat and cheek straps, then led the bay out into the sunlight. The horse was calm, but fresh and eager to be out of the stable; good omens for a fine ride. He mounted up and checked the stirrups and seat of the saddle as Benno's horse was brought, and as his friend took his own seat, the servant arrived with their provisions. They each took a flask and a packet of bread and cheese and stowed them in their saddlebags, and Benno's squire brought their bows and quivers. As he waited for Benno to arrange his weapons to his liking, he felt that stale, flat feeling come over him again.

What is wrong with me? Why does nothing satisfy me anymore?

A minute later, Siegfried looked up at the blue sky above the castle towers, and felt his heart lift a little at the prospect of an afternoon of freedom. He spurred his horse forward and trotted out into the forest, Benno a pace behind. If a gallop through wild woods couldn't cure him, at least for an afternoon he could forget his discontent.

CHAPTER THREE

NOW that the new one—Katerina was her name, apparently—had resigned herself to her situation and had joined the activities of the flock, Odile could go back to her own concerns, relying entirely on the Silent Ones to oversee the swan-maidens. The Silent Ones had always served as spies on the maidens when von Rothbart didn't need them; they were perfect for the task, after all. Although they could not interfere effectively if something were to go wrong, and could not report what they observed to *her* (although they could communicate with von Rothbart directly), they could get her attention when something was wrong. With her father gone nearly every night, the Silent Ones had no need to hover over him, waiting on his whims. Odile left half of them on watch with the maidens, and now had the time she wanted to concentrate on her own magical studies.

She perfected her own transformation spell until it was a marvel of swift efficiency, but she had no intention of showing it to von Rothbart a second time. She was tired of rebuffs when she expected praise; there must be something she could do to change the situation. For the past few days, she had devoured book after book in the library, sitting next to an open window overlooking the gardens in order to enjoy the summer evenings while she sought for a new direction in her work. She *had* to have something to show her father, for he kept up a steady inquiry into the progress of her studies. That inquiry would become painfully embarrassing soon; traces of sardonic amusement already showed in his voice. Her problem was that she couldn't think of any course of study that would please him.

Finally, she tried a different approach to the problem. She cleaned off a wax tablet and sat in her favorite seat with it in her lap and a stylus in her hand, a single lamp burning above her head. She divided the tablet in half with a line scribed in the wax; on the right, she inscribed a word or symbol that stood for a spell she had mastered that had brought forth a word of praise, while on the left, similar signs for spells that had brought indifference, or worse, veiled disapproval.

When both sides of the tablet were full—though the list of spells was by no means the complete tally of everything she had learned—she leaned her chin on her hand and studied the result.

One pattern emerged quickly. Whenever she mastered a type of magic that von Rothbart used, her presentation invariably got a cool reception. In fact, the more powerful the spell, the likelier it was that he would have that reaction.

Ah. But how odd. It puzzled her; it would have been more logical for him to praise her for emulating him, wouldn't it? Didn't he *want* his daughter to follow in his metaphorical footsteps? This discovery only added to her puzzlement, for although she had a pattern, there was no obvious reason *why* he felt this way.

Surely he doesn't think I'm setting up as a rival to him—does he? That's ridiculous. . . .

She rubbed the tablet clean and began another list, concentrating on the accomplishments that he *had* expressed approval of. On the right, the list reflected mild approval, on the left, an actual moment of praise. These lists were much shorter, and there was blank wax beneath both lists; it dismayed her to realize how little she had mastered that had called forth any enthusiasm at all from her father.

Not only am I doing something wrong, but I have been doing it for a very long time, it seems. She compressed her lips tightly, and her eyes stung for a moment. *Can't he see how much I am trying to please him? Isn't the effort worth something?*

Perhaps he didn't realize how much effort she expended on this; after all, he was the one who insisted that she maintain absolute control over her expression and body-language, that she cultivate a mask of cool indifference at all times. She must never show that anything moved her, that anything surprised or angered her. "The more effort something requires," he had lectured her, "the less you should display. Assume that everyone who might watch you is an enemy. You do not show an enemy your weaknesses. Make everything appear as natural as breathing, and that alone will confuse, even frighten, a foe."

She had not been a total failure—for she had actually garnered praise from him from time to time. *I've done a few things right, at any rate. All I have to do is discover what they all have in common.*

But she felt even more dismay when she realized what *this* pattern was—a dismay tinged by anger, an anger that grew with every moment that passed. For the only sorts of magic von Rothbart seemed to approve of were—well, the only word to describe them was *domestic.* When she had learned how to banish the mice and insects from the pantry, for instance.

Or here, the time that he complained about seeing the Silent Ones wielding brooms, and I concocted a way to keep the floors spotlessly clean without needing to sweep.

Kitchen magic! The dismay lessened, the anger and sense of insult grew. Was *that* all she was good for in his eyes? To conjure glorified housekeeping? Her fingers curled into fists; the stylus broke with a sudden snap, and her nails cut into her palms, making her wince with the sudden pain.

She uncurled her fists and stared at the four little red crescents in each palm. It was the pain that brought her back to her senses, made her reestablish her control. Anger would win her nothing but von Rothbart's contempt, and she already had her fill of that. It was only foolish, childish, *womanish* creatures like the flock who gave in to their tempers, or worse, let their emotions dictate their actions.

After the anger came resolution. *I don't care what Father thinks. I am going to master everything he has.* Perhaps it was foolish, but—

No! There is nothing foolish about it!

Resolution gave way to thought as she worked her way out of emotion and into a state of calmness. She should not jump to any conclusions; that was the first thing. She should think things through and not assume insult; this was her *father,* not some stranger. There might be a reason why he was so reluctant to praise her for mastering his magics. He might wish her to save herself, her energies—after all, she herself had noticed how exhausted she was by her efforts. How was he to know that she didn't *care* how much it took from her to manage the greater spells? He might believe she was too young yet, too vulnerable—but at the same time didn't want to forbid her to try. After all, she was supposed to be achieving, learning. If he didn't *encourage* her, but didn't discourage her either, that might be the way to keep her from trying too much, too soon.

And why shouldn't he approve of the—the domestic magics? They make his life easier, and more pleasant.

The last of her anger faded; how foolish she had been! She was very glad now that he hadn't been here to see her lose control of herself so badly. *And this is exactly why he wants me to keep my emotions controlled—look what silly ideas, what flawed reasoning they led me into!* After all, von Rothbart was probably thinking like a father, not a master sorcerer—he only wanted to protect her, forgetting that she was fast becoming an adult, and in no need of protection.

So here was her answer; she would avoid his disapproval easily enough from now on. *I will still work to master his spells, but I simply won't show them to him. What I will show him is more of what he approves of.* "Kitchen magic" was hardly difficult; in fact, the reason she'd stopped doing it was because it offered so little challenge.

At some point when he needs the help, I will do just that—help him, without making any fuss. He'll realize that I am his equal, and he can count on my help from then on. Then, oh then, he would surely open his tower and his own workroom to her, and together they would devise new enchantments, create new spells! He would open to her the secret of where his power came from, so that their strength would be doubled, and she truly would become his equal.

As for what her first little touch of domesticity should be—*Clean something, I think. Clean something impressive.*

She immediately thought of the dim and dusty hangings in the Great Hall; the floors were clean, but one could scarcely make out the figures of the tapestries for all the centuries of soot and grime. Since the tapestries had always been filthy and there had never been any attempt to get the Silent Ones to clean them, she herself had overlooked their state. Probably her father had, too; they must have been new in his great-great grandfather's time, if then.

It ought to be easy enough to work out a way to send the dirt elsewhere without damaging the fabric. If the colors proved to be faded, she would conjure up the old brightness.

She smiled, pleased with herself. She needn't even *say* anything to him; that was the best part of the plan. He'd see for himself what she'd done the moment he entered the manor.

As for the next of his magics for her to master— she picked a direction almost at random, full of relief that she had a course of action at last. *I have the transformation spell; I should work out the binding spell, too, and a counter for it.* Newly energized by her plans, she wiped the tablet clean and put it aside, the broken stylus with it. It occured to her, as she entered the Great Hall and looked up at the tapestries, that there would be other applications of magic to clean fabrics. She could set the spell on *every* fabric in the manor; curtains would no longer collect dust and cobwebs, bed linens and blankets would stay fresh, clothing would not need laundering—

Practical and pleasurable for me, too, she thought with amusement. *And it will further free the Silent Ones for other tasks, which will please Father even more. Well, it isn't a fact yet, and it won't be unless I can work it out.*

The trick, of course, was to remove every bit of dirt without removing other things—the nap of the velvet, for instance, or jewels and bits of gold thread. *Not the Law of Similarity, then.* She nibbled her lower lip as she paced the perimeter of the room, staring up at the tapestries and the banners above them. *I may have to clean each element in the tapestries separately.* That would complicate her work, but it might be the surest and safest road to success. *Let me see; there's an easy spell to take the tarnish off metals—I can find out what it does to the gilt threads up there. . . .*

She chose an insignificant corner of one of the least important hangings, and carefully insinuated her spell into the weave of the tapestry, observing the effect, and calculating changes.

With a little more experimentation, she felt confident enough of her results to bind the three spells she'd chosen together, and set them loose on the walls. By this time, she'd gathered a crowd of Silent Ones, for magic attracted them. She felt their interest as a force of its own. A glowing mist, rather than dancing colored motes, enveloped the tapestries in a rosy haze. It was quite pretty, as if dawn-tinged clouds had invaded the hall to dance up and down the tapestries.

She'd reckoned that it was better to be sure than swift, so the spells worked slowly and there was no perceptible change at first, except for a growing pile of soft dust mixed with soot in the center of the floor. No more than a smudge at first, then a slight hummock, then a real pile—as the filth was removed from the tapestries, it had to go *somewhere,* and she had decided to make a pile of it and sweep it out of the way as soon as the tapestries were clean. Besides, she was curious to see just how much dirt had accumulated up there over the years. It was the sort of thing that gave an otherwise dull task a touch of pride and accomplishment.

Slowly, layer by layer, the hangings showed their true colors, and all the details of their weavings. The sheer amount of detail startled her when she realized how much there was—what she had taken for plain, dark backgrounds proved to be intricate landscapes straight out of a nightmare; sinister caverns with shadowed shapes lurking behind rock formations, and haunted forests peopled by half-animated trees with tortured limbs. The glint of very tiny gems gave an uncanny spark to eyes, catching the light unexpectedly and in startling ways. Not exactly the most *pleasant* of subjects, but very effective. The use of jewels and gilded threads was particularly effective, giving quite a lifelike character to the background figures as well as the mythical beasts of the foreground.

There were one or two faded places where the sun struck fragile colors, but invoking the Law of Similarity put those right, and eventually she was able to stand back and admire her handiwork with pardonable pride. The hangings were quite splendid, all in all—though the swan-maidens would probably find them terrifying. She supposed that was the intended effect; the idea of holding court here was to impress your underlings, and the hangings would make them realize just how inadvisable it would be to anger a sorcerer.

Not that Father has any human underlings to terrify. I wonder how the Silent Ones are taking this?

The banners would be much easier; there were no jewels to work around, and by now she had the knack of the spells. She slipped a bit more speed into the process, bringing up the trophies in all their barbaric glory, then polishing the beams and cleaning the ceiling of its layer of soot for good measure. The last bit of magic swept the formidable pile of dirt into the ash pit below the fireplace, and the Great Hall was cleaner than it had been since the day it was built.

She had timed her work to a nicety, for the rush of Silent Ones to the doorway gave her just enough warning to turn and curtsy as von Rothbart entered his domain.

"I see there is no need to ask you today what you have been doing." As usual, there was very little inflection in his voice, but as was *not* usual, the faint hint of emotion was positive. She rose from the floor and looked up at him with hooded eyes, warily.

"I hope I have not overstepped my authority, Father," was all she said in reply.

His lips curved in a faint, but real smile. "Such usurpation would be most acceptable in the future." He stared over her head at the tapestries, but this was the closest she'd gotten to praise from him in months, and she felt limp with pleasure. "I had half-forgotten what these hangings portrayed. . . ." He stared a moment longer. "I should not be ashamed to receive the Emperor here, now. This is a pleasant surprise indeed, daughter."

She curtsied again, quickly, bowing her head to hide her face, for she was afraid that if he saw her flushed, happy expression, she would lose all the approval she had just gained by betraying her feelings.

As she remained in that pose, he moved past her—and actually laid his hand for a moment on the top of her bowed head! The caress made her dizzy with a fierce joy that burned away every bit of resentment and discontent she'd felt over the past several months. If he'd asked her to cast herself into the mouth of Vesuvius at that moment, she'd have done so without a moment's hesitation. Reveling in her joy, she remained in her kneeling position while he passed on to his own quarters.

It was only when she rose and found herself momentarily off-balance that she realized it might not be only joy that was making her dizzy. *Ah . . . I don't think I should move very far. I don't think I can.* She put out her hand to balance herself, and took a few careful steps to one of the chairs at the side of the room to sit down.

"Bring me honeyed wine," she ordered aloud, hoping that at least one of the Silent Ones had remained with her. *If they aren't—I'll just have to manage.* She was in luck; she put her head down on her knees to clear it, and when she straightened up again, a silver salver hovered at her elbow, with a matching goblet on it. She seized the vessel and gulped the potion down, then leaned back against the ancient wood of the chair, and waited for her weakness to pass. It didn't matter, really; the important thing was that her father had finally shown open approval of what she'd done.

And even if it wasn't impressive magic, it was clever, even if I do say so myself. It was very delicate work, too—it took a light touch. But I must have been doing more than I thought, to be this drained. Maybe it was because I went so slowly at first. . . . It was rather strange that she hadn't immediately felt the effects, but she couldn't think of anything else that would account for the severe drain on her energy. *Well, it's all right. It will come back.* Feeling stronger, she ordered the waiting servant to bring her strawberries and cream, a favorite dish that replenished strength quickly but wasn't as cloying as the honeyed wine. Sorcerers always had a taste for sweets, driven by their need to replenish depleted energy, and there were always plenty of sweet things in the kitchen. When von Rothbart finished a major work of magic, she had known him to devour an entire marzipan figure by himself.

The strawberries were absolutely fresh, and the cream had been slightly sweetened with honey before being beaten to thicken it. The snack and the wine helped a great deal, and she left the bowl and goblet for the Silent One to clean up, rising from the chair to take careful steps towards her own rooms. It still seemed odd that she should have been so very drained—but when she looked back over her shoulder, the amount of work she had accomplished impressed even her. *Filth must have been positively embedded in the fabric by now. Maybe I should be surprised that I'm not* more *tired.*

She shivered; cold was another symptom of energy drain, and she was freezing, hands and feet like ice sculptures. "Put warm bricks in my bed," she ordered without looking back. "And have a warm posset waiting at my bedside." *At the rate I'm walking, even if there's only* one *servitor about, it can get the dishes to the kitchen and complete my orders before I reach the door of my bed chamber. I'm moving like a feeble old woman.*

She wrapped her arms around herself, chafing at her upper arms with her hands to try to stir up her blood as she walked. Just as she got halfway to her rooms, the posset drifted by on invisible hands, and with the scent of cinnamon to spur her on, she put a little more life into her steps.

Curtains belled gently in a warm breeze as she passed open windows, and moonlight poured through onto the floor, checkering her path in light and shadow. She glanced out one of the windows as she went by, and a faint strain of music caught her ear; Katerina was dancing with the little ones, with the older maidens in a larger circle around them. Evidently she'd managed to forget how heartbroken she was.

And a month ago, didn't she swear she wanted to die? Odile's lips tightened in a cynical smile. *Father is right. They are all of them faithless. Perhaps they can fool themselves, but they will never fool him.*

The door to her rooms stood open, and she was mortally glad to let her weary feet take her inside. Once there, she let the Silent Ones disrobe her for a change, and staggered into the bed, now delightfully warmed with the bricks. The posset stood within arm's reach on her bedside table, or she would never have bothered to drink it, but it helped to warm her as well.

She felt herself falling asleep, and tried to get the cup back on the table, but couldn't keep her eyes open. Invisible fingers plucked the cup from her nerveless ones, and she fell instantly asleep.

Odile knew every article of her father's clothing—she should, for she had supervised the making of it—so it was no trick at all to insinuate her cleansing mist into his quarters, even though the door was locked. She had devised a rather neat touch to it, and one that would alert him to the method by which his clothing and linens were cleansed; she'd included a final scent as the hallmark of her magics. She'd chosen the scent of light musk, a little like the scent of a raptor's feathers; it wouldn't interfere with any of his spells, and it suited him. For herself, she preferred rosemary, sharp and cleansing. *Rosemary for memory. It might sting the conscience of some of the flock, though I don't think I'd care to count on that.*

This was the dark of the moon, and unless her father wished it, the flock would remain as swans all night. Only he could counter the spell that required moonlight for their transformation.

Well, I think that I could, but I have no intention of doing so. Not tonight, my ladies. Father isn't here, so you'll just have to languish in your feathers. I intend to enjoy having the gardens all to myself for a change. It only seemed fair to her; the flock had them twenty-seven days out of twenty-eight. On these moonless nights, they tended to slumber on and around the little island, sleeping to make the hours pass faster, she supposed.

She ordered the lanterns along the garden paths lit, and requested the Silent Ones to perform her favorite music, soft madrigals on lute, harp, and flute. Tonight she had done enough work; with the last of the summer flowers in bloom, she would enjoy a few hours without thinking of work or study.

There was a tense expectancy about her father

lately, as if he had found something he had long looked for. He'd spent every night away from the manor; from past experience, she suspected that it wouldn't be long until he was on the hunt. The only question in her mind was, would he leave her and the flock here, or take them with her? He'd snared Katerina on his own, but roughly half the flock had been taken when he'd had the rest in tow.

That could have been only because I was so small, and he didn't care to leave me alone, she thought, a bit wistfully. He hadn't trusted the Silent Ones with her unsupervised care, and of course her mother had been gone by then.

Mother . . . I don't even know what her given name was. She couldn't recall much about her mother anymore, just a vague sense of comfort, a low, sweet voice, and the scent of violets. Her father wouldn't allow a single violet to take root here; the Silent Ones dug them out ruthlessly and the few times she'd seen or smelled one had been when she'd been outside the estate. She hadn't even known that the scent she associated with her mother *was* the scent of violets, until she'd come across some in bloom when she wandered in a wild part of the forest around the manor.

Von Rothbart didn't exactly refuse to talk about her mother, so much as completely ignore any questions on the subject. As a very young child, she'd learned not to ask those questions because when she did, her father would stalk off and leave her alone.

Now I prefer to be alone. How odd. Just as well, really; sorcerers were a solitary lot, and it was as well to make a virtue of necessity. Other magicians might choose to be in the employ of kings and princes, but not her father. *He* would take second place to no man.

And quite rightly, too, she thought with pride. *Baron von Rothbart has blood as fine as any prince, and power that none can match. They should be bowing to him, not the other way around.*

She wondered what he was hunting this time, and where. Although she understood his self-imposed search for unfaithful women, it had occurred to her more than once that it was probably the hunt itself that interested him, and not the final capture. The spells he used to take his quarry were very much alike; the transformation spell and binding spell were items she had mastered—there wasn't much scope there for creativity. *It must be the stalk, the chase itself that keeps him interested.* How many women did he watch before he found the faithless ones? Was such watching tedious—or did he have another version of the Silent Ones to invisibly spy out his quarry?

All women can't be unfaithful, or there wouldn't be anyone left to raise families. Unless they run off with a lover only to find they're expected to raise the children his *unfaithful spouse left behind!* That created an image she had to laugh over, though she doubted her father would have found it funny.

She wandered back to the manor, thinking of finding a book to read, when a huge shadow passed over her head and the flames in the lanterns flickered with the wind of its passing. At that moment, all thought of finding a book flew out of her head; her father was back, and early—which meant—what?

She picked up her skirts and ran toward the steps of the manor, as the lanterns went out behind her, extinguished by her own magic.

When she reached the manor, von Rothbart had made his own transformation. He stood on the steps, his feather cloak cast back over his shoulders, looking out over the lake. She followed his gaze, and saw the flock swimming slowly toward the shore, faint white shapes shimmering in the starlight, with Odette, neck ringed with the glint of gold, in the lead.

They stepped up onto the shore and paraded toward him, heads bowed gracefully, necks curved in arcs of obedience. Odile stood instinctively to the side; he had summoned them here with his power for a purpose, but she was not one of their number, she was a creature apart.

When they stood in a rough half circle before him, he raised one hand in an imperious gesture, and they dropped to the grass, covered, for a moment, by a winglike shadow. When they rose again, they rose as human, beautiful women clothed in silks of purest white and darkest black, hair ornamented with wreaths of feathers instead of flowers or veils.

Von Rothbart surveyed his flock, head raised arrogantly, and Odile retreated a little farther into the shadows as he gave her a sharp glance. She knew that look in his eyes. She was to efface herself for the moment. *Listen and watch; this concerns me, but is not aimed at me.*

"Katerina," he said, in a voice cold as frozen iron. "Come here."

She could not have disobeyed, though she clearly wanted to. His power dragged her to the front of the group, step by reluctant step.

"There is a reason why you are here," he said, words that Odile had expected long before this. "Do you know it yet?"

Katerina looked up, mouth sulky yet defiant. "I have done nothing, sorcerer," she snapped. "What is it you desire? A ransom in gold? An exchange with my husband? It is you who have taken me unwilling from my place."

"And what place would that be?" von Rothbart asked in silky tones. "By the side of your husband? *Or your lover?*"

She gasped, and her hands flew to her mouth in an

involuntary gesture that betrayed her even as she had betrayed her husband.

"Did you think your sin would never be found out?" he continued, and laughed shortly. "You are not the first woman to betray a man; you are here among your sisters in sin for punishment, Katerina. Your punishment is to live as you have for the past months, never seeing another man except in a shape that will inspire no desire except the desire to slay you!"

She stepped back involuntarily, and he laughed at her, mockingly.

She wasn't entirely without courage, this Katerina. "How—" she faltered, "How long? How long will you hold me ensorcelled?"

He raised a single eyebrow. "Until you die, woman. And you should be grateful that you are given such an opportunity to repent. I would advise you to take advantage of it, and avoid the eternal damnation of your soul." His lips formed a chill smile. "And you might pray for others of your sisters in sin who have been given no such blessed opportunities but persist in their delusions and passions until it is too late to repent."

Katerina made an abortive gesture, as if to beg him for mercy. "Who are you?" she whimpered. "Why are you doing this?"

But it was Odette who stepped forward and drew the young woman back when she would have flung herself at von Rothbart's feet to grovel and beg. "Do not hope for mercy from this sorcerer, for he has no heart to feel such emotions," she said as coldly as von Rothbart himself.

Von Rothbart's expression did not change in the least. "The better to avoid the temptation of faithless women," he replied, with a mocking bow. "How else could I be a proper guardian for such as you? It would have been better for Adam had he been created without a heart; he would never have given in to the entreaties of Eve. But it was not only to remind you of your proper punishment that I gathered you this evening."

Odette drew herself up proudly, and stepped forward with her arms spread slightly, as if to protect the maidens behind her. *She* knew what von Rothbart meant, and so did Odile. "If you expect us to repent, why is it that you pledge to hold us until death?" she demanded. "What reason would we have for anything but mourning for what is lost and railing against you? Even God does not demand punishment beyond repentance!"

Von Rothbart eyed her with speculation; Odile was taken aback. She had not expected such a spirited retort from Odette, who seemed to have lost interest in everything of late. Perhaps she had not been sulking on her little island, but thinking.

"An interesting line of reasoning, if entirely feminine," he said at last, and watched her keenly. "Very well, Swan Queen; are you willing to hazard all on your repentance and redemption? For your flock as well as yourself?"

Odette looked suspicious. "I trust no wager of yours, sorcerer."

He made a motion to dismiss her insult. "Listen, before you bandy words about. The spell that holds you all is linked to you, the leader. If *you* can capture the faith of a man who knows you as you are, and hold him as well, then the spell upon you all will be broken and you will all be free." He spread his hands wide in a gesture of generosity. "That, by the by, has always been the case. But he must be utterly true to you, and swear to no other."

"Dare you to swear to the truth of this, Baron von Rothbart?" Odette cried, eyes blazing. "Nay, do not swear upon the word of God, for I do not trust such an oath from you. Swear it upon your name, your power!"

"I swear that it is true, upon my name and power," he said, almost benignly. "He must know what you are, and what you have done to deserve your state, and still remain faithful to you through any temptation."

"And how long must this blessed condition hold before the spell is broken?" she replied, with no trust in her voice. "A year? Ten? A hundred?"

"You wrong me, Odette," von Rothbart retorted. "I am stung! I impose no such impossible conditions. One month, from full moon to full moon, that is all. One tiny month, and you win the freedom of not only yourself, but of all your flock. And tomorrow, when we seek a change of scene, you will even have opportunity for your quest."

Odette stepped back, silent, too suspicious to be anything but alarmed, though the buzz of conversation among her fellows was a mixture of alarm and excitement.

Odile's reaction, however, was of excitement unmixed with any tinge of alarm. It had been a very long time since the last hunt that von Rothbart had undergone where he had brought the flock with him. And if the flock came, so would Odile.

"Tomorrow we fly, Queen of the Swans," Von Rothbart told her, still with a touch of mockery in his voice. "So when the sun sets, be prepared."

CHAPTER FOUR

WOLFGANG, Siegfried's tutor, had a private chamber of his very own by virtue of his importance to the royal family. This was where Siegfried and one or more of his friends often gathered after dinner. Wolfgang had access to the palace wine cellars, and no one ever questioned how many bottles he and his young friends consumed, where anyone but Siegfried would have found the servants reluctant to fetch more than three bottles in a night. Siegfried preferred not to be in his own quarters following dinner. It was too easy for people to find him there.

Tonight, though, only three shared the room—clearly that of a bachelor scholar. Furniture was shabby but comfortable, royal cast offs appropriated by Wolfgang's servant. The huge, canopied bed, fully large enough for a family, was loaded with books and manuscripts except for just enough room for a single person to sleep, and candles jammed into the melted remains of countless predecessors adorned the headboard. Old cushions rubbed bare of nap or with mouse holes chewed in the corners were piled out of the way; these served as seats when there were more visitors than two. Threadbare hangings and curtains kept the chill of the stone walls at bay, all of them banished from the royal chambers years ago when their patterns faded into oblivion or were damaged by moths. For the rest of the furniture: Wolfgang had a desk with one broken leg, held steady by a broken stone column he had found in a ruin; a chair so monumentally ugly that the queen had ordered it burned; a bench padded with an ancient featherbed; and an assortment of stools in various states of repair.

Tonight Benno, clad in a sumptuously embroidered linen doublet of rich blue left open at the throat to show his lace-trimmed cambric shirt, sprawled at his ease on the bench. Siegfried's tutor Wolfgang, in his usual rusty black, rested an elbow on the arm of the chair he occupied next to the cold fireplace. Siegfried, attired more casually in a fine lawn shirt and brown leather trews had appropriated Wolfgang's bed; he, too, sprawled comfortably propped up on a pile of cushions, wineglass in one hand as he listened to Benno and Wolfgang continue the debate that had begun well over an hour ago. A sultry breeze coming in at the window, heavy with the scent of roses, made him feel indolent and lazy.

He listened in a pleasantly detached frame of mind, drunk enough so that his vague dissatisfaction with life had receded into a mellow haze.

Wolfgang and Benno had consumed their share of wine, so at least the debate was on an equal footing. For the moment, Siegfried preferred to listen; Wolfgang was a good talker, and wine freed Benno from the diffidence he otherwise showed for the old man's level of knowledge.

Wolfgang's learning wasn't much help in this case though, and he shook his gray head. "I am confused; more than confused with all of this," he said. "I think that you have me at a disadvantage. Start at the beginning; explain this new fashion of love to me. You say it has rules? How can an emotion be governed by rules?"

Benno, who had been fostered in a French court, was only too ready to impart his knowledge. "The complete knight must have a lady to whom he is devoted. For her honor and glory he fights, it is to her beauty he composes and performs songs, she is the first thing he thinks of on arising and the last on sleeping."

"And this woman is not his wife?" Wolfgang said, puzzled.

"No—love has nothing to do with marriage," Benno replied with authority. "Marriage is about property, lineage, continuing the family line. Love doesn't enter into it—oh, Wolfgang, think! Look at Dorian; he's going to be married to a woman with a face like a cow and a body like a sack of turnips, and how could he be expected to feel anything for her? Marriage is a contract, much like the contract of liege to lord. One needn't love one's lord in order to fulfill that contract. One needn't love one's wife to fulfill the contract of marriage—which is to impart to her the use of one's goods, one's name, one's property, in exchange for children and service."

"Well enough, I can see that," Wolfgang agreed. "That was the same sort of contract that the Greeks and Romans recognized. Indeed, the ancient philosophers say very little about love for one's *wife.*"

Benno shrugged. "In fact—well, it's generally considered rather common and ill-bred to be in love with your wife."

"And the woman you love isn't your leman either—you don't necessarily lie with her." That was Siegfried's contribution. He felt very sorry for Wolfgang; all the logic in the world wasn't going to make sense of the rules of courtly love—but it wasn't about logic, it was about the heart, after all, which knew no logic.

"No—well, sometimes you might have her carnally, if she's nobly born, but it's best if she isn't actually your leman. God's breath, Wolfgang, how could any-one make songs to the beauty of a little peasant girl's hands? If you've got a serf girl or three tucked away, that's all very well, but you don't elevate her to *lover*. That would be sordid, demeaning." Benno sounded very sure of himself.

"Sordid for you, or her?" Wolfgang muttered under his breath. Then he raised his voice. "All right, then, couldn't your lover be a maiden you aspire to?"

Benno shook his head. "Well, she can, but it's better if she's already married if you're going to lie with her—and really, it's better even if you aren't going to lie with her. You don't want to ruin a maiden's honor with your attentions."

Wolfgang sat straight up. "You mean to tell me that the fashionable thing is to make love to another man's wife?" he yelped, actually shocked.

This from the man who has translated the poems of Sappho? Siegfried thought.

"You still don't understand," Benno complained. "You're not supposed to *make love* to her, you're sup-posed to adore her from afar, do everything for her. This is Courtly Love, Wolfgang. It hasn't anything to do with lust, or marriage, it's supposed to be utterly pure and above all that. It's supposed to be all-consuming, overpowering, like Lancelot, or Tristan—"

"Lancelot bedded Guinevere, and Tristan ran off with Isolde," Wolfgang pointed out with complete truth. "That sounds like making love to another man's wife to me."

"Well, Lancelot and Tristan failed to reach the ideal, and that was why they came to tragic ends," Benno explained earnestly. "They weren't *supposed* to let lust get into it, you see? When Courtly Love is pure, it's perfect, and you don't get into situations like that. Don't you see how liberating and glorious it is? You don't *have* to be in love with that doughball you're wedded to, and you don't have to be in love with the pretty peasant you're futtering in the barn. Love gives another person power over you—being in love with your wife could be trouble, because she could rule you, and being in love with your leman is degrading—how could gentleman and a knight allow a peasant to have power over him? The proper person to give that power to is the kind of person who's either your equal or your superior, don't you see? That's why you love a lady above your stature, and preferably a married one with a husband who's conveniently on pilgrimage, or at least disinclined to take exception to your attention."

Wolfgang took a long pull off his wineglass and sighed. "There's no logic to this!" he complained plaintively.

Siegfried decided to put his own bit in. "It's not supposed to be logical, Wolfgang, and the rules aren't logical, either. It's an escape from logic, I suppose."

"Exactly!" Benno beamed on his friend. "Exactly! We have to be logical in our marriages, and although politics is very far from logical, you still can't give free vent to your emotions when you deal with political matters. Courtly Love allows us to give our hearts freedom without compromising our duty or our honor."

"Unless you have the poor taste to follow Lancelot's example," Siegfried snickered. "Bad luck for you, then."

"You're not supposed to follow Lancelot's example," Benno countered, flushing.

"Well, what are the women supposed to do?" Wolfgang persisted. "Collect young knights like so many pretty baubles?"

Benno sputtered at that, but Siegfried, who didn't take the rules of this newly-fashionable Courtly Love so seriously, nodded agreement. "More or less, the beautiful ones, anyway. It isn't done to be in love with your husband, but then, most beauties have been shackled to a drooling old man anyway, so there's no fear of being in love with someone like that. If you're a beauty, I gather the idea is to inspire as many handsome fellows as possible to be in love with you. You're supposed to be gracious, kind, accomplished, and learned, so you can properly appreciate all the songs that are made for you, you can hold your own in conversation, and you can understand the privilege of having someone fighting in tournaments in your honor. But you're also supposed to be distant, a little cool, so that you don't encourage them to do something stupid—like Lancelot."

"And are women supposed to have a single distant—or maybe not-so-distant—love as well?" Wolfgang mocked. "After all, as the peasants say, sauce for the gander should serve for the goose."

"Actually, I'm rather curious about that myself," Siegfried admitted, turning to Benno. "You hadn't said anything about the women picking out someone particular."

"Well—" Benno frowned. "Yes and no. One school of thought says that she should remain aloof from all that; another that she should secretly pick one of her admirers to fall in love with, but never allow him to know for certain that he is her chosen. That's the ideal, of course, but women have been known to take a carnal lover . . . the Church says that they're more fleshly and carnal than men, after all, so it's not surprising."

"The Greek philosophers would say that since a woman's soul is so much simpler than a man's, what she feels could not be love as you are describing in any case," Wolfgang replied ponderously. "The Romans would agree that woman's primary instincts are so primitive that they couldn't even imagine something as sophisticated as this Courtly Love—"

"Oh, hang your Greek and Roman philosophers!" Benno snapped, offended at Wolfgang's tone. "What could they have to say that was relevant here? They're old and dead, and when they were alive, they were as stuffy as an unaired closet!"

Wolfgang bridled, and sat straight up, his face going red with fury. Siegfried decided to put an end to the debate.

"Here now, none of that!" he ordered sharply. "Benno, you're drunk."

"So are you!" Benno retorted. "And so is he!"

Siegfried laughed. "Yes, I am, but I know it, and I'm not picking quarrels. You are drunk and trying to pretend you're not—when you know you'll be very sorry for some of the things you said tomorrow. Apologize to Wolfgang. When you sober up, you'll be glad you did."

Benno growled an apology, but had the grace to look embarrassed at his behavior.

Siegfried wasn't letting his tutor off, either. "As for you, my tutor, the Greek and Roman philosophers don't even agree with each other, so don't say things you know will prick Benno to snap at you," the prince continued, getting a gratified glance from his friend. "Besides, the Greek philosophers say that women don't have souls, either, and what do you think the Church would have to say about that? Would you be suggesting that the Blessed Virgin didn't have a soul? I wouldn't do that if I were you, the priest already suspects that you're half pagan and all heretic. Your favorite philosophers aren't always right, so I wouldn't rely too heavily on them to win my arguments if I were you."

That came out rather jumbled, but it seemed to make sense enough to Wolfgang, who in his turn graciously apologized to Benno, so that in a moment they were all friends again.

"Anyway," Benno sighed, checking the bottle of wine under his bench to see if there was anything left in it, "It's all one to you, Siegfried. Courtly Love doesn't apply to you."

"What do you mean?" Siegfried pushed a full bottle across the floor to him.

"I mean there isn't anyone for you to fall in love with, in that sense," Benno explained earnestly. "You've got the highest rank here so there aren't any ladies superior to you except the queen, and you can't exactly fall in love with the Emperor's daughter, because he doesn't have one. So you don't have to go to all the trouble of finding a worthy object and all the rest. *And* you aren't likely to get married off to a lump of dough, either; you have your pick of the prettiest beauties, any one of whom would be deliriously happy to marry you. So you can be in love with a wife or a mistress or *both,* and you won't be breaking the rules of Courtly Love because they don't apply to you."

"Ah!" Siegfried countered, raising his index finger wisely. "But I don't intend to, you see!"

"What? Fall in love, or marry?" Wolfgang asked.

"Both." Siegfried smiled, having just come up with what seemed to be a perfect plan to him. "I'm certainly not going to fall in love, because I don't intend to wind up so besotted that a woman can order me about—I've had enough of that with my beloved mother, thank you very much. And I'm not going to marry, because I'm tired to death of fetters and restrictions. At least, I'm not going to marry *now,*" he amended. "I'm going to go right on tumbling the chambermaids and peasant wenches, then when I'm *very* old and all the maidens have been making doe eyes at me forever, I'll condescend to marry one. She can bear my sons, and then nurse me." He laughed. "By then I'll be too old to run after pretty women, so it will be nice to have one that has to come to me."

"And if she plays you Guinevere's trick," Benno asked, not quite mocking him, "Then what will you do?"

"I shall magnanimously forgive her and send Lancelot packing to a monastery, probably singing soprano so he won't be tempted by the sin of lust again," he replied, feeling too pleasantly fuddled to be annoyed. "She should be grateful at being forgiven and grateful that I didn't murder her lover, so she'll be even nicer to me. We don't have stupid laws about burning errant wives at the stake *here*. Or if we do, I'll take care to have them changed before I'm old."

"A wise choice, O Solomon!" Wolfgang applauded. "I feel sure that the Greek philosophers would approve, even if the Romans wouldn't. The Romans were very stuffy about marital matters, anyway. Have another bottle of wine."

"Thank you," Siegfried said, bowing graciously to his tutor, and stretching out his arm to take the bottle Wolfgang held out unsteadily. "I believe I shall."

As he took the bottle, he thought he heard a nasty, soft chuckle coming from the window, and when he glanced in that direction, he could have sworn he saw a shadow drop across it for a moment—but he reminded himself that he *was* drunk, and he'd seen and heard things before when he was in that dubious state that proved not to be there.

The next morning he woke without even a moderate headache, thanks to his foresight in taking a good walk around the battlements until his head cleared. Actually, the first part of it was more of a stagger than a walk, but he'd taken care to avoid the parts of the castle that were patrolled by sentries until he'd gotten his feet under him and could give at least a good imitation of sobriety, each time taking a good, long drink of water. He'd taken to doing this ever since the Captain of the Queen's Guards had given him the trick to avoiding morning misery altogether. Wolfgang and Benno had gone straight to bed—actually, he and Benno had lifted Wolfgang into *his* bed, then Benno had staggered off with another bottle tucked under his arm, so he could well imagine what *their* heads felt like this morning.

He pulled back the heavy linen bed curtains, and his servants, who had been waiting patiently just outside his bedchamber door for the first signs of life from the bed, sprang to their feet and bustled into the chamber with entirely too much energy. He climbed out of bed—literally, for the bed was so tall that it had its own set of steps—and the servants swarmed all over him.

So the day began in the usual way, with servants presenting garments for his approval while he stood there in his singlet and hose making up his mind. He rejected the first few garments they offered him, finally approving a leather doublet, silk shirt, and moleskin trews; clothing that would do for paying court to the queen *or* going out riding. He wasn't quite sure what he wanted to do today, but it was as sure as there were angels in heaven that neither Benno nor Wolfgang would be fit company until late afternoon, if then.

I could always have one of the girls sent up. . . . The thought stirred neither his heart nor his loins, the sign that told him that he'd gotten bored with all three of them. It always happened, sooner or later; these three had hung on several months longer than anyone had expected, including, probably, the women themselves.

Bother. I've been bedding them out of habit more than anything. He sighed, for he knew very well that nothing any of them did was interesting or exciting anymore, and not a single one of the three had gotten with child, which would have given him the excuse to pension her off and replace her. *I need something . . . different. A new woman. Or women. Make a clean sweep and start with a new lot.*

Now that thought sparked interest, and he wondered if his current state of ennui had anything to do with the boredom he felt with his women. *Definitely,* he decided. *It's time to pension them all off and go hunting.* And with that decision came a lifting of spirits that he hadn't felt in weeks.

"Arno, stop fussing with those point-laces, they'll do," he said snappishly to his manservant, a fellow who had been with him for as long as he'd *had* personal servants. "The rest of you can go. I'm not my mother that I need three people to comb out my hair."

The other three servants fled, leaving Siegfried alone with Arno, who chuckled at his ill temper. The older man began picking up the discarded garments and restoring them to chests and wardrobes, waiting for Siegfried's next orders.

"Arno, I want you to pension off the girls; tell them I won't want their company anymore," Siegfried said abruptly as soon as the other servants were out of earshot.

Arno chuckled again; long service with Siegfried gave him a certain amount of freedom. "So the rooster tires of old hen and is going looking for spring chicken, hmm? Or were you minded to join the Church and have decided to try a life of virtue?" His sly expression showed just how likely he thought *that* was.

"No vestments for me, old man," Siegfried replied, his temper already improving. "And the quarry I plan to chase today has two legs, not four, if you're curious. Which you are."

"Very good, sire," Arno said with satisfaction. "I'll have things tidied up for you by suppertime."

Siegfried left his rooms and descended the ancient stone stair with a sense of relief as well as anticipation. *Trust Arno; I'll never have to deal with them again.* One thing he'd never been able to manage was telling a girl that he'd lost interest in her—she would always start to weep or rail at him, and he couldn't cope with either reaction. Arno, however, was blithely immune to either ranting or tears, and as a third party, could afford to be indifferent. Of course, if any of Siegfried's current girls had been of higher rank than a manservant to the prince, Siegfried would have had to get someone else to bear the bad news, Benno or Wolfgang for instance—but one was a chambermaid, one was a dairy maid, and one worked in the kitchen, so there was no problem. Arno knew to a groat the size of the appropriate gift for any girl being cast off, and he also knew that Siegfried would want to be generous. With a purse the size Siegfried would give them, they could expect to dower themselves into a good marriage with no questions asked on the part of the husband-to-be. If they made no fuss at all and departed graciously, there would be a fine wedding gift coming, and an equally generous christening gift for the first son. So the girls really had nothing to complain about, once their terms in Siegfried's bed were at an end; a servant's maidenhead (assuming she had one) wasn't worth much unless a noble desired to take it, and a serf's was worth rather less than that.

Anyway, it was all now in Arno's capable hands, and Siegfried wouldn't even have to see them except at a distance. Now he could devote himself to the hunt without a second thought.

He entered through the side door of the Lesser Hall to find most of the castle populace still breaking their fast. The queen, of course, was nowhere to be seen, nor were her ladies-in-waiting; they ate quietly and decorously in the queen's chambers, leaving the Lesser Hall to the men and the noblewomen of lesser rank. Siegfried took his seat at the empty High Table and waited for a page to bring him food and drink while he surveyed the lower tables with an eye to a new conquest.

He had a policy of not taking a new girl from the same class and rank as the old, which meant that the kitchen, the dairy, and the domestic servants were out of consideration. There were serving wenches, however—

Wait a moment—who's that sitting next to Hans the Black? Too old to be a daughter, surely— The couple in question sat among the unlanded knights; freedmen, but only a single step in rank above common trades-men, men who usually owned nothing more than the clothing on their backs, their horse, and their armor and weapons. These were men who moved from court to court, either fighting in tourneys for the prize money, or serving one of the landed gentry in hopes of doing something to earn a small parcel of land and serfs of their own. It wasn't unusual to see a woman at that table, for men who had settled into the garrison often took mistresses from among the servants, or even wives from others of their rank, but Siegfried thought he knew most of them. *She can't be his wife; he's not married; he'd have come to me for permission if he'd decided to* get *married. Sister or some other kin?* The young woman was doll-like in her prettiness, with sweet blue eyes, cheeks that had never felt the touch of the sun or a harsh wind, and golden hair peeking out from under her coif. She wasn't dressed in the homespun of a servant, so she wasn't a mistress. Her gown was of good quality wool, but plain and a touch threadbare. So, if not a clandestine wife, she was a poor relation to Sir Hans, which meant that if she welcomed Siegfried's embrace, she'd be grateful for some fine presents of fabric and jewels. He wouldn't interfere with another man's wife, but anything else was fair game. Hans was of low enough rank that he wouldn't dare protest if Siegfried took his sister, so long as it was with the woman's consent.

When the page arrived with his breakfast of boiled eggs, bacon, and bread, he asked the boy for the woman's identity. The pages knew everything and everybody; they had to, for their well-being depended on knowing who was who and what rank every individual in the Court held. Being asked to carry notes about the way they were, the pages had to *know* relationships among the folk of the castle, or they'd soon find themselves in trouble.

The adolescent had a swift reply, as Siegfried had expected. "That's Sir Hans' widowed sister-in-law, Adelaide. His brother left her in his keeping and she just arrived a few days ago; he's hoping to find someone to take her off his hands, but she hasn't any dower but her face." The page shrugged, and continued, knowing that he could be free with his tongue around Siegfried. "There's plenty of pretty faces here, and with higher rank than the widow of a landless knight—she'll be on his keep for a good while, I guess. Without a dowry, even the Church wouldn't take her except as a drudge."

Siegfried thanked the boy, and turned to his breakfast, thoroughly satisfied. A poor widow? Perfect. No bother about lost virginity, Sir Hans would probably be relieved to find Siegfried taking over her board and keep, however temporary the arrangement, and when Siegfried tired of her, he could provide her with a generous dowry that would see her safely married to a knight of better rank than her brother-in-law. *Ha. Maybe even Benno, if he takes a fancy to her. Benno's had my girls before, and his parents wouldn't object to the wench if some land came with her.* In Siegfried's experience, the only difference in paying off a serving wench and paying off a highborn leman was the size of the pension and the amount of pretty posturing that had to be done when the game was over.

He'd have to court her, of course, but that would simply add zest to the inevitable conquest. He began to watch the woman, finally catching her eye so that she saw he was looking at her and no other. He smiled at her, slowly, and nodded. She didn't simper, thank God—she did blush a little, and said something to her brother-in-law. Sir Hans turned and saw that Siegfried was still looking; he raised an eyebrow to bring Siegfried's attention to *him,* then smiled and nodded, ever so slightly. Siegfried's interest had been noted, understood, and a silent agreement had been reached, all without anyone actually *saying* anything.

Ha! I thought so. He's willing enough, and she will be, too, with the proper amount of coaxing. Good, my way is clear to her bed. No one wanted to challenge Siegfried to a fight, even over a well-beloved woman, but it was better not to cause any distress to a seasoned fighter. It made for unrest in the ranks, and the lower-ranked fighters had other recourses than a direct challenge anyway. A pebble slung at a horse's rump at the wrong time, or interference in a melee— accidents happened, everyone knew that, but accidents could be made to happen, and Siegfried had no intention of giving anyone the motive to cause one.

Siegfried finished his breakfast in fine humor. The woman finished hers long before he was done with his second course of porridge, and she and her brother-in-law rose to make a place for newcomers. As they were leaving, she glanced back and saw that Siegfried was still watching her. She smiled, colored prettily, dropped her eyes, and followed her brother out of the room.

First signals exchanged—next maneuvers to take place after supper. The dance was well begun.

It might be weeks or even months before he got the widow into his bed, however; for the short term, he required something to take care of his immediate needs.

He left the hall and headed straight for the stables; no message had come to him from his mother, which meant he need not make an appearance in court at her side today. As he walked briskly across the courtyard, he took note of the weather, still holding fine for the haying. The sun shone hot and bright, and there wasn't a hint of breeze; it was going to be a brilliant but sultry summer day, and the last thing he wanted to do was spend it indoors.

Already the promise of heat to come made him feel lazy. He waited at the stable door for the head groom, breathing in the scents of straw and horse sweat, waving his hand to chase away flies buzzing about his head. There wasn't much else for them to buzz around, for the queen was very particular about the state of the stables and courtyard, and horse droppings were cleaned up as soon as they appeared. The bandy-legged head groom hurried to greet him, bowing until his long nose touched his knees. Siegfried repressed a growl; the man's manners were more to his mother's taste than his own, but he couldn't help that.

"Prince Siegfried! What is your wish this morning, sire? Your hunter? Your palfrey?" The man knew his horseflesh, at least, and saw to it that the stables were well-provided with good mounts. "I have some stock just up from the breeding farm, sire. Something fresh and untried?"

Fresh and untried, he thought with amusement, *but not in a horse.* "My palfrey," he replied aloud. "I expect to be out all day."

The groom bowed again and hurried off. *He,* of

course, would not be doing the actual work—he barked a series of orders to an underling, and shortly a skinny stripling with bad skin arrived with the reins of Siegfried's palfrey in his hands.

Siegfried took the reins, tugged on the saddle girth to make certain it was firm, and mounted the gentle mare. He took her at a walk out of the courtyard and through the main gate over the wooden drawbridge, letting her set her own pace and pick her own direction.

He rode for some time along the main road, the palfrey's hooves kicking up little puffs of dust as he passed through and past the village, without feeling any wish to stop although the inn there did have very good beer and often had attractive wenches to serve it. His mood at the moment called for the countryside and open air; already by midmorning it was so warm that the birds drowsed in the trees, and only the insects sang. Out in the fields of ripening hay, waves of heat made the air shimmer, and puffy clouds idled through the hazy sky. In a few more days, if the weather held, there would be a crew of men and women out in those fields, mowing down the sweet hay and leaving it to dry in the hot sun. *This is bidding fair to resemble one of those lusty country-folk songs,* Siegfried thought with amusement. *So—will it be a pretty shepherdess, a milkmaid with a saucy smile, a brown girl in the fields, or something different from any of those?*

Hayfields gave way to pastured hills; once he saw sheep grazing off in the distance, and thought about seeing who was tending them. But his mare showed no inclination to move off the road, and he was too lazy to try and change her mind.

After the pasture lands, the road entered the first truly wild woods near to the palace. Merchants didn't much like to pass through here, though the foresters kept guard on the road. Bandits did set up in the woods now and again, usually in fall, when there was traffic for the harvest fair on the road. No bandit would attack a mounted man on the main road in broad daylight, however fine his horse and tempting his apparent wealth, so Siegfried didn't hesitate when the mare followed the road in under the trees.

The deep shade gave welcome relief from the burning sun, and horseflies didn't seem to like the shadows. The palfrey picked up her pace and chose a trail leading off the main track, a path that he knew led to the river. She probably wanted a drink—well, so did he, so he didn't turn her back to the road.

Her ears pricked forward as they drew nearer to the stream, showing more interest than the water alone would warrant, and he strained his own ears to pick up what had alerted her.

Irregular splashing—but too much to be fish jumping. Otters, maybe? Beaver? Either would provide some welcome furs when fall arrived, and Siegfried decided to investigate and mark the place. Cautiously, he reined the mare in and then had her move off the path and pick her way, step by careful step, through the undergrowth. A horse would sound much like a deer to another animal, but the beasts could always tell when a human was stalking them, afoot.

As they came to the river, a patch of dull color on the bank caught his eye.

No animal left that! A pile of discarded clothing lay safely above the water, a beribboned, multihued motley, shabby and patched—but there was no sign of the owner, and he couldn't tell from here if it was male or female garb.

There's also no sign of a fight, so whoever took those clothes off, did it because he wanted to. So—

Water splashed again, and he peered out through the sun dazzle, eyes aching a little. With the sun shining full on the water, it was hard to make out anything on the river.

Yes, there was the owner, surfacing like a porpoise, spitting water and shaking her wet head with a musical laugh that told him these were women's garments on the bank.

She was a gypsy, by the black hair and dark skin, which would account for the gay patchwork of clothing. *Gypsy . . . so that's to be the set of the song! Ha!* He grinned. Gypsy women had a reputation for passion, a reputation he'd never had the opportunity to test.

Either she's completely alone, or she's slipped off from her clan to bathe in the river. In either case, she's alone now, *and I doubt she'd be splashing about like this if she expected anyone to come along.* His breath caught in his throat, and his heart began to race.

The woman reached the shallows and stood up, pulling wet hair away from her face. He bit back an exclamation as his groin tightened and throbbed at the sight of her body, naked as Eve, and as unselfconscious. She wasn't much to look at in the face—rather too brown and angular for his taste—but her body was enough to make a monk forget his vows! High, rounded breasts tipped in dark rose, a flat, tight belly, legs like two young, graceful trees—

He didn't really make up his mind; his throbbing groin made it up for him. He touched his heels to his horse, breaking out from under cover of the brush, just as the woman looked up.

She gasped, and her hands flew to cover herself inadequately. Her pose didn't fool Siegfried; if she'd been afraid, she'd have made a dive into the deepest part of the river where he couldn't reach her. After all, she'd just proved she could swim. *Very nice! Just exactly like a bawdy song! I wonder how many times she's put on this little act?* He grinned, and sent the palfrey forward another step.

She broke her frozen pose and ran like a deer, splashing along the riverbank, fleeing him on a course that took her through the shallows. But she made no effort to get into deeper water, nor did she bolt into the brush where his horse would have trouble going, which told Siegfried that she didn't really want to escape. Sparkling water fountained around her, and she looked back over her shoulder to see if he was going to give chase.

That was all the spur he needed. Digging his heels into his palfrey's sides, he sent the horse galloping after her, water splashing high with every hoofbeat. She hadn't run more than ten steps before he was at her heels; he swung down out of the saddle as the palfrey overtook her, and snatched her up by the waist, hauling her up in front of him to lie facedown over his legs and the saddle.

The moment his hands touched her, she went limp. *So it was a game, little gypsy? Well, we'll just take it through to the final play! And your garments will make as good a bed as any.*

Holding her firmly, he wheeled his horse and returned to the place where her clothing lay, directing the palfrey with his knees to get up onto the bank. Still holding the wench firmly, Siegfried tossed the reins over the palfrey's head, ground-tying her so she wouldn't stray. Then he threw one leg over the horse's back and slid down, slipping the gypsy girl down onto the pile of skirts and petticoats. She stayed limp, and lay completely still where he'd put her, eyes closed, making no move to either fight him or try to run again.

His hands tingled with the feel of her smooth, soft skin, and the sight of her lying on the ground at his feet drove any thoughts whatsoever out of his head.

Quickly undoing the knots his servants had so carefully tied this morning, cursing when his fingers fumbled for a moment, he dropped his trews about his knees and fell upon her like a starving beast.

He was so intent on his own pleasure, so wild with need, that at first he didn't notice that she lay like one dead when he took her, making only a low noise in the back of her throat, her eyes still squeezed tightly shut. It didn't matter; by then he was well seated in her, and even her passivity couldn't dampen his lust.

It was over with a few quick thrusts; the fire in his loins exploded into pleasure akin to delirium, a moment of ultimate satiation that curiously turned to dissatisfaction as if touched by the hand of some evil sorcery.

So as he collapsed atop her, knees weak and body exhausted, his main feeling was of disappointment. After a moment he rolled off and stood up, tying his hose again. Her only reaction was to slowly gather up her clothing around her, clutching it to her body, and cower there, staring at his feet.

So much for reputation! he thought with disgust. *Stupid bitch! If she didn't want me, why did she play with me? Why didn't she fight me?*

Exasperated, he reached into his belt-pouch and pulled out a handful of coins without looking at them, dropping them where she stared. She still hadn't moved by the time he caught his horse and rode off, not even to touch one of the coins.

The encounter left him entirely unsatisfied, although the ache in his groin was temporarily assuaged. *I thought gypsies were supposed to be hot-blooded and lusty,* he thought, disgruntled, his mood entirely spoiled. *That girl was about as lusty as a nun!* In fact, given some of the stories he'd heard about certain convents, the nuns would have been better partners!

His horse, at least, had been perfectly well satisfied

with the browsing she'd gotten, and she picked up her feet neatly as he returned the way he had come. *I am not going back to the palace yet,* he thought, stubbornly, as he left the green shade of the woods and trotted out onto the dusty road again. *If nothing else, I am going to have a good sausage and some well-brewed beer.* By now his breakfast had worn off. If he couldn't satisfy one appetite, well, he could at least take care of another.

By the time he reached the inn, many of the local craftsmen and merchants had gathered there for their own meals and a chance to catch up on gossip. As soon as Siegfried dismounted, of course, the innkeeper hurried over to wait on him personally, and a pair of portly burghers were only too pleased to give up their little table under the trees to him. Or if they were not pleased, they took care not to show it.

But Siegfried was well-liked in the village, and he persuaded them to share the table with him. It didn't take a great deal of persuading; there was an unspoken understanding that if their prince invited them to be a little less than formal with him, they need not fear his offended pride. But the invitation had to come from *him*; that, too, was understood.

In a very short time, Siegfried had a plate of excellent sausage and sauerkraut in front of him—a dish his mother would have regarded with horror, had it been placed in front of her—and a stein of exceptional beer to wash it down. He stayed silent, listening to the gossip of the village, and marveling at how very like it was to the gossip of the palace. *It's a cruder copy of our intrigues,* he decided, his good humor restored. *Just like they try to copy our dress. We must be like a marvelous play to them.*

Although he could while away as much time here as he wished, the rest of the inn's patrons had work to do, and sooner than he would have liked, Siegfried was left alone at his wooden table under the oaks planted in front of the inn. He pondered his empty stein glumly, and was just about to feel sorry for himself, when a comely hand bearing a pitcher refilled the tankard for him.

He let his gaze travel from the hand, to the plump, round arm; from the arm, to the rest of his benefactress.

"Your glass was empty, sire," the woman said, with a little flirt of her rust-colored linen skirts as she stepped back. The prince allowed his gaze to linger, but her only reaction was a broadening of her smile.

"I haven't seen *you* here before," Siegfried replied as he noted the neat figure in the tightly laced bodice and chemise, her breasts displayed by the low chemise in a most satisfactory fashion, a plain apron tied tightly about her waist to emphasize how small it was.

"That's because you haven't *been* here for quite some time—sire." She dipped a mocking curtsy. "I came up from the country to work for Fritz this spring. I'd planned to leave after the haying and harvest— make my way to a city—"

He might have been mistaken about the gypsy, but there was no mistaking the promises in *her* tone and posture.

"Dare I think you could be persuaded to stay?" he asked, his tone as mocking—and as promising—as hers. He liked what he saw: a fine, experienced figure of a woman, who knew what she wanted and what was expected of her. Handsome, not pretty, and with just enough audacity to be intriguing.

And Fritz had no problem with freeing his girls for other duties. He almost smiled at that. The old panderer knew his tastes—the innkeeper had probably hired this wench on, knowing that Siegfried would see her sooner or later, and expecting a handsome reward out of it!

Well, he'll get one.

The woman pretended to consider his words. "I could be persuaded—if I thought there was a good place in it for me," she replied boldly. "I'd rather serve tables at the palace than work in the fields at harvest."

It was his turn to pretend to consider what she had said. "They're very particular at the palace about their servers," he told her, with mock seriousness. "I'm not sure you'd suit. . . ."

She leaned over the table, giving him a good, long look down her chemise. "Would the prince care to try me to see if I'd . . . suit? I'm sure Fritz will grant us a chamber for the interview. He is a very accommodating master."

His hose became uncomfortably binding, but her attitude was so audacious that he nearly laughed out loud. "I believe that would be a good idea," he replied.

She turned with surprising grace and another little flirt of her skirts to display neat ankles and calves, and sauntered toward the inn door. He threw down a coin that would cover the cost of a dozen meals like the one he'd just eaten, and followed.

She was already on the stair when he entered the common room, looking back to see if he'd follow. Her delighted chuckle when she saw him in the doorway was all the encouragement he needed.

He didn't get back to the palace until late that afternoon.

Chapter Five

SUNLIGHT streamed in through three broad windows let into the northern wall of the protected courtyard, windows left open in this warm weather. In the winter, thick and bubbly glass made in small, hand-sized panes set into a pivoting iron frame allowed nearly as much light in the workroom as the open windows did. There were better windows elsewhere in the palace; very few openings were protected only by shutters. This was inferior glass, but it served well enough for the workrooms such as this, the weaving room.

Eight looms stood here, all in use, each with a skilled woman hard at work at it. Queen Clothilde completed her examination of the weaving room with great satisfaction. It had been well worth the expense to have the two new looms built. Now they could provide their own woven tapestries, without having to import them at ruinous expense from Flanders or France, or make them the old way, by piecing and embroidering the designs. The embroiderers could turn their attention to making fine bands of trim for gowns, and larger designs on the breasts of palace livery. Best of all, *now* she could have her pages, heralds, and personal guards garbed in tabards bearing her arms, as she had heard that greater courts than hers displayed.

The queen's most skilled weavers sat at the two tapestry looms, carefully following a design pricked out on precious paper beside them, shuttles of precious colored wool threads heaped in baskets beside them. They worked slowly, an inch or two of tapestry woven in a day was good progress. They also had pride-of-place beside the windows, where the light was best. The other six looms clattered energetically beneath the hands of the weavers, three weaving woolen cloth, two linen, and one weaving very fine thread of plain linen in tight bands that would later serve as the ground for bands of embroidery. The more precious velvets, silks, and plush fabrics had to be purchased, but most of the fabric used by Clothilde's household was woven here. A suit of clothing was part of the yearly stipend of those servitors (including the landless knights and foot soldiers) who were hired rather than serfs, and even the serfs got a stipend of clothing in the form of old clothes handed down from the servants. Personal servants often received gifts of discarded clothing from their masters, after expensive embroideries and other ornamentation was removed, as well as stipend clothing, but that was not very often, as velvets and silks were so expensive they were turned, cut down, remade and used many times before they fell into the hands of servants. Whether "common" clothing was the elaborate livery of a herald or the simple chemise or smock of a kitchen servant, it was made here, in the palace, and mostly from the cloth woven in this very room.

A velvet loom will be next, I think, Clothilde reflected. *I suspect we will be weaving mostly wool plush, but it will be worth it to have the ability to weave velvet when we have the thread. And now that* all *of my embroidery women can work on my page tabards, they should be finished before autumn.* It was the queen's ambition that her court, though small, be regarded as

sophisticated as any in the land; clothing those servants that were highly visible in real livery demonstrated sophistication. A high level of sophistication
implied a high level of prosperity and importance; it
also implied wealth and the strength to defend that
wealth.

She had far-reaching ambitions, plans that were
nebulous shadows now, but if she had the freedom to
act—who knew? If her little court attracted the attention of the Emperor, there could be state visits, invitations to the Imperial functions, and even (dare she
think it?) the personal attentions of the widowed Emperor himself.

A page entered the weaving room, interrupting her
reverie. He looked around for her, then hurried to her
side. "Your Majesty, the minstrel Uwe has returned—
and there is a nobleman with him," the cherubic child
said breathlessly, his blue eyes wide and ingenuous.
"The nobleman would like an audience with you, that
is, he respectfully requests an audience of you."

Uwe—with a stranger? That piqued her interest. She
had sent him off on a mission to find appropriate candidates for Siegfried's bride—but what else had he
found?

"Who is this nobleman?" she asked the boy, not
quite ready to commit to an immediate meeting. She
didn't want the stranger to have the impression that
the Queen had so little to occupy her that she could
give a stranger an immediate hearing—but on the
other hand, she didn't want to offend a powerful man
who might be of use to her.

"Baron von Rothbart, Majesty," the boy replied.
"Uwe said to tell you he has much to interest you
regarding the errand you sent him on."

Indeed? That settled it. "I will see them in the
Lesser Audience Chamber," she told the boy. "Take
your time in guiding them there, however."

The page took her at her word, and left the room at a leisurely walk. Clothilde signaled to one of her maids to pick up the train of her gown and moved briskly to the room she had designated to the page, giving orders to the rest of the servants who accompanied her as she walked.

The Lesser Audience Chamber was just off the Great Hall, through which the visitor would be conducted in order to reach it, giving him an eyeful of Clothilde's improvements. He should be even more impressed when he reached the chamber itself; it was the "lesser" chamber only in terms of size, not of luxury and sumptuousness. The obvious fact that it was easier and less expensive to create the impression of wealth in a *small* room rather than a large one was often overlooked by visitors.

Meant to receive parties of four or less, the room had plastered walls for warmth, covered with floor-to-ceiling hangings so that not an inch of plaster showed. At the moment, only two of the walls had tapestries instead of the draping curtains of an arras; that would be remedied as the new looms produced more work. The only break was a single window, curtained in heavy wool; the curtains were pulled back, displaying the fact that the window was not only glazed, it had a picture in colored glass, just like the one in the chapel, but portraying a sun-in-glory surrounded by stars.

The throne, carved with all the considerable skill of a master joiner, had been overlaid with gold leaf last year, and cushioned in plush. Perhaps it was not of marble, but it was more comfortable, and impressive enough. Clothilde arranged herself in the throne with the help of her handmaiden; a servant summoned by another lady-in-waiting came hastily to learn her bidding, and she sent him off for wine and cakes for the visitor. The sideboard was already laid with a snowy linen cloth, with silver goblets enough waiting, and there were two chairs at the opposite side of the room should she choose to allow her visitor to seat himself in her presence.

The servant arrived just before the two men, and waited at the sideboard beneath the window as they appeared. Uwe preceded the stranger, fell immediately to one knee before Clothilde's throne, and made a deep bow to her, exciting a profound sense of pleasure in her at this sign of his servility. Minstrels were notoriously arrogant. That Uwe should abase himself spoke much for her power, and she knew that this stranger would be aware of that.

Uwe spoke in humble tones, without raising his eyes. "Your Majesty, with your gracious permission, I present to you Baron Eric von Rothbart, who desires to be a great friend to Your Majesty."

"We are always pleased to encounter friends," she said cautiously, then smiled on her minstrel. "You have our permission to rise, Uwe."

As Uwe stood up, she turned her attention to the stranger. A large man, a *formidable* man; it was quite clear he was no stranger to combat. He had the broad shoulders and muscular chest of an experienced swordsman, though he wore not so much as a dagger at the moment, not even a dress sword. His red hair and beard betrayed where his family name, *von Rothbart,* had originated; his face displayed nothing but a pleasant half smile. His costume, however, betrayed a great deal; Clothilde had never seen a mere *baron* in such sumptous garb before. His cloak, curiously embroidered so that it resembled feathers laid over one another, was of rich brown velvet with a creamy satin lining. His gown—for as many mature men did, he wore a long gown, a houpellande, rather than a doublet—was of matching velvet, stitched at the hems with gold bullion in a pattern of owls perched among branches. His shirt, showing at the collar of the gown, could only be of that heavy, fine silk cloth known as samite, so precious that it was generally reserved for altar cloths; it, too, was embroidered in a subtle design in white silk. His pointed shoes in the latest fashion were of fine, gilded leather, soft enough to be made into gloves.

Around his neck he wore a heavy chain of red-gold, the links made in the shape of owls, with a great pendant of enameled gold hanging down on his chest. Strangely enough, given the owl theme of the rest of his garb, the pendant was in the shape of a white swan with a crown about her neck. There were even tiny jewels winking in the gold of the crown.

Every finger beringed, and a baronial coronet of gold and topaz about his brow, this man carried a small fortune on his person. If he wore this much for an unannounced visit, what must he and his holdings be worth?

Granted, he intends to make as much of an impression on me as I wish to on him, but still . . . That much wealth, displayed by a man whose name and title were completely unknown to the queen, made an intriguing package.

The last oddity about the man was that he had in his right hand a staff of ebony, as tall as he, bound with rings of chased gold. The staff was intricately carved, although Clothilde was too far from him to see what the tiny carvings represented, and it was topped with a globe of water-clear, citron-colored crystal. It surely must be crystal, yellow quartz, perhaps. No topaz was ever that big. . . .

All this Clothilde took in, absorbing it in a single measuring glance. She assumed that he was doing the same to her, and was pleased to see that his pleasant half-smile did not waver.

"Please take refreshment, my lord baron," she said,

waving the servant forward, and deciding to dispense with the intensely formal use of the royal plural. "And in deference to the fact that you have traveled far to come here, I believe we can waive some of the strictest of etiquette between us. I will have my servant bring you a seat."

The servant gave a goblet of wine to the baron and offered him cakes, which the man declined. The servant took the refreshments to the sideboard and left them there, returning with a single, low chair. Uwe, of course, could not be seated. He was scarcely above a mere servant in rank, so far as the baron was concerned, and Clothilde was determined not to let this stranger know otherwise just yet. Uwe tactfully removed himself to the sideboard, where he poured himself a goblet of wine and remained standing as he sipped it; an observer, not a participant, so far as the baron was aware.

"This is a gracious gesture, Majesty," the baron replied, in a low voice, like a distant rumble of thunder. "And it is much appreciated." He sat down without looking, rightly expecting that the servant would get the chair under him before a disaster occurred. Once seated, he leaned forward a trifle, resting the staff on both knees. "The matter which brings me to Your Majesty is, however, a delicate one. . . ."

Clothilde was not slow at taking the hint; she signaled her handmaiden and the servant to leave the room, and gave an inquiring glance at Uwe.

"The minstrel is in my confidence, Majesty," von Rothbart said, correctly interpreting the glance. "I encountered him when visiting the court of King Iosef, and when I learned what had brought him, I knew that you would be very interested in my own proposal concerning your son's future, for I believe I can be of great service to you in that regard."

"We are referring to the marriage of my son, Prince

Siegfried?" she replied, allowing her right eyebrow to rise a trifle. "In what way can you be of service to me?"

"I have a daughter—" von Rothbart began, and raised his hand in a gesture of disclaimer. "And under ordinary circumstances, I, as a mere baron, would not dream of proposing to Your Highness that she be considered as a bride for the prince. However, as I am sure you have deduced, I am a baron in name only—and only because I choose not to exercise my considerable power in the realm of the material world more often than absolutely necessary. I possess wealth that kings might envy, and abilities that bring kings to seek *my* aid."

He paused, waiting for Clothilde to make some remark, but she remained silent. The last sentence had given her the answer to the riddle that was Baron Eric von Rothbart.

He was a sorcerer. No other "mere baron" could be so wealthy, so powerful, and so completely unknown to her.

"Nevertheless, it is in the material world that I must *live,* and so must my daughter," the baron continued. "She is of an age to wed, and is enough of a prize that I have misgivings about the suitors that may come to seek her hand, should I make it known that she exists and is eligible to wed. I would see her well bestowed so that I may continue my—studies—with an easy mind."

"As would any father," the queen murmured. "And I assume you wish to present her to me as a bridal candidate for Siegfried. Nevertheless, the choice of bride is to be my son's, not mine, and young men are often swayed by appearances, favoring a pretty face above other considerations."

Von Rothbart's smile widened just a trifle. "In that case, I believe there will be no difficulties. Behold!"

He pointed with the topaz end of the staff to the floor between himself and Clothilde, and without so much as a puff of smoke (which was, to her mind, more impressive than all the flashes and bangs of charlatans) a life-sized image appeared of a young woman.

She impressed even Clothilde. Of her beauty there was no doubt: enormous, childlike blue eyes, a broad, white brow, chiseled cheekbones, a grave mouth, delicate chin, a neck like a swan's, and the most amazing cascade of silver-blonde hair Clothilde had ever seen, hanging loosely down her back, entwined with ropes of black seed pearls. Her gown impressed Clothilde as much as the girl's beauty; of black silk, embroidered with black pearls from the size of grains of sand up to the size of Clothilde's thumb, it embraced the girl's willowy figure in a way achieved only with endless hours of labor and the expertise of a seamstress more skilled than any in Clothilde's household.

Or else, it was made by magic, she reminded herself. But to have made such a gown magically was as impressive, if not more so, than making it with human hands.

"My daughter is sweet of disposition, learned enough to beguile your son with her conversation, and entirely biddable," von Rothbart continued, in the fatuous tones of a fond father, as the girl's image moved gracefully, as if she strolled in a garden. "And lest you think this is only the opinion of a man too easily swayed, let me assure you that she is absolutely obedient to authority. In point of fact, she has never once in all of her life been permitted to disobey. I have given her the strictest of training, and she will abide by the word of her elders even though it cost her dear."

"Your daughter is clearly lovely, and I will take your word on her temper, lord baron," the queen said smoothly. "But there is the matter of the dower. . . ."

"She will be dowered like the daughter of the Em-

peror," he told her promptly, and named a sum that
made Uwe's eyes bulge for a moment. "And, in addition, of course, you will have *my* services to call upon,
from time to time, services which King Iosef found
very useful." His eyes gleamed with dark promises,
and the Queen reined in her imagination with a sharp
tug. "I am not averse to exercising my power in the
material world . . . now and again in a good cause."

"There is the matter of my son's choice," she reminded him. "He and he alone shall have the responsibility for choosing his bride."

Von Rothbart waved his hand and the image of his
daughter vanished. "I think we can take it as read that
he will choose my daughter," he replied negligently.
"In fact, once she appears, I suspect he will see no
one else."

Clothilde thought of love spells and other be-
witchments possible to a powerful sorcerer, and nodded. "Nevertheless, he must have the . . . *appearance*
of making a choice. For his sake, if not for mine."

"I agree completely." The sorcerer nodded. "It is
best if he has maidens to compare with my daughter.
She will outshine them as the moon outshines the
stars, and there will be no question in his mind but
that he has chosen the fairest beauty in all the land."

The queen smiled and extended her hand to the
baron. "In that case, all conditions seem to be agree-
able," she told him. "Uwe will give you my invitation
to the birthday fete, and you may present your daughter to my son at his celebration."

"Your Majesty has made me a supremely happy
man," the baron told her, rising to kiss her extended
hand. "Now, with your permission, I shall take my
leave. I have far to go, and even a man with—power—
at his disposal cannot go from hither to yon in an
instant."

She nodded. Uwe gave the baron the last of his

invitations, and the man departed with a dramatic bow and a swirl of his cape, leaving minstrel and queen alone.

Clothilde sat back against the support of the throne's cushions. "Well!" she said, folding her hands in her lap. "That was—interesting."

"I thought you'd be intrigued." Uwe poured himself a goblet of wine, and sat down on the lowest step of the dais. "Believe me, he's no charlatan; he showed up to give Iosef a little help—for an undisclosed fee, of course—when Iosef's brother started eying the throne a little too closely. That was right after I arrived, and I was just about to leave with the invitation in my pocket."

"God's Blessing, I should think so," the queen exclaimed. "I do *not* need to multiply my problems by adding a father-in-law with a shaky throne in need of propping up! What did he do, kill the usurper?"

"Nothing so crude—as he pointed out to Iosef, that would be murder, which is a sin. He turned the man into a swine." Uwe smirked. "Right in front of the entire court, mind you. I was there, I saw it; it was no mere illusion, and as far as I know, a swine he remains, to this day. Told Iosef that he couldn't do that sort of thing without Divine blessing, mind you—the rule is evidently that the magic doesn't work unless the victim has betrayed someone or otherwise broken faith. Still."

"Still." The queen pursed her lips, then rose. Taking Uwe's goblet from him, she sipped it herself as she thought for a moment. "Not so difficult to get someone to swear to something, an oath he has no intention of keeping. Should it become necessary, of course."

"Of course." Uwe's expression was bland. "And, of course, our prince is a lusty fellow and has a wandering eye. I doubt that a love spell can be made to hold him to one woman for very long. Be a pity if he broke his marriage vows and his father-in-law took exception to the fact, hmm?"

The queen smiled blandly. "A very great pity," she murmured. "A very great pity indeed."

Siegfried couldn't imagine what his mother had been doing that made her smile so much at him that night at dinner, but whatever it was, he was glad of it. Maybe it was just that her pet minstrel was back; she always seemed out of temper when his wandering feet took him off to another court. But as long as the queen was happy, everyone breathed a little easier. When she *wasn't* happy, it didn't do to display anything but sobriety and melancholy in her presence.

For his part, Siegfried was entirely contented when he sat down to dinner beside his mother at the head table. His previous mistresses had quietly and gracefully taken themselves out of his life, with not a single tear or complaint, at least according to Arno. They'd taken their final gifts with expressions of gratitude, and left him free to install that delicious wench from the tavern in the palace as soon as Arno could find her a position. There was something to be said in favor of experience, and there was no doubt in his mind after his little trial of her that she'd had experience in plenty.

Which means it should take a long time before I'm tired of her. He smiled into his cup, thinking about the novel turns she'd shown him in that cozy chamber in the inn—and a couple of things she'd suggested that he'd never even heard of before. With a woman like that in his bed, he could afford to take the time to court Sir Hans' sister-in-law; he could enjoy the chase without going mad with frustration. *But I'll have to*

*make it clear from the start to both of them that I am
the master, and I won't tolerate either of them acting
as if she has any rights over me.* He'd made the mistake of letting that happen only once. It had been the
same occasion that prompted his resolve never to take
a leman from the same rank as his last—or current—
bedmates. The resulting hair-pulling match in the
laundry had even come to the attention of the queen,
and *that* had resulted in a lecture that still made him
want to cringe.

*Never mind. They will both understand from the be-
ginning what the rules are, and that they will abide by
them. They have more to gain from me than I from
them.* There were always plenty of women ready to
take his presents and grant him their bodies. His main
difficulties came from being selective.

The final course of subtleties had been brought in
while he was thinking; as usual, he waved everything
away but a single ripe pear, peeled, cored, and
drenched in honeyed wine. He didn't have much of a
craving for sweets, though everyone else had helped
themselves generously. Uwe the minstrel was singing
some new ballad in the latest style, something he'd
probably written or picked up on his travels. The
queen toyed with a bit of marzipan window from the
pastry palace in front of her as she listened, a definite
smile still lingering on her lips. She'd crumbled most
of the sweet rather than eating it, another sign that
she was well-pleased with something; she only devoured her sweets as everyone else did when she was
in a bad humor.

Excellent, Siegfried thought, watching her out of the
corner of his eye while he pretended to listen to Uwe's
singing, affectations and all. *The happier she is, the
less attention she pays to what I do.* He knew he could
leave arrangements for the new girl in Arno's hands.
And until Arno brings her up here, I can always go

down to the village. It wouldn't be the first time he'd had a girl down there, and it wouldn't be the last. He wondered if he ought to offer Dorian the use of one or more of his discarded lemans; heaven only knew that if the poor fellow was going to be leg-shackled to an ugly mare, he might as well have a gallop with a frisky filly first. It would be a friendly gesture, especially after trouncing him so badly the other day.

I'll have Arno see to it, he decided, feeling decidedly generous. *In fact, I think I'll have them smuggled into his bed, and he can take his choice.* Another generous present should ensure their cooperation. He could imagine Dorian's reaction at finding three toothsome lovelies waiting for him wearing nothing but their long hair. . . .

That's a better wedding present than he'll get from anyone else, Siegfried thought with a chuckle—fortunately covered by the applause as Uwe finished his song.

The end of the song signaled the formal end of dinner, though many of those with nothing else to do would linger over wine and cakes. The queen rose, and her household rose with her; everyone else stood and bowed as she and her ladies—and the minstrel—left the hall. Their departure meant that the less refined forms of amusement could begin.

No more minstrels warbling ballads of Courtly Love—one fighter bellowed out the chorus of a drinking song, and two more chimed in. Several dicing games began on the floor, and an arm-wrestling match or two over the tables, while two of the serving wenches plumped themselves down into the laps of men who'd been eying them all evening.

Siegfried waited a moment to see if anything more interesting developed, but when nothing did, he also left the hall. Unfortunately, he couldn't participate without getting into trouble. The queen would claim

he compromised his rank and dignity, and that the
men wouldn't respect his authority if he acted like one
of them.

Tonight he didn't really regret his enforced aloof-
ness. The afternoon's exertions had eased some of his
restlessness, and he wasn't in the mood for the horse-
play that usually took place after dinner.

He decided in favor of a walk in the moonlit gardens, thinking that it was possible he would encounter
the fair widow Adelaide there. And even if he
didn't—well, the summer would be over far too soon;
pleasant walks in a warm, scented garden would be
impossible until spring.

There was a full moon, which had tempted several
others out into the gardens as well. The perfume of
roses hung heavily in the still, balmy air, and all the
paths through the garden reflected moonlight, making
rivers of light winding among the flower beds. Soft
murmurs of conversation came from secluded bowers;
with a grin, Siegfried kept his distance from all of
them. Not that he'd surprise anything more ribald than
a kiss in the formal gardens, for there was not enough
privacy here for amorous couples to risk more, but
maidens of good breeding would be horribly shamed
by being caught in even a kiss.

Thank God for women of low breeding!

Women who were *not* meeting lovers by prear-
rangement would walk on the paths, or sit on one of
the garden benches placed in the open, talking together, or hoping to be seen by a prospective suitor.
That would be where he would find Adelaide, if she
had, indeed, come out here. Couples who had more
in mind than a kiss would be someplace where there
was no chance of interruption—there were plenty of
places to go in warm weather. It was easy enough to
pitch a tiny pavilion in the orchards or meadows, to
take a boat out on one of the lakes, or to find a se-

cluded nook on the palace grounds but away from the formal gardens. In winter—there was the inn, a couple of hunting lodges, but anything else took the complicity of two or more others to help in getting a moment of privacy. It wasn't the norm for members of the queen's household to have private quarters—only those of very high rank indeed had even a tiny room to themselves. Most slept in dormitories or a room stocked with several narrow beds, or shared a larger bed with one or more fellows. The maiden fosterlings of Clothilde's train, for instance, slept three to a bed in a room just above Clothilde's chambers, a room that itself held four beds. Even her unmarried ladies-in-waiting slept in pairs, in tiny closetlike rooms nearby. Benno and two of the younger nobles shared a similar room, for instance, although they did not have to share a bed, and that was the norm for those who did not reside in a nearby manse. Some of Clothilde's ladies-in-waiting had manors nearby, but those who did not shared a chamber either with their husbands or with other ladies whose husbands were dead or off somewhere on the queen's service. That meant any dalliance had to take place with the complicity of one's fellows, or somewhere inside or outside of the palace where one could find a private corner. *Finding* a private corner took ingenuity and persistence, since it might well fall out that another had already marked that spot and taken possession.

Siegfried found the game endlessly amusing, though others doubtless found it frustrating. Tonight, however, he was in a softer mood, and was content to stroll about the garden, murmuring polite greetings to the ladies he encountered, and smiling with indulgence at the amorous twitterings in the bowers.

He strolled every path of the garden twice over; since he still hadn't encountered his quarry, he decided to seek his bed. *And I'll definitely go back down*

to the inn tomorrow morning, he decided, in pleasant
contentment. It really didn't matter all that much that
he hadn't encountered the widow. She might be having second thoughts, especially if her brother-in-law
had made it plain what kind of liaison she could expect with Siegfried. She might believe—erroneously—
that if she held herself chaste, she could inflame him
enough to get him to the altar. Or she might simply
be shy, modest, unwilling to play the game he had in
mind. She would either change her mind, sooner or
later, or resign herself to living on Sir Hans' thin char-
ity. There weren't many options open to a widow of
meager rank and modest beauty, and the older she
became, the fewer there were. If she were skilled at
embroidery or weaving, she might find a position in
Clothilde's service, but she would then find herself
almost as cloistered as if she'd gone to a nunnery.
Clothilde did not care for losing a skilled worker, and
kept her weavers and embroiderers mewed up away
from the temptations set for them by men. She *said*
she was protecting their souls, but Siegfried had heard
her on the rare occasions when one had wedded out
of the workroom, and it wasn't their virtue Queen
Clothilde was concerned with, it was their craft.

Arno and two of the manservants were waiting for
Siegfried when he climbed the stairs to his quarters.
He let them undress him and climbed into his bed
with a pleasant sense of anticipation for what awaited
him on the morrow. Frogs and the occasional hoot of
an owl outside his window lulled him quickly to sleep.

He drifted from soothing darkness into a dream—
knowing that he dreamed, which was unusual—with
no sense of anxiety. In his dream, he walked through
the gardens as he had this evening, but this time he
was completely alone. It wasn't night, although it
didn't seem to be day, either. There was neither sun
nor moon, only a gray twilight with no evident

source—but since he knew this was a dream, the absence of sun, moon, or stars didn't disturb him.

The garden path led him abruptly into a wall of trees, and he found himself facing an unfamiliar woodland landscape. He hesitated for a moment, with no clues as to what lay beneath the trees.

Should I go on, or turn back?

He turned to look behind him, only to discover that the gardens were gone, vanished completely. Before, behind, all around him was the forest. Evidently he had no choice about entering the woods; he shrugged and went on.

It was darker under the trees than it had been in the garden, but it was still brighter than the moonlight had been tonight. His dream-woods were also strangely empty—no birds, no animals, not even a rustling in the underbrush.

Just when he decided that he was the only living thing in his dream that wasn't a plant, he spotted a dim figure, partly obscured by foliage, on the path ahead of him. That was something of a relief; the dream had begun to bore him. He picked up his pace a trifle, from a slow stroll to a faster walk. As he neared the stranger, he saw that it was a woman.

More than that—a nude woman—and he felt himself grinning, in anticipation of one of his favorite erotic fantasies. His loins tingled and tightened, and he licked his lips. Oh, of course it was only a dream, but dreams were good in their own way—

But the woman moved stiffly, her gait odd and stilted, and as she neared, her expressionless face gave him a sudden chill. The hair on the back of his neck rose, his pleasant anticipation vanished, and in his dream he stopped still on the path, frozen, unable to move.

What is this? He had never had a dream like this before! She continued to approach him, and he saw that her

eyes were glazed, her movements jerky, and her skin
had the chill, blue-gray tinge of one long dead.

Jesu Cristos! It was a liche, some thing out of the
grave!

Fear sat in his stomach, a cold, hard lump that grew
with every passing moment; he wanted to move and
could not. Cold sweat poured out of him; the woman
drew nearer still. It was then that he recognized her
as the gypsy girl from the river.

Her glassy eyes did not seem to see him as she
walked nearer and nearer, arms dangling at her sides.
He tried desperately to move, fearing now that she
would reach for him, and knowing that he could not
bear the touch of her cold, dead hand without
screaming.

But she stopped just short of where he stood. Her
hands slowly rose, and in them she now held a mirror.
She raised it between them until it was even with his
face. Unable to look away, he stared at his own reflection, numb with nameless dread.

The mirror reflected his face for no more than a
heartbeat. As he stared into his own eyes, his reflection shimmered, darkened, then changed.

As his stomach churned and twisted with horror, he
found himself staring at the face of a ravening wolf.
Blood dripped from its jowls, its teeth clamped deeply
into a soft-fleshed arm, clearly ripped from the body
of a girl or a child. It stared back at him, looking as
if it would be perfectly happy to drop the arm it
gnawed and leap out of the mirror at his throat.

And it still had *his* eyes.

With a terrified shout, he wrenched himself free of
the spell holding him—

—and fell, tangled in the bedcurtains, out of bed.

The curtains softened and slowed his fall; he didn't
make much of a *thud,* and apparently his shout had
only been in his dream, for none of the servants

started up out of *their* slumbers to see what ailed him. He lay on the floor in a sweat-drenched knot of sheets and curtains for an interminable length of time, shaking, while his heart pounded and he panted and gasped as if he had been running.

It was a dream. Just a dream. He tried to tell himself that, but was it? Gypsies were supposed to be witches and magicians. Had the girl cast a curse on him in spite?

He tried to reassure himself that it was a singularly ineffective curse, if all it could do was give him a nightmare. A senseless nightmare, at that. . . .

It didn't help. Cold sweat still dripped down his back and shoulders, and every muscle cramped and tensed with the need to flee.

Gradually his heartbeat slowed, his sweat dried, and his logical mind got control over the rest of him.

I am no little child to hide under the bed, scared by a dream.

Or so he told himself. Quietly, so as not to wake the servants, he untangled himself from his bed coverings and got to his feet. He knew where the pitcher of water stood. Feeling his way to the chest where it waited, he drank straight from the lip without bothering with the cup beside it. That took care of his fear-dried mouth and throat and settled the flutters in his stomach. He felt his way back to the bed, pulling his coverings back in place as best he could before climbing back into it.

Jesu preserve me from another such night! He pulled the covers about himself, and shivered a little in the darkness. Logic told him that this was nothing more than a single bad dream—that there was no significance in it—but his heart and guts didn't believe in logic. He wanted to berate himself for cringing in the bed like a frightened child, but at the moment, he *was* a frightened child who longed with all his soul for the welcome light of dawn.

He was afraid to close his eyes again, lest the witch return to haunt him. He lay back into the embrace of his feather bed, fully intending to fight off sleep until morning.

But the next thing he knew, sunlight was pouring in through the gaps in his bedcurtains, and cheerful birdsong from the window made his night terrors seem foolish in a way all his logic had been unable to do.

He reached out and pulled back one of the bedcurtains, as thirsty for sunlight as he had been for water last night. Arno was right at his bedside, pulling the other curtains aside as soon as he moved, as usual, completely oblivious to the fright his master had fought off. Siegfried stared at the sunlight, and felt his fright melt away as if it had never existed at all.

Relief at having survived the night made him unusually easy to please this morning; he accepted the first set of clothing his servants proposed, and made no objections even when they fumbled a little in lacing up the points of his hose.

"Bit of excitement this morning, Prince Siegfried," Arno remarked as he helped Siegfried into his boots. "Found a dead woman in the village millrace. Drowned, so they say."

He furrowed his brow, slightly confused for a moment by the non sequitur, before his mind snapped into alert comprehension. *Ah, of course—this is something I need to know, I may have to give orders about it if Mother hasn't.* "Murder?" he asked cautiously. "Robbery?" If there had been a murder, it was his duty to investigate it.

But Arno was shaking his head. "Captain of the guard says not. Looks like a suicide, he says, and a pity, too. Handsome girl, it was, young—"

"Young?" A superstitious shiver shook him, and an

echo of the horror and chill of last night crept over him. A dead young woman—like the gypsy girl? Surely not . . . surely it could not be. . . .

"Aye. A young gypsy girl, looks like." Arno went on blithely, head bent over his work. "No one hereabouts is missing, and she had the looks of a gypsy and the rags." He made a tsking sound. "A real pity. She wasn't in the water long, at any rate."

"No?" His throat was tight; *all* the fear of last night came flooding back, and he could all but see the staring eyes in the blue-gray, dead face, yet he dared not let Arno and the rest see it, know he was terrified, know his weakness. . . .

"No. No more than half a day," Arno continued, oblivious to the pounding of Siegfried's heart. "In fact, they say she must have drowned last night, just about midnight. Curious."

"Yes," Siegfried managed, his jaw clenched. "Curious. A suicide, you said?"

"The priest ordered her buried at the crossroads, to keep her from walking," Arno reported. Now he looked quizzically up at Siegfried. "Unless you order otherwise. I'm to ask—"

Now he was almost faint with relief for a second time. Buried at the crossroads, she could not haunt him again. "No!" he almost shouted, then quickly regained control. "No," he repeated, forcing an illusion of calm over himself. "Jesu forbid she's free to haunt m— the village! Bury her at the crossroads with bell, book, and candle to drive out her evil!" His tone grew harsh, and Arno's eyes widened with surprise, though he kept his thoughts to himself. "And yes, by Christ! *Stake* her there as well! Drive a spike through her heart! I'll have the witch nailed in her grave!"

"The priest may object," Arno pointed out mildly.

"Hang the priest. Let him tend to the souls of those who deserve tending." Anger burned away fear, and

Siegfried let his anger have its way with him, grateful only that it banished the terror. "He cannot save the soul of a witch; let her writhe in her grave until Judgment Day and burn in hell thereafter!"

A mask of bland obedience dropped over the surprise and curiosity in Arno's features, and he simply bowed as if Siegfried had ordered a new saddle for his palfrey—though the other two servants backed away, their eyes on Siegfried's face as though something they saw there terrified them. "I will order it done, sire," Arno said—and nothing more.

CHAPTER SIX

VON Rothbart led the flock in his guise as a great eagle-owl, followed by Odette, the rest of the swans trailing out in a graceful vee, with Odile bringing up the rear to make sure no stragglers dropped behind. She loved flying; she didn't get to wear her swan form nearly as often as she would have liked, for her studies and duties left her little free time to spend in the air above the baron's estate.

They flew by day, for the eyes of an eagle-owl were perfectly suited to daylight and the "natural" owls hunted equally well by day or night. They flew high enough that it wasn't likely anyone would notice anything but the white skein of swans against the sky, overlooking the darker owl leading them.

Odile had no idea where her father was taking them, for they did not head in the same direction two days in a row. They seemed to be meandering across the countryside, their course determined by chance. She knew very well that her father did nothing by chance, though, so this course may have been determined by the presence of secure places to spend the night.

They made no great speed, either, despite the fact that they were flying. For one thing, being confined to the single lake as they were most of the time, the girls in their swan forms were not accustomed to the kind of exercise that a wild swan got. They flew but rarely, and then for no great distance. For another thing, they needed to feed as *swans* rather than humans, since von Rothbart was not inclined to waste his powers in conjuring food for more than a score of girls. All of these considerations meant that they didn't make a start each day until noon at best. Unless the moon was due to rise late, they had to stop well before sunset—Odile guessed that von Rothbart wasn't going to expend magic in keeping them as swans past the ordinary time of the spell, and having his captives plummet out of the sky to their deaths would not have furthered his plans for them.

The baron had obviously calculated this journey with all those considerations in mind, however, for each day, just as the girls started to tire, or just as the sun sank below the horizon—whichever came first— he would lead them down to a secluded patch of water in the midst of some untenanted wilderness where they would land. There was no one to see the swans glide in to shore, no one to see them suddenly transform to girls as the moon rose, no one to wonder or interfere.

Because of her own nocturnal roamings, much more energetic than the bit of dancing the others practiced, Odile was not nearly so exhausted as the others when they all stopped for the day. This was just as well, since the baron left her in complete charge of the flock at night, flying off she knew not where, and only appearing by sunrise the next day. *She* was in charge of finding them a resting place in their human forms, and sitting guard over them until her father returned.

Perhaps that was why he continued to treat them as he always had, for he was not there to observe the transformations in Odette—or, for that matter, in Odile.

For the first few days, Odile had kept strictly to

orders: flying strongly in the rear of the flock and rounding up the stragglers, then watching over the girls at night as they slept, exhausted, wherever they could find a soft spot of ground beside the ponds and lakes where they came to land. But on the fourth day, there came a change in her actions.

It first happened when Lisbet, one of the little swans, started to drop back, with laboring wingstrokes that showed she was quickly running out of strength. Until then, Odile had simply flown to the straggler and nipped at her until she caught up with the others, but this time it was clear to her, if not to her father, that the little one simply didn't have the energy to keep up today. She hadn't slept well the night before, nor eaten well that morning because of her sleepless night; Odile had expected her to have some trouble, but she had hoped that Lisbet would have the strength to keep up. Obviously, though, she didn't, and it was up to Odile to do something.

She side-slipped in the air and approached the young one, who turned her head on her long neck and looked at her with fearful and pleading eyes, expecting cruelty—a buffeting wing, a painful nip from Odile's beak. It was more difficult to practice magic in her form of a swan than in her human shape, but Odile *could* work some minor changings—and she did, conjuring aid for Lisbet in the form of a partial levitation, to take some of her weight away.

With the load on her weary wings suddenly lightened, the swan shot forward, astonishment in her eyes, and caught up with the rest of the flock. Von Rothbart never noticed.

When they landed on a kidney-shaped pond in the midst of a marsh, Odile took the weight-reducing spell off the youngster just as her webbed feet touched the water, which made for an interesting landing; as usual, her father flew away without even a word.

There was plenty of food here, and tasty by swan standards, so they could all replenish their strength. But a marsh would hardly supply restful sleeping places for humans, a fact that apparently escaped von Rothbart.

While the others gathered together, foraged as much as their exhaustion would permit, and waited for sunset, Odile found a hummock that would bear her weight and made her own transformation to human. With a height advantage, she hoped to find some better refuge for herself and the flock.

Immediately, the dank heat struck her a blow, and the thick, unmistakable odor of the swamp itself, a wet miasma of rotting vegetation, stagnant water, and gases oozing up from the muck, assaulted her nose. A swarm of midges headed straight for her, which didn't improve the situation any. She frowned, a flicker of anger making her clench her jaw. *What was he thinking, leaving us here? Was he even thinking at all?*

Then she shook her head at her own stupidity. Hadn't she wanted her father to treat her as a capable magician in her own right? Hadn't she wanted to become his helper and partner? And wasn't he acting precisely as if that was what she was? So why should she be angry? He had left her a problem, he expected her to solve it without fuss, and that was what she would do.

Fine, we need a secure place to sleep— She swatted at more biting insects in annoyance, then took a deep breath, and circled a bit of magic about herself, creating a barrier the insects couldn't cross. *—no, we need a secure and comfortable place to sleep without being eaten alive by bugs. If the girls don't get some shelter from nighttime chill and insects, they won't be able to sleep, and they'll be too tired to fly tomorrow.* Von Rothbart would probably force them to fly—or if he allowed good sense to dictate his actions, he would be angry that they couldn't.

There are times when Father has not allowed common sense to dictate his actions, she thought with disfavor. *He is more likely to contrive some way to get them farther along.*

If that happened, it would be inevitable that they would be forced to stop sooner than he had planned, and that would throw his entire schedule off. One thing was paramount; the swans must never stop overnight in a place where their transformation could be observed by strangers; having the schedule changed would put that in jeopardy.

It's up to me to make certain there are no problems tomorrow by fixing things tonight. That is my job; that is why he brought me along. If I can't handle a situation like this, I don't deserve to be considered as a partner.

The trick would be to create something using the minimum possible of power, and do so before the moon rose. *I don't have Father's resources; whatever I do, it will have to be clever.* She could, of course, create a shelter out of the thin air, but why? They didn't need something that might vanish early when *she* ran out of power, leaving them all sputtering in the water. What they needed was firm ground to sleep on, warmth, shelter from insects and from damp. All these things could be created without creating them directly with magic.

Dry land, first. I wish I had some of Father's invisible helpers— Then it came to her; she needed helpers, not necessarily invisible nor magical. These waters should be teeming with swamp creatures and more arcane creations; the simplest and least-draining of magic spells to control them would make use of this unique workforce. She took a handful of mud and reeds from under her feet, then carefully spun her

spell around it, feeling power actually drain from her
as she worked. She invested her power in it, using the
water dripping from her hand as the carrier. She wove
in the controls, ordering every creature that lived in
this water to come to her aid—wove in the purpose,
that they should build her an island from the mud and
reeds of the swamp bottom—and spun it three times
around her like a circling breeze to gather in her
power and knit itself tight. She held it like a restive
horse, making sure she had complete control over it,
and let it loose.

Within moments, the first signs that her spell was
working appeared in the form of hundreds of turtles,
three otters, and some other assorted animals, each
bearing a mouthful of mud and reeds, which they deposited on her hummock. They didn't even look up
at her; controlled as they were, she might not even
have been there so far as they were concerned. Each
animal deposited its burden and returned to the water
to bring another load.

*That works. But I want dry land, not an enormous
mud pie.* Odile set her second spell, once again using
her handful of mud and reeds as the catalyst, a spell
to squeeze the water out of what they brought. She
felt more power drain from her, and took a moment
to assess what she had left.

As the water beaded up on the magically firming
mud and ran back into the lake, stranger beasts appeared, also carrying mud and reeds up from the bottom. Undines with weed-braided hair and pale green
skin brought mud up in basketfuls; muskrats patted it
into place. Shortly the hummock swarmed with activity and grew in size by leaps and bounds. Beneath the
waters, those with gills built the foundation; above it,
the air breathers patted and heaped more material
from the bottom of the pond onto the mound. Turtles
and otters worked steadily beside will'o'wisps, un-

dines, and weird creatures Odile didn't even recognize. Odile's spell made the finished mound as dry and firm as any sure riverbank. When she had sufficient land to work with, she spun a third spell of accelerated growth (one requiring significantly less power than the previous spells), and covered the new land with a thick cover of soft grasses and moss as her crew continued to enlarge it.

So much for a dry place to sleep. She waited for a moment, gathering her strength, while she pondered the answer to the questions of shelter and warmth.

As she looked about, the spell of accelerated growth gave her the answer for shelter. She selected one of the animals, a muskrat, and altered the spell on it alone. Instead of mud, she had it bring her a handful of willow shoots. Then she waited; when the island was large enough for all the girls to sleep on it in comfort and without undue crowding, she dismissed her helpers and banished the first spell. As the other spells continued to work, keeping the island dry, and making the grasses and moss thicker by the moment, she planted the willows around the edge of the new land and set them to grow.

By this time, even the weary swans had gathered around the island, eying the new ground with curiosity. Odile kept from smiling with difficulty; it was altogether gratifying to have an audience for her magic, especially one as attentive as this one.

As the trees grew, she paid careful attention to *how* they grew, their drooping branches intertwining at her order to the outside of the island and above it, until they shaped a thick canopy covering the entire island, with plenty of room to stand beneath it. Now she stopped their growth, and altered the spell to make the leaves grow larger rather than increasing the height of the trees—

Larger? She made them *huge*. One leaf could easily

serve as a rain shelter for a cat before she was done!
The leaves overlapped so well that they formed an
actual roof and round walls, many layers thick, proof
enough against dew, chill, damp, breezes, and even
light rain.

As for warmth—now that she had the shelter, that
was the next order of business. She considered spinning blankets of grasses and spider silk, but dismissed
the idea as too time consuming. Instead, she bent and
pulled up grass by hand in the center of the island
until she had a circle of bare hearth. There she kindled
a perfectly ordinary fire.

Well, I suppose it's not ordinary. This was magical
fire, like the one that burned on the hearth in her
room in the manor. It consumed nothing on its little
scooped-out hearth, and gave off an insect-repelling
perfume rather than smoke.

It was dark outside, and the moon would soon be
up, but inside the shelter it was warm, fragrant, and
welcoming. Now that her work was done, Odile was
suddenly very tired. She dismissed the last of her
growing-spells and tucked herself into an odd-shaped
little nook away from the central hearth, but still
within the effective range of the perfume. She couldn't
lean against the willow walls, for they weren't strong
enough to support weight, but they made a comforting
barrier between her and the swamp, and were rather
like a tent with foliage painted on its walls. With her
legs folded under her, her face in shadow, she hoped
that she blended into the darkness.

The last light faded outside the door, and a chorus
of frogs and night insects rose outside, surrounding
the shelter with song. Shortly after that, Odette, still
in swan form, poked her head into the shelter.

She was followed by the rest, who crowded in after
her. As Odette walked slowly to the fire, neck
stretched out suspiciously, the moon climbed above

the horizon. The swans dropped to the grass as if stunned, and the shimmering mist of magic hovered over them all, obscuring them.

The mist lifted; Odette rose, the folds of her white silk dress settling around her feet. She turned away from the fire, and her gaze alighted on Odile.

She said nothing, but her expression was speculative. Odile met her gaze, wondering what was going on in her mind.

Then Odette turned back to the group of girls—weary, but very relieved girls, who hadn't the energy to do much more than find places under the boughs, but had regained enough strength to marvel aloud at Odile's creation.

Odile remained silent, pulling up grass and moss to make a pillow, trying to stay inconspicuous. As the interior of the shelter warmed further, the girls selected sleeping places to their liking and dropped down onto the grass, grateful for the softness and the dry ground beneath it.

One of them commented on the thick carpet of greenery, and Odette smiled crookedly. "And when we are done sleeping on it, we can eat it," she pointed out with undisguised irony. "So our keeper serves us twice with a single gesture. Very efficient."

"Your *keeper* could have left you to make your beds in the mud!" Odile retorted, stung into a reply. "I do not expect thanks, but you may keep your scorn to yourself."

Odette's cheeks flamed, and she bowed her head for a moment. When she lifted it again, Odile was surprised to see her expression was apologetic. "You are correct; I was wrong to accept a gift, then offer derision to the giver," she said quietly. "I was rude, and I beg your forgiveness."

Odile nodded in acceptance and acknowledgment, still too surprised by Odette's reaction to reply. In all the time that Odette had been her father's captive, they had not exchanged words more than a dozen times, and none of those exchanges had led her to think of Odette as anything other than proud and aloof. Was she changing—or was Odile simply seeing more of the real Odette?

She pondered that as the other girls settled into their chosen sleeping places, and dropped into dreams, lulled by the gentle warmth of the fire. Tonight Odile intended to get ample sleep herself. The girls were not going to wander off into the swamp, after all, so there was hardly a need to guard them.

She dimmed the light of the fire, but not the warmth it created, nor the insect-chasing perfume; she gave it the semblance of a bed of red coals, just for the sake of familiarity. Outside the shelter, thick fog caught and held the moonlight before it ever reached the water, swathing the island in a soft, dim glow. As she watched the remains of the fire and listened to the steady breathing of the sleeping girls all around her, she was aware of Odette's gaze still centered on her.

Finally, she turned her head slightly and met the dark eyes that watched her so warily. "What is it?" she whispered. "Why aren't you asleep? You'll need your rest for tomorrow, you know."

"Did you do all this—" a wave of Odette's hand indicated the shelter, "—because the sorcerer ordered you to?"

The abrupt question caught Odile by surprise, and she answered honestly, before she had time to think. "No. He didn't give me any orders, but I knew we'd need a place to sleep, and I didn't see any other way of getting one than to create it myself."

"No?" Odette's soft voice held a touch of irony. "You *could* have just built a cocoon of magic for your use alone—you could have left us to fend for ourselves and find our own place to sleep in the swamp."

"I could have, but then you'd have been in no fit state to fly tomorrow, would you? The baron would be annoyed if you were too tired to fly." Odile wasn't certain she wanted Odette to presume she'd built this shelter out of altruism, so she deliberately kept her tone cool and unemotional.

But didn't I? At least a little?

"You speak as if you are ashamed to admit you were willing to help us," came the soft reply. "And that, quite frankly, puzzles me. I wish I knew what you were really thinking."

Odile couldn't think of an answer for that, and turned her gaze away from Odette's, pretending an indifference she did not feel. Eventually, the silence and warmth prevailed, and sleep claimed both of them.

By the time Odile woke, all of the swans but one were out of the shelter, foraging in the swamp, and morning sun glinted off the water outside, burning off last night's fog. The swan left sleeping was Lisbet, the same young one that had run into trouble yesterday; exhausted by her efforts, she still dozed. The scent from the fire still filled the shelter—which was a blessing, since the miasma of the swamp wasn't to Odile's taste.

Odile stood up and stretched, touching the tips of her fingers to the branches overhead, but moving quietly so as not to startle the sleeping swan, who would react with a swan's instincts if she woke abruptly. She wouldn't think, she'd try to flee, and the blow from a swan's wings was strong enough to break a man's arm.

So Odile made quiet, nonthreatening sounds as she stretched and moved about the shelter to limber up her limbs, stiff from a night spent on the ground. Lisbet woke easily, raised her head from where she'd tucked her beak into her back feathers, and looked around cautiously.

It hadn't escaped Odile's attention that all of the grass on this little island had been nibbled down to within an inch of the roots. The swans *had* eaten their "bedding" once they'd awakened, just as Odette had cynically predicted—no harm in that, but they hadn't left anything for the late riser. So the others had a head start on feeding, which might once again put this little one at risk of lagging behind if *she* didn't get quite enough to eat. Odile weighed the alternatives and the consequences, and decided that a little expenditure of power now was warranted to prevent a similar expenditure at a point where it was more difficult for her to work magic.

She had no need to join the others in foraging for wild rice and water weeds for her breakfast; every morning she used a little magic to "call" her breakfast from the manor. Sometimes the baron shared it with her, and sometimes he didn't, but she always brought in enough food to take care of both of them. She usually repeated the spell at the end of the day, once they'd taken a landing spot for the night; the fact that she forgotten to last night what with all the work she'd needed to do meant she was ravenous now. She was as much in need of sustenance as the swan.

"Wait here," she told the swan, who had gotten gingerly to her feet; she obediently sat back down onto the grass. Odile was grateful that Lisbet was the one of the little swans who took orders meekly; it always irritated her when she had to force someone to accept something she was doing for their benefit.

She banished the magical fire and knelt beside the warm hearth, readying her magic. She cupped her hands over the bare earth and concentrated, building a glowing sphere beneath them that lit up the shelter with the power of a tiny sun.

Then, abruptly, the sphere vanished, and in its place were the items she had "called" from the manor. Rich, nutritious journey-cakes—excellent when fresh, as these were, but rather poor fare when they'd spent too much time in their parchment wrappings—were piled six high on a large patter. Beside them were a pat of fresh butter on a little plate, and a jar of honey, plates, a bowl of strawberries and manchette cake with beaten, sweetened cream poured generously over them, and a platter of thinly sliced ham and creamy cheese. There were far more cakes than Odile and her father could eat, which had been her intention; she took a double handful of them and crumbled them in front of Lisbet, who needed no encouragement to begin gobbling the crumbs. She reserved two cakes for herself, spread with the honey and butter, and two for her father, plain, and continued breaking the dense, crusty golden rounds between her fingers until all the rest were in a form easy for the swan to devour. Only then did she turn her attention to her own breakfast.

As she began eating, a shadow fell over the opening to the shelter, and von Rothbart stooped and entered. He sat down on the grass beside Odile, helping himself to the food.

"You were busy last night," he commented, layering the ham and cheese atop one of the cake rounds, then taking a bite. "I did not expect—all this—when I arrived this morning."

"It was an efficient solution to the problem I was faced with, given that there was no solid land on which to rest," she retorted, keeping her tone level. "But not the one you would have taken?"

"If I had been in your position, I would have kept them—and myself—as swans through the night," he replied. "Then there would have been no need for a shelter."

She thought quickly; was he annoyed, and if so, would he be mollified by good reasons for her actions? "I had several problems here, at least as I saw it. I didn't know what sorts of animals roam this place, nor how dangerous they would be. As swans we would have no defense against something like a wolf or a bear that crept up on us while we slept, and no way to detect something that could seize one of us from beneath the water. But no land-walking predator would be able to cross easily to an island, and no water-dwelling creature could get at us on land. And if anything *did* try to swim across, we would smell like humans, not swans, and there would be the unfamiliar perfume from the fire that would further confuse the scent—" She handed him the second round of journey-cake, and finished her own, dividing the strawberries and cream between them. "I rather think that any night-hunter would fear that combination, and seek some easier prey." She considered a moment longer, as her father ate in silence, and decided to add a little something. "And—a mouse is not a human. I don't know that *I* could have kept them all swans until your return. I knew that I could do all of this; I controlled the swamp creatures to build the land, and sped the growth of plants to make the shelter; that doesn't require as much magic as holding the transformation spell. Only my fire was purely magical."

That was a lie; she knew very well that she *could* have kept everyone in their swan shapes—but he had already shown disapproval of her mastery of his spell, and this would be a test of sorts. . . .

"Good; now I see what your reasoning was, and your actions were well thought out," he said, and there *was* a hint of approval in his voice, that made her lift her head a little. "An efficient use of power, much more efficient than trying to hold the shape-change spell over the entire flock. You were wise not to attempt so difficult a feat."

Odile bowed her head in a dutiful nod to hide her expression, but she felt a momentary flash of anger that he considered her ability so minimal.

"Why feed this one?" he continued, the approval replaced by suspicion as he gazed at the hungry young swan. "You spoil her—"

"Not at all," Odile countered swiftly, daring to interrupt him. "She hasn't eaten or rested well and isn't as strong as the others. I had to support her for half the journey yesterday, or she would have dropped to the ground with exhaustion. Sleeping longer helped her, but that meant that she wouldn't have as much time to forage, so when the flock followed you today, she would be in difficulty again."

"Ah. Another good solution." The suspicion was gone, and he actually smiled. "You prove that placing you in a position of responsibility was warranted."

"Thank you, Father!" she replied, the smile and the words giving her a feeling of heady euphoria. She smiled back at him, her anger completely forgotten. "I want only to please you—"

"And you do please me, more than ever," he told her, and picked up her hand to place a cool kiss on the back of it. "You are showing that you are worthy to be my offspring, and are truly your father's child."

She finished her breakfast in a daze of happiness; he had not given her such a powerful reward in a very long time—not since she was a child and had first demonstrated she had inherited his magical powers, in fact! There was no further conversation between them, but then the baron was not one for much conversation even in his most expansive moods. He finished first and left the shelter, shortly after Lisbet ate the final crumb of cake and joined the rest of the flock in filling what little space was left in her stomach with water plants. When she had finished her own meal and sent back the empty dishes to the manor, he had already taken on his owl form, and was waiting in a nearby tree.

Time to go. The flock had formed up at the far end of the pond; swans were heavy birds, and they would need every bit of clear water to get airborne. She gathered her powers around her, feeling them brushing against her skin as she stood with her arms poised above her head, the center of a whirlwind of force barely visible in the bright sunlight.

She felt her forearms, hands, and neck lengthen, her legs and upper arms shorten, felt feathers appear to cover her like a garment reaching from her nose to her toes. The world appeared to loom taller as she shrank in height; her teeth vanished, her nose and mouth lengthened and hardened, her eyes moved to the sides of her head. Her sense of smell vanished (something of a relief, given the surroundings), her sight and hearing sharpened, and she now saw the odd colors at the edge of violet that only birds perceived. Her vision now encompassed three quarters of a circle around her; disorienting for a moment, until her mind accepted it.

Then, the transformation complete, she shook herself all over, settling her feathers, and plunged into the water to join the rest of the flock.

The great owl launched heavily into the air, laboring upward with powerful strokes of his wings. Odette spread her wings in the next moment and followed, in the half-flight, half-run that a water bird needed to become a bird of the sky. As she got halfway across the pond, the rest of the flock churning the water and air in her wake, she tucked her feet up and rose from the surface of the pond.

Odile followed, last of all, well-satisfied to see that

Lisbet was flying up with the rest of the flock, not lagging wearily behind. She looked back over her shoulder at the island she had created; it did look rather odd, the perfectly circular clump of tightly interlaced willows apparently rising from a pond of clear water in the midst of the swamp. She felt a bit of amusement, wondering what the baron had made of it when he first returned this morning.

Well, although it would remain, an odd island in the swamp, it would gradually lose its peculiar appearance since she was not there to impose her will on it. Some of the trees would die; otters and muskrats would build dens in the bank and it would lose that perfectly circular shape. The trees that survived would drop all their unnaturally large leaves in the autumn, and when they regained their vernal cloaks next spring, they would bear the same foliage as any other willows. Within a year, two at the most, no one would know that a magician had made the place.

And that is as it should be. It was one thing to impose her will on the place where she lived and spent most of her time; it was quite another to do so arbitrarily and permanently everywhere she happened to spend a few hours. At least, that was how she felt about it. She had no idea how her father felt; he'd never expressed his views on the subject.

As they gained height and left the vicinity of the swamp, her experienced eye noted subtle signs, both in the cultivated fields and in the wilder lands, that the summer was coming to an end. Subtle changes in the color of the foliage that only a bird could see told her that the leaves of the trees were fully mature and only awaiting the touch of the first frost to put on their flaming colors, phoenixlike, so that they could die. The hayfields had been mowed, the hay gathered in; the grain fields had taken on the golden shimmer that presaged full ripening. Other crops would wait

for that first frost, for they would continue to improve
in size and ripeness until the cold killed them.

But all these signs of the coming of fall made her
uneasy about her father's plans. Surely he didn't intend for them to spend the winter away from the comforts of the manor? He'd never done *that* before—and
while it was perfectly reasonable to set up an *al fresco*
camp in the late spring, in summer, and even in early
autumn, it was neither reasonable nor comfortable to
do so in the dead of winter!

*But he knows that. He's as fond of his comfort as
anyone could be.*

Her worries, however, were not soothed. Von
Rothbart would suffer nothing in even the harshest
winter; he had power enough and to spare to transport
himself to and from the manor if he chose. But Odile
didn't, not yet—and certainly the flock could not.
While in swan form, they wouldn't suffer too much,
provided that she could produce food for them, but
how could he expect a group of girls clad only in the
thinnest of silk to survive a single winter's night out-
of-doors?

Could Odette's challenge have made him forget all
of that? Surely he didn't expect *Odile* to supply shelter
against the winter's rage for all of them!

*No—he had this journey planned before Odette flung
defiance in his face,* she reminded herself. He had been
on the hunt for weeks before Odette's little revolt.
Whatever alterations he'd made to accommodate her
hadn't substantially altered those plans. The way he
had reacted, with an odd kind of pleasure, rather than
annoyance, proved that.

*He must expect all of this to be over and done with
before the end of autumn,* she decided with relief. *We'll
be fine. He probably knows she won't have a chance
to test his promise on this quest—yes, that must be it.
There probably isn't a susceptible male within miles*

*of where we're going, much less a suitable one to lift
the spell.*

She knew him as well as anyone *could* know him;
of all things he hated, the one he hated most was not
being in control at all times. There was even the slight
possibility that he *intended* to allow Odette her attempt to regain her freedom, and either was entirely
certain she had repented enough that it would succeed, or was equally certain that she was still so unre-
pentant that it would fail. In either case, he must have
it all planned down to the very hour that would see
her freed or bound forever.

Wherever this was to be, it was not in any lands
Odile had seen before; in fact, this was by far the
farthest that she had ever gone from the manor. What
could have tempted him into so long and potentially
perilous a journey? Below her now there were more
cultivated lands than wild; it would be harder and
harder to find suitable places to stop overnight. She
cast her glance downward, to the moving manikins of
field workers at their tasks, bending and straightening
and bending again. There was always the chance that
someone down there was of noble birth, and a
hunter—while they were out of bow shot *now,* they
would not be when they came in to land or rose to
fly. And a trained falcon could circle higher than the
flock could go . . . falcons weren't normally set at
swans, but some falconers were wont to test the skill
and strength of their birds against a strong and difficult target.

*And there is always the chance that someone has
dared convention and law to train an eagle. . . .* An
eagle could *easily* bring one of them down—convention and falconer's law dictated that only an emperor
could fly an eagle, but if one of the many little monarchs far from the Emperor's eye chose to claim such
a bird, there was no one and nothing to stop him.

She shivered, and now turned her wary attention upward, suddenly aware that she was going to have yet another responsibility, to guard against attack from above as well as stragglers. *That's all right; I can make a bird miss her mark. I can even do the same for a bowman. And father's in the shape of an eagle-owl; no falcon would dare attack an eagle-owl, and I'm not sure a falconer could get even an eagle to make a try.* While they might willingly harass an eagle-owl trying to rest in a tree by day, no smaller bird would challenge one already in the sky above her.

There's no way to force your bird to do anything, she reminded herself, *unless you are a sorcerer, and there isn't a magician in the world who would dare to challenge Father. Not even an eagle is going to make a stoop at us, not when there's easier prey about. Besides, you have to fly eagles from cliffs, and there aren't any cliffs below us.*

What was bringing on this sudden spate of worries? She'd never been like this before; she'd always followed the baron's orders, blithely certain that he would take care of everything—

That must be the answer. He'd actually *granted her* equal responsibility this morning—not just implied that she was expected to take care of some limited tasks. Once again, her spirits lightened, and she was only sorry that swans had no ability to sing, for she would have enjoyed being able to carol like a lark.

Father's plans will all end as he wishes, and I will be there to help him, she told herself, with renewed confidence. *He already sees how much I can do—and surely, soon, he will realize just how much more he can accomplish with* me *to help him! He'll realize that all I've ever wanted to do was to please him.*

After that—no, she wouldn't think of what would happen after that. She would concentrate on what she needed to do *now,* and all else would follow.

With that firmly resolved, she concentrated on the task at hand, with one eye watching for trouble from above or below, and the other keeping track of the flock.

CHAPTER SEVEN

TERROR ruled Siegfried's night.

Once more, the ghost-gray gypsy girl approached him as he stood rooted to the spot, sweating with fear. Once again she held up the mirror to his face; he looked for a moment into his own eyes, to see his face replaced by that of a monster—a maddened boar this time, rather than a wolf, a boar with bloody tusks and a mouth dripping foam. He saw his eyes in the boar's face, eyes that glared back at him with insensate rage. With a shout of terror, he wrested himself free—

Choking with fear, he sat bolt upright in his bed, entangled in the bedclothes, staring into the darkness. Sweat soaked, heart pounding, shaking in every limb, it took an act of will to lie back down again; he kept expecting to see the girl's horrible, blue-gray face staring at him out of the darkness. Worse, at any moment, he expected to feel her cold hands seize him.

What was wrong? The girl had been buried at the crossroads, staked into the grave, exactly as he had ordered. She should not be able to night-walk and haunt him like this!

This was the fourth night in a row that the same nightmare had sent him plunging into horror; no matter what he did, how much he tired himself out, the nightmare returned. The only change was in the beast she showed him—wolf, boar, bull, mastiff—all with his eyes, but with the light of madness in them. The only comfort he had was that once the dream was over, he was through with it for the night, and so far it had not returned to haunt him twice in the same night.

I can't go on like this, he told himself, raking his sweat-drenched hair out of his eyes. *I can't. Who knows what she's going to do next?*

There should be one way to be rid of the ghost, one he'd been reluctant to pursue until now, and that was to go to the priest, make confession, perform penance, receive absolution. He didn't like the priest, whom he suspected of telling tales to the queen, but things had gone far enough that he was willing to bear the brunt of his mother's lectures in order to be free of the vision.

With that resolution, he managed to get back to sleep, and woke again just after sunrise. He surprised Arno by hurrying into his clothing, after accepting the first suit that was presented to him, and going straight from the hands of his servants to morning Mass.

His mother and her ladies always attended morning Mass in the New Chapel; much of a lady's day was spent in devotions. It wasn't often that the young men attended the service, however, unless they were interested in one of the queen's women. Older men, who had reason to be concerned with the state of their souls, visiting dignitaries, the most pious of the servants, and those with religious ambitions would be there as well, but very seldom were any of the men of Siegfried's circle to be seen. This did not particularly please his mother, but there wasn't a great deal she could do about it. Nevertheless, the queen had made a prominent display of her piety from the beginning; along with her improvements in the castle had come an entirely new chapel, attached to the old one in a way that left the original chapel as an annex just off the much larger building. The New Chapel boasted colored glass windows (not just painted glass), hanging lanterns, a carved marble altar, and a magnificent carved altarpiece behind it. There were even pews with kneeling stools for the queen and those of rank. The old chapel, now relegated to being the Lady Chapel, had only two plain glass windows and an equally plain altar, with a clumsily carved Virgin and Child behind it and no place to sit or kneel. The queen had hoped these improvements would bring the young men to daily services, but they had not.

Nevertheless, this morning Siegfried was there, head bared and bowed, in the last rows with the older men. He suppressed his yawns as the priest droned through the service and homily, but managed to look reasonably alert through the entire service. When the service was finally over, he performed his final genuflection with relief, and hung behind as most of the worshipers left, chattering and gossiping, taking care to linger in the shadows so that the queen wouldn't spot him and stop to question him. He waited with some impatience until the priest entered his side of the handsomely carved confessional, created from inch-thick planks of black walnut, and was the first to enter the other side of the box and pull the black fustian curtain closed behind him.

The carved screen and the darkness of the box was *supposed* to keep his identity secret, but he knew very well that the priest would know who he was immediately. He kept up the charade, however, and without identifying himself in any way, hurried through the forms, and the priest on the opposite side of the screen surely sensed that there was something wrong just by the nervous quality of his words.

Finally, with the formalities over, he let out his breath, and voiced his real difficulties. "Father," he began, feeling awkward, "I committed a sin with a woman."

"Fornication, I presume," the priest said dryly, his amusement patent. "That is a serious sin, but surely it is not the first time you have committed it nor confessed to it."

"No, but . . . it might have been against her will." He swallowed, finding it difficult to confess what had happened. "And later, after, she drowned herself." There. It was out. The priest would know who and what the girl had been—there had only been one girl drowned around here. He waited, heart pounding, to hear what the priest would say. Would he be outraged, blaming Siegfried for the girl's death?

"*Might* have been against her will? How is that you aren't sure?" The calm voice might have been asking about a child stealing a sweet. Siegfried was surprised; he thought that the fact that the girl killed herself— and *everyone* knew about the body in the millrace— might have called for more concern.

"She ran away from me—and she just—" he felt himself blushing, embarrassed at relating intimate details to a priest. "—when I had her, she just lay there, didn't say or do anything, wouldn't look at me afterward. She didn't fight me though—if she'd fought me, of course I would have let her go."

Maybe. He really didn't know if he would have, not in the high heat of passion.

"And what made you think she would welcome you in the first place?" the priest asked, as if it were a matter of mild curiosity.

"She was bathing naked in the river, in broad daylight—I thought her running was just being coy—" His ears burned, and the back of his neck, and he hotly defended himself. "Father, I saw her swimming, and if she'd really wanted to get away, she would have swum out into the middle of the river where I couldn't get to her, not go running off along the shore."

Wouldn't she?

"So. Tell me if I understand this correctly. You come upon a lowborn gypsy wench, alone, bathing naked in the river, making no attempt at modesty. You pursue her, and rather than effectively fleeing, she makes what you consider to be a token attempt. When you have your way with her, she remains mute and unmoving, although she does not repulse you. Is that correct?"

"Yes, Father," he replied, wondering what was going through the priest's mind.

"Did you have any reason to believe she was a virgin?" came the unexpected question. "Either before or afterward?"

"Not . . . really," he said slowly, then burst out with, "No *virgin* would be flaunting herself naked like that! She was probably there waiting for a lover!"

"And when you left her, what did you do? Insult her? Abuse her? Beat her because she didn't please you?"

"No!" Siegfried said, with such indignation that the priest coughed. "I just threw her a few coins and I left."

"So when you left her, you left her rather better off than she had been before you pleasured yourself with her." Since that was a statement, not a question, Siegfried wasn't sure if he was supposed to answer it, but when an expectant silence followed the words, he decided he should say something.

"I suppose so. She had a handful of coins, I didn't hurt her, and I hadn't—ah—taken anything from her." This line of questioning had the effect of putting him back into the state of mind he'd been in when he'd ridden away; annoyed and a bit resentful that the woman had been such a disappointment.

"Or if you had, it wasn't anything that wouldn't have been lost eventually anyway," the priest said dryly, with unvarnished scorn. "Sooner, rather than later. Even peasants are like dogs in heat; they fornicate as soon as they are able and as often as possible, and the gypsies are impossible, pagans at best, witches at worst, with no sense of morality."

Since that was very nearly the way Siegfried thought, he felt a burst of fellow feeling toward the priest, who at least knew what were the rights of a man of gentle birth.

"So *why* are you here, confessing this to me?" the priest continued. "There is something more than a casual fornication here, to make you seek the confessional with such agitation in your voice."

"I'm being haunted," Siegfried whispered, almost ashamed to admit it. He described the dreams—or visions, whichever they were—and the terror he endured every night since the girl died. There was silence on the other side of the confessional, as the priest pondered his tale. Siegfried waited on the edge of the bench of the confessional, tense with anticipation.

"Well," the priest said at long last. "It seems that the witch has cursed you. With a curse, the—ahem—extraordinary actions taken in her disposal would not protect you." His voice assumed the lofty tones Siegfried usually associated with him. "Your state of sin has left you unprotected, and God cannot protect you unless you undergo penance. In order to have the curse exorcised, you must first perform a fast and penance to show the Almighty that you are worthy of Divine help." He then rattled off a penance that didn't seem all *that* strenuous to Siegfried. He'd have to fast all day, then spend the night in the chapel at a vigil on his knees before the altar, telling over the rosary until dawn. This was no worse than the vigil he'd undergone for his knighthood, and actually less uncomfortable than some nights he'd spent out in the forest while hunting. It was a small price to pay for freedom from nightly terror.

He got the priest's blessing with a sense of profound relief, and left the confessional feeling a great weight lifted from his mind. He hesitated at the threshold of the New Chapel, and decided to go the priest one better, and begin his vigil at once.

Why not? I haven't anything in particular that needs doing, and if I'm going to fast, I'd just as soon be where it's quiet.

He chose the old chapel for his devotions, just off the main sanctuary, for his stint. No one came in here anymore except for the priest (to see that the Presence Lamp stayed lit and that there were devotional and altar candles ready for lighting) and the priest's servant (to keep it clean). No one would see him or bother him here—or report what he was doing to his mother. He knew that the priest would probably tell Queen Clothilde everything sooner or later, but with luck it would be after he'd gotten the vigil over with. At that point, no longer hag-ridden, he'd be able to face her reproaches with equanimity.

He wasn't in the habit of carrying a rosary (very few men were except for those in Holy Orders), but there was a form of rosary inlaid in the floor of the Lady Chapel—large and small stones of a paler color than the rest of the slate floor, for the benefit of those who hadn't their own beads with them. Kneeling behind the altar rail, he kept his gaze on these stones, clasped his hands, and launched into his whispered recitation.

It was chill and quiet in the chapel, with nothing more than the vague murmur of voices coming from the confessional behind him. Soon enough, even that ceased, and he sensed he was completely alone. In the silence, every little sound he made echoed with unnatural volume; the thick stone walls kept sounds from outside to a minimum. He shifted his weight from time to time, as his knees began to ache; this entire task made him acutely self-conscious.

The last time I did a vigil like this was—four years ago! I was a bit more innocent then. He'd been excited, nervous, and full of the certainty that something holy and wonderful was about to happen to him. The solemn speeches by the older knights as he'd readied himself for the vigil had prepared him to experience wonders up to and including the appearance of angels—

Well, nothing had happened, other than a very long and intense session of prayer interrupted by desperate attempts to stay awake. That just might have been the beginning of his realization that God seldom paid a great deal of attention to individual mortals without a goodly amount of ecclesiastical prodding.

A shaft of sunlight coming through the window to his left and falling in a warm patch right in front of the altar gave him something to mark the time. It crept across the floor as the sun rose, then disappeared; it was midday. His stomach growled, reminding him that he hadn't eaten today. He sternly reminded it that he was supposed to be fasting, and went on with his prayers. The repetition began to put him into a dull kind of trance, and when he finally found a position where his knees stopped aching, he fell even farther into a state of half-awareness. Behind it all was the plaintive hope that *this* would be enough to attract God's attention to his difficulties.

The patch of sunlight appeared again, coming from a beam originating from the window on his right. It, too, crept across the floor, marking the passage of time, and seemed to his blunted senses to take an eternity to do so.

Finally, a bit of change entered his vigil. The priest's

servant came into the Lady Chapel in the late afternoon, and did not seem surprised to see him there; in fact, he completely ignored Siegfried's presence. The old man tidied up the altar, carefully dusting each surface and polishing the silver candlesticks, the Presence lamp, and the Crucifix. He chased cobwebs out of the corners, and swept the floor without so much as brushing the prince with his broom. He surveyed his work, then departed with slow, reverent footsteps. Siegfried gave no more thought to him until he heard the footsteps returning.

The servant said nothing as he approached the prince, but Siegfried saw, out of the corner of his eye, that the servant had brought something. He watched the old man stoop down and leave something beside him, an object that gave a soft chink of metal as he set it down. The servant said absolutely nothing, and left as he had arrived, in silence; Siegfried waited until he was gone before turning to the side to see what he had left.

There was an empty goblet and a flat kneeling-cushion, and a metal pitcher of watered wine (which would not technically break his fast). He smiled a little to himself; the priest must have seen him in here when confession was over, and ordered his servant to see that Siegfried's vigil was not unduly arduous. No servant would have brought these things on his own initiative.

Siegfried took the opportunity to get up and walk about a little, stretching his stiff limbs, for there was no vow or rule that required him to pray without pause, and he knew from experience that he wouldn't be able to concentrate on prayers until he'd satisfied the thirst that the mere sight of the pitcher had awakened. When his blood moved less sluggishly, he settled back in his chosen place, then poured himself a goblet of wine and drank it slowly, savoring every cool drop.

After hours of nothing, it tasted like ambrosia and felt heavenly on his dry throat. As the patch of sun left the floor and began to climb the wall, growing reddish in color as sunset neared, he arranged the flat cushion and knelt on it instead of the stone.

That alone was a great relief; evidently the priest didn't see any need to make this penance into an ordeal, since he'd already taken it upon himself to start early. *There's the mark of decent breeding,* he thought to himself before he started again on his round of prayers. The priest was nobly born, of course; most likely a second or third son of someone of rank— the queen would know who—and Siegfried revised his estimation of the man upward. He might carry tales to Queen Clothilde, but he knew how to treat one of higher rank.

The patch of light faded and vanished; the windows darkened from blue to indigo, and the chapel filled with shadows. Siegfried stopped again to drink while he could still see, then returned to prayer as total darkness replaced mere shadows. With no illumination except the Presence Lamp, and that sheltered behind thick, red glass, it was impossible to see anything but the top of the altar.

The priest and the servant came in to prepare for the evening services, which normally were attended by fewer people than the Morning Mass. The servant came quietly into the chapel and lit a pair of vigil lamps on either side of the altar, giving Siegfried the first real light he'd had since the daylight faded.

A few people filed in; he heard their shuffling footsteps and the murmur of quiet voices as they assembled. The priest recited evening prayers, his voice echoing in the near-empty New Chapel; the uncertain mumble of the celebrants giving the responses followed his clear, crisp tones. Siegfried varied his prayers by giving his attention to the service and reciting the responses himself in a whisper.

The Vesper service was soon over; silence fell again, interrupted only when the servant returned, took away the empty pitcher and left a new one.

The priest didn't celebrate all of the offices in the chapel, only one Mass in the morning and Vespers in the evening. The others he held in his own quarters, for he had learned long ago that no one ever attended them. This left the Chapels, Old and New, empty, so that anyone who wished to pray in silence and privacy in between services could do so. That meant Siegfried would have the place to himself until dawn, when the priest would free him from his vigil, and grant him absolution.

It was going to be a very long night. He reminded himself that it was no worse than many another night he'd spent, in many more arduous circumstances, and at least he wasn't cold, wet, or otherwise miserable. Once again, he fell into a trance of repetitive prayer, a fogged state compounded by the fact that he hadn't had any sleep to speak of last night, a state in which he couldn't tell if the time passed slowly or if it even passed at all. . . .

Finally, it was over. The sky lightened, the first rays of sun painted the wall to his right with a square of pale light, and the priest came in. A few moments later, he'd been granted the blessing of complete absolution, and was assured of the fact that (until he sinned again, which would probably be sooner rather than later) if he died, he would go directly into heaven. More to the point, God would now protect him from the gypsy witch and her curse.

Siegfried was dizzy with relief when he returned to his rooms; he hoped that Arno would be there as he climbed the stairs, and it was with pleasure he saw the familiar face as he entered the door.

"Food and drink, and plenty of both," he ordered, throwing himself down into a chair and gesturing to one of the servants to remove his boots. Arno didn't ask where he'd been, but he probably already knew. The priest's servant hadn't exactly been sworn to secrecy, and what one servant knew, they all learned within hours. Arno returned with a page laden with a heavy tray. Siegfried was happy to see manchette bread and meat, hot and dripping with juices, sliced fruit, and a good, strong wine. He did ample justice to everything on the tray, while Arno directed the servants in turning down the bed, knowing without having to ask that Siegfried would want to sleep once he'd eaten.

As for Siegfried, he wasn't in the mood for anything but slumber. He staggered from his chair to the bed and fell into it without undressing.

He passed from groggy wakefulness into slumber immediately, with no intermediate drowsing—

And found himself frozen in a place of mist, the gypsy girl approaching him with her mirror.

He stared at her in confusion; this wasn't what was supposed to happen! He wrenched his gaze free of the witch, and looked around frantically.

This time, he wasn't alone.

Looming out of the mist to his right came a shining being with the glowing shadows of vast wings rising behind his shoulders, and a golden aura all about him, haloing his figure.

Siegfried's terror melted away beneath a flood of gratitude; his prayers *had* been heard, and God had sent him a rescuer in the shape of one of His very own angels!

An angel! Incredible! This more than made up for the fact that no heavenly beings had appeared at his knighthood vigil!

As the gypsy neared, apparently oblivious to the

angel's presence, he waited breathlessly. What would the angel do? Would he destroy her with a touch? Would he blast her with his gaze? Would he simply spread wide his huge, white wings and dissolve her with his light?

The gypsy finally stopped; a look of vague confusion on her dead, gray features. She turned her unseeing eyes toward the angel, who continued to walk toward her, one slow, smooth step at a time, unfurling his wings, which stretched into a span of thirty feet or more. The angel moved between them, with his back to the Prince, until Siegfried could no longer see the witch, only the snowy plumes of his wings.

The angel stopped.

Slowly, he turned, pivoting in place, wings still spread; the gypsy turned to face him, and he looked over his shoulder at Siegfried so that for the first time the prince saw his face clearly. Siegfried felt an emotion at that moment that was deeper than fear—*awe* was the only name for it. That face had such a terrible beauty to it, so perfect, so pure, that now Siegfried understood why, in the Bible, the first thing that angels said when they appeared to mortals was "Fear not." The sight of such a visage could *only* inspire deep emotions, and the likeliest *was* fear—fear that the being possessed of such a state of perfection *must* find a mere mortal an inferior and loathsome creature.

The angel turned away from him and gave all his attention back to the gypsy. As she stared into his eyes, he gently closed his wings around her, wrapping her in them and hiding her and himself from view.

Siegfried stared, unable to imagine what would happen next.

Just as slowly, the angel opened his wings again, and furled them behind his back, holding them close against his body.

The gypsy still stood in the same place, but she herself was transformed.

No longer the gray-visaged horror he had come to know all too well, now she glowed with the same incandescent beauty as the angel, and behind *her* shoulders were the glowing suggestion of something like wings . . . as if they had not yet appeared, but were materializing out of the mist. She still held her mirror, but loosely, as if it no longer concerned her.

The angel held out his hands; with a bow of humility, she placed her mirror in them. The glow about her brightened, intensified, until Siegfried couldn't bear the growing light and had to close his eyes. Even then her brilliance scorched him, burning her fiery silhouette through his closed lids, as the light of the midsummer sun would.

He cried out in incoherent pain.

The light vanished; he opened his dazzled eyes again. She was gone, but now it was the angel who approached him, bearing the mirror toward Siegfried exactly as the gypsy had. He neared the prince, with reproach and pity filling his eyes, a pity so profound it stabbed Siegfried to the heart, holding him in place more surely than terror had before.

Now the angel stood directly before Siegfried, mirror cradled in his hands as carefully as if it were a holy relic. The mirror glowed, catching Siegfried's gaze and trapping it; it filled his vision. Then the mirror itself grew, becoming larger with every passing second, until the glowing mirror became his entire world.

The glowing light that filled the mirror faded, became silver, became a reflection. He saw himself; not just his face, but all of him this time, his entire body, held suspended in the mist like a fly suspended in amber—and it was all of him that changed this time.

The change was worse, more horrible than when it had just been his face that changed. He watched himself become a beast, his body writhing and twisting, deforming, but he was not any of the animals he had been before. This time he became something much, much worse.

Neither man nor beast this time, but a horrible combination of the most detestable, the lowest aspects of each; he watched the creature—which still retained his eyes—as it lumbered through a parody of his own world.

More beasts, or bestial humans, shared that world with him. Clad in his own clothing, the beast fought with more of its own kind, laughing as it defeated opponent after opponent, slaughtering them with unholy joy. It ambled through a travesty of Court life, greeting other monsters only to stab them in the back once they turned away. It swaggered into a church, overturning the altar, and catching up the sacramental wine to guzzle it with another laugh.

Then it was in a garden, trampling the flowers with heedless feet, until it came upon a clutch of young women. Most of them fled, but one froze, and it seized the hapless girl, draped her with gold and gems—then raped her, and left her bleeding and weeping, cast aside in the ruined garden, as it chased after yet another maiden.

He wanted to scream, to vomit, to at least turn away! A single word managed to struggle up out of his paralyzed throat.

"No!"

He woke.

Lying flat on the floor of the Lady Chapel, his face pressed against the cold stone, he felt as if he'd been beaten to the floor and left there. He suppressed the nausea in his guts and turned over onto his back. Then he looked up at the star-filled east window to see that the moon still hung in the sky—in fact, it was barely halfway to the zenith.

He hadn't completed the vigil. He'd barely begun it. He must have fallen asleep as soon as evening Mass was over.

But most importantly, it was painfully obvious that this vigil wouldn't save him. In fact, he began to have the dim notion that nothing this particular priest would assign to him as a penance would come close to absolving him of a very real guilt.

He rolled over again, pushed himself up off the floor into a kneeling position, and felt his head; there was a lump on one temple where he'd hit the stone floor. He ached with chill, and his head throbbed painfully; his stomach churned, and his mouth tasted foul and sour. But none of that compared with the weight that burdened his soul at this moment.

Without looking at the altar, he got to his feet and staggered out of the chapel into the darkness of the night. It was no darker there than in his heart.

He hadn't chosen a direction, but his feet took him into the garden, where he walked in circles for at least an hour before sitting heavily on one of the benches beneath a tree.

I have done something—unforgivable. It wasn't that the girl was a witch, and it wasn't a curse that afflicted him. There was only one answer to the vision that chilled him to his marrow and left him feeling sick and poisoned. The ancients held that mirrors reflected the truth, even when the eyes were blinded by illusion. The mirror that the angel held had only reflected the true state of his own soul.

Am I so vile a creature? The presence of the angel gave him no other answer, and if he told himself otherwise, he *knew* he would be telling himself a lie. He would not add that, trivial though it might be, to the long list of the other sins burdening his soul.

For a long time he held a very different vigil in the garden, groping his way toward an answer, for an answer he *had* to have, if he was ever to find his way out of this darkness.

The moon had gone down by the time he worked his way to a possible explanation that left him a shred, at least, of dignity.

There is no doubt that my behavior to the gypsy was every bit as bestial as I've been shown, he thought miserably. *No matter that she was a peasant, and a gypsy, and not a highborn lady. No matter what the priest said. God clearly does not see it* his *way.* And he had probably been just as guilty in the past of similar behavior with some of his leman. But not all.

Selfish, self-centered, but not entirely bestial. What I was shown is what I could become, but not yet what I am.

There were things he could do to change, and things he *should* do to make amends. He could do nothing for the poor, dead gypsy—the angel had already seen to her—but there was another woman he had almost wronged, and probably would have pursued with the same selfish single-mindedness had he not been visited by those dreams. He could do something about her case, right now.

With heavy, aching head and unsettled mind, he made his way up to his rooms; not even Arno was awake, which was all to the good, the way he felt. A single candle still burned, and he took it to his writing desk.

He pulled a piece of parchment toward himself and dipped a quill in ink; the easiest part was the beginning, a formal salutation to his mother. Now, how to phrase this?

I beg to call your attention to an addition to the Court, Sir Hans' sister-in-law, the Lady Adelaide, he wrote. *From my understanding, she has been left a widow without support, and Sir Hans is now responsible for her keeping. I believe she would make a good*

addition to your ladies; in addition, placing her in your
service would ensure both her gratitude and loyal ser-
vice, and that Sir Hans would not attempt to find a less
worthy disposition for her.

There; that struck the right note—reminding his
mother that impoverished noblewomen made unde-
manding and grateful servants, and that she herself
frowned on even lesser members of her court dispos-
ing of their penurious relatives by making leman out
of them. It would be up to the girl to prove that she
had skills his mother could use, of course—but at least
he had put the opportunity for an honest life in her
path.

He folded and sealed it, and left it on the tray outside his mother's chambers. She'd get it with her other
household missives in a few hours.

As for Trinka, his light-of-love at the inn—he had
an idea or two about her, as well. But those could
wait until afternoon. For now that he had made the
initial steps toward redeeming himself, he felt a modi-
cum of relief, and with that relief all the exhaustion
of the last day was catching up with him.

He undressed himself without waking any of the
servants, fell into his bed, and knew nothing until
afternoon.

CHAPTER EIGHT

QUEEN Clothilde had grown accustomed to the dull routine of her morning household business, so the letter from Siegfried that she found waiting for her came as a complete surprise. She read the astonishing note from her son for a second time, trying to fathom what was behind it.

There had to be an ulterior motive; she couldn't imagine Siegfried making this request just because he had noticed this poor little sparrow lurking about the Court, picking up whatever crumbs fell her way. It wasn't possible that Siegfried wanted to take this Adelaide as a lover himself—he knew better than to try to place such a woman within her personal household. Clothilde closely supervised her women and her few fosterlings; this was *not* the sort of loose household where ladies and female foster children could get into escapades, and everyone knew it. Her son also knew what her wrath would be like if he tried to meddle with her ladies.

Still. He'd all but declared that her brother-in-law was open to such immoral suggestions—by all that was holy, he'd all but accused Sir Hans of being open to auctioning off his sister-in-law to the highest bidder! Could it be that some young friend of his had an eye

to the woman with honorable intentions, but couldn't
get his family past the lack of dowry?

*He can be generous, so long as his generosity doesn't
cost him much in the way of personal exertion,* she
reflected, lips pursed, and scanned the lines about the
girl's expected loyalty and gratitude. Well, that was
certainly true—and was why she preferred to get her
ladies from among those in much the same case as
Lady Adelaide. When you couldn't get a husband because you had no dowry, and very few holy orders
would accept you for the same reason, the promise of
a comfortable life in exchange for much the same
tasks that you would be doing anyway was very
enticing.

And if you had to put up with chastity and the
queen's temper—well, that was no worse than being
in a convent, and at least you didn't spend most of
your time on your knees.

In the rare event that a man was willing to brave
the queen's gaze long enough to properly court a lady
in her household, then was bold enough to ask her
for permission to wed the lady, she actually had given
her permission—provided, of course, that the lady in
question was still going to be free to continue most of
her services to the queen. *If one of his friends does
wish to wed this lady, I'm sure he'll provide a dowry,
without my saying a word.* She nodded; clearly she
had already made up her mind, provided that the girl
had the proper skills.

"Send a page to find the Lady Adelaide, the sister-
in-law of Sir Hans," she ordered one of the others.
"Bring her here to me."

The woman went off to find a page; the queen had
made the deliberate decision not to reveal why she
wished to see Lady Adelaide, for if there was something underhanded going on, the girl's behavior would
likely reveal it.

There was nothing else on her plate concerning household matters this morning, and as she waited for Lady Adelaide to appear, she reflected that there actually was plenty of room in her household for another set of hands. This was particularly true if the woman had skill with the needle. In fact, it was possible that taking her in would solve an ongoing situation before it actually became a problem. . . .

The page entered and bowed, interrupting her thoughts; he was no more than seven or eight years old, but clearly took his duties very seriously. "Lady Adelaide, Majesty," he said, in a piping soprano, and the lady herself hurried in at his heels, flushed and shabby, to sink to the floor, skirts spread about her, into a formal court curtsy before the queen.

Well, she knows her manners, at least. Clothilde surveyed the woman dispassionately for a moment. *Too young and too pretty for her own good. Far too easy for her keeper to find someone willing to take her off his hands, as long as marriage isn't involved. I wonder how she feels about that?*

"You may rise, lady," she said aloud, "And as we are not in formal court, you may take a seat."

The girl did so, properly taking the lowest stool in the room for her own chair, and waiting with her hands folded gracefully in her lap, her large, blue-violet eyes fixed on Clothilde's face. Clothilde fingered her son's letter, and decided to come straight to the point. "The prince has seen fit to bring you to my attention, and recommend you to a position in my household," she said bluntly. "Have you any notion why he should do so?"

The surprise in the guileless blue eyes told her that this was not something that the two of them had brewed up between them. "Why—no!" Adelaide stammered. "I c-cannot imagine why he should take such trouble—I have not so much as spoken to him— n-not that I would dare to—b-but—"

Clothilde, waved her hand, cutting off the flood of words. "Siegfried knows that pretty women with insufficient protection are vulnerable," she replied casually, watching the girl out of hooded eyes. "Especially if their male relations consider themselves to have been—how shall I put this gracefully?"

"Burdened with their keeping?" The girl replied a touch bitterly, having recovered her composure, and showing more sense than Clothilde would have given her credit for. "I am dowerless, Majesty, and my good brother-in-law has made no secret of the fact that he wishes that Rolf had never wedded me. He would be far happier if his brother had died a bachelor. And— he *has* given some hints about the prince's possible interest that I chose to believe were merely a coarse jest—"

The girl now blushed such a deep crimson that it must have been painful to her fair, transparent skin, but Clothilde thought there was a touch of anger there as well as embarrassment. "And you felt—what?" she asked, leaning forward. "You may be frank here, child. We are alone, and my son's history with women is no secret to me."

Adelaide dropped her eyes to her clenched hands. "I told him that the prince's interest was of no consequence to me, as his wife I could not be, and his leman I *would* not be."

Well, there was a real spirit there! "Brave words, child. Did you consider your keeper's possible anger? Sir Hans *does* have the right to determine your conduct," Clothilde pointed out, interested now. The girl showed sense and courage as well as intelligence. She might well be a good acquisition, better than the queen had anticipated. "He can dispose of you however he chooses, and if that disposition meant that you were provided for, very few would chide him, no matter how unconventional that disposition."

"He does *not* have the right to determine that I be thrown into a life of sin!" Adelaide replied, leaving the queen with no doubt that she considered her virtue to be more important than her poverty. "I had made up my mind that if he attempted to force me to such a pause, though I have no vocation, I would go to the Poor Claires. At least there, my soul would be safe."

And the Poor Claires would be the only ones willing to take her dowerless, the queen reflected without pity. The Poor Claires were a religious order that accepted any woman regardless of the poverty or lack of it that she brought with her—and expected every member to work at every task, however lowly, however mean, however difficult. They labored in leper hospitals, they nursed beggars, they owned nothing, not even the habits they wore. They *were* known for the excellence of their embroidery, but that was the only genteel occupation they practiced. *So she is willing to drudge herself into an early grave, nursing lepers and scrubbing pots, if she must. This* is *promising.*

"Have you any skill with the needle, child?" she asked, changing the subject.

Adelaide's flush faded, and she looked up again. "Tolerable, Majesty," she replied with confidence. "I kept myself and Sir Rolf well clothed, to the limit of his purse at any rate, and I was taught fine work by my aunt as a child—my aunt served the Empress."

"Here—" the queen rose and extended her hand, drawing the girl to her feet and leading her to the Queen's own embroidery frame at the window. "Let me see what you can do."

Without hesitation, the girl sat at the frame and began where the queen had left off, in a band of silk and goldwork intended for a sleeve. She worked neatly and precisely, taking care with each stitch to conserve the precious materials—in fact, she took more care than the queen would have. Every stitch was beautifully and perfectly set, following the pattern that had been pricked into the precious damask. After that, there was no question in Clothilde's mind.

"That will do," the queen said, when the girl had finished the leaf she'd begun. Adelaide looked up to see the queen smiling, and smiled in return. "The prince was right to recommend you. I assume you have no other duties and no real responsibilities to Sir Hans?" Adelaide shook her head. "Very well, you can begin at once as a member of my household, and have your belongings brought to my ladies' rooms." She turned to the oldest of her women, the aging Lady Gisele, homely as a plowhorse and just as poor as Adelaide. "Gisele, take this child in charge. Put her in with you, and teach her to share your duties." Gisele looked pleased and grateful—at near fifty, she was finding it increasingly difficult to embroider and complete her other duties, as her hands stiffened and her joints swelled in the winter. Adelaide looked equally grateful; Gisele looked, and was, kind to the younger women. Adelaide would be able to run the errands that Gisele no longer could.

"What state is your wardrobe in, child?" the queen continued, eyeing the much-patched and darned, rusty black gown she wore. True, the patches and darns were made so cleverly as to be *almost* invisible, but not to the practiced eye of the queen. Again, Adelaide blushed.

"I have only this gown and another," she whispered. "And the other—is not so good."

Ah. An opportunity for earning more loyalty inexpensively. "Gisele, take her to the storeroom and draw out linen for shifts and chemises, boiled wool for a cloak, fabric for a winter gown, and something lighter for a summer gown," Clothilde ordered, "Then take her to the shoemaker and get her well-shod for now and for winter. If my ladies appear less than well-gowned, it reflects poorly on us all."

The girl's flush of embarrassment mingled with a look of pleasure, and a melting gratitude that inspired a little more generosity from the queen.

"And as she is in mourning—give her the black gowns from my chest to remake for herself, the ones from my first year as Queen Regent. That should see her through her mourning period." *I shall never wear those mourning gowns again, old as they are. I doubt I could fit them, these days, since they are from eighteen years ago.* "You and I are of the same size—or you are as I *was* when I was in mourning for the king," she told Adelaide, who now looked bedazzled by her good fortune. "I think they will serve you for now, with some slight alterations, quickly and easily done. That will give you the time to sew your own gowns properly." The gowns in question were of an older, fuller cut; worn seams could be cut back or the fabric turned to look as good as new. If the girl was careful, there was a great deal of black-on-black and white-on-black silk embroidery on those gowns that could be picked out, the threads reused. Or, alternately, the bands of trim could be cut off when the gowns were too worn to be turned and remade, and the trim could be applied to her new gowns.

"You may go with Gisele now, child, and fetch your things, then get settled in and begin your duties," the queen finished, and the girl stood quickly, making a briefer curtsy before leaving with the older woman. The queen settled back, well content with the results of her son's request. There had been no question of a wage, of course; Lady Adelaide would have been insulted had the queen mentioned one. The queen's ladies were unpaid—but in return for their service they lived in the Royal Quarters, ate at the High Table, got regular allotments of fabrics from the Royal Stores, got the queen's cast-offs to make into garments for themselves, and received regular presents from the queen herself in the form of pin money, jewels, and other small luxuries. She was a *great* deal better off now than she had been a mere moment ago, knew it, and would work herself to the bone to show it.

Clothilde settled back in her chair, well pleased with the morning's work.

Siegfried descended to the Great Hall to take the noontime meal, feeling better for his sleep—and better for the absence of the angel and the gypsy from his dreams. He took that as an omen that the course he had begun with his note to his mother was the right one.

He didn't quite make it into the hall itself; Sir Hans intercepted him before he passed the door. Evidently the man had been waiting for him to appear.

Siegfried braced himself for the man's anger; only now did it occur to him that Sir Hans might not care for having the young and pretty Adelaide mewed up with the queen's household. After all, even if Siegfried might not be captivated by her looks, there were other men with deep pockets who might be. . . .

But as soon as he got a good look at Sir Hans' expression, he relaxed.

"Prince Siegfried!" the knight called as he hurried forward, his rough, coarse features suffused with relief and good will. "Please, sire, allow me to thank you for your interest in my sister-in-law, and your care for her disposition!"

"The queen has taken the lady into her household,

then?" Siegfried asked, glad to learn of the success of
his letter, and even more pleased that Sir Hans was
happy with the outcome.

"Yes, thanks be to God—and to you, of course,
sire." The older knight clasped Siegfried's hand fervently, then went down on one knee to kiss it. "I am
not a landed knight; it was a sore burden to me to
have the care of her, and I cannot thank you enough
for seeing that burden lifted from my shoulders!"

I misjudged him; he'd have been willing to see her a
wealthy man's mistress, but he's happier seeing her in
an honorable position.

"Ah, no thanks are needed," Siegfried managed,
pulling the man to his feet. "It is a good thing to see
a young and helpless woman placed in a position
where she is safe. I but did my duty to a member of
my court, that is all. Now—if you will pardon me—I
fear my hunger makes me impatient—"

He gestured at the tables within the hall, and Sir
Hans released him, still protesting his gratitude. Siegfried took his seat and waited for a page to serve him
with a feeling of bemusement. He hadn't expected an
outpouring of feeling from the stoic knight—from the
lady, perhaps, but not her brother-in-law. Evidently
Sir Hans' resources were even more slender than he
had supposed, for the feeding and housing of a single
young woman to worry him so.

He ate quickly, for his next task would take him
down into the village to see Trinka, and he wanted to
have plenty of time to make certain he arranged for
her as well as he had for Lady Adelaide. While he
was eating, his mother and her ladies entered the hall,
and the queen took the High Seat beside him. He
stood quickly, leaving his meal half-finished, and
handed her into her place with all due ceremony before resuming his own meal.

"Siegfried, my son, I wish to thank you for recommending that young woman to my household," were the first words out of Clothilde's mouth. Siegfried put down his laden spoon and looked at her in mild surprise, a bit startled by the approving tone in her voice. She smiled warmly at him.

"I'm glad she is going to be useful to you, Mother," he replied. "It occurred to me that unless she was carefully placed, there could be some trouble over her, trouble I wished to avoid by placing her in protection. I judged by her gentle birth and appearance that she had talents you could use in your train. Putting both those factors together, I hoped to do all of us a good turn."

"That was well thought, my son," Clothilde approved, and glanced to the side, where Lady Adelaide sat at the end of the table, as the newest of the ladies. "The lady would thank you herself, but she is too well-aware of her place to approach you, so I do it in her stead. She is an excellent addition to my train, and if you are moved to recommend another such in the future, I will pay careful heed to your words."

Siegfried bowed wordlessly, his hand to his chest, and resumed his meal. *Another omen? It could be— and now, if Mother hears any tales from the priest, she'll be pleased enough with me to dispense with her usual lecture.* How strange it felt, though, to have done something that thoroughly pleased *all* of the people affected by his action! Usually the reaction was the very opposite of pleasure on the part of at least some of the parties.

He had sent an order to have his palfrey saddled and waiting as he began his meal; when he had finished it, he went straight to the stables to find her standing patiently, tied to a ring at the stable door. With a knot of nervousness in his stomach, he took to the saddle and sent her out of the gates, down the road to the village, knowing that if he hesitated, he would never be able to nerve himself to this next task but would find a hundred reasons why it should be avoided, or at least, delegated to Arno.

Trinka was serving a last table of farmers as he rode up to the inn, but quickly left them to another of the wenches when she saw him. "I was beginning to think you'd already tired of my company," she said flirtatiously as he dismounted. But when he didn't respond, she quickly sobered. "Perhaps I was right—"

He shook his head. "I haven't tired of your company, but I must tell you that I have not succeeded in obtaining a position at the palace for you."

The warmth of her initial welcome came as a relief; if she had felt forced into her current position, she might have pretended to warmth, but there would have been wariness beneath it. He thought that now he would be able to see such wariness, though he might have been fooled before.

She was disappointed in his news, but turned her real dismay into a mock-pout. "Ah, well. Is that why you have avoided us? Because you had bad news?" She set down his tankard of beer, and he noted that now she said "us" and not "me." Already she was prepared to distance herself, and go back to the proper behavior of a simple tavern wench to the prince of the realm. That was another good sign, that she had no illusions about her position, and was prepared to be dropped at any time without warning. *So her heart isn't involved with me, thank God.*

"Not entirely—but I am a terrible coward, Trinka," he replied sheepishly. "I cannot bear to disappoint a woman."

Instantly, she softened. "How could a loyal subject ever be disappointed in so noble a Prince?" she purred, and Siegfried fancied he saw a glint of avidity in her eyes. "Your generosity is unfailing."

Ah, good, honest greed! Bless her for being so uncomplicated!

"Why don't we retire," she continued, leaning over him, so that he got a good eyeful of bosom while her warmth and musky fragrance enveloped him. "Perhaps we can talk about this."

If he'd still had any doubts about her, that would have dissolved them completely. He was only too happy to follow her up to the room she used for his visits. This was not *her* room; there wasn't a sign of personal belongings, no clothing stored away, and he had a shrewd notion that the furnishings were far better than the ones she had been allotted for her own use. This was just the inn's best guest chamber, and the wide, soft bed they presently tumbled into probably had very little in common with the narrow pallet she slept on.

Despite her words, she didn't waste any time in conversation.

She had his tunic and shirt off as soon as the door was closed, and slithered out of her clothing before he'd gotten his boots pulled off. As he struggled, off-balance, tugging at his second boot, she growled and tackled him, tumbling with him into the feather bed. He was enveloped in her sweet, musky scent as she shoved him down into the yielding surface. She imprisoned his legs by sitting on them, pulling off his hose and the boot; he lunged for her and grabbed her around the waist, tickling her in her most sensitive parts. She retaliated, but not by tickling; her clever hands closed around his privates, she thrust her magnificent breasts into his face, and within moments he was acutely aware that it had been quite a few days since he'd last had a woman.

He got her on her back with one hand caressing an erect nipple, his teeth gently nibbling her neck, her legs wrapped around him. With a convulsive thrust, he sank into a sea of sensation in which all coherent thoughts drowned until the moment of climax. Then, in the aftermath, it was simply impossible to think for a while.

Only when he had revived enough to be able to converse in anything but grunts, did she reach for the wine waiting next to the bed. She handed a pewter goblet full of cool, fragrant drink to him, and propped herself up on her elbow (carefully arranging herself to display a generous amount of breast) with an expectant look on her face.

She looked as if she intended to make the first move. But he surprised her, both by beginning the conversation, and by the way he began it. "Trinka, I've been thinking a lot about you, you surely can't expect to be doing this—" he waved his hand vaguely, indicating the inn, the wine, and the bed, and left it to her to choose which applied, "—forever. If you could do whatever you chose to make your fortune, what would it be? Your own inn? A shop?"

What he half expected her to say, once she got over her surprise, was that she'd never thought about it. If she had any ideas, he expected that she would aspire to own a brothel. The position of brothelkeeper could actually hover around the edges of respectability, especially in those towns that licensed and taxed such establishments, but a pious ruler or a plague could plunge such an establishment back into disrepute in a heartbeat. In misfortune, people were always looking for something to scapegoat, and ladies of love always made easy targets.

She nibbled that enticing, pouty lower lip as she thought, eyes narrowed, and yes, surprised by the fact that he had asked such a question. "That rather depends," she finally said, "on whether I could do what I wanted to all at once, or in bits."

"At once," Siegfried said decisively. *Well, she does*

have a plan—and since I can't think of how you could establish a brothel "in bits," perhaps it will be something sensible!

"Then I'd go 'round to all the lace-making villages now, *before* the Harvest Fairs, and I'd go to all the old grannies; I'd buy up their old laces, heirlooms they're willing to sell, as well as new lace made for sale, and I'd find two or three of the young ones that were as good as the grannies but were mad to leave their village. I'd take lace and girls to one of the *big* cities—Nuremberg, Vienna, Hamburg—and I'd set up a lace stall in the market selling the lace I had while the girls made new. Once I had the money for a shop, I'd buy a good one, with quarters above for all of us. They'd make lace and each have an apprentice, while I sold it. We'd all go shares in the profits, which would make *them* work harder than if I just paid them so much a piece, and pretty soon we'd have everyone coming to us for lace." She let out a held-in-breath, and looked at him with just a touch of defiance. "I could do it, too!"

"I don't doubt you." He was actually rather impressed; he hadn't expected that much careful planning from any woman, much less one like Trinka. "In the big cities, they don't see good lace like ours unless it's brought in from outside, and then it costs a fortune. If you went to Vienna, you'd have all the ladies of the Court buying from you."

"I've *been* buying lace all along," she confessed, blushing, and looking a little confused, as if she hadn't expected him to accept her dream without an argument. "With every spare coin I had, I've been buying lace for years—it's a safe way to keep money, nobody thinks about trying to steal it. Especially when I see a really special piece, the kind you don't come across very often, I'll do without to buy lace. I know where all the good lacemakers in these parts live. I thought—

I thought I'd take lace into a city, sell it out of a tray at first, then out of a stall, then work my way up until I had enough for a shop and a girl, but what I really wanted to do was to have the shop and a couple of girls all at once. I just couldn't think of a way to get that much money at once."

Siegfried had come prepared to satisfy a much less practical dream than that, and had worried that she didn't have the practical sense to have any sort of plan for her future. In that case, he'd have given her more than enough to convince one of the local peasants to wed her regardless of her past. That had always been a good solution in the past, but now he found he couldn't close his mind to what might happen next. What would become of her when her beauty was faded and her peasant husband had drunk up the dowry?

This, though—this was good. In the closed world of merchants and Guilds, the making and selling of lace was one of the few trades open to women. Not that men also weren't lacemakers, and usually held the position of shopkeeper, but it wasn't unheard of for a woman to do so as well, and get just as much respect as a man.

"Well, *I* think you ought to have your dream now, while you can enjoy prosperity. What's the use of being prosperous if you're so old you're spending all your wealth on physicians, firewood, and gruel?" he said, with a teasing grin. She looked at him suspiciously, and he quickly sobered. "No, I'm serious. You are wasted on my little village, Trinka." Now was a good time for a bit of judicious flattery. "You're too pretty and much too clever for this place."

She still looked suspicious. "I'm not certain I understand you."

With a sigh, he got out of bed and began pulling on his clothing. When he'd gotten as far as his hose and shirt, he reached for his belt and took out a pouch of coins. "Here," he said, putting it into her hand. "Surely you understand this; it's all for you, every bit of it."

With a quizzical glance, she opened the pouch and poured the coins out on the bed—and gasped, turning pale, for they were all gold, and there were twenty of them. "Twenty crowns! Siegfried, are you mad? You can't give me twenty crowns!"

He sat on the edge of the bed with a crooked smile. "Yes I can. I want you to take this money, get a pony, buy lace, hire girls, and go to Vienna. I want you to sell it at ridiculously high prices to puffed-up lords and ladies, and get fabulously rich, marry the Guildmeister, have a dozen children, name the worst brat for me, and live to be a terrible old woman whom everyone is afraid of."

She laughed at this, rather breathlessly, for this was probably more money than she had ever seen in her life. "But—you—"

"But I was going to use that money to buy a Spanish Barb, new falcons, and a new pack of dogs. I don't *need* a Spanish Barb, new falcons, and a new pack of dogs. I *do* need to know that I have made at least one woman's life better, and not shorter." He hadn't meant that last to slip out, but when it did, she gave him a startled glance.

"The gypsy?" she whispered. Now it was his turn to stare. He really *hadn't* thought she was that intelligent! How on earth had she come up with that? "You didn't—" She clapped her hand to her mouth, white-faced, as if she hadn't intended that to slip out, either.

But he shook his head; since it was out, and she had guessed, he might as well admit it. "I didn't kill her, but—I was probably the reason she killed herself." Let her make of that what she would.

She leaped to an entirely different conclusion, much

more romantic than he would have imagined. "Poor thing—she didn't know you were a prince and couldn't marry her, and when she found out, she couldn't bear it." Her face took on a curious expression, half pitying and half exasperated. "That's hardly the end of the world, and no reason to kill yourself, but I suppose it might seem that way under the wrong circumstances."

He shrugged, relieved at the turn of her thoughts, and a little amused; evidently the fantastical notions of the minstrels were trickling down to infect even the peasants! "She evidently thought so, and I—I didn't want to be the cause of anything like that ever again."

"Oh, my poor prince!" She shook her head at him, carefully gathered up her coins and drew on her own clothing, tucking the pouch into her cleavage. Then she looked up at him with a face full of such pleasure that he'd have given her twice twenty crowns to see it. "Trust me, Highness, I am a sensible woman, and very, very appreciative of your generosity!"

So, now I am "Prince" and "Highness." Good. Trinka accepted the transaction, the generosity, and was putting distance between them.

"And," she continued, twinkling, "you may return to the palace knowing that I am putting your generosity to good use. I am going to pack up today, buy a pony and a travel-wagon, and go *right* out on my lace-buying venture! And when I hear that you are going to be wed, I shall send a special lace veil for your bride!"

Touched by the thought, whether or not Trinka ever carried it out, he moved to her side of the bed, took her hand, and kissed it as he would a great lady's. "Then I will have balanced, at least in part, my mistake. Go with God and good luck, Trinka, and show the people of Vienna that our women are a hundred times more beautiful and clever than their own."

If Trinka didn't question Siegfried's motives, and the court paid no attention to this new burst of virtuous and generous behavior, the queen very quickly was apprised of the situation.

As usual, it was Uwe who was her informant, on a beautiful, sun-filled afternoon, the air rich with the scent of late roses and curing hay. She strolled in her garden, attended closely by Uwe, and at a discreet distance by her ladies, becoming more puzzled with every new revelation Uwe reported to her. She was under no illusions as to *why* Siegfried was acting this way—at least, not after what the priest had told her of her son's confession.

So, he'd been the cause of the gypsy's suicide, or thought he was. He'd had a few nightmares, dreams which *could* be interpreted as hauntings (she certainly wasn't going to dismiss the notion out of hand) and had been frightened into pensioning off his whore and arranging for the virtuous disposition of Lady Adelaide. Fine; there was no difficulty there. The problem was that he continued in this pattern of admirable behavior. People were noticing; the old noblemen who had scorned him as an arrogant young puppy were beginning to speak approvingly of him, and say that he had finally outgrown his rakehell ways.

"You actually saw him deliberately *lose* to one of the younger knights?" she said incredulously to her minstrel. This was incredible; Siegfried had always prided himself on never letting another man win a fight unless that man truly beat him.

Uwe nodded, his thin mouth sober. "I have no doubt; he could have won the bout easily, but he held his hand and let Dieter disarm him with a blow he could have countered in his sleep."

"You're certain?" she insisted, a little desperately. If Siegfried began to win the friendship of the younger knights as well as their grudging admiration, things could become very difficult for her plans. "It could have been that he was still suffering from a round of drinking with Wolfgang and Benno."

"Except that it is the tutor who drinks most of the wine lately; the prince waters his wine and drinks it sparingly, and his friend Benno follows his example." Uwe's clouded expression betrayed him. He was as puzzled as the queen at this upwelling of good behavior. "No, he wanted the boy to have a victory and gave it to him as a gift. That is the third time he has done so this week."

The queen glanced at the manicured topiary trees with an absent, unseeing gaze. "Would you say that he is losing respect among the younger knights?"

"To the contrary; they respect him more and fear him less. They no longer worry about suffering inglorious defeat, for they know that if a lady they care for is present, Siegfried will forfeit to them so that they can bask in their victory. There's more, because if he beats them, he no longer mocks them. In fact, he has taken to *instructing* them, showing them the turn of a blade that defeated them, then coaching them until they have mastered it." Uwe frowned. A flock of crows flew by overhead, calling insults down on the humans in the garden. "He gains in esteem with the older nobles as well. He shows them courtesy when they advise him, even when they are clearly talking nonsense. This is not good, Majesty. It will be difficult to persuade them that he is not fit to rule if he undoes all that we have established."

"I am aware of that." Quietly, she gritted her teeth. "It becomes all the more important to distract him with a bride! Have you heard aught from that magician?"

Uwe shook his head. "Not as yet, Majesty—but our plans do not depend on him or his daughter."

She relaxed her jaw. "No, that is true; we can manage fully well with any of the young women you selected."

"And his good behavior with women is unlikely to continue," Uwe persisted, hopefully. "I cannot imagine him going on like this for much longer. Old habits are difficult to change, and I would expect him to be in the bed of another woman as soon as the bloom is off the bride."

"True." Still, it was irksome to have carefully cultivated irresponsible behavior in the prince only to have him reverse his habits and begin acting like a little saint. *The longer he goes without nightmares, the more likely it is that I can find a way to turn him back to his old self.* "Tempt him, if you can find ways to do so discreetly—perhaps through his friends. If not—"

"If not, I shall encourage him in hunting," Uwe said, and smiled, more confident. "Just now, he has a restless energy because he no longer wastes himself in vice. It will be easy to convince him to throw himself into his favorite sport. The more he hunts, the likelier he is to have a natural accident. You know, this spate of virtue may work in our favor rather than against us. He may have changed some of his ways, but he is still reckless in the hunt, ready to risk all for the thrill of the chase."

"True." Her thoughts lightened. After all, it had been a hunting accident that had rid her of the king. "I think I shall develop a taste for wild game. Boar, I believe." Wild boar was the most dangerous game that could be hunted, and the Prince preferred to pursue boar afoot, with few companions.

"A bearskin blanket would be welcome to his tutor this winter," Uwe added slyly. "Or so I would think. The prince has never hunted bear before, so the expe-

rience would have the benefit of novelty, and I think
he would welcome it for that reason alone."

Now the queen's mind raced on other possibilities
that promised danger. "Is there not some ancient custom of the old pagan warriors, of proving bravery by
hunting a stag with only a dagger?" she asked Uwe,
who would surely know these things.

He laughed. "If there is not, rest assured that I shall
invent one," he promised. "And compose an *authentic*
ballad to stir the blood of our young warriors. If they
all fall to boasting, Siegfried will not be able to resist
the temptation of such a hunt."

"He might not be able to close with a stag, though."
She considered other alternatives. "There is much to
be said for waterfowl, as well," she continued, thinking
about swamps and the hazards hidden therein. "Something with challenge. Swans—don't swans prefer
marshy land?"

"Not nearly so much as geese, but we have domestic
geese in plenty, and he would think it odd if you asked
for wild ones, when our own are so much more succu-
lent," Uwe replied. He smiled at last. "I think the
prince would appreciate a gift from his loving
mother—a set of boar-spears, a new crossbow with
bird and bear arrows. And a similar gift for him to
present to his friend Benno would put the seal on
his pursuits."

*Ah, Uwe, I can always depend on you to think of
the most subtle way to accomplish our tasks.* "See to
procuring them for me, then," she told him. "I know
I can leave everything necessary in your hands."

Uwe bowed, and then pulled his lute from his back
and nodded at the circle of benches that they approached. "Would Your Majesty care for some music
for yourself and your ladies? The days grow short, the
nights long, and autumn is fast approaching. There

will be few of these pleasant days in the garden when the frosts come."

Out of the corner of her eye she saw that the ladies had caught up with them and realized why Uwe had suddenly changed the subject. "Indeed, I think that music would be most pleasant," she replied smoothly, and gestured to the ladies. Adelaide hurried up with a basket, taking a cushion from it and placing it on the choicest seat for the queen's comfort. When Clothilde had taken her place, the basket of embroidery beside her, Adelaide and the rest took seats around her, getting out their own work. The queen made it a rule that they never walk out in pleasant weather without their needlework, citing the oft-repeated homily that "idle hands were oft filled with mischief, and idle minds with wickedness."

Uwe struck a chord as soon as they were all settled, and lifted his voice in one of the myriad of ballads around the tale of Tristan and Isolde.

What can he be thinking? she wondered, alarmed at his choice of subject, for Tristan had presented himself to Queen Isolde first in the character of a minstrel. If any of the ladies had any suspicions of the queen's relationship with Uwe, this song could reveal things that the queen would find inconvenient—

Then she glanced around the circle of women, ending her survey with a careful examination of Uwe's features. The minstrel showed nothing more than concentration on his music, the women naught but simpleminded appreciation. She relaxed. No danger there; Uwe had simply picked an easily sung ballad, one that her ladies would find appealing. They were all her loyal creatures, and suspected nothing.

And if all goes well, there will be no danger from anything else, either. She picked up her work with a smile of secret satisfaction, and continued to work on the intricate floral border of a sleeve.

Hopefully, by the time it was ready to put on a gown, this would be a sleeve that she would wear to celebrate being crowned the reigning queen, leaving the title of Regent behind forever.

CHAPTER NINE

THANKS be to God, it's sunset at last. I don't think I could have flown for very much longer. There was a roughly circular lake in the middle distance, and von Rothbart (little more than a dark v-shape at this distance) dropped down toward it, the flock following him obediently.

Odile lowered her head and dropped out of a purple sky streaked with crimson and gold in the west, toward the waters of the secluded lake. Without so much as a zephyr to ruffle its surface and surrounded by towering, dark pines, it lay in shadow, as still and black as her scrying mirror back in her workshop. The others landed, sliding gently into the water, and floated ahead of her like water-lilies among the weeds of a little cove. As her webbed feet touched the water and she landed with a weary flip of her wings, she saw her father standing on the bank, his owl shaped discarded. So tired from the long flight that every muscle and sinew ached, she paddled toward him, heaved herself up onto the grass with an effort, and using the last of her hoarded strength, banished her swan form.

She stood before him in the simple black silk dress that was the easiest to summon and dismiss, determined to learn their destination before he could change the subject. "How much longer?" she demanded, before he could say anything. "How much longer will we be traveling? The others want to know, and so do I; we're all exhausted every night, and *I* don't think we're getting enough rest to recover before we take off again."

He laughed indulgently, as if she were a querulous child, weary from staying up past her bedtime, and not a woman pushed to the end of her endurance every day for the past week. More than once she had been forced to bolster the failing strength of her charges with her own slim resources, with no end in sight. At times she had felt deep regret that she had ever wished to be given the responsibilities of a partner in her father's work.

Now, as he chuckled at her, she choked down anger mingled with resentment. Why should he laugh at her? *She* had been the one doing all the work, not him!

"Tomorrow," he said, as she struggled with her emotions. "Or rather, tomorrow night. We will arrive at the place where I intend to allow Odette to attempt to prove herself, and where I bring about the downfall of a queen as corrupt as Jezebel and as evil as Lilith." His smile held a quality that suddenly made Odile feel uneasy. "She means to betray her own son, her own blood—she believes that I will help her in her scheme. She has no notion that I have merely placed before her the poisoned dainty; she will gorge upon it, and destroy herself in her greed."

"And Odette?" Odile asked, feeling that there was something wrong, but unable to imagine what it could be.

"Ah, Odette will test her virtue against the son, who shares the queen's tainted blood," von Rothbart said dismissively. "If God in His mercy deems that she has redeemed herself through contrition and suffering, which I doubt, then she will succeed. If not, things will remain as they are." He shrugged, for the subject was clearly of no importance to him. "But that is for the future. For now, you may set your mind at rest, daughter, for just after sunset on the morrow, your journeying will be at an end."

Odile sighed, and let her anger sweep away. Her father was right in one respect; the only important thing at the moment was that the end of the journey was in sight. She could discuss her grievances later.

"I will leave you to watch over the flock as usual," he continued, unaware that he rewoke her resentment, which smoldered just beneath the surface of her carefully cultivated mask. "I will come to guide you when the first light is in the sky, for we will need the full day and a little beyond to reach our goal."

With that, and without waiting to hear if she had any objections to his desertion, he cast his own magic over himself, and transformed into his owl form. With his gaze locked intently on the darkening sky, he crouched, then leaped upward, unfurling his wings in a tremendous downward thrust that drove him into the blackness above the trees.

Frustrated and still seething over her father's treatment, Odile turned her attention toward the flock, now wearily foraging among the water weeds. She clenched her jaw, as angry for their sake as for her own.

This sympathy had grown over the course of the journey; she had never been thrown so closely into their company before, and to her surprise they weren't nearly as dull as she had always thought. Since the night in the swamp when she had built a shelter for them, Odette was opening up to her, albeit slowly, and as their "queen" lost some of her suspicion, the rest of the flock followed. There was surprisingly little in the way of complaints about this journey; the entire lot of them seemed to think that it was worth anything just for the *chance* of winning their freedom.

As they cautiously warmed to her and included her

in their conversations (or at least stopped guarding their words when she was around), so Odile slowly gained sympathy for their situation. Their plight was especially poignant now, when they were almost too tired to eat when they landed, sometimes so weary that they fell asleep on the bank before the moon rose, and spent all of their brief transformation still in slumber. There was something incredibly pitiful about the poor things, curled up on the damp grass in their thin silk dresses, oblivious to everything around them but shivering in their sleep. They would have been far more comfortable as swans, and it was a measure of her father's indifference to their welfare that he didn't simply arrange for the spell to remain in force so that they could at least sleep in peace.

As soon as von Rothbart left, the flock drifted toward the shore. One by one, they clambered out onto the shore; watching how hard it was for them to accomplish even that simple task because of their weariness, Odile seethed with further resentment.

But anger was useful in this case; it gave her more energy than usual, enough to reinforce her drained magical power. With that extra boost, she coaxed a rough semicircle of bushes to grow and twine into a windbreak, created another of her flameless "fires" in the center, and induced the grass within the windbreak to grow thick and lush. The swans saw what she was doing and gathered close to her, warming themselves at the fire and tearing tiredly at the grass until the moon rose.

She began summoning food from the manor; she was determined to do what she could tonight to bolster their strength as well as hers. As they assumed their proper shapes, she thrust bread and cheese and sliced meat at them, urging them to eat. "Father intends a long flight tomorrow," she told them. "But he promises that we'll be where he wants us when he guides us to ground, so we'll all get a proper rest at last."

The flock accepted her offerings without hesitation—another sign of improvement in their relationship. "He gave us no time to forage tonight, and what will he allow us tomorrow?" asked Katherine in dismay. "I am so tired now I'll never wake before dawn!"

"That's why I'm bringing food for you," Odile pointed out. "I'll risk his anger if he finds out." She passed Katerina a portion, and the young woman nodded as she held out her hands for it.

"If we do not eat, we won't have the strength to fly, and he will be angry at all of us," Odette said shrewdly. "Thus far, we have given him no reason to be angry with the flock, but I should not care to thwart him even by a little so near to his goal."

Odile nodded, as she took a bite of her own meal. One of the little ones nibbled her bread daintily, and offered a shy "Thank you," that pleased her a great deal, although she did not show it.

The flock ate what Odile provided with birdlike appetites—which was to say, they devoured an amazing amount of food before they were sated; not quite their own weight, perhaps, but certainly far more than one might expect. That was hardly surprising, since they hadn't eaten all day, and by now they must be starving. By the time they finished eating, Odile was even more exhausted than before. If she'd had to do anything more with magic, even something so simple as lighting a candle, she wouldn't have had the strength.

For that matter, I don't have the strength to keep my eyes open much longer. She knew that after all her efforts today, not the least of which was the fetching of so much food, she was actually closer to dropping into sleep than the rest were. *I can hardly keep my eyes open, and the warm fire is only making it harder to stay awake.* She was supposed to be watching the flock, but how could she do that if she was asleep?

I'm not going to watch them, she decided. *Where are they going to go? We're in the middle of a forest, and they're already so tired they couldn't manage to run if a bear was chasing them! Even if they tried to slip off into the forest, they'd transform back into swans before they got very far.* She considered her own soft-soled, silk shoes, identical to theirs, and laughed at herself for worrying. Those shoes wouldn't protect against anything, and after a quarter of an hour of walking in the woods, shoes and feet both would be ruined. Even though some of the flock *had* been peasants, used to going barefoot in all weather but winter, by now they all had equally sensitive delicate feet. You had only to look at their hands to know that, for you couldn't have told anymore which were the fine ladies and which had scrubbed floors.

She yawned, as the others huddled closer to the fire and chatted softly among themselves, speculating about their destination. They no longer watched her out of the corners of their eyes and kept their conversation to inconsequentials around her; their speculations were remarkably intelligent. She decided to lie down in the soft grass, pillowing her head on her arms, listening with her eyes closed.

"He won't have us too near people, I wouldn't think," someone said. "He doesn't want people to know about us, or see us transform."

"But if he expects me to be able to prove myself, our home will have to be within reach of people. A few at least." That was Odette.

"I don't suppose we can expect a castle or something we could live in, could we?" one of the younger girls asked wistfully. "Will he have a manor there, do you think?"

One of the black swans, older and less hopeful, replied with a bitter laugh. "We'll be fortunate if there's a ruined barn or a cave we can shelter in," she said. "Wherever we go, it *will* be untenanted land, probably as forested as this place. People don't build castles in the wilderness."

"No, but they do build hunting lodges, and that might be the answer," Odette replied. "There *will* be a lake. We'll need one as swans, and he's never taken us to a place where there wasn't water. There might be a hunting lodge on that lake, and whoever uses it would be the person I am supposed to win over."

Odile privately thought that there would be no such thing, but decided not to say anything. Once they weren't using all their strength just to fly from one overnight stopping place to the next, she'd be able to husband her resources and *create* a place for all of them to use, even if her father couldn't be bothered with anyone's comfort but his own. *The nights are getting colder, and I have no intention of spending them in anything other than a decent room with a fire and comfortable furniture. And I'm going to sleep during the day in a real bed, even if the swans don't need one.* Once again, she felt amusement at her own expense. *And here am I, planning on creating a shelter for the entire flock. I suppose I wasn't as fond of my own company as I thought.*

The speculations drifted on to other things, and she let herself drift into sleep.

Siegfried reflected with a great deal of amusement that he had not been nearly so virtuous as his mother and her pet minstrel thought. He had not given up women or drink—well, not entirely, anyway. He'd just given up on the single-minded pursuit of both, rediscovering in the process the enjoyment he'd savored in scholastic pursuits before he'd been introduced to the first two pleasures.

Wine was always available, of course, but now he drank it to savor the taste and aroma, not to get as drunk as possible as quickly as feasible. He discovered, when he no longer kept specific mistresses, that there were plenty of wenches among the servants who flung themselves into his path and bed now and again in hopes of generous presents. He didn't disappoint them in the generosity of his presents, and they didn't disappoint him either. He made it very clear to all of them that he had no intention of keeping another woman—or women—but that didn't seem to make any difference to them. It was a bargain honestly kept on both sides.

And although he (and by extension, Benno and Wolfgang) were more moderate in their late-night wine-bibbling *cum* discussions, by no means had they taken to having the discussions without the wine to lubricate their words. The palace cellarer was happier; fewer bottles went missing on a night, and Siegfried found that the less they drank, the better their conversations were. Once again, it seemed a good trade for a slight sacrifice.

Nevertheless, there were some profound, though less visible, changes in his life. Most of them had to do with the way he conducted himself.

Only he knew how hard it was to keep his mouth shut and accept unasked-for advice and lectures from the "old men" of the Court, especially when the lectures had mostly to do with how depraved and degenerate the younger generation was. The only reward he got out of holding his tongue was that when he responded by looking sober and nodding, the lectures were notably shorter than they had been when he made witty retorts. The counter to that was that now the old goats considered it their privilege to deliver the lectures more often. He also had headaches more often now, caused by the strain of keeping his thoughts to himself.

It was easier with the men of his own generation, once he managed to convince himself that it was no stain on his own courage to lose occasionally, or refrain from making jests at the expense of those who lost to him. There was an immediate reward; the others became more companionable without trespassing over the boundary of the respect due to him as their prince. That alone was worth a great deal of the trouble he went to, and if he had to bite his tongue to keep from making clever remarks that would have irritated the others, perhaps that wasn't such a bad thing.

He still had scant respect for the Church in the person of the priest, so that much of his life hadn't changed. He still didn't bother with attending anything other than Sunday Mass. The priest said nothing to him concerning the abandonment of his vigil; perhaps the cleric reckoned it was to be expected, given his past behavior.

He made a point of watching people, rather than ignoring them as of no interest or importance, and tried to think before he acted or spoke. Because of that, he had noticed that the minstrel Uwe was acting rather oddly of late.

Uwe was watching him; well, he expected that, the minstrel was his mother's creature, after all. To a greater or lesser extent, Uwe had always watched him. The difference was that now Uwe seemed to be spending time flattering and courting *Siegfried,* and that was strange.

The prince pondered that as he watched his mother hold her Morning Court. He still didn't spend much time or attention on court or the affairs of running the kingdom; Queen Clothilde managed that very well and he saw no real reason to worry himself about it. What was the point? She was regent, and would rule until he came of age; until she stepped down, he had no real power that she did not give him. He was interested in Uwe, not in the workings of the court or the petitions before the queen this morning.

More precisely, he was interested in seeing if Uwe's influence with his mother had either grown or shrunk. It had occurred to him that Uwe might be working out some long-term plan with Siegfried in mind. Was it possible that the minstrel had a higher position in mind than that of mere minstrel—the position of royal consort? Was he courting Siegfried's favor in hopes of winning him over? Could it be that he actually hoped to marry the queen? Did he, in fact, plan to use Siegfried's influence on his mother to further that goal?

If he does, he's more of a fool than I thought, Siegfried mused, watching the minstrel through narrowed eyes. However much he disliked Uwe, he had to admit that the minstrel was both a handsome man and a clever one. It was not only Clothilde who admired the chiseled features, the square jaw, the keen blue eyes and silver-streaked golden hair of the musician—but Clothilde was probably the only woman in her court who admired the minstrel's mind as much as his lean body. *I've next to no influence on Mother if she's already made up her mind about something. If she hasn't, she's not likely to ask my opinion on something so important, either. Not when she's made it clear how much she dislikes my habits with women. He knows that; he'd have to be blind, deaf, and three times as stupid as the gooseherd to think otherwise.*

No, surely Uwe didn't expect him to do anything to further the minstrel's ambitions with the queen.

But if Mother decides she does *want to wed this minstrel, her courtiers would certainly have something to say about it!* Uwe was a commoner without a single noble drop of blood in him, not even from the sinister side. Granted, he had some small fame for his talents, and minstrels did have a specious sort of rank, but when it came to marriage with even the lowest-born woman of rank in the court, although the women might think it romantic, the men would not. As for marriage with the queen, every nobly-born male in the court would be outraged, especially the single ones, who could reasonably expect to have the queen turn to one of them for a proper consort, if that was what she wanted.

He has to know that. So maybe what he wants is my support in the face of the disapproval of the rest of the court. If the crown prince and heir was in favor of the union, it would be a great deal more difficult to oppose it. There would be no one to use as a focal point for factionalization, and no one to back as an alternative ruler in order to force Clothilde to give up the idea or face losing her rank.

That was far more likely, if the situation was that Uwe's influence with the queen had grown to the point that he would dare to press for marriage. Now, if Uwe's influence was *waning,* he might want Siegfried to plead his case with the queen for him, and that, too, made a certain amount of sense. Although Siegfried would have no influence on his mother if she had made up her mind to be rid of the minstrel, he might be able to remind her of Uwe's past services and loyalty, of his usefulness to her. If Uwe feared she was about to cast him off for a younger man, Siegfried could make some subtle jests about the one or two of the older widows of the court who persisted in making themselves ridiculous by setting their caps at bachelor knights who were younger than their own offspring. That would remind the queen that what was laughable behavior in a mere lady would give fodder for cruel gossip and crude jokes as far away as the

Emperor's court if *she* indulged in it. Of all the things
Clothilde feared, being thought ridiculous was probably one of the worst.

So Siegfried could have a part in turning her attention back to Uwe. Presuming, of course, that Siegfried
wanted to do that.

He watched them for quite some time from the side
of the Great Hall, wondering if either of his guesses
was correct. He couldn't tell. Nothing in either the
behavior of the queen or of the minstrel gave him any
indication that anything had changed between them.
Uwe stood in the ranks of her advisers, all of them
positioned near the throne and ready to be called on
at need. He was, however, just as clearly the *least* of
her advisers, as always; farthest from the throne, and
at least today, never called on for his opinion or even
looked at for more than a moment.

Siegfried finally sighed and gave it up as a waste of
time. Court was enormously boring, and he lacked the
patience to sit through very much of it. He slipped
out, being careful not to disturb anything or anyone,
and retired to the library to join his tutor there.

Wolfgang had acquired a new prize for the palace
library, a copy of one of the plays of Aristophanes—
The Wasps—in the original Greek, rather than the
more common Latin translation. He could never have
afforded such a rarity on his own, of course, but he
was empowered to use the Kingdom Treasury for such
acquisitions, provided he kept them within reason.
Clothilde enjoyed having scholars come to *her* library
to examine or copy manuscripts; it gave her kingdom
elevated status as a place of learning and culture. Siegfried was looking forward to many hours of arguing
over the nuances of translation, as well as relishing
the Greek's cynical brand of humor. *The Wasps* was
a new work to him and, as such, added the enjoyment
of novelty and the pleasures of discovery.

He found Wolfgang exactly where he expected, at the desk in front of the library's large glass window, frowning ferociously at the manuscript. In his old black gown and flat cap, bent over the manuscript stand on the desk, he could have modeled for an illuminated scholar in any *Book of Hours.* The older man looked up at the sound of the prince's footfall on the inlaid wooden floor, and beckoned Siegfried to his side.

"Hang it all, the monk that made this copy must have been under orders to save parchment, he wrote so small! I can hardly make out the letters!" the tutor complained querulously, his gray eyebrows wriggling in irritation. "What do you make of this phrase? All I can make out is, *Therefore, summon the cheeses,* and that *can't* be right!"

Siegfried looked over Wolfgang's shoulder to see what the old man was pointing to—and as he half thought, it was perfectly legible and nothing like *therefore, summon the cheeses.* The carefully inscribed words were beautifully written in the blackest of ink on snowy parchment, and no smaller than in any other manuscript, but Siegfried had suspected that Wolfgang's eyes had been failing for some time. This was just a confirmation of that suspicion.

He had no intention of saying anything about it, though. He just leaned over, as if he, too, found it difficult to read the manuscript, and finally ventured his opinion on the phrase in question.

I am going to have to get Wolfgang a pair of spectacles, he decided, though such things were difficult to come by and might be ruinously expensive. *I can probably get him to wear them if I tell him that they make him look like a great University Doctor.* Wolfgang was very susceptible to flattery, and was absolutely certain that he was utterly immune to it.

The two of them wrangled happily over the manuscript for the rest of the morning, and only put it away when hunger drove both of them to join the rest of the household at the midday meal. As Siegfried strolled into the hall, a page ran to his side and whispered that his mother specifically wished him to attend her as soon as he had eaten.

Interesting. Since I haven't done anything she has any reason to be annoyed about—could it be that one of those notions about Uwe were right? Curiosity heightened his appetite; he ate quickly, but well, and went straight to the queen's chambers, leaving Wolfgang to finish his dinner alone.

Uwe was nowhere in sight when he entered the room Clothilde used for private conversations. She was waiting for him, seated in the carved chair that was so like a throne that the palace servants often referred to it as such. Two of her ladies were with her—their hands full of embroidery work, as usual— and she did not move to dismiss them, so he assumed that whatever she wanted to speak to him about wasn't of a personal nature for either of them.

At her nod, he took a seat, a real chair, and not one of the stools the women used. She watched him for a time, her hands folded in her lap, without saying anything. In his turn, he studied her.

With her hair tucked carefully under a finely embroidered coif and veil, he suspected that there was too much gray in it to hide with herbal washes anymore. On first inspection, her narrow face appeared to be that of a woman no older than twenty, but Siegfried knew what to look for, and noted a few more fine, hair-thin wrinkles at the corners of her eyes and mouth, and crossing her forehead. Clothilde tried very hard to hold off the ravages of Time, but she was only mortal, and was bound to have limited success.

But her neck was still long and graceful, without the wattles and jowls that some women developed; her skin remained a flawless cream, and she still had the figure of a woman a third of her age. She certainly didn't look old enough to be Siegfried's mother.

"Your birthday takes place in two weeks," she said abruptly, startling him out of his thoughts. "You attain your majority." There was an odd quality to her voice, a touch of uncertainty, he thought.

Now, just what am I supposed to say to that? He settled for nodding, and replying respectfully, "Yes, Majesty."

She gave him a sharp glance, but didn't seem dissatisfied with the reply. "Have you given any thought to your duty?" she asked him.

This may be the oddest conversation I've had with her in a long time. "My duty?" he repeated. "Which duty would that be, Lady Mother? I have many duties—"

"The one to wed and produce a proper heir, of course," she not-quite-snapped, and gave a brittle laugh. "You have certainly been doing enough *practicing* for the occasion, but you are more than of an age to take a proper, legal bride."

He had a dozen replies he could have made, none of them respectful or sensible, and settled for a bland answer. "Truthfully, my Lady, I had not—"

"Given your father's example, you should," she interrupted him. "You should do more than take thought about it, you should do something about it, and as quickly as it can be arranged. Two sons in two years are not too many—an heir and a spare, as the saying goes, and the first should come as near to nine months after the wedding as possible." She'd lost that brittle edge and had fallen into the familiar tones of a lecture. "As it happens, I *have* given thought to the need. I have arranged for a celebration, and I have invited several suitable young women and their guardians to attend, all princesses equal to you, or at least not *greatly* inferior. All have been properly brought up, and I understand from Uwe that they all have at least youthful prettiness. Several are held to be beauties, none are older than twenty or younger than fourteen. I expect you to make a choice of one of them."

Her tone of voice left no question but that her last sentence was to be taken as an order, but it was what had preceded that sentence that had his attention.

"You're giving me a choice?" he blurted, taken entirely by surprise. That was the very last thing he had ever anticipated; he had always assumed that the queen would choose someone that suited *her,* inform him when the choice had been made, and leave it to him to go through the paces. He didn't entirely expect to even *see* his bride before she showed up at the altar, and perhaps not even then—it was entirely possible he'd be wedded by proxy. He had simply hoped that whoever she chose wouldn't be too terribly impossible—not a breastless child, nor an old hag, not a creature with a face like a cow nor one so fat it took a horse and cart to move her about. "Mother! I—*thank* you!" he continued, amazed, and touched beyond words. "I don't know how to thank you enough!"

She softened, just a little, and her eyes gleamed with satisfaction. "You thought I was going to shackle you to a baby or a beldam, didn't you?" she asked with amusement. "No, child, our kingdom doesn't require that much of a sacrifice; there are enough suitable young women who are both attractive and well-dowered to allow you to choose one that will make a pleasure out of duty. It seemed to me that if you had that choice, *I* stood a reasonable chance of getting that grandson in nine months." She actually unbent enough to smile slightly. "And if you and your chosen affianced happen to anticipate the wedding, and the grandson arrives in fewer than nine months, well, you are the prince, and no one will point fingers at you."

He could hardly believe what was coming out of his mother's mouth—but she had made her speech before two witnesses, who seemed as bemused as he was. Impulsively, he left his chair and went to one knee before the queen, seizing her hand and kissing it impulsively. "Lady Mother, I will never be able to thank you enough for this boon! I swear to you, if there is not a child in the proper time, it will not be for *my* lack of trying!"

A faint blush colored his mother's cheeks, and she snatched her hand away with an oddly playful gesture. "Enough of that, young fool! Go on with you—I will see to the celebration and the gathering-in of young women, do *you* see to it that there are no inconvenient encumbrances within the palace walls for your bride to stumble upon."

"There are none now, my Lady," he replied, just as playfully, bowing his head. "Has your priest not told you? I am a reformed man."

"Oh, and no doubt the sun will set this night in the east, the moon give birth to a twin, and wine fall down from the rain clouds," she chided, lightly striking the top of his head with her glove. "Off with you! Reform is not in the claiming, it is in the doing, and actions tell more than any protestations."

"Then let my actions speak for me; I will say no more." He kissed her hand again, rose to his feet, and bowed himself out, anxious to find Wolfgang and Benno and share with them this unexpected—and oh, so pleasant!—news.

Clothilde turned toward the door to her solar, where Uwe had been standing just out of sight, listening carefully. Now she dismissed her two ladies and, beck-

oning to Uwe, led the way up to the battlements.
Here, beneath the open sky, they were unlikely to be
overheard—but well within sight of all of the sentries,
they were unlikely to start any unwelcome rumors.
She had been closeted alone with him more often of
late than her cautious soul appreciated; it was time to
make sure they were seen as nothing more than the
queen and her adviser.

And as long as no one is aware of the passage be-
tween the walls linking his rooms and mine, we will be
able to preserve that illusion.

"Well?" she asked, when they had gone a pace or
two down the narrow walkway, her skirts blowing
about her ankles in the cool breeze that made the
pennons and flags above the battlements stand straight
out. "What do you think?"

Wind teased the minstrel's hair, and he brushed it
back from his face with a studiously graceful gesture.
"That the prince, for all his learning, is not in the least
worldly-wise," Uwe replied dryly. "Not once did he
ask what should have been the *obvious* question, when
you pointed out that he would attain his majority in
mere weeks."

"When his coronation would be, do you mean?"
She smiled with pleasure, when she recalled how well
she had manipulated the conversation. "I think I distracted him from that subject very well."

"You certainly picked the best possible subject to
distract him." Uwe laughed, with just a touch of scorn
as his eyes narrowed against the sun. "So much for
his reformation, when you offer him his pick of
pretty women."

"The women you chose to invite to this fête are,
aren't they?" she asked, feeling just a little anxious
when she recalled how often princesses turned out to
be less-than-lovely. "Pretty, I mean. I never trust those
court portraits; court artists are born liars, and their

job is to make their clients look less like themselves and more like what best suits the purpose of the portrait." She allowed herself a tiny grimace. "In any case, I want him to have the maximum possible distraction. I don't expect him to make a choice at once; in fact, it would please me very much if he dithered about it for weeks."

"They are all quite pretty, one or two are enchanting," Uwe assured her. "And speaking of enchanting—Baron von Rothbart has sent a message pledging that he and his daughter have arrived and are staying nearby, and will certainly attend your fete for the prince." Uwe smiled his most charming and winning smile. "He asked me to assure you that he has not trespassed on your hospitality out of respect for you, knowing that the inclusion of his party was not in your original plan. He says that he would not stretch our resources any farther, when he can easily provide for himself."

"Ah!" she exclaimed. "Excellent! I really have high hopes for *that* particular pair."

"As do I." Uwe turned slightly and stared out across the open lawns leading up to the palace and its first line of defense, its moat. Clothilde followed his gaze.

It was a pastoral scene, with sheep and geese grazing beneath the careful eyes of their herders, and more geese and ducks paddling about in the water of the moat. No one had offered a serious challenge to the defenses since her husband's grandfather's time, but she had been scrupulous about keeping them all in repair. One never knew—she thought that none of her neighboring monarchs were tempted to enlarge their lands, but one never knew.

On the other hand, with a powerful magician as an ally, *she* might think about enlarging her land.

"A few more hectares gained along the borders

wouldn't come amiss," Uwe mused aloud. "There are neighbors who would think twice before challenging a sorcerer, if we annexed a few unused fields."

"As usual, you echo my thoughts," Clothilde replied. "But let us not anticipate the future too much. Siegfried might not choose the magician's daughter."

Uwe snorted. "Not if the magician has anything to say about it. He's determined to have his daughter crowned princess, if not queen."

She shook her head. "Never assume," she cautioned. "He might not use his powers to assure Siegfried's choice; he might learn things about my son that he does not like. The girl herself might not care for the boy. What we need to make certain of is that he is so entangled in his choice and his bride that he takes no thought for his coronation."

"And it will be my task to make certain none of your advisers think to remind him of it," Uwe added. "Mind you, that won't be as difficult as it sounds, since Siegfried avoids their company as much as he can, and they are all too old to try to seek him out in his habitual haunts."

Clothilde laughed, thinking of her aged advisers trying to keep up with Siegfried on a hunt, or engage his attention during a passage of arms. "The only place they *could* find him is in the library," she agreed. "And I truly pity anyone attempting to distract Siegfried and his tutor from one of their manuscripts. I do believe that a siege of the palace could break out right below the library window, and they wouldn't even notice."

"Certainly I have seen him completely surprised by the arrival of nightfall," Uwe replied. "No, I believe I can keep your advisers so occupied with the preparations for the fête, the betrothal, and the wedding, that they entirely forget to inquire about the coronation."

"With great good fortune, preparations for a birth

and baptism will keep them all equally absorbed." Clothilde considered how long she could use distractions to hold both the prince and her advisers at bay.

"We'll buy a year of time, at least, perhaps two." Uwe nodded. "A great deal can happen in two years. The bride might die in childbed, and throw Siegfried into mourning. The bride may demand all of his time and attention—the young ladies in question, other than the magician's daughter, are all much-indulged, and very much taken up with the ideals of Courtly Love. As long as the prince remains infatuated with his bride, the lady will lead him a lively dance." He turned and smiled into the queen's eyes as she nodded appreciatively. "That was one of my considerations."

"And if the young lady does not command his attention, many other things may happen," Uwe continued blandly. "After the birth—perhaps we will be preparing a funeral, and not for infant or mother."

"Perhaps we shall," she acknowledged, and slightly raised one eyebrow—not enough to disturb her makeup. "So let us hope that my dear son chooses a lady who looks well in black."

Chapter Ten

SIEGFRIED'S birthday celebration was mere days away, and Queen Clothilde had expressed a desire for swans. Dead swans, not live ones—to grace the feast table, roasted and redressed in their plumage. Such a dish was very popular in the greater courts for major festival occasions, and the queen wished this birthday fête to be regarded with as much awe and wonder in the recollection as any celebration of the Emperor's. She had considered peafowl, but decided on swans as there were only a handful of peafowl that had survived the ravages of foxes this summer, and she wished to keep them for breeding.

Siegfried, very eager to please his mother, had jumped at the chance to contribute to the festivities. Now he and Benno stood on one of the lower battlements, surveying the countryside with their hands shading their eyes, looking for swans in the air. Ducks they had seen in plenty, and a flock or two of geese, but as yet there were no swans.

"It can't be all that difficult to find swans," Siegfried protested. "Last year it seemed as if every time we went hunting for geese, we kept starting up swans instead."

"I don't know, Siegfried," Benno replied doubtfully. "It's a bit early for swans; I don't think they'll start migration for a few weeks yet. I haven't seen any flocks in the air since last fall."

"I'm beginning to think you're right," the prince answered. "Neither have I, but Mother wants roast swan for the banquet, if we can get it, and I hate to disappoint her."

Benno grinned at him, his eyes sly as he squinted into the sunlight. "I can't blame you for wanting to give her what she wants, given the bevy of beauties that's shown up so far. What lucky star were you born under, that you're going to get your pick of the fairest blossoms of the country? I never would have guessed that the queen would be so besotted with you that she would arrange a choice of lovely brides!"

Siegfried was about to reply, when a shout from below interrupted their conversation.

"Hoy! Prince Siegfried!"

Siegfried looked in the direction of the shout to see Uwe approaching up the battlement stairs, burdened with a pair of unwieldy bundles wrapped in deerskin. The minstrel smiled broadly as he neared them, and Siegfried wondered what the man wanted. Although Uwe had continued to display an unusual amount of friendliness toward the prince, it was somewhat out of the ordinary for the minstrel to come looking for Siegfried.

"Hoy yourself, Uwe!" Siegfried said genially, feeling such high spirits that very little could spoil his day. "We were discussing doing some hunting—"

"Ah, then I come in good time!" The minstrel approached, and offered one of his bundles to Siegfried, and the other to Benno. "Here, my prince; I thought I would make my natal-day gift to you a little early, so you have a chance to use it. I rather doubt you'll have much time for hunting winged and four-footed prey after the fête!" He winked broadly at Siegfried, who only chuckled and shook his head. The man could be amazingly charming when he chose, and there was no doubt he had decided to exert some of that charm on Siegfried. It was difficult to resist, and Siegfried didn't see any reason to try.

"And as your own natal day is just past, Benno, the queen thought you might make good use of this, her gift to her son's boon companion and truest friend," he continued, with no diminution of his cheer. "Knowing how much the two of you enjoy hunting together, it only seemed appropriate to equip you equally for the field."

The parcel wasn't heavy, but it was quite oddly shaped, and contained something hard and angular. Siegfried undid the lacings wrapping the package; the deerskin fell away, revealing the finest light crossbow he had ever seen. With an exclamation of pleasure, he held it up; made of the toughest blued steel and cured wood, it was decorated with inlaid designs of game birds made of silver, gold, and mother-of-pearl. With it was a quiver of heavy boarhide to match, ornamented in silver and gold in the same designs. The quiver held perfect bird-bolts, suitable for any game bird from quail to heron.

Benno's gift was identical except that the crossbow and quiver lacked the ornamental silver-and gold-work; he would have to be content with the same motifs as mere gilded carvings in the dark wood and leather.

"Uwe, I hardly know how to give you proper thanks," Siegfried said with genuine appreciation. "This is very fine of you; I've rarely seen such a perfect bow." He cocked the bow experimentally and grinned with enthusiasm when he realized what kind of pull it had. This bow should be able to take a large bird in full flight at a formidable distance. "I didn't have any idea you knew how much I needed a new bow!"

"You mean, you would never have guessed that a

decrepit old man such as I would have any knowledge of hunting equipment," Uwe replied, with a grin and a twinkle in his eyes. "It might interest you to know that a few centuries ago when I was *your* age, I caused notable slaughter among the ducks and pheasant. But I have another gift for you, and that is the gift of information. Know you the whereabouts of the Lake of Black Pines?"

Siegfried knitted his brows, thinking. "Yes—but I haven't bothered to hunt there for years. The last time I was there was disappointing; the only birds I ever saw there were a few paltry teal and some crows."

"When Her Majesty asked you to find swans for the fête, knowing that it was not quite the season, I took the liberty of sending out a few men to scour the countryside to see if they could find any," Uwe said, "And one of them just returned with the news that there is a migrating flock at that lake, believe it or not!"

"Hah!" If there had been anything needed to put the feather on Siegfried's pleasure, it was that. "Well done, Uwe! You have saved us a great deal of fruitless searching!"

"My pleasure, sire," the minstrel replied, and bowed as he returned the way he had come. "My pleasure."

He might as well have been on the moon once he was a few paces away, for Siegfried completely forgot about him in the anticipation of a fine hunt.

"The lake is quite a distance from here, Siegfried," Benno pointed out. "It will take us most of the day to get there, at least, even on horseback."

"There's a full moon tonight," Siegfried replied. "We can hunt by moonlight. We might just as well take some supplies and camp there overnight. . . ." He brightened even more as he recalled the presence of a small village near the lake, a village that boasted a fine inn with excellent beer. "Better yet, we'll stay at the village inn, and we'll take Wolfgang with us!"

"Wolfgang?" Benno laughed, no doubt recalling the last time they'd taken Wolfgang out of the palace. "Do you think we can persuade him into a saddle?"

"I'll put him on my palfrey this time; she has the sweetest gait of any horse in the stables. He needs to get out of the library before he goes blind; he's been poring over that new play too long." Siegfried had no doubt that he could lure his tutor out on the trip; Wolfgang had more than once mourned aloud that his pupil would have little or no time for him once he was presented with his bevy of would-be brides, and even less when the actual bride was chosen. This would be an excellent chance for the three of them to have an outing all by themselves, and the lively discussions that were sure to ensue would keep the journey from growing tedious.

"He can stay at the inn while we go on to the lake," Siegfried continued, planning the thing in his mind. "The peasants will entertain him, I've no doubt, and he can probably find enough in some of their tales for that book of his." One of Wolfgang's ongoing projects was a book of peasant tales; he had a theory that the ballads of the great minstrels eventually trickled down to the peasants, though changed to reflect a peasant's life.

"All right," Benno said, agreeing to the whole project. "I'll go coax Wolfgang out of the library, you go order the horses and gear."

"Right! Give me your bow, and I'll see it's packed up. I'll see you at the stable." Willingly Siegfried took the second crossbow and quiver from his friend, and the two parted on their errands.

From above, the lake looked like every other body of water they had stopped at. Twilight lingered; soft blue dusk-light filled the great inverted bowl of the sky, with only a few stars showing faintly in the east. To the west, the cloudless sky held the last recollections of the crimson sunset in the form of a pale blue glow. It was beautiful up here—but not down there.

If Odile could have shivered in this form, she would have, and she hoped that the others hadn't set their hearts on that imagined hunting lodge, because if they had, they were going to be heartbroken. The waters of the lake, cold, dark, and foreboding, spread beneath them, shaped like a very fat spider with splayed legs, squashed into the forest floor. Mist wreathed the shore, and crept into the branches of the huge black pines around it. Ancient pines they were, perhaps the oldest Odile had ever seen, with their boughs sagging toward the earth in melancholy mourning. Rock cliffs made up most of the shoreline, and in the middle, a single spear of stone stabbed upward, lancing through the very heart of the lake.

The great owl led the way downward, and the flock of swans followed him with exhaustion in every beat of their drooping wings, pale silver vees against the dark water below them.

Odile dropped with them, following in the hollow of their vee, so that all of them touched down on the water at the same time. The feet and legs of swans were curiously impervious to cold, so she couldn't tell how chilly the water was as her feet struck, then glided along the surface, but when they had all settled onto the water, she sensed that it was probably very cold indeed, more so than she would have guessed. It must be fed from a subterranean spring, and the chill accounted for the reason that there were so few other water birds here. Between the cold and the shade of the huge pines, it would be difficult for vegetation to grow, offering little in the way of food for foraging water birds. In this form, she sensed that the lake was very deep indeed, and surrounded by high bluffs and cliffs as it was, there were very few shallow places for plants to take root in the first place.

So I'll have to supply food here. All right, I can do that—but now I see why Father wanted me to come along. It will free him from all of the tedious little chores. There was a touch of scorn in her thoughts, as she watched von Rothbart sail majestically away into the pine forest, leaving *her* to watch over the needs of the flock once again. Well, at least *now* they could get some rest, and she could work on her studies, hopefully increasing her powers. The more magic at her command, the better she would be able to provide for her comfort and the flock's.

She paddled wearily toward the shore, hoping to find a place where the flock could come up onto the shore. After skirting the cliffs into and out of three of the crooked "arms" of the lake, on the fourth she noted that the height of the cliff hanging above them was dropping. As the flock followed her hopefully, she made her way along the fourth limb and at the end of it found what she was looking for, a spot nearly level with the water. Looking back over her shoulder, she saw mist rising out of the water; it was going to be a chilly night. She hopped up onto the grassy bank, followed by the flock, who immediately dropped down onto the grass to rest.

She took her human form, and sought for a good place to create a shelter—but for once, she found that her father had been preparing things ahead of the flock; his magical signature hung in the air at the edge of the grassy shoreline, visible only to those who had eyes to see such things. This must be the only place along the lakeshore where it was easy for swimming swans to get up on the bank, so it would have been no great task for von Rothbart to guess where they would go when they arrived. She walked up to the glowing sigil, and calmly touched it; as she had expected, it began to move. Following it as it led her farther along the shore to the right, she entered a grassy clearing. The sigil moved on, then stopped and dissipated. When she reached the place where she had seen it vanish, she smiled. She would not have to create a shelter, for her father had already done so.

Not that any ordinary mortal would have known that; the clue to her was that the signature of magic at this spot was so strong. It hung about what appeared to be a grove of enormous old oaks growing so closely together that their trunks touched. Each of the trees was so large that four or five grown men could have circled the trunk with outstretched arms and not had their fingers touch; together they were the size of a large house. When she examined them, she realized that there was a dark crevice near the roots of one of the trees, and as she drew nearer still, squinting in the darkness, she saw that behind a screening of vines, there was a door in that crevice. She opened the door, and found that von Rothbart had taken a page from *her* book, as it were. This was no natural grove. Von Rothbart had created this place over the course of many nights, forcing the oaks to grow as she had forced the willows on her island.

So this was why he deserted us every night! She now felt ashamed that she had misjudged him; he had been working fully as hard as she all these nights.

She pushed open the door, which moved easily at her touch, and held up her hand with a faerie-light cradled in her palm. Within the hollow interior, the sorcerer had roughed out a single room, the floor made of the roots grown together to form a solid surface, the walls and roof of the living oak. There were no windows in this shelter, and no furnishings, but it would hold against cold and weather, and it could be heated by a magic fire and illuminated the same way. Or she could fetch lamps and candles from the manor, whichever she chose, though it seemed inadvisable to bring too much flame inside.

She was disappointed; with all those nights to work, she could have accomplished much more than this. Evidently the shelter had not been as high a priority for him as she had thought. *At least he's done* something, *for a change,* she thought, and sent the conjured light up to the ceiling so that she could set about making the place habitable.

Then she turned and went back into the clearing, where the swans awaited her, watching her attentively. The first thing she did was to transport a good supply of corn from the manor, pouring it into a pile in the midst of the ragged circle of swans. It would be some time before the moon rose, and she knew they were as exhausted as she, very hungry and needed food *now* to replenish so much spent energy. Then, while they scooped up the corn in their bills, devouring it so quickly it might have been vanishing by magical means, she returned to the hollowed trees, leaving the door open behind her. Turning this rough space into something livable could take all night, and if she wanted a decent place to sleep, she'd better get about it now.

Besides, if she stopped to rest, she might not have the force of will to take up the task.

Something like a bed—Once again, the easiest thing to do would be to use what she had at hand, which was the living fabric of the trees. Gently, she coaxed a bit more growth, bringing the wood of the roots up to form a low oblong shape, like a hollow bench, just wide and long enough to cradle a sleeping girl. When she had a creation grown to her satisfaction, she made another, then another, until the inner surface of the walls was ringed with sleeping benches.

That done, she turned her attention to the floor, coaxing up a mat of rootlets to weave together into a dense, springy carpet. *Now I need a hearthstone, to protect the wood. I don't want to kill the trees.* After some consideration, she remembered a large, flat stone near the entrance to this grove; with a wrenching effort, she conjured it directly into the shelter, right in the center, and with the very last iota of her power, called up a magic fire upon it.

But calling the fire was the last thing she was able to accomplish. Her vision blurred, and she swayed where she stood. Suddenly overcome with dizziness, she reached for the wall to steady herself, and when that didn't help, sagged down to the floor on her knees.

A moment later, she found herself surrounded by girls. *Oh. The moon must have come up*—she thought vaguely, and tried to get to her feet.

Odette kept her sitting on the floor with gentle but insistent pressure on her shoulders. "Stay where you are," the young woman ordered in a tone of authority. "If you stand up, you'll fall over on your nose."

"But I'm not finished," she protested weakly, thinking about all she had yet to do. "I've only started— there's no bedding, no food—"

"And you don't need to do anything more at the moment." Odette actually patted her shoulder in a gesture of kindness. "Let us take care of you for a change."

Another wave of weakness washed over her, and she decided that she wasn't going to argue. She heard Odette giving orders to the others, and she dropped into a sitting position, leaning against the bed-bench beside her as she rested her aching head against her arm with her eyes closed. For the moment she was perfectly content to simply sit here and let her strength come trickling back. The silence around her indicated that once again she was alone, the others having gone out on whatever errands Odette had given them.

After a time, she heard some of the girls returning. She opened her eyes and raised her head—which seemed to weigh twice as much as it should—and saw that the maidens had brought in enormous piles of bracken, herbs, and grasses, which they were arranging to make soft beds in each of the hollows.

Oh, now that is a good idea, she thought, *And it doesn't require magic, does it?*

More of the girls arrived as Odile watched in bemusement, all with similar burdens, until each of the hollow benches had cushioning material. Then, Katerina helped Odile to her feet and onto one of the primitive beds, which was surprisingly soft and had a pleasant scent from the wild herbs.

Some of the girls settled into beds of their own, but fully half of the benches were untenanted. When Odile took a tally of the flock, she noticed that most of the young women settling in were the ones of noble birth.

Before she had cause to more than wonder about that, the rest arrived, with Odette in the lead.

"Now," the Swan Queen said, in a firm tone, "You've already fed us tonight, and you are in no condition to produce food for yourself, so you will have to make do with what we have found for you." She brought the others to Odile's side with a little wave, and they each placed their gleanings beside her on makeshift plates of leaves.

There was a handful of wild grapes, another of tart gooseberries, last year's nuts (blackened, but still sound), the peeled roots of cattails, a bunch of watercress. Now Odile knew why the "missing" girls had all been those who had some knowledge of the land—

they were the only ones who could be trusted to know what was good to eat and what was not.

As fogged as my mind is, they could poison me with a handful of mushrooms.

But Odette with a proud smile produced the best prize, a fine lake trout. Odile gaped at it, unable to imagine how the woman had caught it without hook or line.

"I drove it up on the bank while I was still a swan," Odette explained. "And one of the little swans gutted and cleaned it for us with a sharp rock. I thought you might be overspent, and I wanted to return the favor of dinner." Having presented her prize, she handed it to one of the others who neatly skewered it on twigs and held it over the magic fire to cook. The savory aroma was enough to drive Odile wild; suddenly she was ravenous, and when the fish was done, she took it in her bare hands, juggling it from hand to hand while it cooled, and picking off bits and popping them into her mouth as she did so. It tasted wonderful, even eaten without salt or any kind of seasoning.

When the fish was a fond memory, she turned to the other offerings, and devoured them all, with words of thanks to the flock as she did so. If the nuts were small and hard to pry from their shells, and the grapes a little sour, it hardly mattered; hunger made everything taste like dishes at a feast.

Meanwhile, Odette shooed the girls into their beds while Odile ate, and the measure of *their* exhaustion could be taken by how quickly they fell asleep. Odette was the last one to take her place, and she watched Odile with a curious expression on her face as the sorceress finished the last berry and licked her fingers clean without shame.

Odile returned the gaze, then dimmed the light coming from the fire (though not the heat; the shelter was just warm enough, and none of them had anything in the way of a blanket). "Thank you again," she said, feeling oddly shy. It was perhaps the first time anyone other than her father's invisible servants had done anything *for* her in a very long time—and even longer since anyone had done anything for her without her having to ask first.

"You've done more than you had to for us on this entire journey," Odette replied with a little shrug. "It seemed more than time to return the favor."

With that, the Swan Queen laid her head down and nestled into her own bed, leaving Odile to follow her example. A full stomach and the cozy warmth left her no strength to do anything else, and the headache that overextending her powers had given her made her long for the oblivion and relief of sleep.

And in a few moments after her head touched the pillow of fragrant grasses, she got her wish.

Siegfried sighed, and laid a calming hand on the shoulder of his restive horse. They had been waiting to ride off for the lake for the better part of an hour now, and that was *after* the queen had indicated that everyone was ready to depart. *I should have known. Of course, when one is the prince, and one's birthday is near and one's mother the queen has invited half a dozen lovely princesses to attend festivities, it isn't going to be possible to sneak off with two friends for a little hunting.*

What *had* started as a simple hunting party of three, with Siegfried going incognito, had turned into an expedition, involving all the visitors and most of the Court.

When Queen Clothilde learned that Siegfried, Benno, and Wolfgang were going hunting, she decided that a hunting party would be just the sort of entertainment needed to occupy the six princesses and their various entourages. The princesses themselves all voiced enthusiasm for the plan—and given that none of them wanted any of the others to have more time around Siegfried than her rivals, they probably would have been enthusiastic even if they had *hated* hunting.

Now Siegfried and his friends were cooling their heels, waiting, while stewards and servants packed up half the palace for what should have been a simple trip, requiring only three horses at most.

Each of the princesses had her own pavilion, as did the queen; several more pavilions were needed for courtiers and hangers-on. Servants would have to sleep in and under the wagons, but there would be plenty of those. With the pavilions came beds, bedding, cushions, carpets, washbasins, camp-baths, plate and cutlery, embroidery supplies, musical instruments, and the appropriate hunting wardrobes. That was just for the queen and the young ladies. Then came the same, in lesser quantities, for the courtiers, servants, and so forth. There was a pack of hunting dogs, both sight-and scent hounds, hence there must be food, the packmaster, and the dog-boys. Most of the falconry mews came, which meant the falconers, cadges, perches, shelters, and equipment. There were beaters and trackers, the huntmaster, a stableful of hunters and jumpers, their grooms and tack. Of course, a hunter had much too rough a gait to ride for pleasure, so each lady also had a palfrey to ride on the journey. One could not depend on the quality of a peasant cook at a peasant inn, so one of the chief cooks and all his helpers traveled as well, and all of the pots, kettles, and miscellaneous equipment *he* would need. And all of these people and animals needed supplies of food and drink, which meant there were wagon loads just of fodder for man and beast. Siegfried had

intended to take two days, three at the most, and return with ample swans for his birthday feast. It took
a full day for this raree-show to be organized, and it
would take another two for everyone to get to the
village common and pitch a camp—and he *still*
wouldn't have his swans!

But the ladies were delighted, the weather looked
to be splendid, and the queen was right; it was the
perfect way to pass some time before the festival
began.

So Siegfried had bowed to the inevitable and allowed the juggernaut to roll over his simple plan,
squashing it beneath the weight of the queen's. He
insisted on one thing only: that he be the only one to
hunt the swans. Let everyone else course whatever
game they cared to—let them hawk for duck and
wood-pigeon, grouse and pheasant, let them chase
hare, boar and deer, let them harry the fox, wolf, and
bear, even. He and he alone, with the help of Benno,
would seek the shores of the lake and the elusive
swans.

When he had that pledge from the queen, he made
no objections, and now, at long last, he rode his palfrey to the head of the procession, surrounded by the
chosen maidens, each of whom had probably arisen
before dawn to dress and primp to show herself at her
best. Finally, the entire cavalcade passed through the
palace gates and onto the open road.

The queen followed behind them, pleased to allow
the prince to ride in the vanguard. Wolfgang was
somewhere behind, with the wagons; no great surprise
there, since given the choice between a horse and a
wagon, he would always select the latter.

Benno rode with Siegfried at the prince's urgent
invitation. He didn't fancy being left to be the sole
focus of all of the six women.

Just at the moment, he was trying to get all of their names straight. It wouldn't do to miscall any of them.

Fortunately, most of the heavy wagons and baggage had gone on before them last night; by traveling through the darkness, urged on by the truly tyrannical wagon steward, they should have arrived at the village by now—or if they had not, they would in a few hours. That would give them time to set everything up before the royal party arrived. By that time, pavilions would have been pitched, the camp established, and dinner would be waiting for them. Siegfried, Benno, Wolfgang, and Arno would be lodging at the inn instead of a pavilion; the accommodations might be of a more primitive quality, but he wouldn't have to endure the shrieks of maidservants finding insects among the bedding, or the flirtatious attempts by the princesses to get him alone for a moment. That could be very unfortunate—he could only choose one, and any of them could claim he had made a secret pledge to her, if she could have a moment with no witnesses. Not that *any* of the six were bad choices, but he wanted the choice to be his, as promised.

As the royal party finally got out of the palace grounds and turned off onto the main road, the six maidens each vied for his attention. There was room for only two to actually ride beside him, but each of the six was determined that *she* would have one of those two prize positions. As he made no attempt to indicate a preference, they maneuvered with the determination of a falcon with prey in view, "accidentally" jostling each other, or causing a horse to start forward or lag back.

Finally, after half an hour of this, the queen stepped in. She invited four of the ladies to ride with her, leaving Siegfried and Benno with only two—the implication being that *she* would see to a fair rotation of time spent with the Prince.

He sighed with relief, though he did his best not to show it, and waited for the two singled out to urge their horses to his side.

To his right, in a habit of garnet wool trimmed in satin, was Ysabeau von Andersburg, her golden hair surmounted by a fine hat with a cockade of rooster plumes, and caught in a net of garnet beads and gold wire. Tiny, rosy, blue-eyed, she handled her spirited Spanish Barb mare with expert skill he would not have expected in a girl who looked like a child's toy.

To his left, Angelique Fortescue chattered like a magpie, rattling on about her delight in the country-side, the outing, the prince's companionship, the queen—if Ysabeau's tactic was to smile demurely, say little, and allow her looks and her riding impress the prince, Angelique apparently planned to batter his ret-icence with a barrage of words. Just as golden-haired as the other girl, Angelique had all the statuesque beauty of Aphrodite, with classical features, marble complexion, and ample proportions. Her chosen color was a tawny gold, with jewels of gold and topaz, her hair confined in a coiled braid held in place by golden pins beneath her riding hat. Her mount was a placid bay gelding of no particular breeding.

Behind him were the other four, who no doubt would take their turns at charming him: Gabriela von Bern, a plump, cheerful maiden with hair the color of her chestnut stallion's coat, garbed in a warm brown and bejeweled with amber—Ursula Brednesi, wearing a small fortune in sapphires, raven-haired and clothed in blue, with the eyes of an angel and a body that would tempt a saint—Honoria von Hansberg, who hid her hair completely beneath a coif of snow-white linen embroidered with silver thread and pearls, but whose violet eyes and heart-shaped face, combined with a body clad in velvet to match, with tiny waist and gen-erous bosom, made hair-color seem irrelevant—and

Evangeline de Luchen, for whom *black* pearls were the gem of choice, clothed from head to toe in the finest deep brown leather, a bare shade lighter than sable, whose fierce black stallion, handled with skill and strength, matched her hair and eyes, and whose piquant and clever features were more handsome than beautiful.

Each one had her own particular beauty. No doubt, each one had her own particular faults. And he had only days to discover them—although he did know one thing already. Although he had gazed into the eyes of each of them, hoping for a sign, for a special spark to spring up between them, lighting a fire in both hearts at once, there had been nothing. Nothing to show that there was anything more in the ballads of the minstrels than fantasy; nothing to show that there was such a thing as love, overwhelming, striking all unexpectedly and at first sight.

Or if there is such a thing, it is not to ignite between me and any of these women, he thought with a stifled sigh.

Well, if he could not choose one for love, he could at least choose by process of elimination.

As Angelique chattered on, he decided that he did know at least one other thing. He *would* grant Angelique a second and even third chance, but if she showed no signs of different behavior, *she,* at least would be out of the running.

Because, beautiful as she is, if she isn't able to bear a silence without filling it, two weeks in her company would drive me to take holy vows and flee to a Benedictine monastery, just to escape her chatter!

Chapter Eleven

ODILE woke slowly to the sounds of birds and an empty "room." She stretched lazily, considering the slant of the sunlight outside the door, left open by the departing swans. She had slept the night through and long into the day; she guessed, as she rose from her bed of bracken and used a touch of magic to freshen her dress, that it was probably mid-afternoon at the earliest.

She brushed a few stray bits of grass off her skirt, and went out into the daylight to see what the lake looked like under the sun. *If this is going to be our home for a while, I hope it isn't as grim as it looked last night.*

Though sunlight and birdsong helped, the scene she surveyed from the shelter was not particularly welcoming. Around her, the forest seemed empty, without the little sounds of life that small creatures made, scurrying about the underbrush. The lake's dark waters did not shelter much in the way of waterfowl, either. The forest surrounding the lake was predominantly of black pine—tall, with heavily drooping boughs and needles of the very deep green that gave them their name, for at any distance, they looked black. There were other trees growing amid the pines, more oaks, some hazels, chestnuts, walnuts, but they were decid-

edly in the minority and didn't do a great deal to
disperse the general air of solemn gloom. The clearing
she now stood in actually extended right to the shore,
though not to the spot where the low bank had allowed them to clamber out of the water. Her view out
into the lake was thus unobstructed, and included a
picturesque, high cliff at the point where this arm of
the lake joined the main body.

The flock was nowhere in sight, but Odile wasn't in
the least worried that they had fled. *This* was the place
where Odette would have her chance to win them all
free of von Rothbart's spells; wherever they had gone,
they would be back, for that chance alone.

*Probably they're off foraging, but I don't think
they'll have a great deal of luck.* There wasn't much
sign of the water plants and wild grains they needed
for real feeding on this arm of the lake, and Odile
rather doubted that the other arms would prove any
different.

And speaking of foraging. . . . She turned back to
the shelter, her stomach grumbling. There were more
than a few things she needed to fetch from the manor,
and after the first decent sleep in weeks, she finally
had the strength she would need to get it all done in
a single afternoon.

*But first of all, food. I could eat a pine bough at
this point!*

She didn't want to waste any time, however, so after
she appropriated a good stock of commonplace foodstuffs taken from the manor's pantry, she made a por-
table luncheon of chunks of bread, sausage, and
cheese that she could eat while continuing to work.
Within an hour, she had brought more creature-comforts
to the shelter, linens, for one. She'd made real beds
of the bracken, by tucking a heavy sheet over the
bracken to make a mattress and pillow, and she'd
added folded blankets to the foot of each bed. When

she stepped back and looked her handiwork over, she chuckled; because she had made the beds of roots, or rather, rootlets all twined and bound together, the beds actually resembled large baskets. With the sheets smoothed over the bracken, they looked like a row of laundry baskets waiting for maids to hang out the clothes.

After consideration of the damage that pests could do, she called a trunk-sized storage cabinet from the manor to seal the food into, and she next brought an assortment of cups, plates and cutlery and stacked them atop the cabinet. Although she planned to bring fresh foodstuffs every night, if something happened to exhaust her, or if any of the flock hungered when *she* wasn't available, she wanted to have some basics on hand. There was also the possibility that something could happen to her, for magic did not render one immune from illness; it was better to be prepared and not have the need.

She also brought a couple of buckets for fresh water, then soap, towels, and a basin—though like the flock, she *could* wash as a swan and it would carry over to her human form. Small things made a difference, though, and she remembered all the wistful wishes of the journey, so the combs, brushes, hairpins, and the like she also brought would make all of them feel less disheveled. And lastly, she created shelves within the hollow oaks to place all these things on, and a curious cupboard to hold her personal possessions.

Then she brought what, for her, was the most important of all; her books and the magical apparatus she thought she might need. There wasn't a great deal; she had gotten beyond the point where she required apparatus to create magic. Like her father, she had entered the realm where only concentration, words and gestures created whatever she needed.

Last of all (and after a rest), just before sundown,

she brought in bags of the grain the swans ate, storing most of them inside the oaks. She dropped one in the clearing, near the shoreline, breaking it open so that she could spread it out where the flock would see it easily as they returned "home."

With that final duty accomplished, she felt justified in simply sitting with her back braced against a sun-warmed boulder, watching the sun set, with the pines circling the lake making a jagged black fence against the flaming sky. It was a dramatic and beautiful sunset, though its beauty had a touch of the uncanny about it. *It's like a woman, a stunning and breathtaking sorceress without a heart—you have to stare and marvel, but you can feel the ice where her soul should be, and you know there are going to be storms wherever she goes.* That didn't stop her from admiring the view, although she could have wished for a softer setting for her temporary home.

She watched the clouds take fire and burn, let her muscles relax, and thought about what she would bring for dinner. And then, of course, when all the work was done, her father appeared.

He walked out of the forest with no warning; he just appeared out of the shadows, like a shadow himself, shrouded in his owlfeather cape. He looked around the clearing with somber approval, even entering briefly into the shelter and emerging to join Odile at the side of the lake.

She rose slowly to her feet, and waited silently for his judgment. For he *would* cast judgment on what she had done, and never mind that he hadn't bothered to contribute even a little to her efforts. For a moment, she clenched her jaw and fought to master her resentment. *I don't know what he's been doing, and I have no right to ask. This is my father's duty, and he allows me to share it.*

"Very neat, Odile," he said, after a moment of gaz-

ing at the sunset beside her. "Very efficient. It did not
occur to me to make furnishings of the oak itself; that
was a thrifty and wise use of power."

*I didn't have much choice, given how little I had left
last night!* she wanted to shout, but instead, she bent
her head and replied with a soft, "Thank you, Father."
For all I know, he was more exhausted than I.

"I see that I can leave you in charge of the flock
with no misgivings," he continued. "There are things
that I must pursue; I will need your eyes and ears
here, during the moonlit hours when the flock becomes human. You are an integral part of this trial."

She perked up a little at that; this was real responsibility, and exactly what she craved. "Give me your
orders, Father," she said with more enthusiasm. "You
know that I will follow them as you wish."

He smiled—a very small curve of the lips, but a
smile all the same. "Obviously, while the flock are
swans, you need not concern yourself about them. Nor
need you concern yourself with the movements of the
young man who will provide Odette with her test, for
I will be marking his path and actions when he is not
with her. But I do wish you to observe the two of
them together, and Odette when she is alone but
human, and mark it all well so that you may report it
fairly to me." At her nod of understanding, he continued. "If the young man should sight me, he would no
doubt regard me as his enemy and attempt to attack
me. He cannot possibly harm me, of course, but such
encounters would accomplish nothing and waste his
time with Odette. You, on the other hand, will not be
seen as a threat; he will concentrate on Odette and
nothing else if you are the observer. Other than that—
keep yourself and the flock tended and fed, and that
is all I shall require of you."

She dropped to the grass in a curtsy. "As you will,

Father," she said, bending her head in submission to his orders. And when she looked up, he was gone.

She didn't rise again, for weariness fell over her shoulders like a too-heavy cloak. Instead, she occupied herself with a task so simple and ordinary that she didn't have to think to accomplish it. She unpinned her hair from its heavy coil at the back of her neck, unbraided it, and began to comb it out.

She didn't often have to tend to her own hair, for at home the invisible servants appeared to take care of it as soon as she removed the first pin. But there was something soothing in letting it down now, and combing it out, so long as she moved very slowly and took the time to untangle knots with exacting patience. *I think I see why so many girls can do this for hours on end. It's hypnotic. Perhaps I ought to do this the next time I want to meditate or enter a trance.*

She hadn't thought about how long her hair had gotten before she undid it; the servants did little more than comb it out, braid it up, and occasionally trim the ends, and they were so deft that they were finished binding it up in minutes. She simply hadn't noticed its length; it reached far past her waist now, which made it difficult for one person to handle.

As the sun dropped below the trees and the sky darkened from flame to rose, from rose to cobalt, a movement, a flash of white across the sky, caught her attention, and she looked up to see the flock circling above, coming in to land.

An unaccustomed feeling of contentment came over her, despite being so very tired. *Everything is ready; if they haven't foraged enough, there's grain, and if they want to nibble a bit as girls, they can share my dinner. They'll have real beds and some comforts tonight. I do believe they'll be surprised and pleased.*

She continued to comb out her hair, pulling the locks she had brushed out over her shoulder to lie across her breast and lap. In the last light, it looked like raw, unspun silk, cobweb-fine and silver-blond. A strange color, given what a violent red her father's was.

Then again, he could make his hair any color he chose, and mine, too, for that matter. He could have changed mine when I was a child, and I would never know. He might not have wanted it to be so obvious that I was his child. An enemy could have taken me to use against him. She considered a moment, and reflected that if he had changed her hair color, it was probably a good thing. *I don't think I'd care for flaming hair. I'm too pale, I've no color at all. Better to look like a spirit than to look like a bleached little stick attached to a red mop.*

The swans glided into view, swimming swiftly across the still mirror of the lake led by Odette; they crossed Odile's field of vision, and disappeared behind the trees. A moment later, however, she heard the muffled padding of their feet as they moved toward her across the grass in a stately progression, necks straight, and heads held high. The others went straight to the grain and began eating, but Odette paced close to Odile, keeping her round black eyes fixed on the sorceress until she was certain she had Odile's attention. Then she bowed her head in an unmistakable gesture of graceful thanks, and only then joined the rest.

As full dark settled on them, the swans shimmered in the starlight, and the lake lapped softly against the shore, sparks of starlight caught in the tops of the wavelets and thrown back at the sky. Odile finished combing out the last lock of hair and leaned back against the tree, watching as the stars came out and glistened in a way no mere gem could match in the soft, ebony sky.

And then, just as a lone nightingale started to sing,

the moon showed its first sliver of pearl above the treetops.

Odile started as someone took the comb from her loose grip.

"Here," said Odette, with the same oddly kind tone in her voice she'd had last night. "Let me finish that for you."

Odile felt herself flush, but nodded. "Thank you," she said, feeling awkward. "I had no idea there was so much of it; the Silent Ones take care of it at home. It's such a bother to do by myself—"

"Especially without a mirror," Odette agreed, deftly braiding the heavy mane of silk, and arranging it in a kind of crown around Odile's head. "I've never known—why doesn't von Rothbart permit any mirrors?"

"Because mirrors show the truth," Odile replied, unable to suppress a yawn. "If you, as a swan, were reflected in a mirror, it would be your human shape that was in the reflection, not the swan. I don't know why."

"Oh." Odette put the final pin in place and gave her construction a pat to test its solidity. "Here, I think this will hold better than the knot you've been wearing."

Odile moved her head experimentally. "It's certainly not as heavy," she agreed, pleased, and yawned again. "I can't believe I'm so tired! I only woke up a few hours ago, and I'm ready to go to sleep as soon as I get dinner."

"I can," Odette said, and the odd, grim tone in her voice made Odile turn to stare at her, startled. She looked into the older girl's dark eyes, and saw things there that she hadn't anticipated. Much of the wariness was gone, replaced by an intent concentration.

"Why?" she asked. *What does she know that I should? And why is she going to tell me?*

Odette hesitated a moment, biting her lip. "Von

Rothbart was here, wasn't he?" she asked. Then without waiting for Odile to reply, continued, "And you didn't feel tired until *after* he was gone, right? Nor is this the first time that's happened. In fact, *most* times that he leaves, you feel tired. No, not tired—*drained.*"

Odile didn't reply immediately, but she knew without thinking back too far that Odette was right. It was something that she simply hadn't thought much about. *Because I didn't want to?* And she knew that Odette had used the word "drained" deliberately.

For she had wondered before how it was that her father managed to accomplish so much magically, and yet have far more power available than she. Not all of it could be marked up to experience and knowledge. Power had to come from somewhere. *And sometimes—it comes from me.*

"He's done it to us, drained us," Odette went on, as if she knew exactly what Odile was thinking. "He's been doing it all along; I noticed it and began to keep track of it—I've seen him arrive when we all felt well, stay for a few minutes, then leave, and we all felt exhausted. That's why we don't *do* much when we're around him; by the time he's finished doing whatever it is he does to pull all of our energy out of us, all we can do is laze about like so many invalids. I've thought all along that was why he caught us and why he's kept us in the first place, and that what we did is merely a convenient excuse. We give him power, more power than he could ever have by himself." She was silent for a moment, as Odile struggled with the growing certainty that Odette was right.

It makes too much sense not to be right. But she could have Father's priorities completely backward. Why shouldn't he benefit from keeping them? Don't they cost him magic to keep them as swans, and to keep them safe? I wonder—is this part of their penance, or—

"Of course," Odette continued thoughtfully, "that

begs the question of why he has agreed to a trial that might release us."

"He doesn't expect you to win free," Odile suggested, hoping she didn't sound as distressed as she felt, for she still couldn't shake the doubts that Odette's words had raised in her.

Odette nodded. "Or—"

Odile slowly closed her eyes, then looked directly into the eyes of the Swan Queen. "Or?" she prompted, searching Odette's face for any sign that the young woman was trying to goad her, or manipulate her, and finding nothing of the kind.

"Or—now that you're grown, he doesn't need *us* for power anymore," Odette said, and bit her lip again. "After all, you *are* a sorceress; I should think that would mean you have more of what he's using. It would certainly be easier to have power come from a single willing and obedient daughter than from a flock of unwilling captives who themselves must take his magic to keep bewitched."

Odile felt her stomach knot, and tasted something sour in the back of her throat. She had words piling up in her mind, a great many of them—but to blurt them out would be a betrayal of her father. Fortunately, Odette saved her from having to answer.

"Odile, I know nothing of magic; this is all speculation—" she shook her head. "I don't mean to distress you, or to upset you. I just didn't want your father to use you without your knowledge, as mine used me."

Odile eagerly seized on the possible change of subject; anything to drive the unwelcome suspicions away, and put Odette on the defensive. She had never heard Odette's version of her capture, only what von Rothbart had said—that Odette had been betrothed to a great prince who would have brought his private army to the king's service, and that when Odette betrayed her father and ran away, it nearly cost her father his kingdom. "What do you mean? Father said that you betrayed your father—"

Odette's mouth twisted into a bitter smile, and her eyes hardened. "I suppose you could say that I did, but only after he betrayed me—" She shook her head violently. "Oh, I don't know why you should believe me, but—if you wish to hear the story, I will tell it to you, in as few words as I may."

Odile nodded, now intensely curious.

Odette looked out over the water of the lake, and the silver path that the moon had written across the water. "My father promised my mother when I was very young that he would never force me to wed against my will. He swore this on holy relics once again when she was on her deathbed. He repeated the promise to me, then promptly broke his promises the moment she was dead. He betrothed me to a man he wished to make an ally, a very powerful prince with an army twice the size of ours, and one border adjoining ours. I can only assume that he had intended to do this all along, since there were betrothal gifts and a portrait of the prince in my room two days after my mother was buried."

"And you didn't like him?" Odile asked.

"I didn't *know* him," Odette replied, her eyes growing angry. "And since my father made it very clear that since *he* needed this alliance, I was going to marry this man even if he was a walking corpse, I had no reason to think that I *would* like him. He was older than my grandfather, he had already buried four wives and was looking for a fifth, and not even a court painter could put warmth in his cold gaze. I had no intention of marrying him."

"And?" Odile prompted.

"And—I persuaded one of my father's squires that I was in love with him, and that we must run away together." She dropped her eyes, and flushed. Now

her voice took on tones of shame. "I convinced him
that we could seek sanctuary in the Emperor's Court,
and find a priest to wed us once we were there—there
are always priests in a large city who will perform
wedding ceremonies for anyone with money. I wasn't
in love with him, of course. I didn't intend to marry
him—in fact, I intended to desert him as soon as we
reached the Emperor's Court. I also planned, while
waiting to appeal to the Emperor, to become involved
with at least half a dozen Princes of the Blood, so that
if the Emperor would not grant me sanctuary, I would
have three or four more suitors to play off against
my father's choice. Needless to say, I would not have
counted that poor little son of a count among them.
So I suppose I betrayed him as well . . . but we never
got there, we never got more than a mile from home,
because your father must have been watching me. As
soon as I passed the bounds of the royal estate and it
was clear that I intended to carry out my scheme,
something happened. A great, dark cloud appeared
out of the blue sky and descended over us while our
horses froze with fear. The squire was struck unconscious, and the very next thing I knew, I was a swan
flying above the road, there was a great owl behind
me that was driving me ahead of him, and that was
all there was to it. The rest, you already know."

Odile suppressed a feeling of triumph after hearing
the story; her father was completely justified in con-
demning Odette. Not only had Odette betrayed the
three men who had depended on her, but she admitted
it! *And she drops words into my ear that she knows
will create doubts about Father. I am a loyal daughter—I would never have gone against my father's
wishes that way! Had I been in her position—*

But there her thoughts faltered in more doubt, more
uncertainty. *Would* she have married this unknown

man had her father demanded it? Especially after he had pledged he would never force her?

What was wrong with her? Why were her thoughts so unsettled? Why had everything become so complicated?

Odette said nothing more, and she didn't seem to expect an answer from Odile. They sat together in uncomfortable silence for some time, until Elke, one of the little swans, ran up to them, providing them both with a welcome distraction.

"Odette!" Elke said, bubbling over with excitement. "You must come and see what the Black Swan has done for us! You must come and see our new home! It is better than last night!"

"And it will be better still when I summon supper for us all," Odile responded to the girl, getting to her feet and brushing her skirt off self-consciously. "Can you think of anything you would like?"

"Oh!" Elke clapped her hands like a small child, and laughed. "More of those honey cakes!"

Odile chuckled weakly. "I believe I can manage that. Odette? Will you come?"

The Swan Queen watched the lake, and replied quietly. "In a little. Please, go on without me."

Odile shrugged, and Elke ran back to the shelter, with Odile following slowly in her wake, her mind on more than just a few honey cakes.

By the time the royal party reached the village of Schwarzbaum, it was well after nightfall, and Siegfried had spent about three hours' worth of time with each of the princesses. Thanks to Clothilde's clever management, all six had spent an equal amount of time in riding at his side. The one thing he could say with surety about the experience was that it had been educational. If his mother had gone out of her way to discover six young women who were entirely different from each other, she could not have managed better. Thus far, he had decided that he could eliminate two from his choice of bride, however; Evangeline and Angelique.

A second hour with Angelique chattering beside him had confirmed his first impression; he would have to be deaf in order to wed her, for the flow of words never stopped. The third hour was precisely the same, in spite of many, many hints that she stop talking. Once, he called her attention to the song of a lark nearby; she couldn't even hold her tongue long enough to hear more than a dozen notes. On another occasion, he asked her if she had any questions about his kingdom, hoping to at least interrupt her chatter with a few words of his own. Even that ploy failed, as she would *begin* a question, which would eventually be lost as she meandered through a dozen more subjects.

Evangeline, on the other hand, was far *too* inscrutable. He literally did not know what she thought on any subject, for any attempt to garner an opinion from her met with clever deflection. That, combined with her ever-so-slightly-superior attitude, was as maddening as Angelique's river of chatter. He would ask her a question, and she would turn it back with another. He would ask her opinion, and she would counter smoothly with an observation of what someone else had said on the subject. Although such a trait would be a valuable diplomatic asset, he really didn't want it used on him. He needed to know what his wife—or would-be wife—was thinking, and he didn't even know Evangeline's most trivial *preferences*. How could he possibly tell if they were compatible? *In fact—how could I possibly tell if she hated me, my kingdom, and everything around her? How could I tell if she was planning on stabbing me in my bed?* Well, that probably wasn't a danger, but he really didn't want to find himself playing King Mark to Evangeline's Isolde.

The other four maidens were still all possible candidates, and he didn't intend to tell Angelique and Evangeline that they were already out of the running and spoil their enjoyment of the festivities. Instead, he would drop hints to some of his unmarried friends—or their fathers—letting them know that the way was clear to the two rejected brides. As Benno had said, any of them would be happy to wed the most flawed of these beauties, given that their faces and fortunes were handsome. So, it was entirely possible that both the rejected maidens would come away from this fête with betrothals—even though they were not betrothed to Prince Siegfried.

When the cavalcade reached the village, he was deep in a discussion of falconry with Princess Honoria, who was not only a devotee of the sport, but to his surprise and delight, actually trapped and trained her own birds. Most ladies left such work to their falconers, but Honoria was firmly of the opinion that the only way to truly know the capabilities and win the guarded trust of a bird was to conduct all the training herself. For that matter, most ladies were content to fly sparrowhawks and kestrels, with only the most enthusiastic handling peregrines. Honoria routinely flew the fierce and temperamental goshawks and powerful gyrfalcons, and had ambitions to one day fly an eagle! If her tally of last year's game was correct—and he had no reason to suspect that she was exaggerating—she could hold her own with the most expert falconers.

"I actually have a surprisingly gentle gos," Honoria was saying, as Siegfried noticed the lights of the village winking ahead of them on the road, and caught the scent of woodsmoke and roasting meat on the breeze.

"I brought her with me; I trapped her this spring as a brancher, and she literally tamed overnight. Any of my falconers can handle her. In fact, anyone who is fearless and steady with her can handle her, and she's rarely yaracky, even when she's quite hungry. She always returns to the lure, and she's never struck at me even when she's missed a kill."

Siegfried was quite impressed. "How is she at the hunt?"

"She takes hares and ducks with ease," Honoria told him proudly. "She's taken foxes, and even a badger! She's absolutely fearless, and I only wish I could have birds of her breeding—to establish a bloodline in the same way that it's possible to breed horses."

Siegfried had to sigh at that, for such an idea was a virtual impossibility, and he was certain Honoria knew it.

It was too dark to see her smile at his sigh, but he heard her chuckle. "I know what you are thinking, and no, I am not such a fool to try such a thing. But what I am thinking of doing is to mark her somehow, perhaps with a silver ring upon her leg, and let her fly free in a few years in a little valley where I know there are no goshawks. I'll trap a tiercel-hawk and release him in the same valley. Then I shall post a forester there to keep an eye on her, and if she breeds, to take an eyas when it is well feathered."

"Now that is a plan which has much promise, my lady," he agreed, liking her ability to find solutions to problems that would make others give up.

I would still like to know just what color hair she has beneath that coif, he thought, as their horses drew near enough to the village to hear a distant murmur of voices. *This one might well do, though; if she is as intelligent on other subjects as she is on the subject of falconry, I would have a great deal to share with her.*

Then, before he had a chance to ask any more questions, a stream of lights poured up the road toward them, and the distant murmur became a chorus of cheers.

Siegfried was not surprised at the enthusiastic reception; there must have been a servant posted on the road to warn the rest when the royal party was near. It would impress and please the guests to have a torchlight greeting, and no one would know that it was only the servants.

Within moments, the servants formed a double line of torches on either side of the road, cheering the arrival of the queen and prince and their guests. Queen Clothilde casually urged her horse past Siegfried's, who moved aside to let her take the head of the procession. The servants had set up the pavilions on the village common, and the torchbearers led the way to the encampment, a neat little village in itself.

The princesses were clearly delighted with the hospitality waiting for them, as well they should have been. Siegfried, who had been a part of the planning, was impressed.

Each of the pavilions prepared for the princesses was a different color, and all of them were lit from within so that they glowed like many-hued lanterns. Small fires set in braziers and oil-filled torches ensured that the grounds were handsomely lit. The pavilions had been set up surrounding a central tent, striped in red and blue, where the nobility would be entertained and fed as sumptuously as if they were back at the palace. Clothilde had brought all her own musicians and had hired a traveling troupe of entertainers as well. If it grew chill, braziers of charcoal with perfumes or incense sprinkled over them would warm the air; if it grew warm, the sides of the tent could be raised to allow breezes to flow through. Already a trio of Clothilde's musicians had begun playing to welcome the new arrivals, and there was a stream of pages carrying food and drink into the tent. Squires appeared to hold each horse and assist each princess from her mount, and escort her into the tent for a belated supper.

Clever. Mother is going to keep them occupied so that they don't miss my presence. I can spend my evening without entertaining the ladies. He saluted the queen when the last of the princesses was safely inside the tent; she gave him a brief nod as Uwe helped her down from her own horse. Siegfried took that as his signal to depart; he, Benno, and the cart holding Wolfgang departed for the inn.

They rode into the village, which stood just out of sight of the encampment; the inn was a handsome little rustic building, two-storied, built in the same style as a hunting lodge. Arno was already there, waiting at the door beside the portly innkeeper, clad in a spotless white apron, who was overjoyed to see Siegfried at last. "Highness!" the man cried happily. "I do not know how we are to serve so honored a guest, but—"

"But just give us your soft beds, good beer, and your fine food, and we will be happy enough," Siegfried interrupted, feeling great relief that he did not need to wrack his brain for more ways to interview his prospective brides, and did not need to produce any more diplomatic speeches.

"The inn is yours," the innkeeper said proudly. "There are no other folk staying as guests, nor will there be until after you have gone."

That was good news, for Siegfried already knew that there were only three rooms above the common hall, and that meant each of them would have his own room. Arno, of course, would quarter with Siegfried, as Benno's man would lodge with him. Wolfgang, without a servant, would take the third room, much smaller than the other two, which usually housed entire families or merchant groups.

"What can I serve you for dinner, Highness?" the innkeeper asked anxiously, as Benno helped Wolfgang down off the cart, and Siegfried gave instructions to the groom who came to take his horse.

"What is in the kitchen tonight?" Siegfried replied.

The innkeeper looked anxious. "Only a game pie, sausages, pickled cabbage—nothing suitable to Your Highness—"

"In that, you are mistaken. That, your fine beer, a good cheese, and fresh bread will be fine," Siegfried said with a hearty laugh, only too pleased to have simple fare for tonight. Since the first princess had arrived, Clothilde had paraded a variety of fantastic dishes at each meal, and he was heartily tired of them. "Perhaps some apple tart to follow. Send it up to my room; the three of us will eat there."

The innkeeper bowed until his nose touched his knees, as Siegfried, Benno, and Wolfgang walked past him into the common hall, a dark room lit mostly by firelight, redolent with the scent of garlic sausage and beer. The peasant farmers and foresters at the rough tables inside stood up and cheered as they entered; the prince gave them a friendly wave, but passed on without stopping, heading for the stairs at the back of the hall which led to the rooms above. It had been a long day in the saddle, and at the moment, he was more interested in dinner and a quiet conversation with his friends than anything else.

A boy scampered ahead of them, up the stairs, and threw open the door to the first guest chamber; light from within streamed out onto the stairs, proving that the bedchambers had better illumination than the room below. "Your room, Highness!" the child said proudly, then turned and opened the doors at the top

of the stairs that led to the other two rooms as Siegfried entered the best guest room.

A fire already burned in the stone fireplace, chasing
the slight chill in the air. A single massive bed domi-
nated the room, a bed that could have (and probably
had, more often than not) held six adults. Unlike his
own bed, this did not have a canopy or bed-curtains,
and the mattress was stuffed with straw, not feathers.
But atop the straw mattress were a feather bed, fine
sheets, pillows, and blankets from the palace, all
brought by the luggage wagons.

This was how most nobles traveled; though they
might *stay* at rural inns, they seldom made use of the
(possibly dubious) bedding provided by the innkeep-
ers. Bedding and sometimes entire beds and other furnishings traveled with the noble, and all that the inn
provided was a room. In this case, since Arno knew
the keeper, and could trust that the beds were clean
and had no unpleasant inhabitants, he knew he only
needed to bring the bedding.

A simple cot brought in the same wagon stood in
the corner for Arno's use, and candles in silver holders
(also from the palace) lit the room brightly. The
prince's silver utensils waited on the prince's small
folding table, and all of his hunting gear was neatly
arrayed on stands beside it.

Three clever folding chairs and a folding stool had
been arranged around the table, furniture the prince
took with him everywhere when he traveled, since
they were relatively compact and easy to transport. It
was just as well that he had ordered them brought
along, since the bed was the only article of furniture
belonging to the inn.

This was because under normal conditions, the precious floor space would be sold to travelers who could
not afford the bed, but *could* afford a space on the

floor. There was no point in burdening precious floor space with furniture.

Benno's room would be like this one but half the size, with a slightly smaller bed. Wolfgang's—as Siegfried had reason to know—wasn't often used for *sleeping;* it was just large enough to hold the bed and a table and washbasin. Rented by the hour, the services of a lady of negotiable virtue came with it; by renting the *room* and not the lady herself, the innkeeper neatly sidestepped any accusations of procuring. *He* only supplied the room; what the tenant did with it (and the lady who was already inside) was the tenant's business.

The lady was probably plying her trade elsewhere for the duration of the royal visit, most likely among the visitors.

A stream of serving wenches poured up the stairs and into Siegfried's room, carrying food and drink, just as Wolfgang and Benno joined the prince.

The tutor backed himself into a corner, bewildered by all the bustling and flirtatious servers; Siegfried was amused to see that none of them carried more than a single dish. Judging by the coyly charming glances that the girls cast at him and Benno, they were probably hoping for attention, gifts, or both.

Arno handled the latter by choosing one of the girls at random, handing her a pouch of small coins, and loudly telling her to see that all the girls got a fair share. Benno and Siegfried disposed of the former with little compliments that made the girls giggle and blush as they filed out of the room.

"Well!" Benno said cheerfully, "Looks to me as if every girl in the village voluntcered to 'help out' tonight."

"Very probably," Siegfried agreed, entirely amused. "We wouldn't have gotten this sort of treatment if we'd followed my original plan."

"By the time this visit is done, they'll have collected a substantial addition to their dowries, if you continue to be so generous, Siegfried," Wolfgang noted, and chuckled. "That may be more of an incentive than a glimpse of their Crown Prince."

"That is entirely likely, old friend," the prince replied with good humor. "Far be it for me to object to a little honest greed, when it ensures our dinner arrives at the table so promptly. Now, no ceremony among friends. Hunger makes the best sauce, so let's do justice to our dinner." He pulled up one of his folding chairs and sat down to help himself; Benno and Wolfgang lost no time in following his example. When they had heaped their plates full, taking his cue from the prince, Arno poured their drink, then served himself, retiring to his stool by the fire to eat.

Nothing broke the silence for some time except the sounds associated with hearty eating; it had been a long time since the midday meal, and they all had good appetites.

Siegfried was the first to finish, and pushed his chair away from the table with a sigh of content. "God's teeth, but it's good to have a *simple* repast for a change!"

Benno sopped up the last gravy from the pie with a bit of bread, and popped it in his mouth. "If I'm faced with another pie of lark's tongues or mess of dormice in honey, I'll turn monk," he agreed.

"Better just retire to the lower tables," Wolfgang advised with a discreet belch. "Ridiculous dainties like that are reserved for the queen's table. Good God, think how many larks they'd have to slaughter to provide everyone with a pie!"

"Ah, Highness, don't let Her Majesty know, but those so-called 'lark's tongues' weren't nothing but slivers of calf liver," Arno offered diffidently from his place beside the fire. "Spiced up till they weren't fit to eat, so's no one would guess."

Siegfried burst into delighted laughter. "You don't say! Damn! And the cook probably pocketed a fine sum, charging up the ingredients for that dish on the household budget!"

"Very likely, Your Highness," Arno agreed. "But I reckon he's earned it, with all the trouble those princesses have given him since they arrived. Hot water at all hours, all manner of things they swear they can't eat, hot possets and sweet cakes at bedtime—"

"I suspect you're right." Siegfried had heard something of this, but it didn't disturb him. The princesses were each so determined that no rival receive preferential treatment that once one made a request, they all made demands so as not to lose status. "So long as he doesn't line his pockets overmuch, I doubt even the household steward will complain."

Then Siegfried yawned hugely. "My friends, I intended to have a fine discussion about our guests with you, but I'm so weary I doubt I could hold up my end of it. Shall we call the wenches back to clear this away, then retire?"

Wolfgang nodded, his old eyes showing his fatigue. "I am relieved to hear you say so. I think perhaps such a discussion would be better postponed until breakfast."

"And I," Benno agreed.

"I'll see to the mess, Your Highness," Arno said promptly, jumping to his feet as Benno and Wolfgang got to their own in a more leisurely manner. Arno saw them to their rooms, then fetched up servants to clear away the debris of dinner. It was notable that this time it was only two scullery boys who arrived to bear away the plates, and not a bevy of giggling girls.

Siegfried stripped and climbed into the bed, leaving

Arno to close the shutters against the night air and tidy up. It was a measure of the fact that he was just as tired as he had claimed, that Arno hadn't done more than cast the last debris of dinner into the fire-place, when sleep overtook him.

Chapter Twelve

SIEGFRIED had planned to wake early, and just as the first sunlight crept through cracks in the shutters, he stretched, yawned hugely until his jaws ached, and grinned to himself. *Good, I haven't lost the knack of waking myself up, the way I used to when I was a boy.*

He slid out of bed and dressed quietly in the same clothing he'd worn yesterday so as not to wake Arno. He was of a mind to slip away alone, and indulge in a somewhat plebeian pastime that he seldom enjoyed at the palace, which didn't precisely fit into the concept of the "noble hunts" his mother proposed.

He intended to go fishing, by himself; with no attendants to bait the line and hand him the pole, or fetch the fish he caught so that he would not get splashed.

There was a fine trout stream near the inn, and trout fishing required little in the way of equipment, but a great deal in the way of skill. Siegfried left his room so quietly he didn't wake anyone, and when he descended to the common room, he found only a couple of early risers there, breakfasting on fresh bread and butter. He borrowed fishing tackle from the innkeeper and slipped away without even the escort of a single servant.

This early in the morning, the trout were cooperative, rising eagerly to his fly, and he returned to the inn before even Benno was awake with a fine catch for breakfast. It gave him an odd little surge of pleasure to devour the freshly fried fruits of his own labor at a sun-dappled table beneath the enormous oak tree in front of the inn, and share them with his sleepy-eyed friends. It was even better to see their astonished faces when he told them who had caught the fish they'd just eaten with such relish.

When the remains were cleared away, Siegfried and Benno had a stable boy bring their horses around, and mounted up. It was time for one of the official hunts: hunting with falcons while the day was still early. Wolfgang elected to remain behind, not being of a mind to hunt with the rest.

As they walked their horses toward the encampment, Benno glanced at his friend with an odd expression. Finally Siegfried laughed and shook his head. "Out with it, friend," he chuckled. "Just what are you thinking?"

"That it would be an odd thing to see you wedded," Benno said mournfully. "I cannot imagine you, who have never been without a half-dozen wenches at your call, tied down to a single woman. The very idea seems preposterous, and yet here you are, and you'll be picking out a bride within days."

Siegfried laughed even harder at Benno's long face. "And why should that change my life?"

"But—" Benno looked at him askance.

Siegfried sobered. "My friend, of the six beauties that my mother has assembled here, there are two whom I do not care to wed, four I am considering, but *none* whom I love—or could love. Nor do I believe that I have struck such a spark in any of their hearts. The only way I would sacrifice my habits would be in the unlikely event that I found a true love to wed; acquiring a consort to please Mother and her advisers is not a powerful enough reason to make me change. My bride will be an ornament to the court, and comely enough to make siring a son a pleasure, but that is all." His smile turned a little cynical. "And I rather doubt that any of them see me as anything other than a way to a crown. No, Benno, nothing will change very much in my life."

"But what about—" Benno began, "—I thought you'd *been* changing!"

Siegfried had no intention of trusting Benno with his dream-visions. "Not because of any plans of my mother's I assure you," he retorted. "I just found some ways to make my life more pleasant. No longer waking up with a pounding head was *certainly* more pleasant, and I decided to let the wenches approach me rather than pursuing them, that's all."

Benno sighed, but with relief rather than regret. "And here I thought you were smitten with Angelique," he teased.

Siegfried shuddered theatrically. "I fear that one is too talkative for my taste. I would never again be able to hear the sound of my own voice. On the other hand, my friend, if you have a taste for her—"

"Not I!" Benno exclaimed, and laughed. "No, the lovely Angelique should only wed a man who is deaf and mute; that way they will both be happy for the rest of their lives! Now, the lovely falconer, on the other hand, never speaks but what she has something intelligent to say."

"Indeed?" Siegfried raised an eyebrow, and urged his horse into a pace slightly better than the lazy amble it currently wanted to take. "Did you speak of aught but falconry with the lady? I did not."

Benno nodded as his horse moved to keep up. "She has some Latin, though no Greek; she has not read the Roman philosophers, but is learned in other areas.

She has read the *Confessions* of Saint Augustine, for instance."

Siegfried made a face and flicked a fly away with his riding crop. "It would be difficult to make love talk out of Saint Augustine. Still, it is something. Do sound her out further for me, and see if she is *opposed* to reading the works of pagans, would you?"

"Surely—what is toward for the morning hunt?" Benno asked. "I can contrive to partner her, if you like."

"We hunt the fields with falcons—at which she will shine, as *you* will not," Siegfried teased, and Benno flushed. In that form of hunting alone, Benno did not excel; he had no rapport with the birds of prey, and after an unfortunate experience with a goshawk that left him with a scarred hand, no longer even tried to man them.

"Then I shall serve as her beater, and flush the game," he said staunchly. "So long as she does not ask me to take up her bird from its quarry."

"I doubt you could offer her a costly enough jewel to give that honor to you," Siegfried replied, as they came within ear shot of the camp. "She allows no one to handle her birds but herself."

The camp was abuzz with activity, as the hunt formed up. The queen was not taking part—no great surprise there, as she had no greater liking for falcons than Benno. About half of the nobles would remain in the camp with her, the other half going out into the field with Siegfried and the princesses.

Some of the nobles had brought their falconers and half their mews—far too many hawks, in Siegfried's opinion. They couldn't possibly put all of them up, and it would frustrate the ones left in their hoods to be taken out and not allowed to fly. He had already left orders with his falconer that he would hunt only with his gyrfalcon, and if he did not find prey worthy of her, he would work her with the lure to give her exercise. Of the princesses, four either had dainty little sparrowhawks on their gloves, or were followed by a servant with one. Honoria, as he had expected, had the gos she had praised so highly on her fist, her falconer following with a fine peregrine.

As Siegfried rode up, he signaled to his falconer, who brought him a glove and his gyr. As he took the bird up, he was pleased that it did not bate and embarrass him in front of Honoria, whose goshawk sat so quietly on her fist that it might have been stuffed.

"Well, my lady," he said, as the hunting party formed up for the ride out to the mown fields where birds would be foraging on the gleanings left by the reapers. "You only spoke the truth of your bird, I see."

"Better still, I can carry her unhooded, if I choose," Honoria replied demurely, astonishing him by gently stroking her hawk's breast feathers and even scratching it beneath its wings. Any goshawk *he* had ever owned would have rewarded such caresses by sinking a talon into his hand. "Valeria is a bird worth more than all the rest of my mews put together, both for steadiness, and hunting spirit. I would not carry her unhooded in company, however," she continued, with a subdued twinkle in her eyes. "It would not be fair to her to tempt her with all the savory little merlins and sparrowhawks about us."

Knowing that a goshawk would happily make a meal of any bird that was smaller, and a good many that were larger as well, Siegfried grinned. "I think we should let the other ladies fly at wood-pigeon and starling until they are tired, which should not take long, and then we true hunters can take the field."

As Honoria chuckled, Siegfried gave the signal to form up the hunting party, with the riders at the front, followed by the beaters and the falconers with cadges of birds. The cadges were unwieldy creations, a square perch of padded wood surrounding the falconer, carried by straps over the shoulders and holding at least one bird on each of the four sides. Siegfried never used a cadge unless he was hunting close by, for they were an infernal bother, in his opinion. He tried not to hunt with more than two birds at a time, but sometimes in duck season the peregrines tired before he did, and he had to fly several over the course of a day.

But he and his men had already planned this hunt well—the nobles who only wished to show how many birds they owned would stop at the first fields and remain there for the morning, leaving the farthest tracts to the real hunters. The gamekeepers had already scouted the best fields for pheasant and grouse, and those would go to Siegfried and those who actually flew their birds, rather than watching their falconer do the work.

"Sound the call!" Siegfried ordered, and the huntmaster wound his horn, signaling to the entire party that it was time to get into the field. The very sound of the hunting horn made Siegfried's spirits rise, and with a grin, he led the way out under a brilliant sun, and a sky so blue it could not presage anything but fine luck.

As Siegfried anticipated, the ladies tired in less than an hour, and retired from the field with game bags of rock-dove and wood-pigeon. Those that were not made into a pie for the high table tonight would go to feed the birds themselves. Siegfried and Honoria unhooded their birds and took advantage of their rank to claim the privilege of the first flights. When a fine hare was flushed by the beaters, Honoria cast her gos without blinking an eye or hesitating a moment. Hare wasn't a good quarry for a gyrfalcon, but it was perfect for a goshawk. Honoria urged her bird on with eager shouts of "Ho! Ho! Hawk!"

Honoria's gos performed every bit as well as she had claimed; the hare zigzagged and doubled back on itself in a vain effort to evade the pursuing talons, but it was all to no avail. When it doubled back, it found the gos waiting for just such an attempt. The hawk hit its quarry so hard that they both tumbled over and over together into the grass, ending with the hawk atop the twitching hare, clutching its quarry and panting in triumph. In a flash, Honoria was off her horse and walking slowly up to the bird, who allowed herself to be taken up off her downed quarry without even a token protest, tearing into the tidbit Honoria offered as readily as if the bit of meat had been its proper quarry all along.

Honoria's gos took two more hare before she declared the bird to be tired, and gave it a leg of the last catch as a reward. She hooded the gos and traded it with her falconer for her peregrine, and it was Siegfried's turn to hunt.

Falcons meant pheasant and grouse, for falcons were the best at hunting other birds, and the beaters and huntsmen were ready to supply that quarry as well. They sent in the dogs to find and point the game, allowing the falconers to get their birds into the air and in position for a stoop. Siegfried was first, of course; he put his gyr up into the sky to wait-on, soaring in tight circles above the field, then signaled to the beaters to flush the first pheasant.

The bird came up out of the bushes in a rush; the gyrfalcon plummeted out of the sky in the lightning dive that falconers called a stoop. The pheasant hardly got airborne before the falcon was on it, hitting it with a hard *crack,* binding to it with its long talons and going down into the grass with it. Siegfried wasn't about to let himself be shown up as a poor falconer by the princess, so he slid down off his horse and went into the brush after the bird. When he found her, she hadn't yet broken training by "breaking in," or trying to eat the catch herself; with a little mantling, she allowed herself to be coaxed onto the glove to devour her own tidbit reward, and one of the beaters got the pheasant for the game bag.

Although Honoria's peregrine wasn't the paragon of birds that her goshawk was, it performed well, and the two of them declared themselves satisfied when the bag reached three birds apiece. Then it was the turn of the others, who went out into the field eagerly, falcons on their fists. Honoria and Siegfried, however, had more care for their birds than to subject them to hours of clinging to the glove of a rider with no more hunting in the offing.

"My lady, is it your intention to return to the camp?" Siegfried asked politely.

"Immediately," she responded. "Valeria and Melisande will be wanting to bathe and sun. May I borrow the services of your falconer as a guide?"

"I will do better than that; we'll all escort you as far as the camp; it is the least we can do for such a fine huntress and her birds," the prince told her with satisfaction, and was amused to see a little high color in her cheeks at the compliment.

"I had rather be called a fine huntress than any other praise," she told him honestly, and blushed a little more as he bowed to her.

Well enough; she's still in the running, he decided. *I think she's not enamored of any man, nor like to be, but we have hunting in common, and I think she would not be inclined to object if I sought other beds than hers. There's much to be said for an arrangement of that sort.*

But before he made any assumptions, he'd have to quiz her on that himself; something told him that this princess would not be shocked by such direct speech.

He left her in the hands of the servants at the camp, and he and Benno continued down the road to the village. He'd already bespoken a bath at the inn, and tonight if the swans were actually at the lake as reported, he would make the first attempt at hunting them. He planned to hunt by night because unlike Honoria, *he* did not possess a goshawk tractable, intelligent, and strong enough to set at swans. That meant hunting with crossbows, which meant he would have to get in close to be certain of a clean kill in a place where he could retrieve his prize. To get that close, he would need darkness as cover.

That was all for tonight, however; this afternoon he intended to relax with his friends, and perhaps see which of the village girls wished to make a closer acquaintance of their prince.

"So, how many of the local flowers are ready for plucking, do you think?" Benno asked, echoing his thoughts, as they neared the inn, and saw Wolfgang waiting for them at the table under the trees.

"At least two or three, which leaves one for you, if that's what you were hinting at," Siegfried laughed. He dismounted and led his horse the remaining few feet, putting the reins and a few pfennigs into the hands of the waiting stable boy. Benno did the same, and they joined Wolfgang, who had already selected wine for them, and was waiting impatiently for their arrival to share it with him.

"By Jove, I cannot see why you waste so much time with nonsense you could perfectly well leave to your falconer," was Wolfgang's irritated greeting as they sat down at the table. "For that matter, if it's game for the pot you're after, I don't see why you just don't

have your servants shoot the damned birds for you
and have done with it."

Siegfried only laughed. "For the same reason that I
went fishing this morning, my friend," he mocked.
"You ask the same question every time Benno and I
go out hunting, and we give you the same answer.
Aren't you weary of it by now?"

"I keep hoping you'll come to your senses and see
what nonsense it all is," Wolfgang grumbled. Siegfried
slapped him on the back and performed the only action that would cheer him up; he uncorked the wine
and poured three tankards full, with Wolfgang's first.
Food came as the wine was being poured, and all three
of them fell to; Siegfried and Benno were ravenous
after their hunt, and Wolfgang could always be
counted on to share a plate of good sausages.

The older man cheered up immediately, and actually unbent enough to ask them intelligent questions
about the morning's hunt—though his questions centered on the princesses, not on the game.

"Well, if you want my opinion, it sounds as if you'd
get along well enough with that Honoria," Wolfgang
offered cautiously, cocking an eye at Siegfried to see
how his opinion would be received. "Assuming that's
what you want. For all I know, you'd rather have a
pretty little empty-headed ornament for the court."

"At the moment, if I were forced to make a choice,
it would probably be Princess Honoria," Siegfried admitted, just as cautiously. "I want to know more about
the others, though, before I make any judgments. I—"

Anything else he'd been about to add was interrupted by the call of a herald's trumpet near at hand.
Every head, including Siegfried's, swiveled toward the
source of the sound, as the trumpeter repeated the
salute.

"It would appear that you are about to have another opportunity," Benno said with a smile, as a dou-

ble line of heralds and pages marched into the village
square, carrying trumpets, standards and all the other
panoply the queen considered necessary to announce
her presence when away from the palace.

Behind the heralds came some of the courtiers, notably those who had not gone in for serious hunting
this morning. They still wore their elaborate and deco-
rative "hunting habits," which were no less encumbered
with trailing, dagged sleeves, bright embroideries, and
ribbons than their court dress. Veils and sleeves in
every color fluttered in the breeze, pennons and standards waved above their heads, all of it creating a
sensation among the villagers. Behind *them* came all
six of the guests of honor, each with the male escort
(an older, married noble) that her father had sent with
her to safeguard her virtue. Somehow they had all
found time to change, for each of them, even Honoria,
had on the ornamental "riding habits" they'd worn
yesterday, newly cleaned and brushed.

Last of all came Queen Clothilde, in a gown that
could not have been less suited for riding if it had
been made of gossamer. The hem and sleeves of this
tawny-gold velvet confection were so long they trailed
behind her for two feet or more, and the hat on her
head, ornamented with a cluster of plumes and ribbons, would have sailed away in the slightest breeze
if it had not been anchored to the gold-mesh net she
wore to confine her hair. A long, gold chain circled
her slim waist, the end of it ornamented with a chatelaine and hanging down an inch or so above the hem.
A heavier chain, the links made in the form of double
initial "C"s, circled her shoulders. She never rode anything but the most gentle and placid of palfreys, and even
then Siegfried shuddered every time she was boosted
into the saddle, firmly expecting the long-suffering horse
to bolt with fright or trip over one of the long, trailing
hems and break a leg.

However, since the queen never rode at a pace faster than a walk, none of this made a great deal of difference to her, only to the pages who had to manage her train, sleeves, and so forth. And to those who had to clean her gowns after she wore them.

"Siegfried!" the queen called out merrily, as the prince approached her to make his bow of courtesy. "The villagers have begged to dance for us! I said yes, of course; it will be charming, and our guests will enjoy it so much!"

Siegfried went to his knee and bowed—but was glad that his bent head hid his expression until he could school it into the mask of dutiful pleasure his mother expected.

Mother, dear, our guests will be bored silly, I expect, unless the sight of a peasant dance is such a foreign experience to them that the novelty alone will give them pleasure. When he rose and kissed his mother's hand, then bowed his head to each of the princesses, he didn't detect anything other than polite interest on their faces—with more politeness in the expression than interest.

Nevertheless, since he fully expected one or more of the dancing village girls to make her interest known to him during the course of the display, he was not altogether displeased with this interruption of his plans for the afternoon.

The innkeeper scurried to his side when he beckoned. "Wine for the ladies, if you please, and beer for the gentlemen." He knew the innkeeper didn't have enough good wine for all the nobles, and better a good beer than a poor wine.

Wine came for the queen and the rest of the women, and foaming tankards of beer brought smiles of relief to some of the male courtiers; the queen graciously accepted a goblet, and servants brought her a chair. Benches from the inn draped in fine cloth served as seats for the princesses, and the rest of the assemblage made do with whatever they could contrive, from an overturned bucket to a tree stump. Those who could not command a seat, stood, trying not to look bored or uncomfortable.

When they all settled in place, a row of excited red-cheeked, blond-haired country girls, dressed in their finest black wool skirts, brightly embroidered aprons, embroidered bodices, and linen chemises, each accompanied by a red-faced, nervous young man, trooped into the square. Two by two they made their bows, first to the queen, then to the princesses, then finally made their way around to the table where the prince and his friends sat to make a final curtsy.

The ever-efficient Arno had already whisked into the inn as soon as the queen made her announcement; by the time the first maiden and her swain made their obeisance to the prince, he was at Siegfried's elbow with a basket. The basket contained the usual "appropriate gifts" for such performers; Arno never allowed the prince to travel without a stock of such things. In this case, the gifts were bright bunches of ribbons such as the girls currently wore intertwined with their braids and the flowers in their hair and the boys had as braided trims on their sleeves, tied to a pretty little silver hawk-bell—a merlin-bell, about the size of the end of Siegfried's little finger, and suitable to be worn as an ornament. As each pair rose from their bow, Arno handed each partner a ribbon bunch, much to the delight of the girls and the interest of the boys.

There were no local musicians, for which Siegfried was thankful; at least they would not be subjected to the meanderings of some senile old codger who had his own notion of tempo and melody. The queen had the foresight to bring along a flute player from her own retinue, and of course Uwe was *always* present with his lute; after a moment of hurried discussion, dancers and musicians settled on a tune they all knew, and the dancers formed up in pairs.

Siegfried watched the capering with every appearance of interest, not altogether feigned. There were four little wenches with bright eyes who cast coy and inviting glances his way whenever the dance afforded the opportunity. One was rather plump for his taste, and one had a face altogether too much like his horse, but the other two were promising, and the looks they gave him had nothing whatsoever of innocence about them.

As for the dance itself, it was exactly what he had expected, a simple country dance with a great deal of rowdy skipping and leaping about, giving the girls a chance to display their calves, and the boys, their athletic prowess. It was neither as graceful nor as intricate as a court dance, but it was performed reasonably well, without any of the dancers falling over each other or their own feet.

A second dance followed, performed by all of the girls, involving garlands of flowers which had probably been made up for this express purpose this morning. At the end of the dance, the garlands were presented to the queen, who loved the scent of flowers and was pleased to receive them. Or rather, her pages received them, and arranged them neatly at her feet. This, of course, was the signal for the queen to present *her* little gifts, more ribbons, but strung with a pierced coin. These were all silver coins of doubtful value; clipped or shaved, or debased in other ways. The queen had all such small coins that came into the Royal Treasury singled out for use as gifts of this kind—for young peasants, who seldom saw a silver coin, such a prize would represent a fine bride price or a good portion of a dowry. The dancers exclaimed over this double portion of generosity, and gathered in little knots to admire their gifts. It wasn't long before many of the boys were trading their bells to the girls in exchange for coins; personally, Siegfried thought the girls got the better part of the bargain. The bells, at least, were full, unalloyed silver.

The three most skilled of the girls took up a position in the center of the square as the rest fell back and stilled their buzz of conversation. Uwe struck up a bright gigue as the three struck a playful pose, then showed the talent that made them the best dancers in the village. As two of the three were the ones Siegfried was most interested in, and they sprinkled their performance with more flirtatious gestures and glances, he enjoyed this quite a bit more than the previous dances.

"Beer all around!" Siegfried called, and serving wenches and boys brought trays full of mugs for the dancers in lieu of any more gifts. Only when the last drop was drained from the mugs did the dancers take their places for the final performance of the afternoon.

Somewhat to Siegfried's dismay, they brought out the inevitable Maypole, and skipped interminably about the object. Maypole dances were very popular with the participants, but invariably boring for spectators. Even the queen's smile began to show signs of strain, as she watched the dancers weaving their streamers with the expected number of mistakes and giggles, until the pole was covered and none of the dancers had more than a foot or two of streamer in his or her hands.

Seeing that they were finally breathless, Siegfried put an end to the display by calling for another round of beer all around, which the villagers were very glad to take advantage of. One or two of the princesses called individual girls over to examine the embroidery on their costumes—possibly with an eye to offering them a position in their households, if the work showed enough skill. The rest of the dancers settled themselves comfortably about, casting surreptitious glances at their rulers and masters.

All except for the sauciest of the girls, the one Siegfried thought was the likeliest of the lot. *She* had another plan to bring herself to the prince's attention, and set about putting it in motion.

Darting over to the table, she seized Wolfgang's hand; as she passed near Siegfried, he caught an unexpected whiff of flower scent from the roses she'd used in her flower crown.

Where did she find roses at this time of year? She must have grown them in a sheltered corner—then taken the time to strip the thorns from the stems, or her head would be perforated by now!

"Come along, gransire!" she said merrily, tossing her head. "I saw you a-tapping of your toes! I reck you can show the boys a thing or twain about dancing, eh?"

By this point Wolfgang had been doing his best to make up for Siegfried's relative abstinence, and had done more than his share of damage to the wine bottles. So when a pretty girl grabbed his hand and wanted him to give her a dancing lesson, he was just well-lubricated enough to think it was a grand notion.

Before Siegfried could interfere, Wolfgang was already on his feet, following the insistent tugging on his hand. "Now then, gransire," the girl said in a coaxing voice, "how do *they* dance, these great lords and ladies? You can show me, can't you?"

"Of course I can," Wolfgang replied, flushed with spirits, and not just the wine. "Here now, you—" He gestured imperiously at Uwe, while the courtiers hid their smiles behind their hands, and the queen watched with amusement. "Give me a bransle, if you please."

Feigning obedience and hiding a smirk, Uwe picked out a tune, and Wolfgang staggered through a few steps, completely unaware of how unsteady his steps were. "Give that a try, pretty one," he said in a kindly tone. "But don't feel too bad if you can't master the steps; they're devilish tricky."

"Ah—let me see, now—" She nodded at Uwe, who began the tune again. "Like this?"

She performed an exaggerated parody of Wolfgang, complete to the staggers, and now it was more than smiles that the courtiers were hiding behind their hands, it was laughter. Siegfried sighed, but decided against interfering. The queen clearly enjoyed seeing the old man make a fool of himself; if he interrupted, she was bound to be annoyed.

Heaven forgive me, but I don't want her annoyed right now; things have been so pleasant, I'd rather she didn't have an excuse to make them unpleasant. Wolfgang will just have to suffer for his indulgence.

Benno frowned and fidgeted in agitation. "Siegfried, we have to do something!" he whispered. "Wolfgang is making a fool of himself!"

"And the queen is in the mood for a fool right now," Siegfried whispered back. "Don't bother; she won't let Wolfgang get hurt physically, and his reputation isn't so clean that he's doing any damage to it."

And chances were, Wolfgang would remember this as his great conquest of the pretty little village wench, and not as the moment when he played the court buffoon. Queen Clothilde did not have a court jester; she didn't much care for buffoonery or the coarse jibes and mime that passed for humor with most professional fools. But she did take full advantage of moments when people were willing to make a mockery of themselves, and her courtiers were alert for opportunities to amuse her.

So when the girl managed to coax Wolfgang into another stumbling repetition of the dance, and parodied him yet again, Siegfried simply shook his head at Benno and signaled patience.

This time it was Wolfgang who insisted on doing the steps a third time, insisting that she still hadn't gotten them right. He tried to grasp her wrist to lead her through the right paces; she evaded him, much to the open hilarity of the rest of the court.

Then she capped her insolent performance by briskly skipping through the pavane three times perfectly, but at twice the speed that Wolfgang had managed—forcing Uwe to make his fingers fly to keep up with her. At the conclusion, she whirled Wolfgang around and around in a circle as if she were playing blind-man's bluff with him. Then when he was quite dizzy, she let him go, to stagger back to the table where Siegfried and Benno caught him and got him to sit down, out of breath and quite bewildered, while everyone else howled with laughter.

"By Jove!" the old man managed, holding his head with one hand and panting, completely out of breath. "By Jove! Bright little wench, isn't she! Lively! By Jove!"

Since it was obvious to both of them that Wolfgang hadn't the least notion what a fool he'd been made to look, Siegfried just sighed, and surreptitiously hid the last of the wine bottles, waving the innkeeper away when he would have brought more.

Now that the entertainment—both planned and impromptu—was at an end, the queen rose from her seat to signal to the rest that it was time to return to their camp. Siegfried left Benno in charge of Wolfgang, and hurried to her side when she beckoned to him.

"Are you certain I cannot persuade you to come back with us, my son?" she asked, with a little pout. "The ladies are all desirous to see more of you, not less."

"Not if I am to fulfill the request of the lady nearest my heart, my queen," he replied with hollow gallantry, more for the sake of the listening courtiers than for his mother's, since he was severely annoyed with her at this point. "You specifically requested swans for your feast, and I specifically pledged that you would have them."

The queen sighed; it was, or so it seemed to Siegfried, a rather theatrical sigh. She didn't get a chance to say anything, however, for Benno suddenly shouted, pointing to the sky behind Siegfried.

"There!" the young man cried, voice rising with excitement. "Look, Siegfried! Just as they promised us! Swans!"

Siegfried whirled, to see the welcome vee of white birds just above the trees, shining in the last light of the sun against the darkening eastern sky, heading in the direction of the lake. There was no doubt of their identity, either; they were too large and too white to be geese; white domestic geese were usually too fat to fly, anyway.

Siegfried forgot about playing the courtier to his mother, and joined Benno, the two of them shading their eyes against the westering sun and trying to count the flock. The queen gave a peculiar, silvery laugh, and called out to both of them.

"Ah, you are entirely too like your father, silly boy! Once the scent of the hunt was in his nostrils, he was not to be distracted by anything else! Come, friends." She gestured to the rest of the court and her guests. "Let us leave the young men to the sport of pursuit, and perhaps when they have had enough, we can persuade them to pursue other quarry!"

With the heralds leading the way, and the rest of the nobles trailing obediently behind, the queen made good her word.

"Are there plans for this hunt, Uwe?" the queen asked casually, as Uwe stationed himself beside her horse with his lute slung across his back and one hand on the palfrey's neck "to steady it." "I am a little worried; shots in the darkness are so dangerous."

She knew that Uwe could only reply obliquely here in public, and took cruel pleasure in forcing him to come up with unexceptional ways to speak of things they dared not say in plain speech. "With Benno at his side, Siegfried should come to no harm, my queen," he replied smoothly, thus telling her that there would be no "accident" tonight. "But there is a plan being carried out—so to speak. An ambush of sorts." He smiled, as if at a joke. "An ambush of love, or so one father hopes. Our friend the baron is arranging for Siegfried to meet his daughter tonight at the lake, in advance of the feast and fête. Presumably he believes that such a meeting will be more conducive to a romance than a public meeting surrounded by strangers."

"What, in the woods? Alone? Without a chaperone?" She allowed her eyebrows to rise a trifle. "With a man of Siegfried's reputation?"

Uwe shrugged. "No doubt the baron will be present. His daughter is much sheltered, and probably unsure in company."

He left unsaid things that they had already discussed; Clothilde's lips curved upward. Should Siegfried take advantage or insult the girl, the sorcerer might well take care of their problem altogether.

"It is very kind of him to give a shy girl the opportunity to meet with my son out of the reach of wagging tongues and spying eyes," she said lightly. "But that shows how much he dotes on her, I expect."

"She will certainly be able to display herself to advantage without having to trouble her little head about what might be said about her," Uwe agreed, his face a mask of genial good humor. "If she is as shy and fragile as you think, it were best Siegfried first sees her in a place where she feels more sure of herself."

"A jewel sparkles brighter in a setting of black velvet than in a cluster of other gems," Clothilde pointed out unnecessarily.

Uwe laughed. "My queen, soon it will be *you* who turns poet, leaving me without employment in your household!"

"Never, Uwe," she mock-assured him, leaning down from her seat and patting his shoulder as if he were a small child. "How could I ever manage without you?"

How indeed, she thought complacently, as she straightened up again and gazed up to road to the camp. *I would be hard-pressed to find a replacement half so willing to soil his hands for my sake. But it would be a very foolish thing for me to tell you that in earnest.*

It also occurred to her that once the problem of Siegfried was taken care of, she might not need him anymore.

Ah, indeed, she reflected, with another tiny smile. *And I will have no such difficulties in removing Uwe; I simply command, and it will be so. If Uwe begins to forget his place, perhaps I should do just that. It is so much easier to be rid of a mere minstrel than a prince.*

CHAPTER THIRTEEN

BY the time Siegfried and Benno organized their hunt, the sun was down and the stars had started to appear overhead, brilliant and clear in the cloudless sky. It was going to be a wonderful night, cool, but not cold, with hints of fallen leaves and smoke on the breeze. The moon would rise at three quarters, granting plenty of illumination to hunt by, particularly when one was hunting snow-white quarry. The hunting party trooped off onto one of the many regular paths that led through the forest to the lake: a half-dozen servants with torches, Benno and Siegfried, and no more. The prince and his friend were the only two who were armed. Perhaps if the swans proved too difficult to kill, he would bring along some of the expert huntsmen on his next attempt, but for the moment, he preferred things as they were. He wouldn't have taken the torch bearers if he hadn't needed extra help, but someone would have to carry out the dead birds, and swans were beastly heavy. The servants wouldn't stay waiting in the forest without the torches, fearful of ghosts and night-walking spirits.

Besides—there was the dark forest to get through before he made it to the lake; torch bearers would be welcome for that. He *could* have carried his own torch, but that would not have been "fitting," and his mother would surely have fussed when she learned about it.

The small procession set out, with waves and cheers from some of the villagers. They hadn't gotten more than a hundred feet into the forest before he was very glad of the presence of the torch bearers. The forest seemed to swallow them up; when he looked back along the path, he couldn't see the least sign of the village. The dense, tall trees cut off starlight—he got only the merest glimpses of an occasional star through the thick branches that met above the path. It was so dark beneath the trees on either side of the path that the darkness itself absorbed the torchlight. He had forgotten that most of the trees in these woods were black pines—tall, with thick, heavy branches and dense needles.

From the darkness came sounds—but not the dreaded howls of werewolves and tortured spirits that the torch bearers feared. Nothing more sinister emerged than the far-off call of an eagle-owl, vague rustlings in the dry leaves, the cracking of small twigs. Those were enough to make the servants' imaginations create uncanny things out there in the dark; their nervousness communicated itself to Siegfried and Benno, and when the death scream of a hare suddenly broke the silence, every man of them jumped, then laughed, shamefaced.

As if we haven't heard all these sounds around the palace, night after night! Of course, then we were all inside four stone walls.

Just when Siegfried had begun to wonder if they were on the wrong path, starlight showed through a break in the trees just ahead. They picked up their pace at Siegfried's signal, and when they reached the spot where the growth thinned, they found themselves right on the shore of the lake.

Siegfried took a moment to have a good look around. Trees grew right up to the edge of the low

cliff on which they stood; as he went to the edge and
looked down, he saw that they were just about three
feet above the surface. Before them stretched the
dark, still water, as reflective as a mirror; the stars
winked back at themselves from the quiet surface.
There was no sign of the swans, but from what the
prince had learned from the villagers, this place was
a veritable maze of little coves and long arms of water,
and the swans could be hidden in any of them.

"You men stay here," he directed the servants,
much to their obvious relief. "Benno will go to the
left, I will go to the right; that way we won't shoot
each other by accident."

The poor jest called up the polite laughter of the
servants, but put them a bit more at ease. They stuck
their torches into the earth at the lake's edge, then
went in search of deadfall for a fire, and prepared to
while away the time while Siegfried and his friend
hunted. Siegfried wasted no more thought on them;
hunt-fever was on him, and all he wanted was to have
his quarry in sight. Already, in his mind's eye, he centered his bow on a fine, fat bird. . . .

He worked his way around the edge of the lake,
noting as he did that the height of the shore above
the water varied from less than a foot to tall cliffs it
would be dangerous to dive from. Presuming one
could swim, of course; Siegfried couldn't, at least,
not well.

So I had better not fall into the water tonight, he
told himself wryly. *Or any other night, for that matter.*
The water looked icy, and it would be no joy to get
back to the fire in soaked, freezing clothing.

Sound carried well across the water, so he took care
with his own steps, making sure of his position before
putting his weight on his foot so that he didn't betray
himself with the crack of a breaking twig. At the very
edge of the shore, he didn't need to fight his way

through the bushes, but there was plenty of debris to pick his way over. It looked, oddly enough, as if very few people hunted or fished here.

Then again, the place has a reputation for being scant of birds and large game, and from all I can tell, it's a deserved reputation. I don't think I've ever been in a forest this silent. The villagers said that the lake had another kind of reputation—not an evil reputation, precisely, but known for evoking unease after dark, as if there were invisible spirits about. Nevertheless, according to the innkeeper, they fished it regularly and hunted it for rabbits, too, so it couldn't have frightened them much.

From across the water came the bark of a fox, then the call of a curlew. As he rounded a point, and saw one of the arms of the lake stretching darkly before him, the splash of a fish near at hand gave him another reassuring sign of ordinary life about him.

Here the cliff was easily twenty feet above the water, and he looked down at it for a moment. Black as the sky above, and not at all inviting, he wondered if daylight would improve it any. Or would it be like a few other tarns he had run across, whose chill, deep water, murky and impossible to see through, turned a sullen gray on a cloudy day, or a dark brown-green in sunlight? Such places seemed to discourage human visitors.

I need to find a beach, or some other spot low enough for the swans to come up out of the water, he reminded himself. *They'll have to come out to graze, to dry off, and probably to sleep.*

Since the ground sloped away toward the end of the arm, it seemed reasonable to think he might find such a low spot somewhere ahead of him. He hesitated, thinking about the possible terrain and vegetation ahead of him.

The ground is clearer under the trees, not as much

underbrush. It would be easier if I worked my way into the woods, so long as I keep the shoreline in sight. Now that the torch bearers weren't surrounding him, his eyes had grown accustomed to the darkness, and it was easier to see that what he had taken for a solid wall of trees was actually more of a forest of trunks. The trees grew so closely together that their lowest branches had long since perished, leaving the area immediately below their boughs fairly clear.

I'll see the swans if they're sleeping on the bank; I can't miss them in all this starlight. But they may not see me under the trees.

He fought his way through the bushes lining the shore with gritted teeth; moving slowly, carefully, and as quietly as a human being could. Only a rabbit would have been able to worm its way through the tangled mess without any noise, but at least he managed to get in under the trees with a minimum of noise and fewer stinging scratches than he had expected.

He took the time to pick bits of branch and leaf out of his clothing; if he had to freeze in place, it was bound to happen that one of those bits would start to itch unbearably. Then he steadied himself with several deep breaths of the pine-perfumed air, before continuing his wary stalking. His caution would have maddened anyone but another hunter with the same patience he had. He would move a few yards, pause to take in everything his senses told him, then move again, step by slow, careful step. His nose and feet told him that he walked on a soft floor of old pine needles; better and quieter footing than the dry leaves and twigs at the shoreline. His ears picked out fewer noises of wildlife than he would have expected, but there were *some;* none of the sounds he associated with deer, for instance, but the little scuttles and scurries that might mean rabbit or other small game. The darkness beneath the trees was not as absolute as he'd feared, though it was so thick he barely made out the trunks of the trees nearest him against the general gloom; they were a dark ashen gray against the black of the deeper forest, or black shadows against the star-light on the lake. By contrast, the shoreline to his left was *quite* bright; it was easy to stay just within the forest with that light to guide him.

He judged that he had gotten very close to the end of the arm of the lake, when regular splashing ahead of him made him freeze for a moment, as he took stock of the sounds.

There was quite a lot of it, and it didn't sound like fish; it sounded like a flock of waterfowl coming ashore.

Now he went into a true stalk, crouching to make his silhouette as small as possible, working his way closer to the splashing noises with such painful slow-ness that his muscles ached with the strain. He ignored the ache, all of his attention centered ahead as intently as if the only thing of importance in the world was the cause of those sounds before him.

When he reached the bushes, he crouched further; putting his crossbow aside, he parted the branches, twig by twig, leaf by leaf, until he had a spy-hole through to the other side.

Yes! His heart exulted at what he saw; here was the beach he had been searching for, and here were his swans, arrayed so perfectly for him that they might have been following his directions!

There must have been at least two dozen of them, perhaps more—most were out of the water and up on the bank, preening, shaking out their wings, or graz-ing. The rest, still in the water, waited patiently for their turn to jump up on the bank to join the rest of the flock.

He had never seen birds so huge or so magnificent before; they were so large that if another hunter had told him the size, he would have thought the man a liar. With wingspans of better than six feet, their heads would reach his chest with their necks still curved in a graceful arc.

They must weigh upwards of forty pounds! he thought in awe. *And I've never seen plumage so perfect!* They would make a fine show on the banquet table, roasted and redressed in their feathers—better, by far, than peacocks, which for all their pretty colors were often scrawny, tough, and not particularly savory.

With great care, he reached for his crossbow, and put a bolt into the slot by feel. It was already pulled and nocked, and he had two more bolts in his belt; he needed only to stand up, aim, and shoot, and he would have at least one in the bag. Given that he was between the swans and the water and that they'd have a hard time getting into the air under the trees, he could get off three shots, and bag three—then he might still get off more shots as they tried to escape, in the air or on the water. That would be chancy, though, without dogs to retrieve the bodies from the lake, and he really ought to be content with what he could take on the land tonight.

Or I can wait until they settle again, and try to bag three more; it might take all night, but I'll have six, and six birds of this size would be enough to make even Mother surprised and satisfied.

With that in his mind, he put the bow to his shoulder, ready to sight, and stood up.

The birds saw him at once, and did something he had never expected, action that took him so completely by surprise that he wondered for a wild moment if they *wished* for him to kill them.

They ran—ran away from him with their wings half-spread in panic, then huddled together under the protection of a huge tree trunk, cowering away from him, with their heads averted behind those half-spread wings. Stranger still, this all took place in complete, unearthly, silence.

He had expected the squeals and calls of aroused and frightened swans; he had figured they would try to flee past him to the water. He had never seen a flock of swans behave like *this*.

Suddenly, from behind and above him, came a strange, angry cry, like nothing he had ever heard in his life, a melding of a trumpet and a woman's scream of outrage. He didn't even have time to react to the sound—a white shape arrowed down out of the darkness and landed in front of the huddle of terrified swans.

A swan more magnificent than all the rest pivoted to face him, spreading her wings wide to shield the others, defying him to shoot with an angry hiss. She stretched out her neck, her black eyes wide in anger, completely without fear.

He had only just caught the glint of metal around her neck when the moon rose over the trees and touched the entire flock with its silver rays.

As one, the swans, including the defiant one, dropped as if they had all been struck by lightning. They shimmered, and a cloud of mist rose out of their prone bodies, rising in a strange, wraithlike column above each bird. His crossbow dropped as he gaped at them—and he rubbed his eyes as they suddenly blurred in a confusion of silver and white. He looked again, but his vision was no better—and he felt a curious twisting in his stomach that forced him to look away for a moment.

Then his eyes cleared, and he looked back—but the swans were gone.

In their place stood a huddle of frightened young women, with one dazzling beauty facing him defiantly, her eyes sparkling with anger.

He backed up a pace, crossing himself involuntarily,

and shook his head. *Blessed Jesu!* he thought numbly. *What witchery is this? Am I mad?*

He closed his eyes, then opened them—nothing had changed. He faced a single woman robed in a strange gown of white, her arms spread to protect the huddle of white-clad maidens behind her, head high, eyes blazing. On her head she wore a thin coronet, though in the moonlight he could not have told whether it was silver or gold. And now he saw what he had missed before—behind the white-clad girls was a row of terrified maids in *black* gowns.

No matter how logic told him that it was impossible, his own senses told him that there had been *magic* here. The swans had become women, as if he had stepped into a tale of Arthur and Merlin, Tristan and Isolde. As one part of his mind grappled with that, another, more whimsical, wondered about the girls in the black gowns; had there been black swans he had not seen in the darkness, hiding behind the white?

Whoever heard of black *swans?*

"Begone, varlet!" the first maiden cried out angrily. "Leave us in peace! We have harmed nothing of yours!"

He dropped the crossbow to the ground from fingers gone numb with shock, and rather than turning to go, took one slow step after another, until he stood face-to-face with the woman. If this was evil, some form of spirit unhallowed by the knowledge of God, he wanted to confront it. These women were on *his* land, and he would not leave his people to face them unwarned. If they were shape-changing witches, he would know that, too. The nearer he came, and the clearer he saw her, the more his mind stilled and his heart pounded.

Is this an angel? Surely nothing so enchanting could be evil . . . surely evil would be ugly, not as lovely as a vision of paradise.

But he had seen an angel—in his dreams, at least—and he thought she was too earthly to be angelic. The anger of his angel had been a tangible force, and though there was anger in this maiden's enormous dark eyes, it was not *that* powerful. Further, it was swiftly fading, transmuting into puzzlement, and surely an angel would not be puzzled by him.

Her fragile loveliness made him want to go down on his knees to her, but it did not inspire the awe of the divine he had felt even in his dreams. She had none of the angel's strength, either. Whatever she was, it was mortal.

He came within touching distance, and looked down at her. "Who are you?" He spoke the words before he took thought, saying the first thing that came into his mind.

Her anger rekindled at his presumption. "Who are *you?*" she countered, raising her head with pride, as if she and not he were the ruler here. "How dare you threaten us with weapons? How dare you come upon us like a thief in the night? How dare you approach us without invitation?"

Not the words of a witch or an evil spirit, either. Surely such would have answered his question with destruction for his insolence or an immediate attempt to beguile him.

He answered the pride with a humility he had never felt before, and dropped to one knee, free hand on his breast, head bowed for a moment.

Then he looked up, so that she could see *his* expression. "I am Prince Siegfried, my lady," he said with quiet pride of his own. "These lands are ruled by my mother, Queen Clothilde. I humbly beg your pardon if I have affrighted you and your maidens. But you see, I came here as an honest hunter, and but moments ago, you all appeared to be, as it were, fair game. Though had I known that the game was so fair,

I would never have raised a bow against you, unless it were Cupid's and not mine." He raised his head a little more, and smiled winningly up at her, with an expression that had won forgiveness from women many times before. He invited her to share the jest, hoped she would, and prayed that this was not all some strange vision that would fade when he blinked, leaving him alone in a moonlit glade. His heart still pounded so loudly that he was certain she could hear it, and he felt a strange giddiness, a lightness in his heart and a sense of intoxication stronger than any wine.

It was her turn to step back an involuntary pace when he gave her his name, and another, hand going to her throat, when he rose.

"I am—Odette—" she faltered, staring at him, as her face alternately flushed and paled, going from pink to white and back again.

Behind her, as they stared at each other, the maidens slowly straightened and stood, then when he showed no signs of attention toward anything but their would-be protector, silently slipped away until only Odette was left in the clearing with him.

He fought the unwonted paralysis of his mind and speech as he continued to look down at her, filling his mind with her face so that if she vanished in the next moment he would always have that much to carry inside him. In the moonlight it was not possible to tell the true color of her eyes, though he guessed they were blue, so wide were her pupils; some nameless, lambent shade, they held mysteries he had not dreamed of until this moment. Her hair must have been spun of moonlight itself, so silken silver it was, and her brow was encircled by that coronet—which meant she had some high rank, surely. A face sculpted of alabaster by master artist could not have been wrought with purer lines, and the full, trembling lips betrayed the fear she was determined not to display.

He could not think, but his body acted for him. He took her unresisting, delicate hand and went once again to his knee, dropping a kiss so gentle on the velvet-skinned back of it that it would not have bruised a rose petal. The cool hand continued to tremble in his, but she did not withdraw it.

"I am very sorry that I frightened you, Odette," he said, putting as much earnest feeling into his words as he could, hoping she would hear it. "I would not have done so for the world."

He let her hand go at her slight tug of resistance, and stood up again, full of earnest dignity of his own. "Now, since I am disturbing you and your maidens, I ask your leave to go."

"No!" she cried sharply, startling him and herself as well. Her hand flew to her lips, then she managed a faint, shy smile. "Please—do not go. These are your lands, then? It is we who trespass . . . and we who should be gone from here since we did not ask your leave to be here."

"No longer," he replied firmly. "You might not have come here at an invitation, but now you are my guests; I will vouchsafe as much to anyone who should challenge you. Stay or go as you will—but I hope you will stay."

Once again her cheeks flushed, then paled, and she looked down at her hands, nervously clasped to hide their trembling. "If you would allow us to remain— you are too gracious."

"Not gracious enough," he told her, feeling bolder by the moment. "But I would like to hear who my guests are, and why they have come. May I beg the honor of your company for an hour?"

She looked up, and he read his answer in her eyes.

Odile was as contented as she had ever been; curled
in a little nook she'd formed to fit the curve of her
body in the tree trunk, a magic light above her head
to illuminate the pages of her book. Here and now,
she felt free to devote her time to herself alone; she'd
seen to the care of the flock, and until the mysterious
suitor arrived, she need not waste her time spying on
Odette. If this situation continued, *she* would be perfectly, if selfishly, content.

"Odile!" Sofie, one of the little swans, came running
into the tree-shelter in a high state of excitement.
"Odile! He's here! He almost shot us, but Odette got
between, and he's with her now!"

Odile looked up from her book, and for a moment
her thoughts were a muddle before she managed to
sort out the sense of what she'd been studying from
the excited girl's words. She leaped to her feet in
alarm, the book tumbling unheeded to the ground,
as one word penetrated her confusion. "Who's here?
What's all this about shooting?"

"Prince Siegfried!" Sofie forgot every bit of dignity
she had ever acquired and squealed like any peasant
wench, bouncing on her toes and clapping her hands
in excitement. "Prince Siegfried is here! He came
hunting while we were still swans and he almost shot
us, but Odette flew down and protected us until the
moon came up, and now he's with her!"

Odile had no difficulty recalling her father's orders.
Watch her, he said. "He is, is he? Where are they
now?"

"The low spot, where we all get out, by the big oak.
Do you think—?"

Odile interrupted her, but tried to be as gentle

about it as possible, for the child couldn't help the fact that she had more hair than wit. "I don't think anything, since I haven't seen him. I don't even know if this is the prince. He could be some nobody hoping to trick a poor girl into— Oh, never mind. Just go on about your business, and leave them to me. Don't bother them! If he is who he says he is, we mustn't interfere with Odette. If he isn't—" She smiled grimly, secure in the new knowledge she'd been gathering of more powerful, darker sorceries. "I will deal with him myself."

She slipped past Sofie and out into the moonlight, gathering it about her in one of the simplest spells of invisibility, one that confused the eye into seeing only moving shadows that looked nothing like a human form. Thus protected, she trod her way carefully to the grassy bank where the swans usually came ashore, taking care not to disturb a single twig.

She realized as soon as she got within earshot of the two that she needn't have bothered with stealth; she could have ridden a battle charger through the woods right up to them and they'd never have noticed her until the horse trampled them.

She also knew as soon as she saw the man's carelessly discarded weapon that he was what he claimed to be; perhaps she was sheltered from the great world, but she knew fine and costly materials and workmanship when she saw them. Only a prince could have afforded hunting gear of glove-tanned deerskin, finely dyed and worked with silk embroidery, with a silk shirt beneath a jerkin fitted closely to his body. Only a prince would have a silver-ornamented crossbow, or be so careless about dropping it in dew-damp grass, because only a prince would be followed about by people whose sole purpose in life was to pick up after him.

But oh, they made a handsome pair—that was not

to be denied, and for a moment Odile felt a pang of
jealousy as she saw the expression on Siegfried's face,
the look in his eyes. No man would ever bend such a
look to her—not her, the pale, poor shadow to
Odette's delicate, luminous beauty—

Don't be ridiculous, she scolded herself immediately, as she slipped into the shelter of a tree trunk,
completely unnoticed by either of the others. *What do
you want with a stupid prince? Magic is worth a hundred princes—if you learn enough, you can even make
a suitor out of a mouse or a bird if you want!*

Besides, this was to be Odette's chance for escape
from the punishment von Rothbart had inflicted on
her for so long. Nothing must spoil that chance!

*If she and the others escape, then Father will no
longer have their care; he can spend more time teaching me.*

The surge of jealousy hadn't a chance against *that*
promise; she turned her attention to the low-voiced
conversation on the other side of the tree trunk.

" . . . I cannot tell you," Odette was saying uneasily.

"Cannot, or *will* not?" Siegfried asked.

Odette shook her head. "Please—not now. Do not
press me further," she begged. "Later, perhaps, I can
tell you more. When I know enough—"

"To trust me?" As Odette bowed her head in embarrassment, he touched her hand. "Don't look
away—I understand perfectly. After all, a moment ago
I was pointing a crossbow at you, so you have no
reason to trust me!"

At his careless-sounding chuckle, Odette looked up,
and smiled weakly.

"Let us pretend we are at some ball, some fête,
and have met by chance," he continued. "We are two
strangers, but I have seen you from across the room,
and I am—"

"Oh please," she cried, falling in with the pretense.

"Don't, I pray you, say that you are dazzled by my beauty!"

"Too much of a commonplace? Let me say, then, my lady, that I am intrigued." He backed up a pace, then bowed formally, from the waist. "Good evening, my lady. Allow me to present myself."

Odette smiled, showing a dimple that Odile had not even known was there. She made a brief curtsy. "You do me great honor, Your Highness. How may I serve you?"

"Well, since I do not seem to have brought any minstrels with me—" He pretended to examine his pockets, then his game bag, while Odile stifled a chuckle and Odette openly laughed with delight, "—I think we should stroll beside the lake, and discuss— the weather, perhaps?"

"Perhaps. Or perhaps I shall frighten you back to simpler maidens by discussing the philosophy of the Greeks?" Now she tilted her head and gazed at him with challenge in her eyes.

"That, I promise you, would only encourage me to reply with the poetry of the ancient Romans," he retorted, "which is far better a discussion topic by moonlight than Plato and Socrates."

You have an interesting way of trying to ensnare this man, Odette, thought Odile with amusement. *Anyone else would be trying to seduce him, not challenge him. Or is that the point? Perhaps you are being cleverer than I thought; perhaps so many women have tried to seduce him that a challenge is more exciting to him.*

Oddly, though, Odette didn't act as if she had thought any of this through; she acted as if every word she spoke was spontaneous. Perhaps it was neither craft nor cleverness, but pure instinct that guided her. Odile had come to know her fairly well over the past few weeks, and she thought as she watched the changing emotions flitting over Odette's face that all of this was as much a surprise to the Swan Queen as it was to Siegfried. Odette was not very good at covering what she thought and felt with anything but a stony mask; the mask had been put aside, if Odile's past experience was anything to go by.

And if my past experience is anything to judge by— Odette is as entranced as the prince.

The two moved off slowly, walking side-by-side, but without touching, as any well-bred strangers who had just met. Odile followed, flitting from shadow to shadow, but she might just as well have followed them openly for all the attention they paid to their surroundings.

For quite some time they spoke of ancient poets, of Virgil mostly; poetry held very little interest for Odile, and she ignored the words in favor of the unspoken messages passing between the two. Words were only weaving a net binding the two of them closer together. They could have been talking about the weather, or the hunting season, or the price of cattle; it wouldn't have mattered.

"Tell me about this place, your kingdom," Odette urged, when they seemed to have run out of complimentary things to say about Latin poetry. "This lake—"

He gave her a curious glance, puzzled; perhaps he wondered why she didn't already know, but he was perfectly willing to tell her whatever she wanted to hear. "This lake is called the Lake of the Black Pines," he began, leaning up against a tree trunk without taking his eyes off Odette's face. "It lies in the far northeast corner of our land; the village nearby is the only habitation for miles 'round about, and the rest is wilderness. It is said that there was once a stone tower here, used as a hunting lodge by some long-gone ancestor, but the hunting hereabouts is not good enough to keep it up, and it fell into disrepair so long ago that I have never heard of anyone using it. I don't even know where it lies."

Hmm. Unless I am greatly mistaken, that would be where Father has taken up his abode, Odile decided. *And I think, Prince Siegfried, that you would probably be very surprised to see what it looks like if he has.* She amused herself with a brief vision of Siegfried's face if he came upon the tower, repaired, furnished in all the luxury von Rothbart demanded, and tended by the invisible servants.

"I have not seen your tower, but I have not explored the lakeshore to any extent," Odette replied. "It might be hidden."

"So it might," Siegfried agreed. "My father was a great hunter, and his father before him; the men of my line all seem to share that trait, so I suppose it shouldn't surprise anyone that the game is so thin near where a former hunting lodge is. I only come here because—"

Here he stopped, and looked profoundly embarrassed.

"Because you had heard there were swans here?" Odette prompted. He nodded.

"My birthday is soon, and there is to be a great feast on the occasion," he replied awkwardly. "My Lady Mother specifically requested swans for the feast."

"Well, *I* would rather you disobliged her," Odette told him impishly—another expression that Odile had never seen her show before. Really, the Swan Queen was displaying facets tonight that Odile had never suspected under that somber exterior!

Siegfried looked away for the first time, at a loss for words—then with an effort that was visible to Odile, though not to Odette, he returned to the pretense that they were two newly met strangers with no shadow of magic about either of them. "The streams here are known for trout, and I expect that since very few of my ancestors are notable fishermen, the lake is as rich with fish life as the forest is barren of large game. At any rate, the villagers seem to be well provided for in that area."

"You would not have come here alone, certainly?" Odette tilted her head to the side, in an unconscious, but very birdlike, pose.

"No—my friend Benno hunts the other side of the lake, and we brought servants. We have a large hunting party, actually. The queen brought many of the guests to amuse themselves, and I brought Benno and my tutor Wolfgang."

Odette brightened, seizing on a "safe" subject. "Your tutor! Then he must be the one who taught you so much of philosophy and poetry!"

Gladly Siegfried took his cue from her. "Yes—and Wolfgang has been as much a friend as a tutor for many years now. In fact, we are working on a translation together."

Once again, Odile ignored the topic of discussion in favor of the subtle expressions and the language of their movements.

But just as things were getting truly interesting, the two were interrupted by the fierce call of an eagle-owl somewhere nearby.

Odette started, and jumped away from Siegfried as if he had suddenly come out in plague spots. *That isn't Father, silly girl!* Odile thought, half annoyed, half amused. *Father would never announce his presence that way!*

But Odette wasn't taking any chances. "I must go, *now*," she said, edging farther away. "And so must you."

"But wait—surely I can see you again!" Siegfried called plaintively, sounding exactly like someone in a tale.

Odette turned back, her face still and white. "Tomorrow evening," she said, as if the words had been pulled out of her all unwillingly. "Here. After moonrise."

With that, she fled; after a moment more of lingering, Siegfried went away as well, leaving Odile to return to the shelter, feeling as if she had been pulled away from a story before it had rightly begun.

Chapter Fourteen

SIEGFRIED fought down his impulse to run after the strange maiden who'd called herself Odette, for something deep inside warned him that he would jeopardize any rapport he had thus far built with her if he did. Running after her would only frighten her, and make her sure she could not trust him.

Blessed Jesu! he thought, straining his eyes to watch her as she flew over the grass, with steps so light she barely touched the ground. *I have never seen anything like her! What is she?*

She hadn't forbidden him to watch her, and he followed her longingly with his eyes until she disappeared into the dark shadows of the forest. It seemed to him that a faint perfume, too faint to be identified as anything but a hint of sweetness, drifted after her on the light breeze.

Only then did he turn and retrace his steps, making his way back to the place where the servants waited, wandering along the shoreline with no attempt to conceal his presence from the wildlife. Sticks broke beneath his feet, rocks skittered away from him.

I am enchanted, in every sense. I have never seen a female, woman or girl, so utterly incredible. Why did she suddenly run away? For no reason that *he* could see, she had gone from warily friendly to ready to flee. Something had frightened her—no, *terrified* her.

Something also turned her and all those other girls into swans, too. Could it be the same thing that frightened her from me? Could she have been trying to protect me from it? Was that why she forbade me to follow?

Who, and what, was she? The question spun around and around in his thoughts, making him dizzy. Her sad, solemn eyes seemed to hang before him in the darkness, calling up an ache inside him, a desperate need to turn the sadness to a smile. With the moon high above his right shoulder, casting brilliant light to show him the way, his progress unimpeded by the need to skulk through the underbrush, he saw the light of the servants' fire sending a long streak of reflected brilliance lancing across the water long before he expected to. He hadn't even begun to digest the things that had happened to him in the last hour; he wasn't ready to face others yet. He shivered in the chill air, and felt the grip of nausea on his throat.

But what am I going to do in the meantime if I don't return to the servants' camp? Sit down here and dangle my feet in the water? He'd asked himself the question facetiously, but he then realized there could be unseen peril here. If the lake played host to swans who turned into women, what else might lurk *beneath* its waters? Perhaps it was a glimpse of something rising for a moment above the surface that had affrighted the maiden. It might not be a good idea to stand in one place all alone in the dark beside this lake.

He did pause with one hand against the rough bark of a tree to prepare himself to face the servants and their curiosity, although his thoughts felt as unsteady as Wolfgang after a long night of drinking. Taking deep breaths of the cooling air, he stared out at the still water, and decided exactly what he was going to tell the servants. What he told Benno, when his friend appeared, would be very different. In fact, now he wanted very badly to see Benno, to hear what Benno might think.

He kept his mind clear enough to find the easiest way back to the servants, taking the line through the trees rather than pushing his way through the underbrush. The moon was still low enough to send brilliant shafts through the trees deep into the heart of the forest, so that he didn't find himself blundering into trunks.

Soon enough the leaping flames ahead of him rivaled the moonlight, and he knew he would have to face a circle of inquisitive servants. He set a disappointed expression on his face, and strode into the circle of firelight. The servants jumped to their collective feet, but he waved them back to their seats, and chose a spot on a fallen tree-trunk for himself.

"Nothing," he said with feigned disgust. "I didn't see a thing, and I gave up. Wherever the swans are, they've hidden themselves well, or perhaps they flew off as we were making our own way here."

"There might be islands," one of the servants offered respectfully, waving vaguely at the dark expanse of water. "They might be on an island."

"It's true enough that I couldn't find a spot where a water bird could come ashore for as long as I walked." Siegfried hoped that would prevent the ever-helpful servants from dashing out in an attempt to locate the birds for their master. "I turned back when I came to a bramble patch too thick to cut through; no point in trying to find a way around it in the dark."

"No, sire," the same servant said respectfully. "If my prince will forgive my speaking out of turn, it's as dark as the inside of a pocket in these woods; you could be hunted by an entire pack of wolves and never know it until it was too late."

"A bit hard to fire off arrows in the dark and expect to hit anything, Peter," another added laconically as an aside to his fellow. "You couldn't hardly defend yourself, no matter how good you was. I bet there's bears there, and wolves, too."

Siegfried nodded absently and stared into the fire, bent over with his elbows resting on his knees and his hands loosely clasped before him. He hoped he was giving a good imitation of disappointment, the kind that put him in a mood where he really didn't want anyone chattering at him.

Seeing that he didn't need or want any entertainment from them, the servants lapsed back into their own gossip, quiet mutters which didn't interest Siegfried nearly as much as the lovely creature now monopolizing his thoughts.

Why did she come here? Where is she from? What is she? How could a swan suddenly turn into a maiden except by magic? But what kind of magic would do such a thing, and why? Who could the magician be?

He took refuge in his scant store of magic tales gleaned from the songs of minstrels and the ancient Greek and Roman manuscripts he shared with Wolfgang. *What do I know about swans who turn into women?*

The only similar tale he could think of was the myth of Zeus and Leda—but it was Zeus who had turned into the swan, not the maiden. It didn't seem to Siegfried that Odette could be a pagan goddess. *Why would a goddess be frightened of anything? And she was frightened. Even when goddesses were caught by their spouses doing something wrong, they were never afraid—*

She'd once crossed herself, too, which meant she was a Christian, which made it unlikely that she was a pagan goddess.

Given that—then either *she* was an enchantress, like

Circe, who transformed herself, or she was in the grip of some dreadful enchantment herself. What reason could she possibly have for turning herself into a swan, of all things? For that matter, why would she turn an entire flock of other girls into swans? Swans made fine targets for hunters; it would be a stupidly risky choice of form, if it had been assumed by choice.

He moved so that his feet were closer to the fire; it was getting much colder now that the sun was well down.

If Odette herself was the magician, why would she have waited so long to transform when threatened? A heartbeat later, and he would surely have killed one of the swans, if not her.

She must be under the enchantment herself. She wouldn't have taken the risk of being a bird of quarry if she'd had any choice.

What had she told him about herself? Her name, which he had not recognized; she had given him no title, though the rest of her flock treated her with the deference due a queen. She had said that the flock had arrived at the lake no more than a few days ago. Everything else had been questions of her own, which he had been dazzled enough to answer. Perhaps that had been foolish, but he couldn't help himself, and even now he did not regret a single answer.

He looked about him as the servants forgot his presence and raised their voices to a normal conversational level. They only disturbed him for a moment, then he went back to his ruminations.

She's nobly born; she can't be anything else. The manners, the mannerisms, are too ingrained for her to have merely been tutored in them. No peasant, no merchant, would behave as she did. She addressed him by the correct title; she accorded him the precisely correct amount of deference due to the heir of one kingdom from a visiting prince. Such things were subtle; second nature to one born royal, difficult to master for one who was not.

He shifted on his log; it wasn't the most comfortable seat he'd ever had.

She had acted, once she discovered who he was, with relief—and that was odd, now that he came to think of it. Why would that be? Had she been expecting him, or someone like him, to appear at the lake? Had she been told about him? By whom?

That implied things about her that he didn't want to consider. A latter-day Circe *could* have transformed herself, and yet could be frightened of a greater power than herself. A witch—as he had thought the poor gypsy girl was—

He shoved the unwelcome thought away. *She can't be trying to trick or trap me, no matter how arcane her origins. I can't believe that . . . she's too sweet, too gentle.*

But then there was that folk tale—"The Woman Without a Shadow"—where a perfectly sweet and innocent-seeming woman had sold her soul to the Devil, and being desperate to get it back, lured young men into pledging *their* souls to the arch-fiend for love of her. That was why she had not had a shadow; the lack of one betrayed that she had no soul. Had Odette possessed a shadow? He couldn't remember, and a shiver went up his back, a chill passing over him that the warmth from the fire couldn't counter.

No, that can't be right—why would the Devil turn her into a bird? That doesn't make any sense. No, she's as innocent as she is beautiful.

But what if a sorceress had plans to usurp a throne—wouldn't she pretend to be an innocent victim, to lure her prey into her trap?

Oh that was ridiculous, what was there to covet about *his* land? *Why would she pick this place? No, that can't be right at all; she didn't seem to know any-*

thing about my kingdom, and surely a sorceress with plans for a kingdom of her own would have studied the place she planned to take!

But what if a greater magician intended to use her—

What greater magician? I've never heard anything about such a sorcerer, and anyway, why wouldn't he just use magic directly against us and take the throne quickly and easily? He couldn't imagine a plot so convoluted; it made no sense to expend that much time and effort on something that could be accomplished in a straightforward manner.

Granted, she is beautiful enough to put anyone off his guard. . . .

He lapsed into rapt contemplation of that beauty as he stared at the flickering flames. Even given that moonlight was particularly flattering, he couldn't recall another woman he had ever seen who was quite so near to perfection as Odette. Her silver hair had gleamed like the finest silk in the moonbeams; her eyes, large and soft as any doe's, held an immensity of sorrows and mysteries. A clear, broad brow promised intelligence, and her conversation fulfilled that promise. Soft lips, full and tender, had tempted him to steal a hundred kisses.

She may not be the trap, a nasty little voice warned him, *But what if she is the bait?*

He wanted to ignore the ignoble voice, but grudgingly admitted to himself that the cautious thought might provide the answer to all of those unanswered questions.

Why she was afraid, for one thing—why she had insisted that he leave, for another. If someone out there intended to catch a prince, he would want to bait his trap temptingly, and make sure that he had firm control over the bait. What firmer control could there be than control over the very form his bait took?

Now he felt his neck grow warm with embarrassment; could he have been so foolish as to walk straight into such a trap?

But if there is such a sorcerer, he cannot control how the bait feels about her role. If Odette had been in accord with this postulated enemy, she would have painted him a tragic tale of captivity and begged him to save her from it. Wouldn't she?

He tried to remember the nuances of her expression, and could only recall the beauty of her eyes, of her slim, delicate hands, of the slender body imperfectly concealed by her white, silk gown.

He was lost in these reflections when Benno returned, preceded by the sound of cracking brush and kicked-up leaves, striding through the brush with no more attempt to hide himself than Siegfried.

"Nothing and nothing," he cried, disappointment clear in his voice. "Not a swan, not a goose, not even a feather. I did find at least one source of the lake, though—that was why I turned back. It's fed by a river, and I didn't fancy trying to cross it afoot and in the dark."

"I had no better luck than you," the prince replied, but with a signal of hand and eyebrow to tell his friend that there was more, much more to it than he was willing to speak of before the servants.

Benno gave a quick nod, then suggested that they all return to the inn, since there was no luck out here for them on this night.

The servants—who would be returning to camp rather than the inn, but could expect several rounds of drink from their prince by way of reward for their service—gathered up their extinguished torches and thrust them into the fire without waiting to hear what Siegfried said. But Siegfried was quite ready to leave; with his mind unsettled and his heart fluttering, he wanted to talk with his oldest and most trusted friend in private. He didn't trust himself to make any conclusions or decisions at this point.

It took longer than he liked to walk back to the village; he wanted very badly to spill out his heart to Benno, and from the sidelong glances that Benno cast at *him*, curiosity was eating his friend alive. The servants kept their pace to a swift walk just short of a lope, no doubt thinking of the good beer waiting for them in the inn, so he had nothing to complain of there, at least.

When the lights of the village appeared ahead of them, he stretched his legs a bit farther, forcing the servants to do the same; he heard a bit of muttering, but knew that they wouldn't dare to complain aloud. If they wondered why he was so anxious to get back himself, they would probably consider his reputation and the way that the village girls flirted with him, and make up an answer to suit themselves.

He was first through the door of the inn, for the servants paused to douse their torches in a bucket of water placed to one side of the door for that purpose. Warmth and the pleasant scent of roasted meat met him as he opened the door and crossed the threshold.

As always in a small tavern, every head turned to see who it was who had just entered. "Keeper!" he called. "We've had a frustrating night of it—beer and sausage for my men, and wine for me and my friends! And bring me something to eat; use your best judgment!"

He scarcely paused to acknowledge the bows of the patrons, hurrying up the stairs to his room, with Benno hot on his heels. As he'd expected, Wolfgang was already asleep in his own little cubby, overcome by his own overindulgence. Arno started up as he entered his chambers, but Siegfried waved him off.

"Go fetch the wine and food from the innkeeper, then go to bed," Siegfried ordered. "I can manage for myself for once."

"Sire." Arno paused long enough for a perfunctory bow, and took himself off. Siegfried dropped into a chair at the fireside table, and Benno did the same, but leaned forward over his crossed arms, looking at him with eyes wild with excitement.

"Something happened out there!" he half whispered. "Something that has *you* in a state! You have to tell me what it was, or I'm going to go mad!"

Siegfried nodded, but put his finger to his lips. "Not now; as soon as we're private," he cautioned, then quickly switched the topic to the unsuccessful hunt, declaring out loud as Arno led a trio of inn servants up the stairs that he had never seen a lake so barren of game or the least signs of game.

Arno knew his master's moods and knew when it was wise to leave him alone. Without a word to Siegfried, he quickly and efficiently directed the serving girls in the placement of dishes and tankards, then shooed them out without allowing them so much as a flirtatious glance, following them and closing the door behind him.

Siegfried took his time in cutting slices of chicken he didn't want and pouring wine that he did. Benno looked ready to burst, but he took his time in drinking down a full goblet and pouring another before he began.

"I found the swans," he said abruptly.

"And?" Benno's voice rose in pitch with indignation. "You didn't chase everyone else out just to tell me that you found the swans and missed your shots or discovered you couldn't shoot them!"

"Well—partly. I found them, and I couldn't shoot them—because they weren't *just* swans." Choosing his words with care, he told Benno everything that had transpired; it wasn't difficult, for every moment was etched into his memory so clearly that he doubted he could ever forget it. Benno forgot his meal, forgot his wine, forgot everything as he leaned over the table to fix Siegfried with an unwavering gaze. Siegfried found the look in his eyes a bit disquieting, however, since there was as much alarm as excitement in it.

When he finished, he downed another goblet of wine and poured himself a third, feeling very much in need of it. Benno didn't touch his and finally leaned back and toyed with the chicken on his plate, frowning.

"I don't like it, Siegfried," he said, his frown deepening. "I don't like it at all. This smacks of witchcraft, black magic—you shouldn't go back there tomorrow night."

"I know it's dangerous—" Siegfried began dismissively. Benno interrupted. "It isn't the danger to your *body* I'm worried about, it's the danger to your soul!" he countered. "What possible good could this do for you? If you just want a girl to bed, there's plenty right here in the village; why go chasing after some fey half-swan half-woman? There's something very nasty about all this, and I don't trust any of it, not one bit!"

Siegfried laughed incredulously, for this was not what he had expected to hear from Benno. "That's a fine statement, coming from *you!* Have you suddenly turned priest on me, to be so concerned about my soul? I thought *you* were the one who always wanted to see magic at work with your own eyes!"

But Benno was not to be deterred by mockery. He leaned forward over the table, his meal forgotten again. "Siegfried, I'm serious. I don't trust any of this. It's too much like a trap, and the only thing I can think of is that somebody wants your soul or worse, if that's possible." He shook his head vigorously as Siegfried started to laugh. "Look here, friend, I'm trying to think in a responsible way! This could be an attempt on your land! What if some enemy wants to take you captive, or even kill you? What if this is a plot to keep you from choosing a bride? What if—"

"What if, what if, what if!" Siegfried exclaimed, all of his own concerns vanishing in a sullen anger at his best friend's apparent betrayal. Why was Benno the doubter all of a sudden? What was Benno risking? Nothing! This was Siegfried's adventure to pursue or not, and Benno's cautions only made him more determined to meet Odette tomorrow night. "What if the sky falls? What if I were to die in my sleep? If anyone wanted to interfere with me, they've chosen an awfully roundabout way of getting to me—anyone able to turn girls into swans could just as easily turn *me* into a wild boar when we're out hunting!"

"Well, what if that's what they plan?" Benno asked stubbornly. "Witches need your hair or something in order to cast a spell on you, and maybe this swan-maiden is supposed to snatch some of your hair for just that purpose!"

"Then I'll take my chances," the prince replied, beginning to feel more exasperated than angry. So Benno was worried about him and wanted to wet-nurse him; fine, maybe all this business of picking a bride had begun to wear on both of them. "Come, be of some help, Benno! Have *you* ever heard of anything like this in your life? If I had not been standing on my feet, I would have been certain I was dreaming!"

"Well—other than children turned into gingerbread by a wicked witch, no," Benno said darkly. "Or men into pigs, by the enchantress Circe. And I think you're being foolish to make a joke about it."

Siegfried closed his eyes for a moment, summoning patience. "You didn't see Odette," he finally said quietly. "I have never seen another woman to compare to her, and if I had to fight my way through a hundred Circes to get to her side, I would do it."

He opened his eyes again to see Benno staring at him, slack-jawed with amazement.

"If I didn't know better," Benno finally managed. "I would say that you sounded as if you were—enamored."

"Enamored?" Siegfried lifted one corner of his mouth in a lopsided smile. "Don't you mean lovesick?"

Benno frowned fiercely, his eyes clouding with anger. "Dammit, Siegfried, this is *not* funny! You're acting as if you're already under an enchantment! Are you sure this woman didn't get some of your hair? Or did she get you to look into a mirror, or something?"

He stifled the urge to tell Benno that he was under the enchantment of Odette's eyes, and held his tongue. "No hair, no mirror, and at this point if you were to ask me if I had fallen in love with Odette the moment I saw her, I would have to admit to it. So, what do you think I should do? And don't tell me not to go out there tomorrow night, because that is *not* an option. I would like some advice, though."

"You let *me* look the place over tomorrow in the daylight, and you let me come with you tomorrow night," Benno replied immediately. "If I can't make you see sense, I can at least try to protect you—from yourself, if not from this woman."

The notion of Benno trying to protect *him* was ludicrous, but Siegfried nobly refrained from laughing at him. "All right," he agreed. "I can't see any objections to either. She didn't tell me to come alone, and if there are two of us, she might be a little more forthcoming about herself and why she's here. Who knows? With you along, she might look different to me. I doubt it, but there's always a chance."

Benno's snort showed what he thought of that statement. He made no other comment, but drank down his wine in a single gulp and held out his goblet for Siegfried to refill. The prince did so, and now found that the appetite he thought had deserted him was back with a vengeance. He attacked his chicken ravenously, while Benno watched.

"If this paragon of yours can convince *me* that she's no witch, I promise I'll leave you alone together," he finally said, though he looked as if the words had been wrung from him unwillingly. "But I warn you, it's going to take a great deal of convincing."

The prince pushed his plate away, taking only a soft roll to play with, pulling bits of bread from it and rolling them into little pills that he piled on the plate. "If you can manage to clear your mind of your suspicions for a moment, can you think of anything that might help, here?" he asked, trying not to show his own impatience.

Benno shook his head, but his irritation softened. "Look, Siegfried, I know that what you want to hear from me is—'go ahead, my friend, she sounds like just the woman for you! Woo her, win her, and carry her off to your castle!' And I—I would love to tell you just that, but it isn't that simple. We're *not* in a tale. You know yourself that you have duties and obligations to your mother and to your kingdom, and I never thought that I would be the one to have to remind you of them! Just because a woman's a half-magic creature, that doesn't mean she's a fit bride for you or will be a fit queen when you're king. You don't even know her rank. What if she's a peasant? I know that you'll say it doesn't matter, but it *will* matter to Queen Clothilde, and it *will* matter to the fathers of the girls you reject in favor of her. I feel as if I'm betraying you in some way—" he sighed, "—but I know I would be betraying you in a worse way if I didn't play devil's advocate right now. You always tell me that you need me as a friend because I tell you the truth, and I'm trying to tell you the truth now."

Siegfried's irritation melted. "Just—promise to keep

your mind open to every possibility," he said at last. "That's all I can ask of you."

Benno drank his wine, and set the empty goblet on the table. "I can promise that," he replied with a nod. "I can definitely promise that—if *you* promise to listen to me when I give you advice."

"I will promise to listen," the prince responded.

But in his thoughts were other words. *I will promise to listen to your advice—but I won't promise to act on it.*

With dinner over, the dishes whisked efficiently away, and the tables and chairs rearranged for entertainment, the large pavilion took on a quieter aspect. Clothilde was altogether pleased with the refurbishment of this pavilion, which had been commissioned for her wedding to Siegfried's father. Windows screened with cheesecloth had been let into the sides, and a frieze of flowers and vines painted on the canvas around them. New banners and streamers decorated the exterior, and clever lanterns suspended from the roof lit the interior. A carpet beneath Clothilde's chair served in place of a dais, with the rest of the seats arrayed in a half-circle on the plank floor on either side of her. Uwe sat on a stool at the queen's feet, and played for the enjoyment of the queen and those guests who still remained—mostly female. The male guests for the most part had long since departed for the heartier entertainment to be found around their campfires. Since there was no place large enough for the queen to entertain all of the bridal candidates at night, once the feasting was over, the men deserted the feasting tent, leaving it to the ladies and a few indolent or elderly men. The women danced round-dances with each other, when so moved.

Clothilde had been a bit disappointed that Siegfried hadn't at least made a token appearance tonight, but since he didn't yet seem to be taken all that much with *any* of the young women, perhaps that was to be expected. If she knew her son, he would spend his time hunting rather than courting any of these maidens, knowing that the one he selected would be, as betokened by her appearance here, a willing and even eager bride. Why work to obtain something he already had? Siegfried had never been inclined to put more effort into anything *he* hadn't planned than he had to.

There is still the enchanter's daughter, she told herself. *Siegfried has yet to meet her, and I must admit that she is far more attractive than any of these young ladies.* She already had doubts about the suitability of a couple of them, anyway. There had been hints in the behavior, disturbing glances cast her way, that made her reconsider Uwe's assessments. Princess Honoria, for instance, although she seemed uninterested in anything but her hawks, showed all the indications of having a very strong will of her own and a disinclination to be led. Not all of them were going to be as tractable as Uwe had thought, and she decided to do what she could to cull those out herself.

Not overtly, of course, but a hint or two to Siegfried about a tendency to nag, a hint of a sharp temper—that would take care of the problem before it became one. She, of all people, knew that Siegfried was not to be forced into anything, and if one led him, the reins had better be invisible. It was better to coax, cajole, or—better still—make him think that whatever you wanted him to do was all his idea in the first place.

She watched the girls carefully, without seeming to watch anything. There were definite signs there that more of the girls than Honoria had minds of their own; a couple of them watched Clothilde even as she watched them, though not as skillfully, their manners betraying them. Those two would *not* sit back and accept the position of mere princess. By all rights, whoever Siegfried married could and should be queen, and Clothilde could and should retire to the minor position of dowager—they clearly knew their rights, and would not sit by tamely while Clothilde ruled after the wedding. They would use whatever weapons they had, their youth and beauty not being the least of those weapons, to urge Siegfried to claim his throne from his mother. If they were clever, they would point out that a man of eighteen, a warrior and knight in his own right, should no longer be ruled by a mere woman. She had no doubt that such words, murmured gently in bed by crimson lips, would find receptive ears.

Never, my dears, she thought silkily, wondering if *she* had ever been so transparent. She rather thought not. After all, one of the reasons that Uwe had chosen these six was that in his estimation none of them was a match for her in intelligence.

They were, all of them, gently reared in the bower, far from throne and council chamber. *She* had learned the craft of governance at her father's side and the craft of guile at her mother's. It was too bad that her mother had not lived to see her wedded to a king, nor her father to see her become queen regent in her own right, but they would both have been proud of her for at least a week—following which, they would have begun schemes of their own to wrest some of that power and control from her hands for themselves.

They taught me well, Clothilde thought with some amusement.

And as for experience—well, there was *something* to be said for increased years and the knowledge that came with them. Whatever time stole from the face and body, it at least compensated with additions to the wits.

Uwe glanced up at her briefly, so briefly that only she read the message in his eyes. *So. The enchanter has put in an appearance! Good; it will only be a matter of time before Siegfried encounters the girl.*

It occurred to her at that moment that she might have something to fear from the enchanter's daughter. What if the girl was a sorceress herself? What if *she* would not be content with the title of princess?

Clothilde watched her guests swaying together in a gentle pavane as she considered these possibilities, then smiled, as if in pleasure at the pretty picture they made, when a solution came to her.

She still had her little book of "herbal recipes" from her mother. One was the recipe for the love potion that had gained her this throne in the first place; by making sure both Siegfried and whichever maiden he chose drank it together on their wedding night, she would inflame their passions and fix their interest on each other for a time. Another was the fertility drink she had downed faithfully for a month until she conceived the prince; a woman in the throes of passion would happily agree to anything to give her man an heir, and a pregnant woman concentrates on the well-being of her child-to-be to the exclusion of all else. Then—

Then we see. It amused her to think that the daughter of a sorcerer would be vulnerable to a simple love potion, but that ability to look for unexpected weaknesses was one of the things that had made Clothilde queen. It had certainly worked against her husband.

She smiled again in recollection; it had been a perfect plan, perfectly executed. She knew where the young king hunted and where he generally paused to refresh himself. She had simply surrounded herself with a party of her homeliest maidservants and arranged for a hunting excursion of her own. The king stopped to admire the hawks and the huntress, and she coyly, charmingly offered him wine from her own flask—well-laced with the love potion.

A week later, the betrothal of the daughter of Graf Hohentaller with the king was proclaimed to all the kingdom. In a month, she was queen.

The prime indication for her that none of these beauties was her match was that none of *them* had tried to slip Siegfried a similar potion. Surely, they'd had ample opportunity by now.

Ah well, she thought, sitting back into the comfortable embrace of her chair. *This latter generation is no match for mine in any way. This is just one more proof that it is I who should be holding the reins, and not my son.*

Chapter Fifteen

ODILE stretched in her narrow little bed and yawned, blinking at the entrance to the tree house. The swans had pushed the door open when they left, and of course had not shut it after themselves, but she didn't really mind. The fresh air was pleasant, and the light didn't bother her. *Full daylight; early afternoon, I think. Good! Plenty of time for myself before sunset and moonrise.*

She'd been sleeping less of late, feeling less tired, since she'd finally completed all the work she wanted to do to make this place a comfortable dwelling. She was even sleeping less than she had at home, which meant she had more hours free for practice and study.

Von Rothbart was gone most of the time, although she suspected he wasn't far off. And while it made her feel guilty to admit it, his absence was a relief. She didn't feel compelled to second-guess her actions and decisions, nor to look over her shoulder to see if he was watching her. Whatever he was up to, it kept him too occupied to watch for Odile's missteps and mistakes, and as a consequence, she thought she was making fewer errors.

As usual, she was alone. The swans were all out foraging or drowsing at this hour. It would have been nice to have an invisible servant of her own to fetch and carry for her, but Odile didn't quite have the nerve to try summoning one. As gentle and tractable as von Rothbart's had all been, Odile had learned from her reading yesterday that if they were not firmly bound, they would exact revenge on whoever tried to enslave them. According to a new book she had begun perusing, they weren't *precisely* demons, but. . . .

But it's not worth the risk to try to subdue them. Not to me, anyway. This book clearly was a tome of gray magic—not white sorcery, but not quite black, either. So far, everything Odile had learned or created was simply useful magic, the exercise of power that harmed no one. She wanted nothing to do with anything dubious, and she had sent the book back to the library without a second thought.

It made her wonder why her father went to so much trouble and danger to have the services of silent spirits, when he could get the same service at no hazard from human serfs. He could even put a simple spell of silence on them if he didn't want to have to hear other human voices, and as for obedience, who would dare to disobey a man with von Rothbart's powers? Granted, a spell of silence might annoy the servants and make them rebellious, but surely he could *command* simple silence from them, couldn't he?

Odile had very vague recollections of things being different when she was very small; there *had* been human servants when her mother had been alive. Was it only her mother's death that had given her father such a distaste for humanity? Or had he only tolerated human servants because she had wanted them?

For that matter, the servants could only have been in Mother's quarters; I certainly never left them until after she was gone. And once there was no reason to keep them, Father probably got rid of them as soon as he could, and never wondered if I would have been better off with some companions.

That thought brought a flash of anger. Abruptly, she shoved aside her light coverings and got out of bed; that was enough daydreaming for today. She had work to get to, and there was no telling what might turn up to interrupt it. Outside forces over which she had no control were in motion now, and the outside world was sending visitors, even intruders.

Possibly even a lovesick prince looking for Odette. As she took a gown out of the closet she'd made and shook it on over her head, she made a face of distaste. If Siegfried showed up before his appointed time, she would just avoid him altogether. Her duties of keeping an eye on Odette did not include playing reluctant hostess to her suitor.

Getting her hair braided and pinned up without help was too much of a bother, so she sat down in the sunlight bathing the doorway and brushed it out, then left it loose. It wouldn't hinder her reading, nor her magical exercises, and since there wasn't much of a breeze it wouldn't end up getting tangled in every leaf and twig if she just tied it back with a ribbon and ignored it.

As she picked up her book from the shelf where she'd left it last night and walked out barefoot into the afternoon sunshine, she had an unexpected revelation that made her smile, the muscles at the corners of her mouth stretching in a way that felt odd.

I thought I was going to hate it here—but instead, I'm going to regret having to leave! Odile had never thought she would actually come to take pleasure in the wilderness, but there was so much to watch and learn, and so many new things to try, that she wondered how she was going to be able to bear being back in her father's lands. She hadn't seen much of daylight at home, since she kept the same hours as the swans and her father, and the carefully controlled and manicured grounds of the Rothbart estate were so tame that virtually everything inside the manor and outside showed the sorcerer's heavy hand. She had more than once thought that the sculptured trees and bushes took the place for him of furniture or artwork, and the grass was certainly a substitute for carpets.

And although the invisible servants made life effortless, they were also spies that could move about without detection. For the first time there was no sense that her father had eyes watching her even when he wasn't there; she could do whatever she pleased so long as she obeyed his simple orders. Freedom! That's what this was. And if living in a shelter formed from the trunks of a grove of trees and cooking or summoning meals and clothing was the price of freedom, she'd pay it twice over and call it cheap.

I might feel differently in the dead of winter, she reminded herself as she sat down in her favorite spot, cradled in the roots of a huge willow, where she could put her back against the trunk and dangle her feet in the water. *Keeping everyone warm and fed would be no joke, and we probably wouldn't be able to leave the tree most of the time.* She wrinkled her nose at the thought of being crowded into that small space with dozens of restless, claustrophobic swans. Swan leavings were slimy and smelly at best, and nervous swans made lots of leavings.

Then again, I can't imagine Father putting up with living in the wilderness into the winter, either. If we're here that long, he'll make other arrangements, I suspect.

That made her wonder where *he* was, when he wasn't taking her reports. Now and again, she had sensed his presence although she had not seen him— but always after darkness and moonrise. Where was he during the day? And what was he doing with his time?

He might be setting up a trap, she thought uneasily. As she knew from her own experiments, establishing the transformation spell was arduous and difficult; was there someone hereabouts that he felt deserved the punishment of being added to his flock?

But there won't be a flock if Odette succeeds. . . .

Maybe he was arranging for Odette's success; maybe he was doing something about getting places for the swan-maidens to go once they were no longer under his control.

One of the swans had told her that there was a strange island in the middle of the lake, a tall, tree-crowned rock with steep, vertical sides that looked like an owl. Was that where von Rothbart had made his lair?

It would be like him, she thought, irritated again. *He could have his servants and soft bed, his meals prepared for him, and his luxuries without having to share them with us.*

She forced herself to find a more charitable explanation. It could be that he just needed a more defensible dwelling place than they did; he wouldn't be able to sleep anywhere that wasn't completely secure. It was difficult to kill him, but not impossible, and if any of the swans' relatives came looking for revenge, they were probably intelligent enough to know not to come after a sorcerer when he was awake and alert. Odile didn't know the exact parameters of the spells protecting her father's life, but she could make some good guesses.

He can't specify invulnerability, because that's impossible, but he's probably protected against weapons made of steel, iron, bronze, copper, lead, and wood. He's probably done something about poison and strangling. I know he's guarded from drowning or being drowned, and against fire. I suppose you could bury him alive and smother him, or wall him up in a cave and starve him, but only if he wasn't conscious, because the minute he woke up, he'd have himself out of there.

Two things she knew he had *not* warded himself against were silver and gold; she knew that because when she was just learning her first incantations, he'd twice showed her spells that needed a drop of the sorcerer's own blood. The first time, since it was a moon-spell, he had cut his finger with a dagger made of silver, and for the second, sun-spell, he'd used a needle of gold. Unless a sorcerer was willing to traffic with real and undisputed demons to obtain true invulnerability, the best he could do would be to ward against common weaponry.

Not that there're too many knights careening about with swords of silver or gold, so I expect he's safe enough.

She had her own little silver dagger to use when she needed to shed her own blood, for she had already warded herself with similar protections. The only one she hadn't needed was the one that warded against drowning, for she could swim like an otter, and had been able to for as long as she could remember.

She had the dagger with her this afternoon, although she didn't usually carry it; it was sheathed and in her lap as she read, and she ran her finger up and down the smooth silver hilt in a self-soothing circular motion. There was something she wanted to try, although she wasn't quite sure she was ready for it yet; it was a scrying spell, but not one that would see into the future. It was a more difficult spell than anything she had yet tried. She wanted to see into the past— her *own* past. For that, she would need to let a single drop of her own blood mingle with the water of her scrying glass.

That was what she was studying today, searching through the deceptively straightforward spell to make sure there were no hidden catches or pitfalls. Too many times she had uncovered such things and she was not about to let her guard down just because this

was a book von Rothbart himself used on occasion.
When sorcerers wrote their grimoires, they never intended to make life easier for those who followed (or attempted to follow) in their footsteps. On the contrary; most sorcerers appeared to be so jealous of their power that, although they could not resist the notoriety that publishing would bring them, they left the path of the would-be initiate strewn with pitfalls.

And Father is no different from any of them. He hasn't warned me about trouble for years, and I doubt he's going to begin again.

This was a completely harmless spell of white magic, though, and one that the author of this grimoire himself had written was an odd, though complicated bit of sorcery, one he considered useful only to impress clients. Unlike another version, which could be used to discover lost secrets or hidden treasures, this one revealed only the past of the one whose blood was used. So unless one could somehow obtain the blood of the one who had known the secrets or hidden the treasures, it was of little practical use. This was Odile's fifth reading of the spell, and so far the only thing she'd discovered was a simple bit of deliberate transposition that would result only in simple failure if the instructions were followed exactly. She'd found *that* on the first reading, before she'd even begun to look seriously for tricks. It might not even be deliberate; it could be a copying error.

But she never attempted a new magic until she'd searched the text seven times, so she perused the instructions in their crabbed black-letter printing with the same single-mindedness she'd given them the first time. A frown of concentration creased her brow and she lifted her hand to her forehead to shade her eyes against the glare of sunlight off the water before her.

"Ah, hallo."

Odile shrieked and jumped, the book tumbling out

of her hands and heading for the water. She snatched it up a hair's breadth from disaster with her left hand while she pulled her dagger from its sheath with her right, twisting up onto one knee to face the intruder. Her heart still pounded with the fright he'd given her.

The young man gazing back at her after a startled step backward of his own didn't appear to be anything like a bandit or robber, though. In fact, he was dressed in a fashion very similar to the clothing worn by Prince Siegfried the night before. Hunting costume, certainly; expensive deerskin and fine linen, with buckles and buttons of stamped silver. He was armed with a crossbow, but he carried it on his back, unstrung; his sword was still in its sheath, as was his dagger. In short, just at the moment, he was at a greater disadvantage than Odile.

She did *not* like being frightened like that, and irritation made her clamp her jaws tight. *She* was not going to speak first; let *him* make the first move!

Guileless brown eyes blinked at her as she regarded the dagger in her hand. As she got slowly and cautiously to her feet, still holding tightly to the precious book, he cleared his throat.

"Sorry. Didn't mean to frighten you—" Now his eyes passed quickly up and down her body, assessing her. She was suddenly conscious of her bare feet and unbound hair, and flushed, but evidently the evidence of her black silk gown, simple though it was, outweighed the bare feet. "Truly don't mean any harm, my lady," he continued, with a little bow. "I thought you'd heard me tramping up through the bushes—"

But as he straightened up, his eyes narrowed, as if a thought had just occurred to him. "Beg pardon, but you wouldn't be the Lady Odette, would you?"

She surprised him and herself by breaking into a nervous laugh. "Lady *Odile* von Rothbart," she corrected him, and added, "And it's *Princess* Odette, not mere 'Lady.' Surely you don't expect to find a princess dangling her feet in the water, do you? Furthermore, if you've had her described to you, you must know that I'm nothing like her." She smiled bitterly. "If you had even a glimpse of Odette, you would never mistake a plain little creature like me for a great beauty like her."

"Ah." The young man fidgeted uncomfortably, clearly unable to come up with an answer that was both gallant and truthful, or at least that was Odile's cynical assessment of his discomfort. "But by your words, may I assume you do know the la—ah, princess?"

Von Rothbart had given Odile no instructions regarding the intrusion of *friends* of Siegfried's, and she felt just malicious enough toward all men at the moment to answer him honestly, but in a way that misdirected him if Siegfried had just let drink do his talking last night.

This could be a drinking chum or a confidant, or even a young fool who heard enough to make him curious. Let's just see how much he's been trusted with.

She put on a haughty air at odds with her bare feet and loose hair. "I know the princess quite well, actually, but you'll have some difficulty getting to speak with her, I'm afraid. She's not available until moonrise, and I believe she has a prior engagement." She took some pleasure in treating him as if she were Princess Odette's social secretary, seated at a table in a receiving room, rather than a barefooted, bare-headed sorceress standing beside a wild lake. If he didn't know that Odette was flouncing about in white feathers at the moment, this should really confuse him.

"Ah."

Odile decided to be the one asking questions. "And just who might *you* be?" she countered. "I do not believe that the princess has made more than a single acquaintance in this country, and you, sir, are not he."

The young man flushed the most vivid crimson Odile had ever seen. "Ah—beg pardon, Lady Odile—failed to introduce myself. Landsknecht Benno von Drachheim at your service." He made a much better bow this time, and Odile sheathed her dagger and graciously extended her hand for him to kiss, all the while holding in an unexpected burst of hysterical giggles.

Benno kissed her hand without any hesitation, and only straightened after letting go of it. "My—ah—friend Siegfried is the acquaintance you mentioned," he said carefully. "He told me some things last night that frankly seemed rather fantastical in nature. That your princess was—had a double nature. I thought perhaps, given the—ah—*unusual* quality of their meeting, that I ought to—"

Odile interrupted him, unable to bear with this chasing about the barn any longer. "He told you that he'd seen a swan that turned into a maiden, and you thought he was mad or bespelled or worse, so you decided to come see for yourself. Well, have a look about you." She indicated the shore and the lake with a wave of her hand. "I rather doubt you'll find the princess; she's shy of being seen in her current form. That's understandable, considering how many people there seem to be with crossbows and bird-hunting quarrels hereabouts." She eyed the bow at Benno's back ostentatiously, and he flushed again.

"He did say that, my lady." The young man abruptly dropped his silly-ass manner, and she blinked in surprise. "And I was not prepared to allow my friend and my prince to go unwarded into a moonlight encounter with someone who might be dangerous." He stepped forward deliberately, and it was her turn to step back a pace. "I do not know how you have come here, or what you and this princess intend, but I warn you, no magic will save you if my prince comes to any harm. And you would do well to tell me now just what your plot is."

A thrill went through her, not of fear, but of excitement. The moment he turned from idiot to dangerous, Odile glanced about for an escape route. She couldn't get past him, and there was a good chance that if she bolted, he would be able to run faster than she and chase her down, for *he* wasn't hampered by long skirts. But there was a perfect way to escape that would even provide a place to hide waiting at her back, if she could just distract him for a moment. If she could manage that, he wouldn't be able to seize her when she turned to flee.

And she had the means of distraction in her hand.

Before he could move again, she readied a small spell in her mind, and flung her book straight at his head.

He was so startled that he didn't even duck, but she didn't intend to hit him; the last thing she wanted to do was hurt him even slightly. Just before the book reached his face, it vanished in a clap of thunder right in front of his nose.

Now it was his turn to yell and jump back—while she took advantage of the moment to turn and dive into the lake behind her, arcing gracefully toward the dark waters.

Then she hit the surface of the lake and plunged beneath it, and fought back a gasp. The water was very cold; she knew that already, of course, since she'd been dangling her feet in it, but it was still a shock when it closed over her body. She managed to hold in most of the breath she'd taken as she struck the water, and once out of sight she added to the momentum she'd brought with her from her dive with powerful strokes of her arms and legs. The silk gown hampered her a little, but not as much as one of heavier material would have, and the color helped hide her in the somber water.

Odile could swim underwater for quite some distance, and she used that ability now. She knew where she was going; an overhanging rock she could hide beneath farther down the arm of the lake that formed a kind of grotto. She surfaced near it and quickly ducked under the shelter of the overhang when she heard the young man crashing through the brush, looking for her.

He wouldn't find her, of course; not unless he could swim, and most nobles couldn't. Only peasants learned to swim; nobles had boats and bridges to get them across the water. Even if he could swim, would he be willing to dive into the frigid water, and chance ruining his clothing? She didn't think so.

Odile had learned to swim only because she hadn't known she shouldn't, and one of the Invisibles helped by keeping her from drowning. Her father had seemed indifferent when he saw her cutting through the waters of their own lake, so she'd kept improving her skill. Now she felt another thrill, this time of triumph. She had tricked this man and escaped him, all by herself!

Another touch of magic surrounded her with a shell of warm water, and she stopped shivering as she waited under the ledge, clinging to the rock to avoid making any noise, breathing slowly and quietly, listening. She wondered what the young man was thinking right now; from his point of view, she had all but vanished, and he must feel terribly foolish to have been outwitted by a mere female. She *had* considered taking her swan form, but the memory of that crossbow prompted her to forget the idea. He might not shoot at her, but then again, he might. True, she was warded against the steel of the arrowhead, but she wasn't so certain of those wards that she cared to test them in a manner so potentially fatal.

Better to hide and wait for him to go away. It was annoying that she was losing all this study time to him, but what could she do about it?

At least my book is still safe, and he can't possibly get into the tree. The book had gone back to its place on the shelf within the tree house, and she'd followed her usual precaution of shutting and hiding the door when she left. She'd had no intentions of letting this upstart get his hands on it!

The crashing of brush neared, and stopped just over her head. She heard him muttering angrily to himself; too far away to make out the words, but there was no mistaking that tone. She smiled wryly. Little enough actual magic had been used in her escape, but *he* didn't know that, and presumably he had been impressed, and perhaps even a little frightened. Clearly, though, he had not been frightened enough to take himself off; he still wanted to get his hands on her to interrogate her about Odette.

If he actually sits down and thinks, he'll realize that I could have hurt him, and didn't, she thought. *Right now, though, he's just angry that I managed to deceive him. What could he expect? After all, he threatened me, and I was perfectly within my rights to escape.* She heard him blundering off again, and wondered how long it would be before he gave up and left.

It had better be soon, or I'll have to make myself invisible in order to get out of the water. She had no intention of spending hours under this ledge until her fingers and toes were withered as a dried grape, but she also didn't want to waste magic if she didn't have to. Besides, being invisible didn't imply that she would be undetectable. There would be a "hole" in the water where her body was, she would leave footprints, and as water droplets fell from her body, they would be-

come visible again. If he was at all intelligent and
saw any of those signs, he would have a target for
that crossbow.

At that moment, as she waited for him to go back
to where he came from, she was torn between amusement at her situation and anger at being put into it.

Men! Jesu! she thought with exasperation. *Stubborn,
unruly, quick to anger and slow to think! Why on earth
does Odette want to bother with these creatures? Why
would anyone want to bother with them? It's easier
being a swan!*

". . . so I looked for about an hour, but there was no
sign of her," Benno concluded ruefully. "My own stupid fault for threatening her, of course. I lost my temper and as a consequence lost a source of information
we can hardly do without."

Siegfried rubbed the side of his nose with his finger
and sighed. This wasn't the worst thing that could have
befallen, but why had Benno acted so precipitously?
If he had simply treated the girl without threats, they
might have learned all manner of things. "She must
have been one of the other girls I saw with Odette—
but why was *she* there, and not the princess? I would
think that they would all be swans at the same time, but
she clearly implied that Odette was still ensorcelled."

Benno shrugged. "I can't even begin to fathom all
these magical goings-on. She was wearing black, and
didn't you say that the girls you saw were all in white?
Maybe the black ones are swans by night and girls by
day, and the white ones are the opposite. Maybe *she's*
the one that put the spell on them. Your guess is as
valid as mine. I'm just angry at myself for letting her
escape like that."

The prince was impatient to plan his own journey to the lake, and didn't really care to hear any more about Benno's. "I'm still meeting Odette at moonrise," Siegfried declared, with a look to Benno that warned his friend not to object. "Nothing you've told me is changing that."

"And I'm still going with you." Benno's answering glare was just as stubborn. "I trust the woman even less now than I did before. And she had better have an explanation for that *other* girl and why she wasn't a swan."

Siegfried tapped the table with his finger as he thought, suppressing his irritation with his friend. After all, Benno hadn't seen Odette; to him, the swan-maiden was not a great deal different from the maid he'd met this afternoon. How could he realize that? "You know, this Odile might not *be* one of the swan-maidens at all!" he exclaimed. "Wouldn't they need some kind of keeper or herder? What better and safer guardian than another maiden?"

"I suppose—but that would make her a good candidate for the one who put the spell on them in the first place," Benno pointed out. "And that is what strikes me as wrong. She didn't act that way; if I had seen her at a court, I would have said that she was a functionary of Odette's, not a captor. It was as if I spoke to your mother's seneschal, not to the queen herself. I did not have the feeling that Odile was the one responsible for what was going on, although she clearly knew a great deal about it. She has power, and she might be in league with someone far more powerful, but I think she is to that person what the seneschal is to your mother. She may be able to perform some magic, but she's not the witch who cast the powerful spells."

Siegfried saw this as a good way to change the subject; neither of them knew enough to make any valid conclusions about either girl, and until they had more information, the horse that Benno persisted in beating would remain just as dead as it was when he started. "Are you implying that my mother is a witch?" he asked, grinning.

Benno looked alarmed for a brief moment, then caught his expression and grinned back. "No. Why? Is she?"

Siegfried mimed a blow at him, and he ducked. "That's a fine thing to say about your queen!" he chided. "I suppose I ought to report you for treason, but I like you too much. You will, however, be happy to hear that my day was just as fruitless as yours. I didn't even get to hunt properly; only one of the princesses ever courses with hounds—Honoria, of course— so naturally all the rest of them stayed in the camp, and since I had already spent sufficient time with Honoria, according to Mother, so did I." He made a face. "We spent the entire afternoon listening to Uwe and reading poetry aloud. Uwe is pleasant enough to listen to, and at least he's acquired a few new tunes, but unfortunately Uwe didn't get much chance to play."

"I thought you liked poetry," Benno objected.

"I like *good* poetry," he countered, "Not the drivel that passes for poetry in their circles."

Benno's eyes lit with sympathy and understanding. "Blessed Saint Joseph!" he exclaimed with mock horror. "Don't tell me they all trotted out scrolls from their pet troubadours and read them!"

He groaned and nodded. "Worse than that, their ladies trotted out paeans of praise to the princesses. It was so bad it was very nearly comic. Blue skies/ blue eyes, lady fair/silken hair, angel's face/fairy grace, moon/June—"

"Loon, buffoon," Benno laughed at his mournful expression. "I prefer my wild swan chase to your afternoon! I think I would rather wade through another couple of bramble thickets than have to listen to that much bad poetry and smile through it all.''

''I was hard put to keep from laughing—when I wasn't fighting to stay awake,'' Siegfried nodded, but kept his next thought to himself. Benno would hardly approve.

The only thing that made it tolerable was that I knew I would never have to endure another afternoon like it—for I have no intentions of wedding any of them. They could all take their bad poets to whatever poor fellow did marry them, and he pitied the man if he had to listen to such drivel on a regular basis.

Poor little princesses! I pity them, too; they are trying so hard to win me, and I am already won. . . .

He would not, could not confess this to Benno, not yet, but he woke this morning knowing with the certainty of the sun rising that he would never be able bind himself to anyone but Odette. The mere prospect of taking anyone else to wife made his heart grow cold. It was insane, of course, but it was a glorious madness, and he would die before he sacrificed it on the altar of duty.

After all, the queen had pledged him that he could wed where he willed, and as soon as he secured Odette's consent, he had every intention of holding his mother to that pledge. No matter if it cost him his throne, he would woo and wed Odette, the swan queen.

And that was another thing that Benno did not yet need to know.

Odette unexpectedly encountered another knot in Odile's wet hair, tugged it too hard, and apologized. Odile shrugged. ''Pull away, it's my own fault for being too lazy to braid it in the first place. It wouldn't be a mess now if I'd just braided it."

"Well, you couldn't have known you were going to find yourself diving into the lake, could you?" Odette continued her self-appointed task of combing out the snarled, wet hair and braiding it into a neat coronet. She'd found Odile sitting beside the lake in the moonlight, dry and wearing a new gown, but trying without success to get the tangles out of her long hair. Odile was frustrated to the point of tears, and just about ready to cut her hair off entirely. Odette immediately took the comb from her and without being asked, took over the task herself. Odile, both surprised by the kindness and touched, thanked her profusely.

"It never occurred to me that your visitor last night might have told a friend about us." That was noncommittal enough, and kept her from betraying that she had spied on every moment the two spent together. "It should have, though," Odile continued, with a grimace Odette couldn't see. "Men call *us* gossips, but they tell more tales to each other than we ever do." Still feeling spiteful toward the importunate young man who was the cause of all her current difficulty, she added. "The young fool probably thought he'd find a veritable harem of loose women here! He probably thought we were pagan sylphs or gypsy witches, trying to seduce every man coming along with our bodies!"

"Oh no, no—" Odette said hastily, "I am sure Siegfried would never have said anything that would give him *that* impression!" The abrupt silence that followed her outburst led Odile to think Odette had spoken without thinking. After a moment, the princess added lightly, "I wish I could have seen his face when you dove into the water, though!"

"So do I," Odile chuckled, feeling a little better. After all, she had outwitted the young man, trounced him thoroughly, in fact, and that was some comfort. If she'd just braided her hair, she wouldn't even be undergoing this inconvenience.

"There! You're done!" Odette had finished while she'd been thinking, and gave her hair a little pat of approval.

"And just in time, too, unless I miss my guess—" Odile caught sight of one of the others running toward them, skirts held high in both hands, presumably to warn Odette of Prince Siegfried's approach. White silk fluttered behind her in an echo of swan wings. Odile turned to glance at Odette, and saw her face take on a brief pallor that had nothing to do with the moonlight.

"Odette—" the maiden said as she reached them, dropping her skirts to gesture behind her.

"I should go—" Odile said, and before Odette could object, she leaped to her feet and ran off into the darkness beneath the trees.

But not far. No, although she suffered a twinge of guilt over her actions, she paused in the deepest shadows just long enough to make herself invisible, then stole back to within listening distance.

Odette waited for the two men who approached her looking remarkably composed, the center of a half-circle of the others, who watched and waited with her. In the moonlight, they formed a remarkable tableau, looking every bit as magical as forest spirits in a tale. The prince looked a little surprised to see that she was not alone; Odile could not tell what the other man felt.

It was her intruder from this afternoon, though. Although he tried to remain expressionless, as he searched the group of girls, she wondered if he could be looking for her. If so, he didn't find her, and his expression as he examined Odette and her escort was full of wary suspicion. The maidens moved not a single muscle; the only movement was that of their diaphanous white gowns and the flowers and swan feathers ornamenting their hair, fluttering a little in the faint breeze.

Siegfried, looking completely confident and at his ease, bowed to Odette; she acknowledged his courtesy with a regal inclination of her head. If last night she had been the half-terrified, half-angry, fey spirit, tonight she was all queen, in command of herself, if not of her fate. After a dubious glance at his friend, the other young man did the same.

Benno von Drachheim, Odile recalled. *But if he's a genuine landsknecht, I'm the Queen of Sheba. He's a knight, no doubt, but it's his father who's the landed one; he's just the heir, if he's anything. The title's no more than a courtesy for a son, assuming he didn't just appropriate it.*

"I hope you will permit me to present my friend, Landsknecht Benno von Drachheim," Siegfried said, with the same formality he would have used in a lofty hall. At least the young man hadn't claimed a title he didn't have. It should have been amusing, but Odile felt no inclination to laugh.

Odette slowly extended her hand for him to kiss, head held very high on her long and graceful neck, face marble-pale in the moonlight. Benno dropped a very perfunctory salute on the back of it before it was withdrawn. "I had not thought you would come as anything but alone," she said to Siegfried, as if Benno weren't there—a nice little bit of byplay that clearly made Benno uneasy. "I hope you have not confided in anyone else; you could be creating danger for us. Not all hunters would hesitate to kill us. Some would think us creatures of the devil and think it their duty to remove us from the world."

Siegfried only smiled. "My friend is concerned for me," he replied, with a glance at Benno.

Odette turned a gaze on Benno so cold that it

should have coated him with a rime of frost. "And
what was it that made him concerned?" she asked
icily. "Does *he* think we are unholy demons? Does he
believe there is anything we could possibly do to harm
you? Did he think my companions and I would fall
upon you and tear you to pieces with our bare hands?
Or did he suppose that we were the perpetrators of
the curse we suffer under, and not the victims?"

Even in the moonlight, Odile saw Benno flush. Put
that way, the young man's suspicions sounded both
ridiculous and crass. Odile smiled; that was one score
for Odette! *I never realized that she was this clever!
She uses honesty and truth as any warrior would use
a sword!*

"So you *are* cursed!" Siegfried seized on that eagerly. "It was as I thought!" Abruptly he dropped to
one knee before the startled maiden, and seized her
hand before Odette could shrink back. "If there is a
way that I can free you from it, tell me now! I swear
I shall do so, no matter the cost!"

Be careful, Odette! Odile warned, tense with worry.
*Don't forget what the conditions are! Don't do any-
thing yet!*

From the appalled look on Benno's face, that was
exactly what he had most feared the prince would
say—but Odette gently took back her hand, and shook
her head.

"Do not swear so rashly before you know what you
swear to," she replied, her voice faltering, just a little,
as she looked down into the prince's eyes. "But if you
truly wish to hear *all* of our story, I beg you, come
apart with me. What I have to tell you is not for any
ears but yours, for if you should change your mind, I
would not wish any others to know what I have to tell
you. They might not hold their tongues as you would."

She glared at Benno now so that he winced—but
then her expression softened, unexpectedly, and as she

urged Siegfried back to his feet, she extended her hand to the chastened Benno.

"I can see that you are the true friend to your prince—and I must ask you to trust me long enough for him to hear me out. I swear to you, by whatever saint you ask, that I will not permit him to make any offers before he has heard all, both good and bad. Will you grant me that much trust?"

Odile gave Odette more points in the skirmish between herself and the prince's interfering friend. Put so graciously, how could a man who claimed to be a knight and a gentleman do anything other than acquiesce?

He did, and with better grace than Odile had expected. "I ask your leave to question your maidens, however," he added, before Odette could draw Siegfried aside. "The one I met with this afternoon was singularly uncooperative, and did nothing to allay my mistrust."

The corners of Odette's mouth actually twitched, but she gave no sign that she had already heard the tale from Odile. "So long as you make no threats, nor offer them any insult or harm," she replied pointedly. "But if any of them feel you have done so, you must not be surprised if they choose to depart from your presence, however abruptly. We may have no weapons, and no strong hands to protect us, but the night is a friend to us, and will conceal us from those who would harm us."

Yes, and I personally would like to see you led into a bramble patch if you treat them as you treated me!

Before he could reply to that sally, she turned away from him and walked away. With her skirts trailing on the grass behind her, she moved swiftly and gracefully along the bank. She glanced back once, and Siegfried followed on behind her.

And final score to Odette, Odile thought with great

amusement, as she observed the crestfallen look Benno cast after them. *Check, and mate, in one move!*

Then, obedient to her father's orders, she followed silently in their footsteps, leaving Benno to cool his heels and allay his suspicions among the other swans.

Chapter Sixteen

ODETTE did not take Siegfried far from the clearing and his friend, just far enough that there was no chance that Benno would be able to overhear them *or* keep a watchful eye on them. She chose another, smaller clearing for her conference, one bordered by the lake so that moonlight flooded it completely. Odile followed at a discreet distance, and when they stopped, she tucked herself into the shadows and whispered a little spell that would bring every word they spoke to her ears. She should have done that last night, but she had been too surprised to think of it. Her father would want to know exactly what they said and did, and if she could not give him an accurate accounting, he would likely never trust her with anything again.

The thought of going home and being confined to the estate again was suddenly unbearable; she thought that she would be willing to sacrifice a great deal for the sake of this new freedom she had tasted. It was even worth the guilt she felt for playing the spy.

And I made no pledges or promises to Odette that I would keep my distance, she consoled herself. *I am simply making certain that she adheres to the conditions Father set for her. Surely she expects that he will have some sort of watcher on her!*

"In a way, your friend is right; I am not what you

think." Turning to face Siegfried, Odette broke the silence abruptly, and with a curiously unadorned choice of words. When Siegfried made as if to reply, she quieted him with a shake of her head. "No, Siegfried, you must hear me out without interrupting, or I will never be able to tell you everything that I must. Yes, I and the others are spellbound; cursed to be swans by day and our own selves again only by moonlight. And yes, the spell was placed upon us against our will. But our captor believes that we all deserve this curse by our own actions, and I, at least, cannot deny that I deserve *some* punishment, though I wonder if any man, even the most severe critic, would say it should be as harsh as this. We think him cruel and even evil—but in his own eyes, he is surely executing a just and proper retribution upon us. There may even be some who would agree with him. You may be one of them, once you have heard me out."

Odile nodded, and mentally congratulated Odette for her complete honesty, and for being scrupulously fair to von Rothbart. *Good for you, Odette! Fair, even-handed, there is nothing anyone could object to in what you've told him. But you can't leave it at that—you have to tell him everything!*

"You—" Siegfried began in a tone of protest.

Odette again silenced Siegfried with a look. "Hear me, and judge my crimes, for crimes they are, for yourself. I broke the betrothal contract my father had made for me, I deceived one of his squires into believing that I was in love with *him* so that he would help me to run away. I intended to go to the Emperor's court and petition for redress, and while I was there, find a husband to *my* taste. So, I broke a holy vow, I betrayed my father once by running and twice by subverting his man, and I betrayed the young squire in his turn. For this, I have been cursed. Now, say what you will, and judge me for yourself."

Odile wanted to cheer for the princess. *Oh, most excellent! Surely even Father would admit that you have exceeded his conditions!* Odette had given no reasons for her actions, and no excuses; as a prince himself, Siegfried was well aware that duty came before all else, and that the vows a prince—or princess—made, were the foundation upon which the throne stood. Odette had made it even harder to win him now—and if she succeeded, no one could cry "foul."

Odile's heart leaped and pounded, and she waited breathlessly for Siegfried's reply.

"You must have had your reasons," Siegfried said quietly, as Odette also waited, her chin up, staring into his face to read what might be written there. "Why did you break the betrothal contract?"

"It was made without my knowledge or consent, and when I was told of it, I would not agree to it, even when Father raged at me. Father himself vowed to Mother as she lay dying that he would never force me to wed anyone I had not chosen." Odette seemed to relax a little; whatever she saw in the prince's expression must have reassured her. "He broke his vow first, and although that does not excuse my actions in the least, he also betrayed his trust to me. That is the main reason. As for my other—" She hesitated. "It was my conviction, not held by my father, that the man he wished to wed me to would in his turn betray us both and seize Father's crown at the first excuse."

Odile held her breath, hoping for an encouraging sign, as the prince nodded slowly. "The Most Holy Father himself has said that a vow made *for* someone else is not valid unless it is consented to. This is only common sense! You did not give consent; you were not even consulted, and you refused consent when you were asked. The vow of betrothal was not valid from the beginning." He said nothing about Odette's other reason, but she seemed content enough with that. "Now—what of your father's squire?"

Now she hung her head, and there was no mistaking the regret and shame in her voice. "For that, I have no excuse or reason of any kind. It was selfish, petty, and cruel. I wanted to take something from Father as he tried to take my freedom from me. I could have attempted escape alone, in the guise of a page. I could have hired a mercenary to protect me, using the jewels given me by my mother. I did neither. I caused the young man to break *his* sacred vow of fealty, and I used him shamelessly."

"And you have done neither more nor less than many women before you, and many who will come after you." Siegfried's voice sounded calm. "You must know that the Church holds that women are weak of will and inclined to sin by their nature." He paused, then chuckled. "All of which has always sounded rather specious to me, coming as it does from priests who keep mistresses and live as any noble."

Odette looked up, startled, and moonlight glinted from the tears on her cheeks.

No, that is not feigned, I would take an oath on it! Odile's heart ached for Odette, and yet she was nearly bursting with hope and pride. Von Rothbart had always told Odile that the only way the maidens would be worthy of release was if they showed true repentance, and if those were not tears of shame—

Then I will eat my slippers without sauce! Odile didn't think she would be dining on silk and leather any time soon.

"It was wrong of me, and I made an innocent suffer," Odette protested weakly. "That is a terrible sin, worse I think than breaking any vow."

Siegfried shook his head. "If he was the squire to a king, he was fully old enough to know his duty and take responsibility for his *own* actions. Lady, forgive

me for playing the devil's advocate, but *I* am a man,
and you are not, and I know full well how a man
thinks. It was possible that he had designs upon you
that you were too innocent to think of. If he had a
dishonest hedge-priest in his pay, he could easily have
overcome you and carried you off to the altar, thus
securing your hand and dower for himself! If he used
you shamefully beforehand, you would have been
forced to wed him! Can you vow that this was not
the case?"

Another surprise to make Odile's eyes widen. *Well!
I had not thought of that! I wonder if the reason he
thought of that is because he considered the idea at
some time?* She was still suspicious of Siegfried to a
certain extent; after all, von Rothbart was not likely
to have chosen a naive and romantic boy as the subject of Odette's trial, but someone who had plenty
of experience with women and was not likely to be
persuaded by tears and a lovely face alone.

Odette opened her mouth—then closed it again.
"I—cannot say." Her brows creased in thought, and
she blushed, her mouth pursing in chagrin. "I was so
intent on my own plan, and so certain I could bend
any young man to my will, that such a thing never
entered my mind. It could have been. It could well
have been." Only Odette knew what was going
through her mind at the moment, but Odile thought
that she must be reviewing some of the things her
gallant squire had said and done in the light of this
new possibility and arriving at an answer that she did
not like. She shook her head, and her mouth twisted
as if she had eaten something sour. "Oh, this does not
reflect on me any better—for not only did I intend
that this man break his vows for me, but I was *stupid*
enough not to pay any attention to what he did and
said! I was so overconfident in my ability to wheedle

and charm that I never thought someone else might be tricking *me*!"

There was no mistaking the chagrin in her voice, and indeed, Odile would have been just as chagrined in her place. *Poor princess! Bad enough to sin deliberately, but how much worse to sin and discover that you were being played for a fool as well?*

"I think you have been punished enough, my lady," Siegfried said, interrupting both of them in their thoughts. "And I, at least, absolve you. Now, who is it that holds this curse over you, and how can it be broken?"

"Baron Eric von Rothbart, a sorcerer of—frightening power." Odette shivered all over, and Siegfried caught up both her hands. She did not try to take them back.

Odile waited uneasily to hear what she would say about the sorcerer—for he would want to know if she had exaggerated anything he did, or twisted the truth in any way.

Please, please, make it the truth, and make it plain and unadorned, she thought desperately at the princess. *I don't want to have to tell him something bad, not now that you've done so well this far!*

"This is what he does—" Odette said slowly and carefully, choosing her words before she spoke them aloud. "He seeks out women who have betrayed the men to whom they are duty-bound, and he places this curse upon them. But we wrested from him the pledge that his curse is bound upon us in such a way that if a man be willing to take one of us to wife, pledging faith to her until death and keeping it, knowing the maiden's sin in its unvarnished fullest, the curse will be broken for all of us. But—*but*—" She held up a cautionary finger. "If that man betrays his bride in turn, the curse will rebound and remain upon that unhappy maid and all the rest for all time. That admit-

ted, he laid it upon my shoulders to be the one to
make the trial for us all. And I believe, although I do
not know for certain, that he meant for me to meet
with you, in specific. I believe that is why he brought
us here, so far from his home. And if you feel that
you have been entrapped—so be it. I will accept responsibility for that as well. But I never intended to
lay traps for anyone, least of all you."

Siegfried did not answer at once, and Odile held
her breath, waiting to hear his response. "That—is a
hard condition to bind a man to," he said at last,
ignoring entirely Odette's words about von Rothbart's
trial and possible traps.

*Really? Is it so difficult, then, for a man to actually
be faithful to one woman for his lifetime?* Odile felt
her lip curl in disgust, and she wondered just how
blatant a womanizer this Siegfried was. *I begin to dis-
like men more with everything I learn about them! How*
dare *Father be so harsh with women, when men are
so perfidious?*

"I know it," Odette said—sadly, Odile thought. But
if she was thinking the same acrimonious thoughts as
Odile, she didn't voice any of them. Odile's sympa-
thies were aroused by that single, sad phrase more
than everything else Odette had said put together.

*She sees her chance of release slipping away—and
she won't run after it, because that would violate Father's conditions! She even warned him that we'd come
here just for that purpose, and that* wasn't *strictly one
of the conditions. Unfair!* Odile was as angry at her
father as she was with the rest of mankind at that
moment; her cheeks flushed, and she longed to be able
to place a curse on traitorous men to match the one
her father had placed on the swan-maidens.

*Worse! They deserve to be loathsome worms by day,
and toads by night!*

"Nevertheless—my Lady and my Love!—I *will* bind

myself to it!" Siegfried cried, just as Odile clenched her fists in anger so hard that her nails bit into her palms. To her shock and delight, Siegfried went once more to his knee before Odette, both her hands still held tightly in his. "If you can tell me as honestly as you just proclaimed your guilt that you can love me, then I will bind myself to that pledge and to you, with all my heart and soul, and for all time! I am *glad* that the sorcerer chose me to be the one to redeem your curse, for otherwise I would never have seen you, and known the only woman I could ever love with all my heart!"

Odette gasped, then burst into tears. Siegfried leaped to his feet and took her into his arms, as gallantly as in any troubadour's tale.

Odile clamped her teeth on a cheer, and contented herself with dancing a little jig in place. *You did it! You did it! You did it just by being yourself, without anything that Father can claim was unfair! Oh, Odette, you are wonderful!*

"Odette, I believe that I loved you from the moment I saw you, and never until that moment had I believed such minstrelsy could actually be true," the prince murmured into her hair as she wept on his shoulder. "Listen; my mother has pledged that I have the right to choose my own bride. A day hence, I am to declare my choice at a fete in celebration of my birthday. If you can tell me that you return my feelings, or even that you could *learn* to love me, I will declare before the entire court that I will wed no woman but you, and cleave to you all my life!"

He took her shoulders, and set her a little away from him, so that he could gaze into her face. "Can you at least learn to care for me, my princess? If you do not love me now, can you learn to in days to come?"

Odette's eyes streamed tears, but she managed a

tremulous smile. "Learn? May God forgive me, but the moment I saw you, I had no thought of any other but you—I would rather suffer this curse for all my days than bind myself to anyone *but* you!"

And that, too, Odile would swear was genuine. Odette had paced the clearing restlessly all last night, refusing offers of food; now weeping, now staring at the moon, now whispering to herself, she had given the impression of someone placed in a situation for which she had made no preparations.

And now I know what that was; the breaking of the curse did not depend on her winning the prince specifically but on winning a man. If he had renounced her and fallen short of the mark, if she had been heartwhole, there was still plenty of time for her to try with another, even the prince's friend. Last night, she realized that she couldn't bear to pursue another man, and yet all of the others depended on her to pass the test and break the spell. No wonder she was agitated!

Odile felt a great wave of well-being wash over her; she could not have envisioned a more perfect solution for all of them! Within days, the swans would be free, and her father would in his own way be free as well! He would have time to turn his attention to his daughter for the first time in years, and he would find—

He will find that I am accomplished enough to satisfy even his most exacting demands! Then at last he would be proud of her; he would give her the praise that she had longed for, he would change his plans to include her as an integral part of his work!

Together, we can do so much, see so much—why stay here, when we have the power to travel to the East, to Africa, anywhere we wish? We could spend our lifetimes delving into new mysteries. . . .

She hugged her arms tightly to her chest to try to contain all her happiness, as Siegfried and Odette murmured little tender whispers to each other, exchanging vows and kisses that Odile didn't bother to note. Then, just for a moment, Siegfried left Odette alone in the clearing, coming back again quickly with his friend Benno. With Siegfried's hand in hers, Odette tremulously repeated what she had told Siegfried.

Benno frowned as he listened, and looked penetratingly from Siegfried to Odette and back again. But evidently even his skepticism was overcome, for when Siegfried again made his declaration, he threw up his hands, but his frown had changed to a smile.

"I suspected the like," he said, shaking his head. "You were entirely *too* well-behaved and obedient this morning, Siegfried. You are never like that unless you have something occupying your thoughts."

Odette looked limp with relief, and Odile shared her feeling; Benno represented the last hurdle to overcome. Opposition from the man Siegfried had called his best friend—

There's no telling what he would have been able to convince the prince of, and meanwhile, poor Odette is gowned in feathers and unable to speak in her own defense. For that matter, he could have made up some story that would have resulted in the prince being chained up for his own good, and then where would we be?

"There is just one thing I would like to know," Benno continued, frowning again. "Just who *was* that maiden I spoke to this afternoon? And why was *she* not a swan, if you all are bound to that form except by moonlight?"

"That—was Odile; she is in a manner our keeper," Odette replied slowly. "She is von Rothbart's daughter, and something of a sorceress herself. She sees that we are fed and protected, both as swans and as ourselves, and she has been a faithful guardian to us."

Siegfried placed his arm around Odette's shoulders,

and glanced about in alarm. "Where is she? Could she be spying on us? Is she likely to harm you?"

"No, no!" Odette cried immediately, making Odile flush with unexpected shame and pleasure that the princess had defended her. "No, she is good and kind of heart; she protected us and worked herself to a wraith to see that we were sheltered and nourished on our journey here! If you had seen her, you would know how carefully she cared for us. I am sure she would never harm any of us, least of all myself!"

"Well—she didn't do anything to me, and I was— very rude," Benno replied, sounding ashamed himself. "If she's enough of a sorceress to make herself vanish the way she did, I suppose she could have saved herself the trouble and made *me* vanish instead. I'd be a lot of good to you as a toad."

"She could have dumped you in the lake to cool your temper, and then where would you be?" Siegfried laughed, relaxing again. "You cannot swim any more than can I."

He turned to Odette, looking down into her eyes, which gazed back up at him in shameless adoration. "Will you permit me to remain with you until moonset, my Lady?"

Odile chose that moment to steal away; nothing Siegfried or Odette could say would be of any interest to her father at this point, and she wanted to let the impatient swan-maidens know what had happened between the lovers. Besides, the idea of staying to spy on amorous confidences made her feel embarrassed and uneasy.

She remembered to make herself visible again before she reached the clearing; there was no point in letting anyone know she had this particular spell, for it would only arouse suspicions she didn't want to answer at the moment.

The one called Mathilde spotted her returning from

the same direction Siegfried, Benno, and Odette had gone, and pounced on her eagerly. The others followed suit as soon as they realized she'd been in a position to overhear what was going on.

"What happened? Do you know? Did you—" they surrounded her with a confused babble, and she waved her hands at them to make them calm down.

She had already decided on a harmless deception. "I've been keeping watch for trouble. When the prince passed me and returned with his friend, I guessed that all had gone well—and since it was no longer just the two of them, I slipped in to where I could hear." She smiled in triumph. "Odette fulfilled every one of Father's conditions and beyond, and Siegfried has not only pledged to wed her, he swears he will announce it to his court tomorrow night, and he has won over his friend as well!"

Never in all the time that she had known them had she ever seen the maidens really happy—and what followed her news was an outburst of joy so overwhelming that for a few moments she feared that their wits were in danger of being lost. Pairs and trios of friends hugged each other breathless; the little swans leaped about like crazed young lambs. Some clasped hands and swung each other around until they fell to the ground, too dizzy to stand, only to rise and do it again. All of them babbled at high speed, their words completely unintelligible.

At just that moment, the prince's friend returned. He surveyed the scene, hands on hips, a wry grin on his sensitive mouth, then approached Odile as the only one sane enough to speak to.

"I see that my news has traveled before me," he said laconically, raising an eyebrow at her.

Odile shrugged. "Once you joined them, they were no longer in private, were they?" she replied evasively. "I do have some interest in this, after all—and a duty to see to."

"You do. And I understand I owe you an apology for some ungentlemanly behavior." He eyed her as if he expected another sharp retort, but she said nothing. "Well, I do apologize."

"And I forgive." She gave him a long, sideways look. Now that he wasn't trying to be offensive, she had to admit that he was, in his way, as handsome a fellow as his friend. "I hope you didn't blunder into too many brambles."

"Just enough to teach me my lesson," he told her ruefully, and she laughed at his expression. "I don't suppose you could teach me that vanishing trick, could you?" he continued hopefully.

"What, so that you can use it to sneak up on unsuspecting maidens and spy on them when they think they are private?" she countered, and laughed, excited by the new sensations she was feeling. Triumph, pleasure, a tingle she suspected was due to the fact that she was actually *flirting* with the fellow in a way—

Is this what I have been missing, kept close for so long?

"The only way I can teach you is if you are willing to learn to swim," she continued quickly, a bit of caution intruding, warning her not to reveal that she *could* become invisible. "There was nothing more to escaping your unwelcome attentions than that. I swam away and hid beneath a ledge where you could not find me. That is all." She laughed at his crestfallen expression. "Surely this is not the first time you've been outwitted, mighty hunter?"

"By a pretty maiden, yes," he said woefully, and she was almost embarrassed at how warm that word "pretty," spoken entirely without the wish to flatter, made her feel. "My trouncing would be easier to accept if you'd done it with magic rather than cleverness."

By this point, the rest of the maidens had left off their celebrations, attracted by the conversation. They watched and listened avidly, eyes shining in the moonlight. Odile had no hesitation in playing to her audience, and neither, it seemed, did Benno.

"So you do admit I defeated you?" She smiled so widely that the corners of her mouth ached. "Doesn't the victor customarily get a prize when a warrior is defeated?"

"Custom says you may have my mount, my weapons, and my armor," he replied, falling in with the joke with a good humor she hadn't expected him to possess. He spread his hands wide. "Since in our contest I had no mount but my feet, no armor but my virtue, and no weapon but my wits—"

"Oh, pray, do *not* burden me with your wits, it will leave me forever at a disadvantage!" she cried teasingly, and he struck his breast as if she had hit him there with an arrow.

"Ah! Lady, you have not only defeated me, you have slain me with your cruel and clever words!" he cried. "See, I die at your feet!"

He slumped to the ground and sprawled out, groaning theatrically, which gave the other maidens a chance to swarm him and help him back up, fussing over him. Odile stood back, laughing, very much amused, and just a little jealous as they made much of him.

At that moment, a pang in her middle reminded her that none of them had eaten, and *she* was the only one who hadn't foraged as a swan. Let Siegfried and Odette live on love if they chose, but she had a duty to her charges, and to Benno as a sort of "hostess."

The provisions in the tree would not do, here. While Benno was occupied with the others, she left the group and sought out a quiet place where she could fetch fresher and tastier viands from the manor. She made

reckless inroads on the wine cellar, and plundered the pantry of ham and cheese, breads, honey, and jam, then attempted a more complicated conjuration that gathered the apples and pears, walnuts and chestnuts from the orchard before bringing them to her circle. The effort left her a little tired, but quite satisfied; she rejoined the group and gathered up the four little swans to help her carry the feast, then led them back in a glow of accomplishment.

"And here, sir, I furnish your funeral feast!" she cried, holding out a platter laden with food as they approached the group gathered like bees around a drop of syrup. When the others saw what they carried, to their credit they left Benno to help with the food and drink. They spread out the food with the grass serving as their table, and Benno sat back at his ease while the others waited on him, each one more eager to feed him some little dainty than the last.

He *did* keep glancing over at her, though, and now and again addressed a remark to her, which she tried to answer as cleverly as she could. There was no reason to feel jealous of the swan-maidens, really—how could they help themselves? They were all accustomed to centering their lives about *men*—they had been bred and taught that all their powers must be bent toward pleasing and serving fathers, brothers, husbands.

They've never learned to read or write, most of them—never thought of going beyond the bounds of the world they lived in all of their lives, she thought with growing pity. *And now, for the first time in how many years—here is a man that they can give all their attention to! No wonder they're acting like little foolish children!* The pity grew and eclipsed the jealousy, especially when she noticed that the few remarks Benno addressed to *her* were clearly phrased to test her wits and her learning, while those he addressed to the others were empty, flowery compliments. That pleased her enormously, and made her warm with pleasure again.

Why has Father shunned the company of others all these years? she wondered. *How can he have forgotten the enjoyment that there is to be had in simple conversation?* She revised her plans for the future. *I must, I shall show him that the life of a hermit is an empty one*, she decided, her resolve growing. *And with his powers, we should be welcome at every learned court in the world!* The idea of spending every night in brilliant and witty converse among courts both great and small, made her dizzy for a moment. Or was it the wine?

She checked the bottle at her side, and determined that it was barely touched. No, it wasn't the wine—it was intoxication of another sort. She cast a smile at Benno, and blushed to get a dazzling smile in return.

It wasn't until Siegfried and Odette joined them that Odile realized belatedly that the hours had sped by. The expression on Odette's face—a painful kind of joy—made her glance involuntarily at the sky. There was light both in the west and the east; the moon was setting, and the sun about to rise.

"The moon—" she said aloud, and conversation stopped dead, as the others followed her glance.

"It is about to set," Odette said gently, and Siegfried squeezed her hand. "I came to warn you, lest you all be caught unawares."

Odile stood, quickly, her eyes on Odette's. "I'm sorry," she said impulsively, knowing that the princess would understand what she meant.

"You needn't apologize—this may be the last time, after all—" Odette tried to smile, but it was obvious to Odile that if anything, this transformation would be the most painful she had ever undergone. Odile impulsively went to her side and took her hand for a moment—the one not claimed by Siegfried. She would have said more, but she saw at that moment the shimmer of light and power that presaged the transformation drop over Odette like a veil. Odette felt it envelop her, and, dropping both their hands, stepped away.

For the first time, Odile couldn't bear to look; she averted her eyes as Odette and the others dropped to the ground and the shimmering power eclipsed their forms.

She felt something powerful driving her to act. *No! I won't let them go alone this time!* she thought defiantly, and like the others, dropped to the ground, her own power spinning the spell about her, blurring her vision and reshaping her form.

When the others rose as swans, so did she; with a single backward glance at the two men standing in the clearing, mouths agape, she followed the flock into the sky, dark silhouettes against the growing light of the dawn.

"So. Are you *quite* out of your mind, Siegfried?" There was more than enough light from the rising sun for the prince to read his friend's expression. It was compounded of equal parts of perplexity, astonishment, and disbelief.

Siegfried could only laugh; it was the single expression his full heart would permit him at the moment. Not even the finest wine had ever filled him with such sweet intoxication. "If feeling altogether unlike myself is being out of my mind, then that might be the explanation." He put out his arms and spun around like a giddy child. "Jesu! I have never known such a woman! I could fight the whole world to be at her side!"

"Fortunately, you will only have to fight your

mother and six disappointed princesses," Benno replied dryly.

Siegfried stopped his spinning to grin at his friend. "Mother can protest, but I will be of age to make my own decisions. As for the princesses, *I* was not the one who promised that one of them would be my bride. In any case, five of the six would be disappointed no matter what, so what does it matter if one more is added to that number? What odds is it, anyway? I would give up the kingdom and make my way as a masterless knight, so long as Odette was at my side."

Benno fixed him with such a look that Siegfried had to laugh again.

"You really mean that!" Benno exclaimed. "By Saint Valentine, you really *are* in love with this woman! I have never seen anyone so—"

"Happy?" Curiously, the question sobered him slightly. "Benno, if this is happiness, I have never experienced true joy before this."

Benno sighed and shook his head. "Truly, you are not at all like yourself. Have you listened to yourself? You have been spouting the worst poetry I have ever heard in my life, and grinning as you do so! You must be in love; only lovesick loons can tolerate such twaddle."

The words hinted at disgust, but the expression on Benno's face was a curiously soft one. Benno put one hand on his shoulder.

"My friend, be as lunatic as you wish," he said soberly. Only that, but Siegfried heard more than the words, as he was intended to.

"Thank you," he said quietly, then peered up at the eastern sky. The rest of the hunting party had already begun the journey to the palace; they would arrive just in time to dress for the grand fête to celebrate the prince's birthday, and to hear him name his choice of bride. "We'd better get back to the inn. I'd like a few hours of sleep before we make the trip back to the palace. Tonight—will be—"

"An event," Benno replied dryly.

There seemed no better description than that, so Siegfried just threw back his head and took in a breath of the pure morning air that only added to his intoxication.

"An event, indeed!" he agreed. "So let us hasten to meet it!"

CHAPTER SEVENTEEN

ODILE had not thought she would be able to sleep when she returned in the gray dawn light to the tree shelter. Too much had happened, too many emotions had tossed her this way and that. But she went ahead and lay down in her bed, and the next thing she knew, she woke with a start, staring at bright sunlight beyond the open door. It was at least noon, perhaps later. How had she managed to sleep? She barely recalled lying down.

She hurried through her preparations and ran out into the sun to see how much of the day was left. It was just about noon, and she was relieved that she had not slept the day away as she had first feared.

What woke me, then? There was nothing in the clearing in front of the shelter, and no sign that anything had passed there. She thought perhaps that von Rothbart might have come seeking her and caused her to wake, but there was no sign of her father. *Odd. I expected to find him waiting for me.*

She searched all of the usual places where he would wait for her, and found them empty. Not a magical message, not a note, not even so much as a feather.

Now what should I do? He gave me no way to find him; it never mattered until now, but how do I tell him what has happened?

She was at a loss and began pacing the clearing uncertainly. If all went well, this was the last day that her father's spell would hold the swans. By tonight, Odette would be the prince's betrothed, and the transformation would never take place again. *How can I tell him if I can't find him? I know he's going to be angry with me if he doesn't find out until after it's already happened. . . .*

She tried to tell herself that von Rothbart had only himself to blame, but that was not much comfort. He *would* find a way to place the blame on her, telling her, perhaps, that she had not used enough initiative.

Maybe if I don't think too hard about it, I'll have an idea of how to find him come to me. Meanwhile, there was always the chance that he *was* laired up upon that island; she walked slowly toward the lakeshore, hoping that she might find some sign that he was there.

But if her father was not waiting for her to awake, as she approached the water's edge, it was clear that Odette was. The regal swan with the golden band about her neck glided slowly up and down the bank, her posture stiff with tension.

Odile knew what she wanted the moment she saw the swan, without going through any of the mime she usually did to communicate with the others when they were in bird form. It was, after all, fairly obvious. "You want to follow Siegfried back to his palace, don't you?" she asked.

Odette's head bobbed up and down, her eyes fixed firmly on Odile's.

"Do you know how to find him? How to find his palace?" That worried her a bit; Odette was *her* responsibility, and it would be bad for everyone if she got lost.

Again the swan's head bobbed eagerly, her black eyes shining.

She and Siegfried must have talked about this last night. Of course! She knows when he plans to leave the village, and she can follow him from the air. Then she can find a place nearby, perhaps a pond in the garden where she can wait. As soon as the moon rises, she'll become herself, and Siegfried can make his announcement with her at his side! It made perfect sense—and naturally Odette wanted to make certain that her "keeper" wouldn't prevent her from leaving, or somehow force her to return.

Father didn't say anything about keeping them from leaving, and if he *wants them kept confined, he should have done something about it. I certainly don't have the power or the knowledge to establish such a perimeter.*

"Well, what are you waiting for?" she teased. waving her hands like a goose girl shooing her charges away. "Go! Or even with wings you won't be able to get there before the moon rises." She made a face, and laughed. "Wouldn't *that* make a pretty sight! You in your fine gown and your dainty shoes, trudging along a dusty road like a peasant!"

Odette did not wait for further permission; she revolved in place and with her back to Odile, spread her wings and took off. In moments, she was a white speck in the blue sky, beginning the turn that would take her over the village that had taken its name from this lake.

And in the future, will they call this place Schwannsee? she wondered. *Will people come here to see the place where the tale began someday?* Ah, that was getting ahead of things; Siegfried still had to declare himself. Vows made in the dead of night sometimes looked odd in the light of day.

She sighed and sat down on the bank. It was then that another explanation for her father's nonappearance occurred to her.

Simply put—he didn't have to be present in order

to keep an eye on all of them. He was an extremely powerful magician, and there was no reason why he couldn't be scrying them, watching them from afar.

But—if that were the case, von Rothbart himself should arrive very soon to hear from Odile's own lips what had transpired, and woe betide her if she left out anything, or if her version differed from what he had observed.

He let Odette go to Siegfried, so I suppose he must approve of what I've done so far. . . .

Clothilde had planned a leisurely breakfast at dawn, followed by a pleasant ride back to the palace. Her plans were interrupted the moment she exited her pavilion.

One of the pages hurried to her side as soon as he saw her, and bowed clumsily. "Majesty, there is a visitor to see you. He says that he must speak with you."

She raised her eyebrow and glanced up at the sky; the sun was barely above the horizon. What could be so urgent that it could not wait—and why had the page referred to the petitioner as a "visitor?"

"Majesty—" Now Uwe strode toward her, joining the page. "Baron von Rothbart wishes to speak with you before you make the journey back to the palace."

"Ah!" Now she understood. "I will certainly see the baron." She glanced around, realized that there was only one place where she could hope to have any privacy, and shrugged. "Uwe, tell the baron to come to my tent—and you, boy—" she addressed the page, "—have a servant bring me tea and bread to my pavilion to break my fast. Bring enough for three."

The servant would bring far more than just tea and bread, if he had any sense.

She turned with a sweep of skirts, reentering the turned-back canvas flaps. Her maidservant scrambled to set up chairs and a small folding table, articles she had just collapsed in anticipation of packing up. As the queen took her seat, the same servant ran off with a fire-pot and returned with coals from a nearby cook fire which she tipped into the brazier she set up at the queen's feet. The warmth from the little brazier was welcome against the chilly dawn air.

Von Rothbart and her breakfast arrived together; she signed to Uwe that he was to join them, then signaled to the maid to leave and drop the flaps of the door behind her. The baron bowed deeply before her, and only took his seat when she graciously indicated he should do so with an inclination of her head.

He made no move to help himself to the pastries brought by the maid. "Gracious Majesty, what I have to say is brief, and I shall not delay your departure if I can help it. Your son has met my daughter, as I had planned."

"Yes?" The queen had no intention of waiting another minute for her meal, and took a comforting swallow of hot, honey-sweetened herb tea. "Was the outcome a good one?"

The baron smiled broadly. 'I believe I can say without any fear of being contradicted that your six lady guests will return home disappointed—unless, of course, they found someone other than the prince among your courtiers. In short, he was so enamored, so completely enraptured by the woman he met, that he declared himself on the spot."

There was triumph in his voice, and for a moment, his eyes gleamed like those of a hunting owl's. The queen felt a strange chill as those eyes fell on her— and just for a split second, she wondered what she had bargained with.

She shook it off, and did her best imitation of a

proud and pleased mother. "How wonderful! This will be a fine match for all of us, baron, I do feel certain. I must confess that I was growing concerned, for I had not heard from you directly, and my dear son showed no signs of interest in any of the young women I had brought here for the fête. I had *so* hoped for a love match for him; it is a hard thing for a young man to be bound to a bride in a marriage of expedience."

"Believe me, if you had heard and seen him, you would have no doubt that his heart has been thoroughly captured," the baron replied with a brusque laugh. "Now, I would like to bring my daughter to your masquerade so that he can make his selection known with her at his side. I trust that there is room for two more at the fête?"

"Of course, certainly!" the queen replied with enthusiasm. "I shall have a word with my servants before we leave this morning, and remind them to add your names to the list when we arrive at the palace. I shall make it my first order of business. Will you require masks, or—?"

"We have costumes, Majesty, but thank you. I think even you will be charmed by them. And there is one other small, very small request that I have to make of you. Could you arrange for all mirrors in your ballroom to be draped?" As he made his request, the baron gave her the strangest, and most penetrating gaze she had ever encountered. So intense, it felt as if he reached inside her mind and backed her into a corner—she found herself pressing her back against the back of her chair, and wondered if she had completely misread the man.

"Why, yes, we can do that," she heard herself saying, "Uwe, see to it, would you?"

Then as if nothing out of the ordinary had ever occurred, the baron was his old, charming self again, with nothing more in his eyes than a gleam. Clothilde

gave herself a mental shake; what on earth had so
disturbed her about this gallant man? She must be
suffering from lack of sleep. She vaguely recalled giving Uwe an order—

*Ah, I have given him so many orders I begin to lose
track of them.*

"Thank you, Highness," the baron said suavely.
"My daughter is shy, as I told you. She finds herself
unable to look at her own reflection in a mirror without becoming intensely self-conscious. I want her to
be poised, confident, show herself to be the fine lady
she truly is. Of all times, this would be the worst for
her to feel as if she would like to retreat into the
corner!" He rose, went to one knee, and kissed her
hand. "I must go—for we, too, have much to do to
prepare for your fête. Until tonight, then?"

Clothilde smiled brightly. "Until tonight, Herr
Baron."

Von Rothbart rose and bowed himself out; Clothilde
waited until she thought he was out of hearing distance before turning to Uwe.

"Now I see why my son was so desperately eager
to go swan hunting again last night," she said dryly.
"And to think I was under the impression he was
trying to indulge my fancies!"

Uwe only smiled sardonically, and helped himself
to a slice of apple cake liberally dusted with sugar. "It
would seem that we have this much; the prince must
be obsessed with this young woman to have declared
his intention to wed in so short a time."

"Obsession is a good thing, for us," the queen replied, making a mental inventory of the stillroom, and
wondering if she had enough attar of roses to complete the love potion. She decided that she did, if she
gave over her plans to make rose water for the cook
and substituted violet instead, at least until she could
purchase more. He was only going to make the win-

ter's supply of rose pastiles anyway; violet was a perfectly good substitute for sweetening the breath.

Uwe gave her an odd sideways glance, as if he wondered what she was thinking. "Yes," he replied, his voice betraying none of his thoughts. "Obsession would be very good for our plans."

She laughed at him, laughed at his suspicions, even if he didn't voice them. "By all means, then, we must encourage these young lovers in their continuing devotion to each other. A swift wedding, I think, then a long honeymoon, free from responsibility—"

"I should think that the king's hunting lodge would be remote enough for them to have privacy," Uwe said smoothly. Clothilde smiled. The hunting lodge was *so* remote that it might just as well have been in another kingdom, yet in her husband's day, it had been a gem of masculine luxury, and could be so again. Opened up, aired out, and refurbished, it could be ready in time for the wedding; staffed with her most trusted servants, neither Siegfried nor his bride would have anything to complain about. She would cheerfully sacrifice the best of her own furnishings to create a feminine bower in the midst of all that masculinity. She made a note to have it stocked with fine fabrics, embroidery materials, and so forth. An infatuated young woman often wished to create special garments to refurbish the wardrobe of her beloved; such work would occupy hands and mind and perhaps keep her from thinking that *she* should bear the title of queen. And if they found themselves snowbound from December to May, well, so much the better. If Siegfried grew at all restless, there was plenty of fine hunting, so odds were *he* would not mind the isolation.

"Well! If we are to have all in readiness, we had best get on our way!" she exclaimed, and rose with alacrity. She pushed aside the flap and walked out into the chaos that was really as tightly organized as any

of her endeavors. Already half the camp had been
packed up onto wagons, and the rest was well on the
way to that state. Her servants had only been waiting
for her to leave before starting on her pavilion; the
moment Uwe stepped through the door a dozen servants swarmed it like mice swarming a crust. He
hadn't gone a dozen steps before the furniture was
out and the pavilion itself was flat on the ground.

Her horse and Uwe's stood ready in the hands of a
groom; everyone else in the court cavalcade was in
the saddle and ready to be gone—including the six
princesses. She almost felt sorry for the poor things;
they were so eager to get back to the palace and don
their costumes for the fête, each of them hoping, no
doubt, that evening's end would see *her* as Siegfried's
betrothed. Little did they dream—

She stepped into the linked hands of a groom, and
he boosted her into the sidesaddle. Arranging her leg
over the horn and her skirts over the back of the
saddle, she took up the reins and clucked to the palfrey, sending the little roan to the head of the
procession.

She took a quick glance at her head groom, who
nodded to indicate that everyone was in position; with
that, she urged the horse into a fast walk.

Soon, soon, now—things were falling into place. It
was almost happening too quickly—and yet, it could
not happen quickly enough. Until Siegfried was firmly
under control again, she would not feel completely
easy.

Odile relaxed as soon as Odette was well away—and
in a moment, she realized why she felt at ease, at long
last. If her father had not wanted Odette to leave, *he*

would have put spells in place to prevent it. Hence, either her father knew what was happening, or he had anticipated it would happen. Perhaps he had even done some scrying into the future to see Odette and Siegfried together.

Whatever had happened, she was no longer responsible for anything other than the safety of the flock. It could not be long now, before she was free even of that. And then—

And then, the world.

She stretched, reveling in the feeling of new-won freedom, and tense muscles relaxed, knots caused by worry in her shoulders and neck released.

Now, I suppose I should wait and see what Father has in mind.

She settled in her favorite lakeside spot with her grimoire; it was too chilly to dangle her feet in the water, but she could move to another position among the gnarled roots, soak in the sunlight, and keep an eye on the swans from there. *Their* tension was visible from across the water; they would not trust in their release until the moment it happened.

And then what will happen to them, I wonder? she thought, watching as they nibbled nervously at lake weeds. *Where will they go? I have no idea where their homes are, if they still have homes. By now they've been given up for dead; their families might well consider them to be apparitions or evil spirits. Or else they'll think the girls ran off with men. Either way, they'll never believe the real story, and never accept them back.*

There should be some room for them in Odette's court, shouldn't there? Siegfried would be able to find places for all of them as ladies-in-waiting to Odette— and even the little swans, peasants though they were in origin, acted and dressed as nobility now. If no one revealed their secret, they would be accepted as the

way they appeared, provided they weren't so foolish
as to reveal it themselves.

Silly things; they just might give themselves away.
Well, that was hardly *her* concern. Let Odette worry
about it.

*She can always turn them into her handmaidens. I
suppose they can learn enough about housekeeping and
maid's duties to make themselves useful.*

Because she faced the island, for the first time since
they had come here, Odile saw her father leave his
secret lair and approach the shore.

Movement caught her eye at first, as she mused in
the sun, her book lying neglected in her lap. She
glanced over her shoulder at the island she had suspected to be his roost, and spotted the wide-winged,
dark shape rising from it, heading straight for her part
of the shoreline.

Although there undoubtedly were eagle-owls lurking in this forest, and although eagle-owls did hunt by
day as well as by night, it was unlikely that there were
any ordinary owls roosting on that island. True owls
seldom used islands as their lairs, preferring the
deep forest.

The owl drew nearer, and she made out its huge
eyes, glowing with a yellow gleam against the darker
plumage. It stared right at her; without a doubt, it was
von Rothbart. She got slowly to her feet, and waited
for him, one hand on the trunk of the willow beside
her, the other holding the grimoire. The owl was in
no hurry to get to the shore; with slow, graceful wingbeats he moved powerfully through the air, giving her
plenty of time to prepare herself. As he drew nearer,
she was caught and mesmerized by his enormous eyes,
eyes which somehow still held the enigmatic force and
concentration of the man behind them.

He wafted in above her head, near enough that the
wind of his wings sent stray tendrils of her hair flying

and drove her skirts against her legs. As with a true owl, there was no sound of wingbeats; he flew in an unsettling and ghostlike silence. He dropped down into the clearing behind her as she turned, and she averted her eyes from the blurring of his form as he transformed from bird to man.

When she looked back, her father waited, settling his feather cloak more comfortably about his shoulders, watching her closely.

"I trust you have a great deal to tell me," von Rothbart said, as she moved toward him, then dropped into a curtsy before him. She raised her eyes to his, but saw no censure there, only expectation.

"I do, Father," she replied as she rose. Clasping both her hands on her book, she gave him her verbal report, watching his face for clues to his mood. Would he be pleased that Odette had exceeded his demands and *still* won her freedom? Would he be angry that she had escaped him?

In the end, she couldn't tell; his mask never dropped, not even for a moment. She was left looking keenly into his face, no more certain of his feelings than she had been when she began.

"I think—Odette has truly earned her prince and her freedom," she ventured at last. "Father—she has worked for this, she has proved herself repentant."

Still, she could not read his expression as he pondered what she had told him. Finally, after a silence that reawakened her tension, he spoke.

"It would be fitting for you to see the end of the story, as you have seen the beginning," he said at last, still with no hint that he intended to drop his mask, even to her. "I have in mind that we shall attend this fête, you and I."

She did not trouble to ask if he had been invited; if von Rothbart wished to attend Prince Siegfried's fête, he would be permitted to do so. That was beyond doubt. Whatever von Rothbart was determined to have, he found means to get.

It was also beyond doubt that if he intended *her* to be there, she would attend with him.

She felt very uneasy from the moment he made the announcement, however. A strange, queasy feeling settled in her stomach, and all the tension that she had lost earlier returned, redoubled.

There was something wrong, some secret he still retained for himself and had no intention of sharing with her. He gave her no chance to question him—with an enigmatic quirk of his lips, too inscrutable to be called a smile, he gestured. And with that gesture, she found herself dropping to the grass, feeling her body twist and change into the familiar form of the black swan.

It happened too quickly for her to feel indignant. When she shook her head to clear her eyes, he was already back to the shape of an eagle-owl, fixing her with his enormous yellow eyes. With a jerk of his head, he launched himself skyward.

It was not so easy for her to take to the air; for all its apparent size, the eagle-owl's body was light for his wingspan. Her body was a much heavier load for her smaller, narrower wings. She plunged into the water, as he circled overhead, waiting for her. Spreading her wings, she plowed the air with them as she first paddled, then ran across the water, gaining enough speed and momentum that she was able to tuck up her feet and achieve true flight.

At last, she soared into the sky to join her father. He waited only long enough to see that she was following him, then without a backward glance, he set his course.

He also set a pace that required all of her effort to match as he drove his way through the sky. She was glad that she had been keeping up her flying exercises, or she never would have been able to follow him.

There was no question in her mind why there was so much urgency in this journey; Odette had left much earlier, which implied that the palace was far enough away that if they meant to arrive in time for the fête, they had to move swiftly.

She wondered where *he* was getting the strength for so swift and prolonged a flight. From the moment she had transformed, she'd been aware of a steady drain of energy; despite the exercise, despite that she was fit and rested, this was hard, grueling flying, and took more out of her than she had expected.

We must be working against a headwind, she thought, when she had breath to think. She wished fervently that it was a tailwind instead; every wingbeat was labored, and her wings felt as heavy as if her bones were lead.

They passed over a patchwork of farms and villages, with intervening stretches of forest; this was, by far, the most populated section of country she had ever seen. There were farmers working in the fields, children at play in the yards of their homes. A few folks with donkeys or horse-drawn carts crawled along the roadways, their shadows stretching out before them in the light of the setting sun.

This was already more people than she had ever seen. *How many people are going to be at this celebration?* she wondered, and felt a twinge of alarm penetrating her weariness. Until she'd met Siegfried and Benno, she had never seen *men* other than her father. Tonight there would be many people at the fête, at least half of them men. How many strange men and women would she be forced to confront?

If she could have, she would have called to her father and begged him to let her go back to the lake.

How could she possibly stand before all those strange faces, face all those alien eyes staring at her?

It was too late at this point. Over her right shoulder the sun touched the horizon; in the distance, the gray-white walls of what could only be the palace rose above the trees like a marzipan subtlety at a feast, softly touched with rose by the last rays. Only now did Odile have some sense of how prominent Siegfried and his family must be; this was an enormous edifice, several times larger than her father's manor, with seven multistoried towers rising far above the walls of the main building. Surrounded by a moat, enclosed with triple walls, this was the dwelling of a king of the first order.

People swarmed the courtyards and gardens, tiny, brightly colored creatures, all very busy. Her initial thought was that she and her father would probably land and transform somewhere within the grounds, but the presence of all those people precluded any such thing.

Once again, her father apparently had something in mind; he swerved off a little to the side, and led her over the turrets of the palace itself. Their wings cast shadows on the palace walls, and the windows of the highest tower gleamed at her as they passed a few feet below her. On the other side of the palace, within the third wall, was a horse-pasture, but oh! it was a pasture for the horses of a king, and no less. With ponds and meadows, wood-lots and fine fences, any horse would consider it heaven-on-earth. On the palace side lay stables as extensive as her home manor. Beyond it, the pasture stretched rich and lush across an expanse that dazzled her. Some of those acres were out of sight of the palace altogether, and at the moment, the pasture and stables were devoid of any sign of people—who were, presumably, all very much involved in preparations for the fête.

Von Rothbart led the way to the plot of trees nearest to the stables. They landed next to the woods in the last fading light of sunset; rather than landing in a tree as a real owl would have, von Rothbart landed on the ground and waddled into the shelter of the shadows. Odile followed, flaring her wings and dropping lightly down onto the grass. She walked slowly under the boughs, finding it easy going, for the horses had grazed and trampled away the underbrush. The owl waited for her, just far enough into the shadows that it was not immediately obvious where he was.

He transformed as soon as he saw that she had landed safely; she made her own change, and stood beside him, a little dizzy with exertion. He looked her up and down, and shook his head, clucking in disapproval.

"This will never do—so plain a gown, for such an important fête? You are an important personage, a lady of rank, not a simple knight's daughter. We will have to clothe you in something more festive."

She hesitated, one hand on her throat, not certain what he meant for her to do. She had no idea of how to clothe herself for a grand court, much less for a great occasion at a grand court! Where should she begin?

He laughed shortly at her expression; he evidently read it correctly and knew her confusion. "Never fear, daughter. I have experience enough in such things for both of us. I shall see to your festal garb."

He gestured briefly, and she felt a tingle running all over her body, as if thousands of butterflies were beating their wings frantically against her. She glance down in startled amazement, seeing her gown as a black blur about her, a mist of shadows that billowed and swirled exactly like storm clouds, obscuring her body as it roiled around her.

Then it stilled, and settled into the folds of the most

incredible gown she had ever seen in her life. In heavy black silk-satin, embroidered all over in a pattern with a suggestion of feathers, encrusted with jet beads and tiny black gemstones that reflected light in a million minuscule facets, this was nothing like the simple gowns she had grown so accustomed to. Beneath the heavy overgown with its long, elaborate train and divided front panel, was an underdress of black gossamer silk, and beneath *that* were so many black silk petticoats, each as light as a breath of air, that she wondered how long it would take to put them on naturally.

Her arms and neck were laden with heavy jewels; black sapphire and black pearls, set in ornate frames of dark gold. But the crowning touch was the enormous span of wings, real feather wings, springing from the gown at her shoulders.

These wings were also ornamented with jewelry, a conceit she never would have imagined on her own. Dark, pigeon's-blood rubies, emeralds and sapphires of the deepest green and blue-black, in settings of the same, dark gold, the decorated wings were so enormous she could not imagine how the dress supported them. Yet they felt weightless to her, as if they were not there at all.

Her father handed her a mask on a delicate, filigreed wand; the mask was the head of a black swan, surmounted with a crown. As an unexpected breath of cool air passed across the back of her neck, she put her free hand up to her head in startlement. Her hair had been built up, braided and twined with more jewels. She could not for a moment imagine how she looked; she only hoped that it wasn't *too* ridiculous.

Her father was also costumed, but although he wore a cape that replicated two huge wings flowing down his back, he was not disguised as an owl. He had the armor and helmet of a warrior, and with the wings, he looked like nothing so much as an avenging angel.

"This will be a masquerade," he told her, "so I have provided appropriate costumes for both of us. I think we will make a striking couple."

He offered her his arm, and she took it gingerly. He led her out of the woods and up toward the stable, using the shadows of the stable-yard to cloak their entrance through the walls to the main courtyard. Or—perhaps he cloaked them in invisibility; she could not tell.

They were certainly visible enough as they entered the courtyard.

The court was full of carriages and bustling people, both servants and gaily clad courtiers. Not only the inhabitants of the palace had been invited, it seemed, but everyone with pretensions of noble blood for miles around. In the chaos of the courtyard, their entrance without a carriage went unnoticed; they could have alighted from any of the vehicles being pulled out of the way by anxious grooms. Their costumes, however, excited a great deal of attention and no few glances of sheer envy; Odile hid her face hastily behind her uplifted mask to hide her blushes and confusion.

She was glad to have her father's arm to cling to; she felt light-headed, fever-hot and chilled at the same time. Perhaps it was the sudden press of so many strangers, the sense of urgency and hurry. She felt the pressure of strange eyes on her skin, and wished herself anywhere but where she was.

Von Rothbart basked in the attention, and took his time strolling across the cobbles to the entrance. People instinctively gave way before him, and many bowed or curtsied, assuming that anyone so clad must be of high rank and great wealth and power. It was easy enough to tell which of the people were guests, even without livery; guests wore costumes, even if the costumes were nothing more than a mask with their court dress. No one possessed costumes as elaborate as theirs, however. The sheer span of Odile's wings would have forced people to give way to her had she used them in that way.

Just how am I supposed to dance in this? she wondered, licking her lips nervously. But there was no denying the fact that she and her father were impressive; from the looks that some folk gave her, she thought she might be the most outlandish thing they had seen in their lives.

Those waiting at the door cleared away at their approach so that she and her father sailed through without impediment. They passed from the torchlit courtyard under the twilight sky into the brilliantly illuminated interior. Candles gleamed from many-branched holders set into the wall; more candles shone from chandeliers made of dozens of gilded deer antlers suspended from the ceiling. Before them stretched the entrance hall, a short passage that led to an antechamber, which in turn led to the double-doors of the Great Hall. A line of guests stretched to the doors, now flung wide to admit them; at the door stood a liveried herald to announce the names and titles of the guests before they made their entrance.

Von Rothbart led Odile to the line with the assurance of one who attended such functions every day. Odile kept her mask before her face, surveying the room and the people from behind its shelter, as they slowly made their way toward the herald. The other guests made no attempt to conceal their curiosity; Odile's dress was the richest in the room as far as she could tell, and her father's was as impressive, though in a more subtle fashion. No one here recognized them, and there was much buzzing of conversation behind them, much whispering behind hands before them, as other guests speculated as to their identity.

Finally they reached the herald, who deferentially asked her father for his identity and consulted a scroll he held in his hands when von Rothbart replied.

The herald cleared his throat and stepped into the room. As the guests within the Great Hall caught sight of the extraordinary couple waiting to be announced, the hum of conversation stilled for a moment, and the herald's voice rang out into the expectant hush with the tones of a trumpet call.

"Baron Eric von Rothbart—and daughter."

Chapter Eighteen

OUTSIDE, thunder growled in the distance, and dim lightning flashed beyond the windows, silhouetting the trees black against the glass. There was a storm approaching, but that didn't seem to concern anyone as they stared at Odile and her father. In that moment of silence, Odile took in the entire hall, slowly moving her gaze from left to right, from behind the security of her upheld mask.

The air was warm, and laden with the warring scents of many perfumes. Between walls swathed in drapes of umber and gold fabric and cascades of late-autumn flowers and greenery, groups of brilliantly costumed guests milled on either side of an "invisible" passage where those to be presented to the hostess moved in a steady, stately progression. The end of this "corridor" led directly to a canopied dais on the far side of the room that stood beneath a pointed arch of stonework marking a recess in the wall; beneath the burgundy canopy were two wooden thrones. On one, the taller and more elaborately carved, sat a crowned woman; on the other, looking absently out the window nearest to him was Siegfried. The queen, a regal figure in scarlet velvet trimmed in ermine, greeted each guest gravely as they presented themselves to her, but the prince paid little or no attention to them. Siegfried's costume for the masquerade was minimal; a fine suit of court dress in white satin and black velvet, with a simple black-velvet domino mask that dangled from his hand.

Von Rothbart led Odile down toward the thrones, making way for the next guests to be announced, and following in the wake of those who had come before. If they had been the objects of attention before, they were now the objects of intense scrutiny and comment by the rest of the guests. Conversation ceased as they approached and increased as they passed; Odile kept her mask up firmly before her face and stared straight ahead, but her father basked in the attention, sauntering along in no particular hurry, gazing about him as if the other guests were nothing more than vaguely interesting plants in a garden. As they neared the vicinity of the dais, Odile found herself the object of some painfully direct attention from a half-dozen groups of people, each clearly associated with a particular young woman of very high rank. The groups shared a costuming "theme" with their putative leader, with their masquerade garb being less elaborate than hers.

The women themselves were not all as intent on Odile as their followers were. One made no pretense of being anything other than bored with the entire affair; her costume was also that of a bird, though not as elaborate as Odile's. She wore a gown of brown velvets and silks with dagged sleeves that resembled wings, and the mask of a fierce hawk—not the sort of thing one expected a young woman to wear! Her followers were dressed as other woodland creatures: stags and foxes, songbirds and the like.

Of the others, two—one all in black, with black gloves and a sinister black feline mask whose followers were also dressed as cats, the other her exact opposite, all in white, with no mask at all, and abbreviated angel-wings fastened to her shoulders with a retinue of sylphs—showed a great deal of interest in young men lurking on the edges of their groups. But the other three (in fairly conventional carnival costumes, Spanish, Magyar, and Slovak in theme) leveled glares at her that were both suspicious and threatening, and Odile wondered why, even as she flushed further. She was deeply grateful for her mask, which she clung to as to a shield.

Then, before she could regain her mental equilibrium, they stood before the queen. Odile lowered her mask as she dropped into a deep curtsy, her skirts pooling around her, and did not arise until the queen gave her permission. Queen Clothilde smiled coolly at them as von Rothbart bent over her hand, looking Odile up and down with a measuring glance. *She was beautiful once—she is handsome, still. I can see where Siegfried got his good looks. But there is something very cold and hard about her; I would not care to cross her will.* "Well, Herr Baron," she purred. "I understand—everything—now that I see your daughter."

Thunder growled nearer.

Siegfried was still staring out the window, paying no attention to the queen and her guests. Was he watching for Odette? *Of course he is—the moon isn't up yet, and he must be wild with impatience.*

"Indeed, Highness," von Rothbart replied, and chuckled, a deep rumble in his chest. He took Odile's wrist in an unbreakable grip and drew her forward until she stood by his side. "So now, may I formally present my daughter, Odette, to you?"

The moment he spoke the wrong name, a chill, then a strange tingling, swept over her, and for a moment the queen's face blurred, as if Odile gazed at her from beneath a foot of rippling water. *Odette?* she thought, startled, as Siegfried's head snapped around and he riveted his gaze on her. *Why did he call me—?*

"Odette!" Siegfried cried joyfully, leaping to his feet and reaching toward her, before checking his movement as if he only just realized where he was. "But—why—how—"

"All will be explained in time, Prince Siegfried," von Rothbart said smoothly, as Odile felt her mouth taking on the curves of a smile against her will, and watched her free hand reach for Siegfried's, then pull back modestly. "For now, simply take joy in this evening, and let matters become clear later."

Odile struggled against the spell that had seized her, but to no avail. She no longer even controlled the blinking of her eyes; she was trapped inside a body that glanced flirtatiously at Siegfried, only to blush and look away.

Von Rothbart moved aside in answer to the queen's beckoning finger, taking a place to one side of her throne where the two whispered together. Von Rothbart did not take his eyes off Odile, however, and as for Odile—

Siegfried had a chair brought for her, and insisted that she seat herself beside his throne. Her eyes and mouth smiled, her hand rested in Siegfried's; only her thoughts were hers.

This is Father's doing! He's made me look like Odette—dear Jesu, he's using me to make Siegfried break his vow to her! When the bonds of the spell closed around her, von Rothbart's intentions were only too clear. If only there were mirrors! The reflection in a mirror would betray her real identity to Siegfried—

But if there were any mirrors about, they had been hidden by the draperies and flower garlands. Was that her father's doing, as well? Had he planned all this from the very beginning? He must have! How else could this all have fallen out so perfectly? She, Odette, and even Siegfried had been manipulated like pawns on the chessboard for von Rothbart's pleasure, with

the outcome of the game determined before it even
began!

Dismay turned, in a flash to anger, and anger to
rage.

He never *intended to keep his word! He* always
planned to betray Odette! And he's using me *to do it!*

Inside, she was afire with fury; outside, as cool as a
snowmaiden. Her body sat beside Siegfried, watching
politely as more of the invited guests presented themselves to the queen. He held her hand and murmured
tender endearments that *she* didn't listen to, though
her body bent toward him and murmured back. Siegfried couldn't tell the difference, as her body responded
anyway with modest flirtation, actions choreographed
by her father.

Anger built and built with no way of expressing it.
She was so angry now that there was nothing real for
her except the anger and the terrible helplessness. . . .

The last of the guests were presented; one of the
groups she had noticed earlier stepped forward, their
costumed lady at their head—this was the Magyar
group. They performed their bows, and the lady made
a graceful little speech; Odile struggled to regain control of her rage and herself.

*This is energy; this is power. But it isn't going to do
me any good unless it's focused!*

As she used her anger as a weapon, she threw herself with all her might against the spell controlling her.
As an ironic counterpoint to the raw struggle going
on beneath her tranquil surface, the musicians played
a sprightly folk melody, and the group performed a
clever dance especially for the queen and Siegfried
designed to showcase the grace and beauty of their
leading lady.

One by one, each of the six groups came to perform
before the dais, as Odile pounded against the magical

bonds holding her a prisoner. Like a wild thing in a trap, she beat against the barriers with all her strength.

At last that strength failed her, and she fell back within herself with intelligence dimmed and energy exhausted, having made no more impression on the spell than a single raindrop on the face of the sun. Bitter defeat rolled over her in a black tide, until she was as overcome with cold despair as she had been with fiery rage.

Meanwhile, her body smiled and shyly caressed Siegfried's hand, and made complimentary comments on the dancers. Von Rothbart said nothing, and hardly moved at all; she longed with all her soul for something to demand his attention and distract him for just a single moment. If only she could get a single crack in the walls of magic imprisoning her! The storm in her heart mirrored the nearing storm outside—and she made as little impression on her sorcerous bonds as that outer storm did on the walls of the palace.

When the last of the six groups finished a stately pavane, the six ladies came forward as a group, and waited expectantly before the thrones. The prince paid no attention; he was too busy looking into Odile's eyes. "Siegfried," the queen said, with a touch of sharpness, "You must dance with your guests now." The look in her eyes promised trouble if he did not obey, as did the tone of her voice, and with a sigh, Siegfried rose.

"It's just this one dance," he whispered, before turning away from her. "They'll learn the truth soon enough."

The truth? Look at me, you idiot, and see the truth!

Odile's mouth smiled, her voice answered, "Of course. It is only courtesy," as her mind screamed at him to look, really *look* at her!

But he didn't; he just smiled fondly, and went off to partner the six young ladies in a kind of ring dance

in which he was the only male. They all knew now
that they had no chance of winning him, but three of
them kept trying anyway. They might just as well have
been cronies of his mother's for all the attention Siegfried gave them; he was polite, gallant, and never
touched them any more than the dance required.

Odile's body stared straight ahead; without Siegfried
to beguile, her father wasted no time or effort on making her perform. Instead, he now whispered confidences to the queen, who smiled and simpered like a
flirtatious virgin half her age. Although Odile could
not even turn her head on her own, she did have the
queen, her father, and the queen's minstrel in her line-
of-sight—and a strange little tableau they made.

Von Rothbart, wearing the mask of a fond father,
betrayed nothing of his true intentions and feelings as
he traded compliments with the queen, and, occasionally, the minstrel. The queen also wore the mask of a
devoted parent—but *her* mask slipped now and again,
showing the ice beneath the surface warmth, the steel
beneath the silk. It did not take Odile long to realize
that the queen truly hated her son; did her father
know that also? What plot had the two hatched between them?

Von Rothbart had never before involved another in
his schemes. And this bid fair to destroy Siegfried as
well as Odette! Why would her father harm a *man*
when he never had before? Why was he helping the
queen to break her son's heart—and perhaps his mind
as well?

Or was this plot even deeper than the queen knew?
Was this entire subterfuge a trap to catch a queen as
well as a betrayal of his daughter and Odette? Was
Siegfried no more than incidental to this disaster?

The minstrel, all smooth blandness, let *his* mask slip
less frequently than the queen, but in the few instants
that he did, Odile was surprised to see the venom

directed at the queen *and* von Rothbart. For Siegfried, there was only contempt; for herself—nothing. She was a nonentity to him. What part did the minstrel play in all of this—and what did he expect to gain? Had her father promised him something? Or was he not involved at all?

She was just as much of a nonentity to the queen, who made no effort to speak to her, though there were a few remarks directed *at* her that she was clearly not expected to answer.

For the moment, Odile was too exhausted to care, and far, far weaker than she should have been.

And why, do you suppose, is that? a tiny voice asked in the back of her mind. *Could it be that Odette was right—that you and she and all of the swans have never been anything to your father but a reservoir of power he could dip into at will? Could it be that this was the only value you ever had to him, other than being a convenient puppet, spy, and bait for a trap?*

Yes. Oh, yes. Anger, now sullen, smoldering, and heavy, stirred in her again, uncoiling from her gut like an ancient dragon newly awakened.

Yes, she answered her own voice. *Odette was right.* There was no reason why she should be so depleted—unless her father had stolen her power to in turn fuel the spell to steal her body.

In a blinding instant of chilling epiphany, it all came clear to her, and found voice in three poisonous words.

I . . . hate him.

There had *never* been love, there had *never* been care, or pride, or anything but the same cold calculation a farmer uses when admiring a calf he is raising for slaughter, or a cow who gives unusually rich milk. She had never been a person to him, only a possession—and no one worries about the feelings of a possession. No one loves the calf destined to become veal.

How long had he been using her? She stared at that
face, that familiar face, knowing that at any time she
would have sold her soul for his approval—knowing
that if he had ever come to her and *asked* for her help
she would have given it without a second thought.
*Would I even have betrayed Odette after she and the
others became my friends?* With a sick feeling in the
pit of her stomach, she knew that, had her father said
and done the right things, she might have. She might
very well have, if he had offered, not only approval,
but affection. And had he been an iota less arrogant
and self-confident, had only a second thought about
his own power and ability, he might have done that.
"Help me, my daughter," he might have said, "I depend on your help to unmask this traitorous queen,
to prove to Odette she is not ready and her suitor is
not worthy. I cannot do this alone, I need the daughter
I love to work with me at my side."

*And if he had, it would have been just as false as
this mask he wears now.* Everything he had ever said
or done was with the intention of getting more from
her than he pretended to offer, even in illusion.

Her anger built again, and with it, some of her
strength—but she was clearer in her mind now, and
determined to hoard the dearly won power. No more
flailing against the walls of her prison; now she would
hold her power in reserve, and wait. He could not
hold her forever . . . eventually he would have to drop
the spell, if only when he revealed his true intentions
to the queen and her son.

And meanwhile, she would use her anger to destroy
the connection between them that made it possible for
him to take what he willed from her.

Siegfried returned, the dance complete, and beckoned to her to dance with him, alone. Now, sensitive
to the nuances of the magic imprisoning her, she felt
the pressure increase around her. Her body rose—she

willed it to walk stiffly, unnaturally, but it did no such thing. It moved gracefully, and far more seductively than she ever could have on her own.

They danced, and if she had been in control of herself, she would have fled in sickened and acute emotional pain. This "dancing" was none of hers!

Siegfried seemed oblivious to the fact that his demure and modest beloved had somehow transformed into a seductress, a mate-devouring Lorelei, entrancing her would-be spouse into her clutches with the promise of passionate carnal love. Her body moved in subtle ways she hadn't dreamed possible, and she went from writhing in anger to squirming in shame.

Siegfried, blinded by love, blinded also by sorcery, gazed at her in abject adoration. Nothing she did broke the spell of enchantment or disturbed his lovelorn gaze.

Is this how Father sees women? she cried out in anguish. *Even me?* How could he think of *her* like this? *She* had never done anything to make him believe she was a Jezebel like this!

But he was willing to use her however he wished, so why shouldn't he degrade her as he chose? If he thought of her as a fatted calf, why not think her a man-eating whore as well?

If she could have wept, her tears would have burned furrows down her face, so bitter were the dregs of degradation that she drank at that moment. Those unshed tears drowned every last bit of feeling she had for her father, washed it away in hate-filled revulsion.

This dance, too, came to an end, to the polite applause of the court and the disgruntled glances of her "rivals" and their entourages. Siegfried caught her hand and kept her from returning to her seat when the music ended; she felt tension building to a climax.

Siegfried, don't! Look at me! See me, *not the illusion!* She thought at that moment that nothing could have made her feel worse—until a ghost of movement caught her attention, and she looked over the heads of the courtiers to the windows.

Peering into the hall, with a face as pale as one drowned, eyes black with pain, hands beating in utter futility against the glass, she saw Odette.

And Siegfried, spell-bound and spell-blinded, saw . . . nothing. Nothing but *her.*

He gestured grandly for silence, and the crowd hushed obediently. "Tonight you are gathered here to honor my natal day," he said proudly, "but also to honor my choice of a bride. Out of all of the lovely maidens who have graced our court with their gracious presence this night, I regret that I can wed only one." He looked about with a fatuous smile on his face, and Odile screamed inside her mind.

Look! Look! Oh, you fool, you idiot, look and see! Look at my father, your mother, and see the trap they've laid for you!

"I wish that I could grant each and every one of you a prince and a kingdom of her own," he continued, as Odile's body smiled on. "But only one maiden has won my heart, and it is to her that I will pledge my troth, now and forever."

As the real Odette watched in horror from the window, and Odile screamed soundlessly behind her own eyes, Siegfried dropped to his knee beside the Black Swan.

"This is she!" he cried, taking her hand in his and kissing it. "This is the maiden, and no other, that I will take to wife, the enchanting daughter of Baron von Rothbart!"

And into the silence that followed—Eric von Rothbart laughed.

Only then, as von Rothbart roared with triumphant laughter and the storm broke above the castle, did the spell slip. Just a little—but just enough.

With a strangled cry, Odile shattered the spell holding her, and shattered the illusion von Rothbart had wrought. She leaped away from Siegfried, toward the fatal window—she whirled, and Siegfried saw her real face.

And behind *her,* the tortured face of Odette in the window, gazing at him in despair.

Lightning flashed, and thunder rattled the windows; with a cry of absolute agony that echoed from floor to the rafters of the hall, Odette reached for Siegfried from the other side of the glass, reached for him, and was stopped by the glass.

The cry should have shattered the coldest heart, but von Rothbart only roared with laughter again, as Odette melted into the Swan Queen, whirled with another cry of despair, then spread her wings and allowed the tempest to carry her away.

Now von Rothbart spoke, his voice full of contempt as the crowd stood, numb and silent. "So, Prince Siegfried, *this* is how you keep your word? You vow yourself to Odette, then swear to Odile before the sun rises a second time?"

He might have saved his breath for he was speaking for the benefit of the crowd, not to the prince; Siegfried was already at the door of the hall, calling Odette's name as he ran. No one tried to stop him; they all seemed turned to stone with shock.

Only Odile could still move, and she picked up her skirts and ran, right on his heels, driven by that once-beloved voice.

Clothilde's cup of pleasure was full to the brim, without room for a single drop more, as Siegfried fled into the tempest, wildly calling out after someone only *he*

had seen. She didn't understand what the baron meant by his taunt, but she didn't particularly care. Nor did she care why the baron's daughter had run off after him. As the courtiers milled in confusion, as the storm increased in fury and lightning struck the trees just outside, she stifled her laughter behind her hand, hoping that she could feign being horror-struck instead of hysterically pleased.

He'll never be king! was her only thought at the moment. *They think he's mad—they'll never accept him as king! The throne is mine—mine—mine!*

But the storm had a will of its own—and the power to set every plan at naught.

A flash of blinding light that filled the Great Hall changed her elation in an instant to primitive terror. The thunder that struck at the same instant drove her backwards to cower, trembling, beneath the canopy of the throne. A sudden burst of wind shook the glass, threatening to collapse the windows, and a second lightning strike nearby sent half the court screaming out of the hall to seek shelter somewhere less exposed. In the next instant, the windows shattered in a shower of shards, and the storm winds drove the rain into the hall. The wind swept away the warmth and perfumes, replacing it with cold and the faint scent of brimstone. All the candles blew out at once, leaving no illumination but the continuous lightning.

Only von Rothbart stood in the center of the hall, defying the storm—or was he conjuring it? Those courtiers who had not fled cowered against the walls, while lightning struck again and again, while the winds howled insanely about the chamber. Clothilde huddled in her throne, her heart pounding as loudly as the thunder that drove her back against the wood; the very stones beneath her feet shivered. Icy cold bit to the bone, but she could not move; fear, and von Rothbart's glowing eyes, held her where she was as her rich garments were whipped wildly by the wind as if the heavy velvet were as light as gauze, and the canopy tore away from the frame above her.

"Daughter of Eve, temptress and betrayer, you play traitor to your perfidious son as you did to his father." Von Rothbart's voice was impossibly clear over the thunder, as if he spoke mockingly into her ear. He moved ponderously toward her, step by deliberate step. *"As your tainted blood runs true in your son, he in turn betrays his own vows, a blackguard poisoned in the womb by his harlot mother!"*

How could she hear him? She was near-deafened by the booming of the storm, the banshee wailing of the wind, yet every word burned in her ears!

"Your poison must be purged," von Rothbart went on, his eyes shining with demonic glee, raising his hands above his head to emphasize his words. *"Never again will you betray another, for death is the wages of sin! Look up, witch, and see the Hand of God bringing your punishment to the very walls of your iniquitous den!"*

He gestured upward, and her eyes followed his gesture involuntarily. She saw a white-hot bolt of lightning race in through the broken window and strike the wall above her head, at the point of the archway that sheltered the dais. Helplessly paralyzed, unable to move to save herself, she watched a fierce, white fire race along the seams of the stonework. Thunder shook the stones to their foundation; she *saw* them moving.

Half the arch trembled, rocked, and fell. She watched the massive blocks of stone descend, and did not comprehend what was happening until it was too late.

She could only watch, clutching the arms of her throne in impotent terror, as the stones hurtled toward her; her mind, her ears filled with the screams of her courtiers mingled with the howls of the wind, and the sound of von Rothbart's mocking laughter blending with the thunder.

Odile did not follow Siegfried once past the doors of the palace; at the moment, *he* was unimportant. Nothing he could do would change what he had already done, however unwittingly.

It was Odette she followed, leaping into the arms of the storm winds and transforming herself as she did. She spread her wings wide and let the wind bear her up; the Black Swan was strong enough to ride the worst tempests, her wings powerful enough to make the wind serve *her* purpose. Odette, transformed out-of-time back into her swan shape, again fully under von Rothbart's magic, could only be fleeing back to the flock. *He* would not let her escape him now.

Odile drove her wings with powerful, deep strokes of her shoulders, and grimly followed on. Without her father draining her, there was no exhaustion; had fury not settled into her heart, she might have found exhilaration in riding the winds. But there was room for only two concerns in her thoughts tonight, and both of them centered on her father. He would not succeed in destroying Odette. And Odile would make him pay for his own double betrayal. The thousands of ice lances of rain beating down on her would not even slow her down; the lightning spears could not frighten her, nor the thunder shake her determination.

She pushed on, using the wind to add to her speed, following instinct rather than sight in rain so thick as to be blinding. She concentrated solely on flying, speeding through the skies, leaving no room for thought.

Abruptly, the rain ended; she blinked ice water out of her eyes, took her bearings, and kept going, but now she did not have to work so hard to stay in the air.

The winds are slacking. . . . That, and the end to the rain told her she had come to the edge of the storm. When she broke through into moonlight, she caught sight of a far-off glimmer of white that could only be Odette, and a farther gleam of moonlight on water that was her—their—goal. They were nearer the lake than she had thought.

She lost sight of Odette briefly when the swan descended below the tree-line, but she already knew where the Swan Queen was going. *Now* her wings began to feel heavy, as heavy as her own heart. What would Odette say—what must she be thinking? Would she ever believe that Odile had been coerced, tricked, and betrayed, just as she was?

It does not matter what she believes, so long as I can make it right.

She arced down to the water and back-winged at the last possible instant, to make her landing as short as possible, and as near to the shore as she could. Odette was not there, but furtive glimpses of white among the trees gave her all the clue she needed as to where the flock was.

She drove herself up onto the shore and transformed on the run; one moment, waddling awkwardly, the next, running surely on two swift feet, the clearing before the tree shelter her goal.

But when she saw what awaited her, she stopped abruptly on the edge of the clearing, one hand on a tree trunk.

Moonlight poured down on the clearing, as if the moon was trying to pour balm on a heart wounded past healing. In the center of a fluttering, helpless group of maidens, Odette lay prostrate on the ground, weeping. Her sobs, so deep, so full of absolute despair, shook answering sobs from Odile's throat; the Black Swan's eyes stung and swam, and a sick lump lodged in her throat.

Half the swan-maidens wept with their leader, the other half tried in vain to console her. Nothing any of them could do or say made any difference, and Odile recognized in her disconsolate weeping the desolate sound of someone who wanted only the release of death, for there was no more hope in the world for her ever again, only pain.

Suddenly, it was no longer important to Odile that Odette understand her role as unwilling fellow victim. Whatever *she* felt was insignificant compared to the despair that held Odette's heart in its stygian darkness.

So she stayed, frozen, at the edge of the clearing, unable to go to Odette but unable to leave. Hours crept by, the moon traveled slowly across the sky, and still Odette wept, as if she could fill the sea with her tears, and still not weep enough.

The moment he saw Odette, and saw who he had *really* pledged to wed, Siegfried's guilt and grief drove him in an instant past sanity and into a kind of focused clarity that made him see that he had only two choices at this moment—either to give up and drive his own dagger into his heart, or to follow Odette and attempt to save her, somehow. Stricken, he watched her take on swan form and be wrested away by the tempest outside. With thunder and von Rothbart's laughter deafening his ears, he ran—ran—seeing only her despairing eyes, feeling his heart torn and bleeding by what he had done to her.

He must have found the stables, he must have had

the sense in his frenzy to select a horse, because in his next moment of clarity, he discovered himself on the back of the fastest courier-horse in the herd, racing headlong through the storm on the road to the lake. Rain lashed him, lightning blinded him, thunder deafened him, and none of these things held him from his wild gallop. Not even concern for the horse induced him to slacken his pace. Lightning struck the road in front of him, and the horse shied. The moment it faltered, he urged it on, cruelly, with whip and spur, wresting its head around and cutting at its flanks. Maddened by pain and the tempest raging about its head, the horse responded with hysterical energy, somehow keeping its feet as it pounded through the darkness.

He was not in much better condition than the horse, driven by the whip and spur of his own tattered emotions; soaked to the skin, numb with cold, eyes burning, muscles aching, and the bitter taste of bile in his mouth. Only the lightning flashes showed them the road ahead of them; there was the sharp scent of ozone in the air whenever a bolt struck too near to the road.

Abruptly they broke out of the storm into moonlight; he shook the last of the rain out of his eyes and shouted to the beast to encourage it. The beast responded to better conditions and the prince's continued goading by putting on more speed, though no mortal horse could have matched Siegfried's neverending demands. Whenever it tried to slow, he spurred it savagely. The black-and-white landscape swept past him, the lathered horse strained beneath him, he never seemed to get any nearer to his goal, and the nightmare ride stretched on with no sign of the end.

Odette! Sweet Jesu, what have I done?

Hours—days—years later, the horse plunged into the blackness of the forest. It did not get as far as the lake, for its strength gave out. Finally, the poor beast could no longer answer to the demands of whip and goad. It stumbled, recovered as he fought to wrench it to its feet, then stumbled again and went to its knees.

He knew the horse was done when it stumbled the second time and was ready when the horse failed beneath him. He tumbled off its back, falling heavily to the ground and bruising his shoulder. Somehow, he got to his feet and raced headlong into the tree shadows, leaving the horse to live or die on its own.

He stumbled through the underbrush alone now, with branches tearing at him, roots and stones tripping him. The storm he had outraced was catching up to him; he heard thunder growling behind him, and caught the occasional flicker of lightning. He must have fallen a hundred times; he barely felt the bruises, but struggled to his feet, and ran on, his sides aching, and his lungs burning.

He burst into the clearing where Odette lay, prostrate and beaten by despair, surrounded by her weeping maidens; before his courage could fail him, he flung himself down on his knees beside her and gathered her into his arms.

A hateful, familiar chuckle rumbled like the approaching thunder; he looked up, torn between guilt and rage, but saw only the maidens cowering away from a shadow shape.

"How charming," said von Rothbart.

CHAPTER NINETEEN

ODILE felt the darkness of her father's presence only a moment before he laughed, by the way her skin crawled and the faint tug she felt toward a darker shape among the trees. She froze before he made his presence known; the flock responded to his cruel chuckle by shrinking away from him as Siegfried started and looked up. She shrank back into the shadows and cloaked her own presence from him. This might be a coward's move, but until she was certain he could drain no more power from her, she would not reveal herself. She could probably stand against his draw on the flock, but she was not certain she could withstand a direct attempt to steal her magic. If he did not know she was here, he could not mount a special trial on her.

She sensed the pull on her increase as he *tried* to extract power from her—and from the others—but she resisted successfully. The pull increased. It felt exactly like a cord connecting Odile with her father, stretching tighter, tighter; she clutched the tree trunk and continued to resist, clenching her jaw and closing her eyes to concentrate. If she did not keep her wits about her, she would find herself answering the pull by coming out into the open.

It was tempting, so tempting, to sever the cord at

that moment and let it snap back on him. That might have disoriented him long enough for the swans to flee. But doing that would surely reveal her presence, and it would have snapped back on *her* as well, and she was none too certain that she could absorb that shock. Such a tie worked both ways, and all actions at this point would have multiple repercussions.

If her father noticed her resistance, he made no sign. Perhaps he didn't; his attention was taken up with marshaling his powers and mocking the prince. Since he wasn't aware she was here, perhaps he marked down the resistance to putative distance from him.

Von Rothbart used words like arrows, aimed directly at the heart. Why had she never *seen* that before? "How very charming, and what a fine display of loyalty, Prince Siegfried," he chuckled. "You abandon lovely Odette for my daughter, then run off from my daughter to throw yourself at Odette's feet. Will you next seek to court Odile when Odette sprouts her feathers and rejoins my flock?"

Unfair—and blatantly untrue! Odette had been there, she had seen the truth of the matter! Did he think to drive a wedge between the lovers with such an accusation?

But it was Odette who sprang to Siegfried's defense before the prince could gather his wits to speak. Dashing her tears from her eyes as anger replaced grief, she faced von Rothbart squarely, and leveled accusations of her own. "There was no treachery here save your own, sorcerer!" she retorted, in a voice harsh with weeping. "*You* are the cause of all our grief, *you* transformed your daughter into my image, and you and no other laid the trap beneath his unsuspecting feet. It was trickery, and no true betrayal, as well you know!"

"Nevertheless, it was to my daughter he pledged his

troth," von Rothbart replied implacably as Odile grew
hot and cold with renewed anger at being used so
shamelessly. "He swore to wed *the woman that stood
beside him* and no other." He laughed. "He is for-
sworn, Swan Queen. You have failed the test and so
has he, and you are mine for all time!"

In answer to that, as lightning flickered in the sky
and thunder growled angrily, Siegfried leaped to his
feet, drawing his dagger. His face was dark with outrage, his mouth twisted into a snarl. Odile shivered,
seeing him in that state, and prayed silently that he
did not feel the same hatred for *her*. "You will have
her only when I am dead, warlock!" he shouted, taking a fighting stance, balanced on the balls of his feet,
ready to strike out at his enemy.

The sorcerer had drawn his own silver dagger in
automatic response to Siegfried's challenge, but now
in confident bravado, knowing that Siegfried's weapon
could not harm him, he cast it away. Odile watched
the dagger spin away, glittering as it flew, with an avid
hunger. *Here* was a weapon that von Rothbart had
cause to fear!

She marked where it fell; not so far from her hiding
place that she could not find it, if von Rothbart was
sufficiently distracted.

"I have her, with or without your death, Prince
Oathbreaker," the magician mocked, "But if you wish
to contest me for her, be my guest. See? I have cast
away my own weapon! Take the first blow! I will not
even defend myself."

Thunder rumbled, underscoring his words, and his
mocking smile grew darker, more sinister. "But be-
ware, Prince. I will not attack *you*—but if you attack
me, I will be freed to work my will upon both of you,
by whatever means I choose. You may strike the first
blow, but *I* will strike the second."

Siegfried, so afire with rage he probably was not

even thinking anymore, paid no attention to his words or his warning; he charged the sorcerer with his dagger in hand. He did hold it properly, prepared to defend against an attempt to take it from him, but of course no such attempt was forthcoming. Von Rothbart simply stood there, a sinister smile on his lips. Siegfried raised the dagger at the last moment, feinted, and made his strike. He plunged the dagger into von Rothbart's unprotected chest, penetrating the showy breastplate and sinking it hilt-deep into the area of von Rothbart's heart.

Siegfried jumped back with a shout of triumph—and stared, dumbfounded, as the sorcerer waved his hands in a mocking half-bow, and laughed at him. A moment later, as lightning flashed and thunder rolled directly overhead, the hilt dropped from the sorcerer's chest and fell harmlessly away, the blade dissolved by von Rothbart's protective magic.

Siegfried's shout of triumph turned to a gasp of dismay, and the maidens wailed aloud. Odette ran to his side and clutched his arm. But while Siegfried had attacked the sorcerer, Odile had crept to the place where von Rothbart's dagger lay and had snatched it up. Now, with the dagger securely in her possession, she went back into hiding.

"I warned you, Prince Siegfried," von Rothbart said, with an avaricious hunger in his voice that made Odile's skin crawl. "Now it is my turn. You struck the first blow. I shall strike the second."

Now that it was von Rothbart's turn to act, he did not hesitate. With a completely impassive, masklike face, he strode forward and seized Siegfried's throat in his right hand. As the prince struggled, the wizard lifted him bodily off the ground, half-strangled, holding him kicking and frantically tearing at the magician's fingers. Von Rothbart merely stared at his captive, as if Siegfried were nothing more than a vaguely interesting insect he had not yet decided to swat.

Odette flung herself at von Rothbart, and the magician cast his captive aside to make a grab for her, probably intending to hold her out of Siegfried's reach and continue to taunt them both.

He's enjoying this!

Odette avoided his outstretched hands, leaving a single shred of white silk in his grasp as she whirled out of his reach. With a cry, she cast herself over Siegfried, protecting his body with her own.

And that drove the rest of the flock to interfere.

Before von Rothbart could act, or Odile could form any plans, the entire group of swan-maidens interposed themselves between the sorcerer and his victims. If he flung any destructive magics at his chosen victims, he would have to do so only after cutting down most of his precious captives.

But the desperate ploy could only bring temporary salvation, as Odile knew only too well. With all the power her father had at his disposal, this was nothing more than a distraction. Von Rothbart had very direct ways of dealing with distractions.

A lightning bolt lanced into the waters of the lake, as von Rothbart roared his displeasure and gestured imperiously for the swans to make way for him. "Begone!" he shouted, his face scarlet. "Out of my way, shameless harlots! Get you gone, or suffer with your queen!"

The maidens trembled visibly, their faces averted from his direct gaze and blanched with fear—but they refused to move away. Odile clutched the dagger and wondered where they had found their sudden courage.

With a growl von Rothbart gathered his magic; Odile felt the ominous weight of the power he massed beneath his control, and it was her turn to tremble.

Behind the shelter provided by the maidens, Odette

helped Siegfried to his feet. The prince now thrust her behind him, and prepared to face von Rothbart again. It appeared that he was quite ready to attack the sorcerer with his fists for lack of any other weapon.

But first, the wizard brushed the maidens aside with a sweep of his arm; fueled by his power, a wall of force parted their ranks, as if a giant's arm shoved them out of the way. They fell to either side of an invisible corridor, dropped prostrate on the grass, the mists of his magic gathered about them to hold them in place so that they could not interfere with him again.

In the moment that he dropped the maidens to the ground, Odette and Siegfried exchanged a *look* seen by only Odile.

Though Odile was on the opposite side of the clearing from them, the emotional weight of that look struck her and held her dumb.

Instinctively, she knew that they had gone beyond themselves in that moment—beyond despair, beyond grief—and that, somehow, they had joined their spirits in a way not even von Rothbart could sever. But a cold dread came over her as she realized what that wordless, weighty exchange of glances meant. An unspoken pact had been made in that instant.

Their love was too strong, their mortal frames too weak; without each other, they would die. So rather than be parted for even an instant, they had chosen to enter death together—trusting that von Rothbart could not pursue them beyond that veil, and could not stop them before they crossed it. Trusting, in fact, that if they "tried to run," he would strike at them in fury and slay them on the spot—

—or if he did not, they could find their release in the cold waters behind them.

As one, they turned and ran, arrowing their course, as Odile had feared, for the lake.

Von Rothbart stared after them in baffled fury. *He had not yet realized their decision; he only saw them fleeing, and did not know that they were courting a killing strike.*

But Father is not that impulsive—and he has more skill and options than they know. He's only been toying with them until now.

As Odile watched in horror, she could almost hear the thoughts in her father's mind. He knew they could not escape his reach, and he gathered his power again—a death-blow for Siegfried, and a transformation for Odette. The prince would die, and Odette would still be von Rothbart's prisoner, trapped in her swan feathers—

Odile's own anger rose in a cresting wave, white-hot and fierce.

No, Father! Not again, never again!

All of his attention was on the two figures running from him, illuminated by incessant lightning above their heads; none of it was spared for a look behind. This might be her only chance.

She did not stop to think, for if she had, she would never keep her courage. She dashed out into the clearing, running as hard as she could. At the last possible moment, she raised von Rothbart's own silver dagger above her head, clenched in both hands, and drove it with all her might into a point between his shoulder blades. The impact rocked her with shock; she let go as if the dagger's hilt burned her, and jumped back out of von Rothbart's reach.

There she stood, frozen in place, her hands tingling. *What have I done?*

Convulsing with shock, arms flailing in a vain attempt to reach the hilt, von Rothbart whirled and stared at his attacker. His face twisted with pain, his eyes blank, his mind clearly refused to believe *who* had struck him. He took a single step and reached out for her—

Even now, if he had *asked* for help, she might have saved him. She could have; she could have pulled out the blade, stopped the bleeding, helped him heal the damage. All he had to do was ask. . . .

But he did not. With his dying strength, he flung a spell at her designed to *force* her to his side, to wrest from her the help she would have given, with no care for what it cost her.

"No!" she cried in fury, and called on her own power, hoarded for just this purpose—and channeled a bolt of lightning from the heavens above to the hilt of the dagger penetrating his protective magics.

The lightning answered her call, eagerly coming to her summons.

She shielded her eyes in the crook of her arm, and still the bolt blinded her as it struck. White heat scorched the air. The simultaneous clap of thunder knocked her to the ground, her hair stood on end and her skin burned. . . .

When she looked again, blinking away tears, there was nothing to be seen of von Rothbart. Nothing! It was as if he had never been there.

Fearing he had somehow escaped destruction, she crawled desperately to the spot where the lightning had struck.

And there, in the middle of a place where the grass was burned black, was a man-shaped pile of ashes, a puddle of melted silver slowly cooling in the midst of it. As thunder rolled, and lightning continued to strike overhead, she finally grasped the fact that he had *not* escaped, after all. This was all that remained of the mighty sorcerer, Baron Eric von Rothbart.

She blinked, slowly coming to understand that he was gone, truly gone—and he would never return.

Jesu . . . what have I done?

She was not granted the leisure to answer that question.

"Odile! Odile!" Two of the maidens, Mathilde and Jeanette, came out of the darkness, and tugged insistently at her arm, tears streaming down their faces. "Siegfried and Odette—"

"What? What?" she replied, dazed. What could possibly be wrong now that her father was gone?

He's gone . . . gone. . . .

"They've thrown themselves over the cliff!" Jeanette sobbed. "They've thrown themselves into the lake!"

Sweet Jesu! She gathered her scattered wits about her and ran for the shore, followed by the sobbing girls. She followed in the direction she had last seen the two heading, and spotted the knot of more of the maidens who stood on the shore, crying and clinging to each other, pointing out into the lake.

In the continuing lightning flashes she saw a dark form—Siegfried—floating face-down in the water at the foot of the cliff; there was no sign of Odette.

A surge of anger fueled her; after all of this, all she had endured, all she had sacrificed to stop him, von Rothbart would *not* win!

Kicking off her shoes as she ran, she launched herself into the dark lake in a flat dive, striking the icy water with a shock. She did not let it stop her; after all the shocks she had endured tonight, this was by far the least. Propelling herself through the water with arms still aching from the blow that had killed her father, she reached Siegfried and rolled him over. She did not pause to see if he was still breathing, but took a deep breath and struck down into the depths, hands outstretched, calling on what little power she had left to help her. Down there, in the cold blackness, the Swan Queen drifted. She would not allow the lake to have her. She *would* not.

Her lungs screamed for air, but she would not give up her search, even though little sparks dazzled before her eyes and her chest was afire. Within the water, within her mind, she coaxed the last of her magic to help.

Bring her to me! Bring her to me now!

Her hands touched something soft, floating—she seized it, and knew it for Odette's sleeve. With a final burst of strength, she fastened both hands in the soft fabric and kicked out with both legs, hauling the lifeless body to the surface.

By the time she reached air and broke through the water, gasping for breath, there were four more bodies in the water with her—Elke, Ilse, Lisbet, and Sofie, the four little swans, who, being peasants, swam as well as she did. Emboldened by her example, they had come to the rescue, and she thanked God that they had, for she was spent.

Elke and Ilse already had Siegfried between them and were halfway to the shore; the other two took Odette's limp body from her and followed the others, leaving Odile to drag herself along in their wake.

But when she crawled up onto the shore, the maidens were weeping even harder, and there was no sign of life in either body. It seemed that all of their effort was in vain.

For one moment, she too despaired. But she was not going to give up. Not yet.

Not until I have no more options to try.

"Stop that!" she ordered sharply, and a sea of white, tear-streaked faces gazed, startled, at her. "My power is gone—but *you* have magic in you, magic enough that we might yet save them. Will you give it to me?"

They looked at her as if she had spoken a foreign language, and her temper finally snapped.

"Now!" she ordered. "Decide! *Yes or no?"*

They looked at each other helplessly as Odile stifled the urge to take their magic without consent. She would *not* continue the path that her father had taken. But time was slipping away, and with it, any chance, however fleeting, of saving the lovers.

As one, the swan-maidens turned to Jeanette as default leader. She put her hand to her throat, and ventured a tentative, "Ye—es. . . ."

That was all Odile needed. As ruthlessly as her father would have, she stripped every vestige of energy from them that they did not absolutely require to remain alive themselves.

Von Rothbart had never taken power from them so abruptly, or so completely. Some of them fell over in a dead faint, the rest just dropped to the ground, as utterly spent as she had been a moment before.

As they collapsed, she poured that energy into the two soaked, limp bodies beside her, forcing the water out of their lungs, the air into them, strengthening the hearts that beat so feebly, calling the spirits back from the darkness in which they wandered. The other maidens sprawled on the shore, those who were still conscious too exhausted even to watch as she worked.

If Siegfried and Odette had been truly dead and gone, she could not have revived them; she knew that. But they were not—quite—dead; their spirits had not escaped their bodies, and she could use the tether of lingering life to drag them back, use their love to call each to the other.

Two chests began to rise and fall; with the returning breath, a bout of coughing drove the last of the water from their lungs, and they began to stir. Siegfried was the first to revive; he groaned, turned on his side, and opened bloodshot, dazed eyes. Then, when he saw Odette, he sat up abruptly, taking her into his arms just as she opened her eyes.

Odile released the remaining power back to the rest

of the flock, who in turn began to stir weakly. She staggered to her feet, weary almost to death herself. She was so cold she couldn't even shiver, drenched and dripping, and wanted nothing so much as a warm place to lie down.

Fortunately, there was one very near at hand.

Using tree trunks to support herself, she staggered the few feet to the tree shelter, collapsing in the darkness and warmth onto her own bed.

After a long interval of simply lying in the darkness immersed in the most basic sensation of all, that of knowing she still existed, she finally regained the ability to put a simple thought together.

I just killed my father.

She lay unmoving as she absorbed the full knowledge of that thought. Then, at last, her own tears began.

She wept as she had never wept before, mourning, not the death of the sorcerer, but the loss of the father she had *thought* she had.

He never was. And now, he never will be.

She cried for herself, that she had been lied to, manipulated, and used all her life. That she had never been more than an object, a possession, of no more importance than a cup or a vase, valued not for what she was but for what purpose she could serve. Just as easily discarded, just as easily broken.

She sobbed, unconsoled, for all the things she had never had, yet had *believed* that she had. She cried for the loss of her innocence, and with it, the loss of what had been, for her, a comforting and comfortable world. All illusion, all delusion, and now, all of it gone. Worst of all, the knowledge that all of it had been one more lie.

Finally she ran out of tears. She lay with aching eyes and burning cheeks, and stopped thinking about what she had lost—remembering, instead, what she had won.

Freedom. Hadn't she been willing to do almost anything to keep freedom, once she had tasted it? Well, she *had*. And now she need answer to no one but her own will and conscience. The whole world lay before her, and if she faced it alone, she also faced it as herself, not someone else's puppet or shadow.

Friendship. True, she might have lost the friendship of Odette and the other swan-maidens, but there were more people in the world than the flock. She could find other friends, other companions. She had learned how to do that, after all; learned how to give, and how to accept, how to ask instead of demand. She had learned that respect was not the same as fear, and that it was much more to be desired.

Knowledge, of herself, as much as anything else.

I have gained—myself. And that is no small thing.

She got up slowly, for her arms and legs ached cruelly from all of the unexpected exertion. Her damp dress was ruined, the ornamental wings no more than tattered stubs. She tore it from her with distaste, shaking off the last rags, and dropped the jewels atop it. Standing naked and free of the last remnants of the fetters her father had put on her, she felt a small part of her burdens lift from her.

I am no longer his creature.

When nothing of what her father had created remained, she toweled herself off roughly until her skin tingled, then took the clothing that waited for her on the shelves above her bed. She took down her hair, removing the rest of the jewels from it and discarding them, combed it out roughly, and twined it into a simple braid.

Now I am myself.

Only then did she walk back out into the clearing. The first gray light of dawn painted the sky above

the clearing; the storm had passed, and the last flickers
of lightning illuminated the towering clouds on the
horizon with orange flashes. As the sun rose, the moon
was setting. The maidens of the flock stood in little
clumps, singles, and couples, watching the moon go
down with anxious faces. Siegfried and Odette, shivering, clung to each other, as they, too, watched the
moon. Siegfried had proven his faith to Odette, even
to the point of death; was the spell broken, or had
von Rothbart lied as he did so easily? And von Rothbart himself was gone, dead beyond doubt—but would
his will and his magic persist beyond his death? When
the last moonbeams vanished, would the maidens become swans once again?

*If they do—I'll find a way to break the spell if it
takes me the rest of my life.*

Odile had no idea that she had spoken that thought
aloud until she realized she was the focus of every eye
in the clearing. She shivered, and looked back at them
all with eyes that asked for forgiveness. Her part in
this had been unwitting—but how could they know
that?

Although Siegfried looked at her with some doubt,
Odette squeezed her hands and smiled warmly on her.

"If the spell still holds us, it does not matter," Odette said boldly, much to the startlement of the rest of
the maidens. She laughed at their expressions, and
shook her head. "No, truly, what *can* it matter? The
sorcerer is gone, he rules us no longer! Odile, dear
friend, you have done so much for us already. Do not
drive yourself into a wraith just to keep us from
sprouting a few paltry feathers! If we are swans by
day and maidens by night, at least we are free!"

"And any man who truly loved you would guard
you by day for the sake of the hours he could spend
with you at night," Siegfried added, putting his arm

fondly and protectively around her shoulders. "*I* will undertake to keep you all safe, if that be the case."

"Until I find the cure," Odile replied stubbornly. "I *will,* I swear it, for I owe you all that much. What my f— von Rothbart did, I shall undo, though I cannot restore all the years he stole from you, nor give you just retribution for what you suffered."

"Look!" Katerina interrupted, her voice full of incredulous joy as she pointed at the horizon. "Oh, *look,* all of you!"

The moon had set while they spoke, and not even a hint of it remained above the horizon; the sun arose in a sky made glorious by the remaining clouds, which caught the golden rays and reflected them back in tones ranging from silver to rose. *The moon had set*— and the maidens were maidens still.

With little cries of joy, they celebrated, each according to her nature. Elke, Ilse, Lisbet, and Sofie spun around and around in a mad dance until they were dizzy, the others embraced, or, like Jeanette, dropped to their knees in heartfelt, thankful prayer.

Siegfried and Odette fell into each other's arms.

Odile alone watched the sun rise, soberly.

And now what? The end of the tale? And they lived happily ever after? No one ever explains how one manages that. Siegfried and Odette will, surely, but what of the others? And what should I do now, to live happily ever after. . . .

She heard the hoofbeats of approaching horses long before anyone else did. She turned, and the others gradually became aware that there were people arriving. Many people; from the sounds, there might be a hundred.

Threading their way through the forest, and led by Benno, was a crowd of folk on horseback, with several riderless horses in tow.

Despite their bedraggled finery and exhausted faces,

Odile recognized them with a sense of shock. *Clothilde's courtiers—the guests from the fête—*

But they no longer looked so festive. Their garments, stained with soot and rain, storm-tattered and torn, were no longer fit for a feast. Their eyes, full of fear and sunk into their pale faces, told of a long night full of horror, spent without sleep. Their faces were lined with fear and the terrible knowledge that a world they had thought stable and unchanging had come down about their ears—and they had not yet found a new center for it.

Only Benno looked anything like his old self, and his face overflowed with anxiety that transmuted magically to joy when he saw Siegfried. Then he stood up in his stirrups and whooped, waving his hat in the air, before vaulting out of the saddle and running to embrace his friend.

Self-consciously, Odile withdrew to the side of the clearing, feeling very uncomfortable and at the same time wishing with all her heart that she did not.

How wonderful it would be to have a friend like that—and a place to belong. The thought of the manor, empty now, but full of the memories and contaminated with von Rothbart's magics, filled her with nausea. Of all the places in the world, that one, now, was the last to be called "home."

The others dismounted slowly, but seemed very much relieved to find their prince alive and well. Quiet and subdued, they let Benno do all the talking. Which he did, at a high rate of speed, interrupted by Siegfried and Odette who related their side of the tale.

"Siegfried, this is like a miracle!" Benno laughed at last, holding his friend at arm's length. "Dear God, we were so afraid, with you running like a madman into the night and—" Then his face fell abruptly. "Blessed Virgin, I forgot. Siegfried, you are the king now. Your mother—the sorcerer was not content to drive you into the storm—he had some business with the queen as well. Lightning struck part of the Great Hall; the wall above the dais collapsed, and she was under the worst of it."

Siegfried paled, but Benno wasn't finished. "So was Uwe." His face darkened with anger. "But he didn't die until he'd told us the truth; he was afraid to die with such sins on his soul. Siegfried, she was in league with that sorcerer, and *he* was the intermediary! She intended to keep you from the throne forever—by beguiling you with women if she could, by arranging an 'accident' with the sorcerer's help if she couldn't. Once you had sired a son, she intended to be rid of you."

Odile bit her lip as the last piece of the puzzle fell into place for her. *That was why we came* here, *why it was Siegfried and not some other prince. That was how von Rothbart knew the doings of the court. And that was what drew him here in the first place—the chance to catch, not a young maiden, but a queen, a woman already heavy with the sins of betrayal.* She watched as Benno explained the little that the minstrel had confessed before dying, watched Siegfried's face reflect so many changing emotions that she wondered which one he would settle on.

It looked for a moment as if anger and hatred would win—but Odette placed her hand on his arm before he could speak, and put in her own soft words.

"If it had not been for her, the sorcerer would never have brought us *here*," she reminded everyone. "That, to me at least, balances some of her greed and vanity; we would never have found each other if it had not been for her. Let the past bury the past, let her answer to God and not to us for her sins, whatever they are; I for one do not intend to waste a moment's more thought on her." She turned a face full of soft wonder and pure happiness to Siegfried. "It would be one more sin to waste time on *her* that we could have spent in joy!"

Siegfried's expression softened, and he nodded. "God alone may judge her," he said, loud enough for everyone to hear. "Let her be buried with the honors of her rank and estate as queen regent; let the rest be as God wills, for we have no way of knowing her thoughts or her heart."

It was as if a burden had been lifted from the hearts of the courtiers; their gloom fell away, and Odile wondered at the wisdom Odette had just shown. And Siegfried, too, in following her lead—

I should take the same advice. Let my father answer to God; I have a life to find. It would be difficult advice to follow—but wouldn't it also mean that she wrested a little more of herself away from him?

That declaration set off a torrent of activity in which Odile found herself caught up with the rest. The weary courtiers surrounded all of the maidens, even Odile; before she knew what she was about, she found herself lifted up by one of the young knights to perch pillion-wise behind Benno on Benno's horse. Siegfried appropriated one of the led horses, and took his place at the head of the procession back to the palace, with Odette on the saddlebow before him.

By the time Odile thought to protest, they were underway, forcing her to hold onto Benno's waist to keep from falling off. No one had asked *her* if she wanted to go back with the rest!

"Wait—" she protested unsteadily. "I don't—"

"Don't you want to see Siegfried and Odette wed and crowned?" Benno asked, over his shoulder. "From all *I* understand, you've been rather helpful in all of this. I should think you deserve to take part in the celebrations."

"Yes, but—"

"Have you anywhere else you need to go?" he continued, as if she had not answered.

That was a very good question, and she thought it over. "Not immediately," she replied, still trying to get used to this entirely novel mode of transportation. She had never ridden a horse before—and being perched sideways on a pad behind the rider was a bit precarious, to say the least! "At least, I don't think I have anywhere I need to be."

"Good." Benno seemed to consider it all settled. "The others want to stay with Odette, why don't you do the same, at least until the celebrations are over?" He managed a charmingly crooked smile over his shoulder. "I think you'd enjoy it. Siegfried's people are very good at contriving entertainment. I can't imagine that the swans held very many fêtes, did they? It would be a bit difficult, I should think, and the menu likely to be limited. Water-weed, corn, and grass don't seem festive to me."

She was both taken aback and rather amused by his flippant assessment of the situation. "No, you're right; there were no fêtes, if I recall correctly," she responded, trying to sound dry and proper, and not certain she had succeeded.

"Good. Then stay a while, until you make up your mind about where you want to go. Odette wants you to stay. Siegfried does too. And—" he added, with a lift of his eyebrow, "—so do I. You're the most intriguing lady I've ever met. And—"

Was he blushing? Yes, he was! The back of his neck was a distinct scarlet!

"—I want you to teach me how to swim."

CHAPTER TWENTY

IT turned out to be a winter wedding, after all.
Siegfried was crowned immediately, in a sober
ceremony attended only by a handful of the most
important courtiers, the ones he had appointed as his
Privy Council. Since the funeral of his mother had
preceded it by no more than an hour, anything more
elaborate seemed inappropriate.

And a proper royal wedding took a great deal of
time to organize, as well. Siegfried was determined
that his Odette have the finest celebration ever seen,
and the swans were just as determined as he that this
celebration be an occasion to be remembered for
generations.

So the wedding took place on Twelfth Night, as a
fitting conclusion to the festivities of Christmas. On a
crisp, clear winter morning, with fresh snow lying like
swansdown over everything, Siegfried made Odette his
bride, and the Swan Queen in truth. The feasting
began in mid-morning, with tables spread in the courtyard for anyone who cared to enter the palace gates,
and every space in the Great and Lesser Halls taken.
No less than four sets of musicians, six jugglers, two
acrobats, and two real minstrels entertained. The
dancing began when dinner was cleared away, and
didn't end until dawn.

Odile had contributed her part as inconspicuously as possible. She'd helped with the rebuilding of the Great Hall; with careful and near-invisible use of magic. Claiming she knew something of glass making, she'd had the shards of the windows taken to a deserted workshop, then melded them back together with magic when no one was about. The stonemasons reset the panes, and no one seemed to notice that the quality of the glass was much higher than it had been—and no one noticed that it was now virtually unbreakable. She'd "assisted" with the lifting of the stones from a discreet distance, then made certain that the mortar set hard, and in half the usual time, once the stones were in place.

When repairs were completed, she joined the household in their frantic preparations for the wedding— and took a great deal of amusement from her invisible help. Bolts of ornate silks were "discovered" among the common woolens; trims, beads, ribbons, and the like appeared in the most unlikely places just when they were needed. At the Harvest Fair, when Odette and her ladies went shopping among the cloth merchants, their purses never seemed to have a bottom . . . every coin spent was replaced by a mate, until the Fair was over.

All of this wealth came from von Rothbart's manor, of course. The invisible servants, released by von Rothbart's death, were no longer there to keep it up, and Odile had decided that, whatever else befell, she was *not* going to reside there. There was a great deal of wealth in the place, however, and why should it go to waste? Why should gorgeous draperies, fine carpets, and luxurious furs gather dust, moths, and fall to pieces, when she could give them all new homes?

So silks and trims and ribbons made their way, a bit at a time, to the stores of Siegfried's castle, either taken from the stores of the manor, or plundered from the "linens" and furnishings. Von Rothbart slept on silk, but why waste perfectly good fabrics on beds and curtains no one would ever see again? Odile knew every inch of the manor—except for the master's tower—as intimately as any housemaid knew the palace. She took the gemstones and beads from the tapestries; the gold and silver threads became little coils of bullion for embroidery. Coin from her father's hoards ended in Odette's household purse. The fur bed coverings and rugs turned up in the queen's solar and other chambers. As she had brought food from the manor to feed her swans and herself, now she plundered the riches of the place to provide for Siegfried and Odette and the rest of the flock.

She thought, from the sly, conspiratorial glances Odette gave her from time to time, that the queen knew what was going on. And if Odette knew, so did Siegfried. At least once a day, one or both of them would go out of their way to give her quiet but nonspecific thanks, which was exactly what she felt most comfortable with.

Siegfried's people, with the exception of Benno, were uneasy around her—not that she was at all surprised by their reaction! She was a magician, a sorceress, and they all knew it. So until the wedding, she decided that her best course of action was to appear to be just like any of the other maidens. . . .

Almost like any of the other maidens, anyway; to her chagrin, she discovered that she was the only one of them who didn't actually know how to perform the most basic of "female" tasks—how to sew! It was such a novelty to find that there was something that she couldn't do, once she got over her embarrassment, she took a great deal of amusement in acquiring that skill.

There were other things she didn't know how to do, as well. She couldn't ride, or hunt, and Benno took particular delight in teaching her to enjoy both. Like him, she preferred to hunt, not for the quarry, but for the pursuit. On clear winter days, a company of them would go out riding, and if she came home without actually shooting anything, no one commented.

Odile gradually made another change in herself; she stopped wearing black. With the rainbow of fabrics being worked with for the wedding, and a court full of ladies more than willing to advise her and help her, she finally escaped the last vestige of being her father's daughter.

It was the oddest thing, but once the flock ceased to be swans by day, they lost that pallid, transparent appearance. The change was greatest in Odette, whose hair had deepened in color to a true pale gold, and whose cheeks and lips now warranted the poetic descriptions of "roses and cherries." Only Odile retained her transparently pale complexion, her spun-silver hair.

As a consequence, most of the colors that looked marvelous on others of the flock made her look like a corpse. Anything warm-colored, from red to gold, looked hideous, and pale tints only made her look bleached and faded. Brown was impossible. Black still suited her perfectly—but black was the last thing she wanted to wear.

Ah, but deep cool colors, emerald and sapphire, *did* look just as well; those were expensive colors to dye, but what good was being a sorceress of you couldn't manage a paltry color change in your wardrobe?

And so she shed the last mark that von Rothbart had put on her, and she found that a change in wardrobe had an oddly uplifting effect on her spirits as well.

When she met Siegfried's tutor Wolfgang, however, her real cup of pleasure overflowed. Here was exactly the sort of person she had dreamed about meeting— learned, scholarly, even witty at times—conversant in

Latin and Greek, acquainted with the writings of the ancient scholars. As Siegfried became more and more occupied with the business of state and the concerns of his kingdom, it was Odile who joined Benno and Wolfgang in late-night conversations that ranged from philosophy to alchemy, from the poetry of the Greeks to the rhetoric of the Romans.

Wolfgang certainly knew what she was doing; how could he not, when new volumes appeared in the palace library every day or two? She plundered the manor library as ruthlessly as the rest of it, with the magical tomes going into her personal hoard, and the others into the shelves of the palace. Some of the books would not make the journey; she had come to recognize the "feel" of them from a distance, a kind of residue of her father that suggested the magics within were too contaminated to use safely. And, of course, she had no intention of taking *anything* from his tower. But the rest were useful, and Wolfgang was in transports of joy, having so rich a treasure trove suddenly spread at his feet.

But it was Ilse, one of the "little swans," and not Odile, who made the real change in Wolfgang's life and status.

One night, not long after the wedding, when the guests were departed and only the king's household gathered about the fires in the Great Hall in the evening, a storm set in that brought everyone to the fire especially early. The winds howled around the walls of the palace and it seemed that winter would never end; with all of the entertainers gone, the evening bid fair to be tedious. Then Ilse suddenly jumped up out of her seat by the fire and skipped over to where Wolfgang sat. "Master Wolfgang," she said, with an impish parody of officiousness, "we have all heard each other's stories so often we know them by heart.

You, so they tell me, are a learned man—and *you* never help to entertain the rest of us. Tell us a story!"

The other three joined in her demands, as the older swans laughed, and the courtiers hid smiles. "Yes! Tell us a story! You must know *hundreds* that we haven't heard!"

Ilse sat down on a cushion at Wolfgang's feet, and looked up at him with a face full of mischief and expectation.

At first, Wolfgang was a little confused, then embarrassed, but at last he gave in to Ilse's pleading and cleared his throat self-consciously. "Well," he said— and fortunately, he did *not* see the bored or incredulous expressions of the courtiers, only the eager ones of the four youngest maidens, "I have never told a tale before, so perhaps I should tell a short one."

"And if we like it, you must tell us more!" Ilse demanded instantly.

Hesitantly at first, then warming to his subject, Wolfgang began to relate the story of the youth Narcissus. Odile was quite familiar with the tale, of course, but it was entirely new to most of the company, and Wolfgang proved to be astonishingly adept at storytelling.

Perhaps he learned more than just the stories themselves from all those years spent listening to others, Odile thought, as she watched even the courtiers who had been the most bored begin to lean forward in their seats, the better to hear the old man.

When he was done, it wasn't just Ilse who demanded more, and within a few nights, Wolfgang had gathered the nerve to embark on a multi-evening recitation of the saga of Odysseus, beginning with the contest of the goddesses and the theft of Helen by Paris. With every night that passed, Wolfgang's status rose in the minds of Siegfried's court. It was apparent now that he was a great deal more than they had thought—and their new regard had an unexpectedly good effect on Wolfgang as well. He gradually ceased to drink; the intoxication he found in the faces of his listeners was much sweeter than that in the bottom of a bottle.

As spring neared, and courtiers actually began seeking the old scholar's advice (feeling that anyone who knew that much would at least have the wisdom of the ancients at his fingertips), Siegfried proposed that Wolfgang be added to his Privy Council. There were no dissenters, and Wolfgang took his place among the king's advisers in a ceremony that delighted all his friends.

And *that,* in turn, meant another change for the old man and, indirectly, for Odile.

Directly after the ceremony, when Wolfgang was closeted with Siegfried and the rest of the councilors, Odile found Ilse sitting all alone in the chimney-corner of the library. Since Ilse couldn't read, that was a very strange place for her to be—and since the girl's face was full of woe, Odile knew that there must be something wrong.

She hesitated a moment, and thought about going back to her own room before the girl saw her, but something in the girl's expression made her decide to say something. "Ilse, you look as if you just lost your best friend!" she said, walking into the library. "Did you quarrel with Sofie? Can I help?"

Ilse, of all the little swans, was the most direct, and the one least likely to hide anything from anyone. She took one look at Odile, and burst into tears.

Odile dropped to her knees and took the girl's hands in hers, seriously alarmed now. This seemed more serious than a simple quarrel with a friend. "Blessed Virgin, Ilse, what on earth is the matter!"

Ilse never thought before she spoke—so her words came straight from her heart. "I—I—I—" she sobbed "I w-w-want to m-m-marry W-W-Wolfgang!"

That was the last thing Odile would ever have expected, and she stared at the girl for a moment in sheer astonishment. "You do?" she managed, incredulously. "Then why on earth *don't* you?" She warmed to the idea, and continued, "I think that would be wonderful for both of you! Wolfgang is *very* fond of you!"

That only brought forth a torrent of tears. "I h-h-haven't any *dowry!* " she wailed.

Oh, my— Odile was torn between sympathy and laughter, and had to stifle the laughter lest poor Ilse be further traumatized. Instead, she comforted the girl until she stopped crying, dried her tears, assured her that the idea of a young girl like her marrying an old scholar like Wolfgang *wasn't* absurd, and sent her off to wash her face. She made no promises—not yet.

But she did lie in wait for Wolfgang until he left the Council chamber, and came directly to the point with him—feeling absurdly like a gossipy old village marriage broker.

To her great relief, Wolfgang was not only *not* horrified by the idea, he went as red as any peasant boy, and stammered out a confession that he thought Ilse was the most delightful girl he had ever seen. "But she *can't* want to shackle herself to an old man like me!" he protested. "She'd waste her youth—she's so sweet, so pretty—there must—"

Odile stopped the flood of protests with an impatient shake of her head. "She was once betrothed to a miserly, miserable old bastard who beat all his previous wives and worked them to death," she pointed out. "*She* thinks you hung the moon—and that a great thinker like you needs someone to take proper care of him. If you can manage to scrape together enough courage to propose to her tomorrow, *I* will take care of the rest today."

Wolfgang agreed, and went off in a kind of glowing

daze. Odile went straight to Odette's chambers, where she was fairly certain of finding the entire flock, sewing and gossiping together.

She was right—and even more fortunate in finding that, for once, there were no "outsiders" among the ladies. That meant she could post a page at the door with orders that the queen and her friends didn't want to be disturbed. This shouldn't take too long, for after all, it was *bad* news that was long in the telling, not good news.

Then she went in, took a seat off to one side, and waited for the conversation to come to a lull before clearing her throat. By now the rest were so comfortable in her presence that conversation no longer ceased when she entered a room, and the current topic was an interesting one for all of those here—Ilse, and her infatuation with Wolfgang—so it took a while for the buzz to die down.

When it did, she coughed to get everyone's attention. She got it, in no small part because she usually did *not* spend afternoons in the queen's solar with the rest of them. "Majesty," she said, with a little bow to Odette, "this situation with Ilse has shown me that there is at least one more thing I can do for the flock to make up for what you all endured." She met the eyes of each of the maidens in turn, and sighed as she saw only friendliness and curiosity. "I'm sure that you know—or surmise—that the baron was a man of wealth. As chatelaine of his household, I know where that wealth was kept. There is no reason why his hoard should not be divided among you to provide dowries."

Well, *that* certainly put the cat among the pigeons! She had to wait for the excited babble to die down until she could continue, but she flushed with pleasure and a little excitement herself as she waited. Finally

Odette signaled for quiet, as the only way to get the babble under control.

"This is going to take time," Odile warned them. "I can't bring a great weight at once, and coin is heavy. You saw me bringing food and corn, so you know what I'm talking about. It will probably be a month or more before I have enough for everyone, and if there's no objection, I'd like to fetch over enough for Ilse's dowry first."

Ilse went pink, then red, and for the first time since Odile had known her, was left completely speechless. Odette answered for the flock.

"I think that would be perfectly correct," she replied, with a gentle twinkle in her eyes. "And if there are any more of you who have—how shall I put this?—potential suitors?—I think that a hint that *I* am to stand in place of your parents as the person to ask for permission to court would not be amiss."

Given the number of pink faces, Odile was fairly certain that the surplus of unwedded young knights among Siegfried's train was about to take an abrupt drop. Hiding her smile, she absented herself, and set to work on her latest task.

When spring truly arrived, in a torrent of flowers and birdsong, there were so many weddings being planned that it was decided to make them double and triple ceremonies, so as not to encumber the priest and the chapel overmuch. There was a new priest; the old one had been less than understanding about the presence of the swan-maidens. After he had sent two of the girls running from the confessional in tears, and had made the paramount error of calling Odile a "witch" to Odette's face, Siegfried had turned him out of his place and had found a more reasonable man. The new priest, a gentle old man with a fine sense of humor, was a better match. What he lacked in energy, he made up in wisdom, tolerance, and understanding.

When he could, he often joined in the late-night discussions.

It was with spring well in flower that Odile sought a private audience with Odette. The arrival of spring had reminded her of a queen's duty to her kingdom—"an heir and a spare"—and she wanted to give her friend a little help with that before she left. She could not stay here forever, after all; sooner or later, she would cease to be a welcome guest.

"I have—a little something for you," she said, with a touch of shyness. "Two somethings, actually. My belated wedding presents." She held out two pendants; one of silver, with a modest sapphire, the other of gold, set with a pearl. "This—" she held up the gold ornament "—is a—ah—fertility charm. This—" the silver, "—is the opposite. Wear the one you want constantly for three months. If you change your mind, don't wear either for a month, then switch." She found herself with burning ears, as Odette regarded her with a look of curious surprise. "It took me a while to find spells that were—gentle. *Men* seem to want things to happen all at once, and they don't seem to care what harm that does. These work, though, and they won't hurt you at all. I tried them on rabbits."

Odette accepted both, placed them carefully on her dressing table, and surprised Odile with a spontaneous embrace. "You keep doing so much for us. Odile, isn't there anything you want for yourself?"

She shook her head, and the arrival of a page gave her the excuse she needed to leave.

She went out onto the walkways on the walls of the palace, and chose a spot where the wind was in her face and she had a good view of the countryside. It was time to think about her own future, now. She had done all she could for the flock; she had done her best to make up for what von Rothbart had put them all through. The rest was up to them.

What do *I want for myself?*

The truth was, she didn't know. If a home was a place to live, she had that, and she had already decided to let it molder away—though it was more likely, given that von Rothbart had brought other sorcerers there on occasion to impress them, that once word spread that he was dead, some rival would come to take the place for his own. That was a good enough reason for her *not* to be there. Contesting with another sorcerer of von Rothbart's ilk for possession of the manor would serve no real purpose now that she'd gotten everything she wanted out of the place.

Whoever takes it, is welcome to it—though if they're anything like von Rothbart, I hope the traps he set for trespassers still work. A malicious wish, perhaps, but the world would be better off with fewer sorcerers like von Rothbart.

She could travel, as she had considered doing, and there was a certain restlessness that the spring had set off in her. Impulsive acts were just not in her nature, though; she couldn't imagine just taking off to see the world without a clear plan in mind.

The sound of booted feet on the walkway made her glance to the side. She expected to see a guard come to ask her courteously if she required anything; she did *not* expect to see Siegfried.

He smiled at her and nodded, but said nothing at first, only leaned on the wall beside her and gazed out at the countryside, his eyes half-closed against the brilliant, warm spring sunlight. It was only after they had both watched a hawk make a stoop on something in one of the distant fields that he spoke.

"I come up here all the time," he said idly. "The wind seems to clear out my head. Especially after Council meetings, when I've had to do more mediating between two stubborn old goats with opinions instead of ideas than I have been doing decision making."

She laughed, and brushed a strand of hair out of her eyes. "I can see that you would need fresh air after that. Isn't Wolfgang any help?"

"Wolfgang is occasionally part of the problem. Not often, but occasionally." But he laughed anyway, and shook his head at the folly of "stubborn old goats." "I could use—no, that's not strong enough—I truly *need*—someone to act as a mitigating force in my Council. Furthermore, there is no one on my council with any actual experience of magic, and given the antecedents of my beloved Queen, I begin to think that could pose a serious weakness."

She turned her head and saw that he was looking at her with one lifted eyebrow. "Are you preparing to flout all custom and insult your other Councilors by having a *woman* on your council?" she asked incredulously.

"Why not? Once you're on, they won't dare object to having Odette as well, which I also want and need." He shrugged. "Odette reminded me this morning that you have a remarkable ability that very few people possess, and I don't mean sorcery. You don't look at a situation and see what can't be done, you look at it and find solutions. As a ruler, I find that talent rare and useful, and I wouldn't care if the person who had it was a man, a woman, or a blue-faced ape." He made a sour face. "Actually, a blue-faced ape would probably be equally useful in breaking up arguments by flinging things at the offenders. I don't suppose you'd care to do that, would you?"

Now she was forced to laugh. "I doubt it would be as effective—but you *are* serious, aren't you? You want me to become a permanent part of your court and Council?"

"And I'm not the only one." He made a little signal with his hand, and up the stairs came Odette, Wolfgang, and Benno.

"Please stay," Odette said, reaching out and taking Odile's hand in both of hers. "Sooner or later, all of the rest of the flock will go off with their young men as wives and chatelaines of their own keeps, and only return to court on state occasions and fêtes." Her huge, dark eyes were wistful as she gazed at Odile. "That's only right; they need to be where they can raise families, and they can't do that if they're dancing attendance on me. But—" she gestured helplessly with her free hand "—the ladies that Clothilde gathered to make her court—they don't understand—"

Odile nodded; she had met with that more than once. Those who had never *experienced* what magic could do to someone had nothing in common with those who had. And those who had only heard of magic in tales tended to look on those who had lived with it as odd at best, and suspect at worst.

"Please stay," Wolfgang said, taking her other hand. "You have no notion how *wonderful* it is to have a fresh mind about! And I could use some help with those ancient monuments Siegfried chose to appoint as Councilors. They seem to think nothing should ever change!"

"Please stay," Benno said softly. He didn't move, but there was something in his eyes that made Odile's heart beat just a little faster. "I would really be very grateful to you if you would. We could all use a friend like you."

Then he grinned, and his eyes sparkled with silent laughter. "Besides, you still haven't taught me to swim, and you promised."

"If you'll stay, I'll not only appoint you to the council, but I'll appoint you Court Magician," Siegfried said firmly. "Maybe even Seneschal, if I can hammer it past the council. I've already talked to Father Timon; he says that he'll vouch for you to any ecclesi-

astical authority if they challenge you. He'll even get
a dispensation from Rome for you to practice magic."

"If you'll stay, I'd like you to take the Dowager's
Tower," Odette said. "It would be absurd for you to
try and do anything in just one little cubby of a room.
You need space for a workshop, a library, a
stillroom—well, lots of things. You know what you'll
need better than I. You'll have all the privacy and
space you need, and a very nice view as well."

"All I can promise is splendid conversation, and a
great deal of contention," Wolfgang admitted. "But it
won't be dull, I pledge you that."

Benno shrugged. "I can't promise anything but my
company, if you enjoy it," he said, and left it at that.
But once again, the glance he gave her promised more
than that. She was glad that the brisk wind cooled the
heat she felt rising to her cheeks.

These people are my friends, she thought with wonder. There was no reason for them to ask her to remain here—as Siegfried had inadvertently admitted,
having an openly-practicing sorceress in his court and
on his council had the potential to cause serious problems, not the least with the Church. Odette could just
as easily have preferred to see the daughter of the
man who had imprisoned her go far, far away.

And what had she expected to find in travel? A
chance to see more than the narrow world of von
Rothbart's manor—to learn new things, and see new
sights, to speak with other scholars. All those things
were here, after all.

She smiled at their expectant faces; if they had not
already known what she would say, they had at least
known that they had gifts of their own to offer *her*—
the most important of which was themselves. And
those gifts were far, far too precious for any sane person to reject.

"I don't believe that there is anyone in the entire

world who could offer as much to me as you do," she said, with a wide smile. "So—I suppose we'd better go evict the rats from the Dowager's Tower and prepare to appall the rest of your Council, Your Majesties!"

Benno gave a great whoop of joy, and flung his hat in the air. The wind caught it and it sailed into the moat, where it astonished a family of ducks. Odette linked arms with her, and they led the way down the stairs followed by the men.

"You'll have to have a title, of course," Siegfried continued blithely, clearly as happy with her answer as Benno. "Otherwise the other Councilors will be insulted—I made Wolfgang a baron, but—"

"No," Odette and Odile said together, and laughed. Odile continued. "Please, *not* baroness."

"A title alone won't serve; she'll have to have land as well," Wolfgang reminded him. "Being landed will give her weight enough with the others for her to be taken seriously."

"I don't want to claim the sorcerer's land, either," Odile said forcefully. She didn't have to state the rest; Odette squeezed her hand in understanding.

"I know what will serve!" Siegfried said, and as they paused on the landing, he took her shoulder and turned her towards him. "I hereby grant to you the royal holdings of the town and environs of Schwarzbaum; I change the name to Swan Lake, and I endow you with the title of countess. Countess Odile von Schwannsee, and that even gives you an entirely new name; how does that strike you all?"

"Wonderful!" Odette applauded. Benno and Wolfgang nodded, pleased.

"Countess Odile von Schwannsee," Odile repeated, softly. Nothing less like the name of von Rothbart could possibly be imagined. "I like it, Your Majesty," she said, with a heart so full that her spirit sang. *Is this what real joy is like?* she wondered, and laughed

for the pure, spirit-soaring pleasure of it. "I like it
very much indeed!"

She lifted her face to the sky and took in an intoxicat-
ing breath of spring air so full of life that it purged
the last of her old self completely away. The story was
not at an end—it was just beginning.

And we will all live happily ever after.

Mercedes Lackey

The Novels of Valdemar